DON'T CALL THE WOLF

Don't Call the Wolf

ALEKSANDRA ROSS

HARPER TEEN

An Imprint of HarperCollinsPublishers

HarperTeen is an imprint of HarperCollins Publishers.

ISBN 978-0-06-287797-0

Typography by Chris Kwon
20 21 22 23 24   PC/LSCH   10 9 8 7 6 5 4 3 2 1
❖
First Edition

For Babi, who was Irena first

❧ PROLOGUE ❧

A WHITE CASTLE ONCE STOOD in the forest, with spires that soared to the lower floors of heaven and dungeons that stretched ever downward, or so the legend went, to brush the very chimney stacks of hell. To the villagers who prospered in its shadow, the castle encompassed the entire expanse of earthly life. Its mausoleums housed the bones of ancient lords, its throne bore up their beloved queen, and its crib cradled their tiny, treasured princess.

But then, the world grew dark.

Slowly at first. With small things, things that scuttled and slithered. In the treetops, *nocnica* danced on their spider legs and looked for humans to strangle. In the rivers, *rusalki* circled unsuspecting swimmers, whispering in their ears before they dragged them under. In the castle grounds, three hundred *nawia* glided across the lawn and left the smell of frost and rotting flesh. And within the castle itself, *psotniki* stumped across the marble floors, chuckling softly as they plucked the eyes out of sleeping nobles.

And then, gliding over the treetops, came a Golden Dragon.

They said, afterward, that its wings blocked out the sun. Formed of gold, it was like nothing they had ever seen. Some said it was the most beautiful, the most heavenly of monsters. Its claws were glass. Its teeth were crystals. Its eyes were so dark that in them, they said, was held the ruin of worlds.

With sunlight glancing off wings of gold, the Dragon took the castle spire in its claws. It ripped. It tore. The villagers came out from under their doorways and shielded their eyes. They watched as gold and fire blazed on the threshold of heaven. They watched, realizing too late what they saw, as in that topmost chamber, the Dragon devoured the young queen and her daughter. Too late the knights drew their swords. Too late they charged up the spiraled stairs. Too late they paused in the dim stone hallways and heard, far above them, the echo of glass claws on stone as the Dragon launched itself from the white walls. It flew east across the forest. And there, in the Moving Mountains, it made its roost and awaited the onslaught of knights.

And they came.

Heartbroken and furious, the king gathered his knights. Banners flying and swords chiming, they galloped down the drawbridge and through the dark woods.

One by one, they were picked off among the twisted trees. Many survived, only to be lost among the unforgiving Mountains. And of those who remained—those who conquered the Mountains, who eked out the hidden trails, who scaled its peaks, who outwitted its monsters—those who were battle-hardened, or brave, or talented—those last, doomed souls were crushed in golden jaws.

Below, the trees grew thicker. The villagers mourned. In a bid for the vacant throne, the more ambitious nobles put on old-fashioned armor and rode out to face the dragon and prove their worth. Not a single one of them returned.

The kings of other lands arrived. Some brought gold and silver. Some wielded chipped blades and rode scarred warhorses. Some employed magicians and soothsayers and made offerings to the saints of dragon slayers and kings. And when those kings were dead the armies came. Led by drummers and trumpeters, black-coated soldiers rode in military formation, sabers rattling and rifles primed. In all, within ten years of the Golden Dragon's attack, ten thousand warriors crossed the borders into the forest. They were professionals, they were aristocrats, they were the civilized and the elite and they were men and women already living legends of their own.

They were not enough.

Ten thousand souls went into that forest, and ten thousand souls were lost.

In the end, the cleverest and the bravest were the people who fled. The ones who took what they could carry and ran and never looked back. The ones who abandoned fortune and birth and everything familiar and left the kingdom to the Dragon.

Of course, some stayed behind, and the dark things found them. For in the wake of the Dragon, these things grew braver.

Evil wrapped itself around the little village. Evil walked the crumbling streets, evil lurked between stuccoed buildings. It looked down from the rafters with glowing eyes. It rattled its claws in the corners. It strangled the villagers in their beds. It dragged them to the depths of rivers. It snatched them up on quiet roads. It beckoned from shadowed eaves. Evil sang to them in the dark, candles burning, nights eternal.

In time, the forest darkened. Its borders closed. For a long time, there was no hope.

And then, from the darkness, rose a queen.

⚹ 1 ⚹

"LADIES AND GENTLEMEN," BEGAN PROFESSOR Damian Bieleć, "we live among legends."

He paused, bracing his hands on the sides of the lectern.

"For we have lived through the fall of Kamieńa. We have lived through the advent of the Golden Dragon. And in the midst of both these tragedies"—Damian Bieleć's voice fell to a carefully crafted whisper—"we have seen—nay, we have *borne witness to*—the last of the Wolf-Lords."

A thrill ran through the auditorium. Shining heads bent toward one another. Their owners ignored the tight collars digging into throats as they murmured their admiration for a brilliant speaker, their interest in a fascinating subject. The air rustled with low voices, and Damian Bieleć waited before proceeding.

In the back of the auditorium, leaning against the doorframe, Lukasz put his hands in his pockets.

Outside, it was June. Outside, children were laughing, parents were scolding, and carriages were clattering. The streets were filled with fire breathers and ice-cream vendors. Outside, the world was a riot of summer and sales, of bartering and bickering. Miasto was the greatest city in the world, and it was at its peak. But in here, in this moment, no one cared about the outside.

Because in here, in this ageless dim, legends were being told.

"For a thousand years, the Wolf-Lords did not leave the Moving Mountains," Professor Bieleć went on. He inhaled deeply, nostrils flaring, as if he could actually smell the cold shale and hot smoke of that lost world. Then he said: "Until seventeen years ago."

Another pause.

"Until the Golden Dragon."

His listeners were on edge. Lukasz could feel it. He could also see it, betrayed in the glances cast over shoulders, in the subtle twitches of those elegant faces. It was half fear, half hope. Maybe they had even come for the same reason as Lukasz had: Not just to listen to fairy tales, not just to learn of the Wolf-Lords. But to see for themselves whether the gossip rags were true.

Whether there really was, somewhere in these hallowed halls, an Apofys dragon on the loose.

"For ten centuries," Bieleć was saying, "the Wolf-Lords lived in isolation and in a state of barbarism that we can only imagine. They carved out niches among the shifting rocks and weathered the tides of those Mountains. They hunted dragons and made blood pacts with wolves."

Somewhere near the front of the auditorium, a projector rattled to life. A map of Welona loomed, with the ocean to the north and Miasto—where they were now—marked by a star in the south. To the northeast, a black stain marked the kingdom of Kamieńa. And still farther east, beyond the forest, a line of crosshatching represented the vast, legendary Moving Mountains. A Dragon, rendered in golden ink, wrapped golden claws around forest and mountain.

There were sounds of awe from the audience.

"Because seventeen years ago, the Golden Dragon attacked the kingdom of Kamieńa," recounted Professor Bieleć. "And shortly thereafter, the Wolf-Lords left the Moving Mountains. Were they pushed out by the dragon, which had claimed their ancestral home as its roost? Or were these dragon slayers as foolish as the king of Kamieńa, and were they, too, killed in its pursuit?"

He chuckled, and Lukasz cracked his knuckles. *Ironic*, he thought. Bieleć wanted to criticize Wolf-Lords when there was an Apofys running amok upstairs?

"But all we know," Bieleć murmured, lowering his voice, "is this: In the end, only ten Wolf-Lords remained. Only ten came down from the Mountains."

The map trembled in place for a moment. Then Bieleć made a small signal, and the slide changed, the projected image shuttering up and out of sight. A photograph took its place, black pigment stained brown with age.

"These ten men were the Brothers Smokówi."

The photograph had been taken from a distance, with a low line of black trees cutting a stark line in the background. In the foreground, ten men were seated on black warhorses. Nine of the ten horses each had a set of antlers on their bridles: some ending in elegant curls, others simple and spiked. The men had serious faces. They wore leather and fur.

They looked, in a word, barbaric.

"These ten," whispered Damian Bieleć, "became the Brygada Smoka."

A crest ratcheted onto the screen: a wolf's head, flanked by crossed antlers. Below the image ran lettering familiar enough that even Lukasz could recognize it.

ZĄB LUB PAZUR

"Tooth or claw," translated Damian Bieleć. The projector's beam cast his face in alternating light and shadow. "The motto of the Wolf-Lords. And later, the motto of the great Brygada Smoka."

Lukasz placed a cigarette between his teeth and fished out his lighter. Almost reflexively, he ran his fingers over the case. He knew the etching by heart: crossed antlers and a wolf's head.

When he looked up again, he could have sworn he saw Bieleć's head twitch toward the lighter's flash. The professor paused a split second before he resumed his talk.

"Their—their beginnings were modest enough." He faltered. "The brothers began by hunting lesser dragons, collecting bounties on Lernęki. Living off the troves of Dewclaws."

There was a skittering sound overhead, and a few pinpoints of dust fluttered down from the vaulted rafters. None of the listeners looked up, but Lukasz's focus shot to the chandelier and the shadows beyond. A wisp of smoke, scarcely larger than a cat, rolled across the rafters and disappeared into darkness at the far end of the hall.

He relaxed. Just a *dola*. Nothing more.

Lukasz settled back against the doorframe, watching Bieleć through the hazy air.

"And then," continued Professor Bieleć. His knuckles were white on the lectern. "The brothers arrived in the town of Saint Magdalena, where for three hundred years, a Faustian had terrorized the countryside."

The slide changed again. Amid the wreckage stood a man and a boy. A Faustian dragon sprawled behind them. This photograph had been taken among the ruins of a cathedral—now nothing more than splintered pews, shattered glass, and scorched stone. So fresh was this kill that its antlers had not yet fallen, and its still face was crowned with glittering, staglike horns. . . .

Darkness tipped one of the tines.

The man in the photograph was tall. He was handsome and hawkish, smiling and savage in leather and fur, broadsword strapped across his back. He beamed, like a proud father, arm around the boy, as if congratulating him.

Lukasz knew better. The man was holding the boy up on his feet. It did not show up in the monochrome photograph, but the boy's pant leg was soaked through with blood. At the memory, pain stabbed through his knee.

On went the professor.

"The last of the Wolf-Lords." The professor's voice fell to intonations usually reserved for worship. "Their exploits are chronicled in photographs and newsprint. But we know so little of *who* they were. Of how they must have felt—how lonely they were—the last of their kind in a world like ours."

The slide changed. The brothers in one of Kwiat's famous bathhouses, cast in shadow by flames burning in the stone pool behind them. The image shuddered, disappeared, was replaced. Brothers standing on a dock, while behind them a pair of Tannimi hung nose-down from cranes like enormous, grotesque salmon. A *click*, and a new image appeared. Brothers smoking with swords propped on their shoulders, a Ływern stretched out across the cobbles beside them. As the photographs changed, the brothers changed: from leather and fur to sleek black uniforms, from wild beards to fashionably short hair. From savages to celebrities, each moment captured. Immortalized on celluloid film, even if they were dead.

As the slides changed, Bieleć's voice became hushed and hallowed.

"Bound together by blood, by fire, by the loss of the world they'd left behind and the fear of the world they'd entered. Cursed, lonely, destined for the outskirts of civilization. *By tooth or by claw*, they promised. The Brygada Smoka. The last of the Wolf-Lords, and the greatest dragon slayers in the world."

The whole room held its breath, with the exception of Lukasz. *Then again,* he thought, *perhaps this is worship.*

Lukasz glanced down at his hands. Realized, a little distractedly, that he'd forgotten his gloves. When he looked up again, the slide had changed once more.

The last pair of Smokówi brothers smiled for the camera. They wore black army uniforms trimmed in silver braid and gleaming with medals. One had spectacles and artistically messy hair that did nothing to soften the brutal slant to his cheekbones. The second man was younger, with black hair and eyes whose blue had evaded the colorless camera flash. All the same, they had a wicked glint.

Lukasz knew those eyes very well.

They were his.

"But then," whispered Professor Bieleć. He spoke, it seemed, into Lukasz Smoków's very soul. "But then the Brothers Smokówi began to disappear."

Lukasz waited for the auditorium to empty before he strode to the front of the room, where Professor Bieleć was folding his notes into a briefcase.

Lukasz could feel the Apofys in his bones. He'd spent the morning reciting its curriculum vitae: the demonic taxidermy collection devoured, the pagan amulet exhibition plundered, and four Unnaturalists gutted. And Damian Bieleć, newly promoted department chair. By default.

"Dewclaws don't have troves," observed Lukasz, snuffing out his cigarette in an ashtray. "Only bits of metal and trash."

Bieleć shot bolt upright. Up close, he did not seem quite as impressive. He was small and pale and, without a podium or a captive audience, even a little pathetic. He'd probably escaped the dragon because he simply wasn't very appetizing.

Bieleć took in everything from the black army cap on Lukasz's head to the tall leather boots.

"L—Lieutenant Smoków—" he began. "I didn't realize—"

While Bieleć gathered his wits, Lukasz licked his fingertips and reached into the projector to snuff out the gaslight. He didn't mind the tiny sear of pain. If you hunted dragons, you got used to burns.

Lukasz interrupted:

"Heard you've got an Apofys on the loose."

Bieleć wiped sweaty hands on his elegant suit, eyes running

down to the old-fashioned broadsword at Lukasz's side. *What was it Eryk used to say?*

Lukasz remembered the eyes, darker than mountain skies. The laugh, easier than a falling blade. Teeth brighter than dragon bones.

Dress us like gentlemen, and we'll hunt like wolves.

"Aren't there two of you?" Bieleć was asking. "It's really quite a dangerous creature—"

Hand still in his pockets, Lukasz fiddled with the cap of the lighter.

"You want it dead or not?" he cut in. "Just show me where to find it."

"Well—it's—" Bieleć struggled. "Well, it's in the department of Unnatural history. You should be able to find it. The hallways are very clearly labeled, and we've even put up a sign—"

For a second time that afternoon, Lukasz felt uneasy. Maybe Franciszek had been right after all, about that whole reading thing.

"I'd rather you showed me," he interrupted as casually as he could. "Just as far as the department. After that, it'll find me."

Bieleć blanched.

"Well . . ." He hesitated. "Very well, I suppose. Could you take this, please?"

Lukasz took the briefcase and the projector and followed Professor Bieleć out of the auditorium. They moved in silence through the *uniwersytet*'s lobby. It had the kind of richness designed to make a man like Lukasz feel small: an enormous gold globe to his left, a mural of the country's founding covering the entire wall on his right. Jarek would have loved that mural. A wide pink velvet carpet ran from the auditorium doors to a white stone desk inlaid with gold lettering. Two clerks, one male and one female, each of astounding beauty, sat behind it. And flanking either side of the desk, twin white staircases curled up to a second story, which promised more velvet and gold.

They left the professor's belongings at the front desk and at the top of the staircase took a sharp left at an expansive stone atrium. They entered a dingy hall, hemmed in by doors on either side.

"My apologies for the lighting," said Professor Bieleć. "We've turned the lamps down. Evacuated the whole wing, you understand. In case the dragon wishes to, erm, *explore*."

The walls had auburn wallpaper and the doors were oak, with brass plates inscribed with what Lukasz presumed were numbers and names. The only light was the dim brown glow of gaslights. They took a right and entered another identical hallway.

"You know," began the professor, "when this—this is, um, handled—if you're available, I mean—I would love—be honored, really—to interview you and your brother." The professor seemed to hesitate before asking in a small voice: "Are you sure you wouldn't like to wait for your brother?"

Lukasz swallowed against the tightness that rose suddenly in his throat. *Your brother.* How much longer would people describe the Brothers Smokówi in the plural? When would this morning's events make it into the newspapers?

When would the world realize that they were down to their last Wolf-Lord?

"It's just," continued Professor Bieleć, misinterpreting Lukasz's silence, "I have a special interest in historical peoples."

"What's historical about the Wolf-Lords?"

"Well, they're extinct, of course."

Bieleć was so short compared to Lukasz that he could see the hair thinning over his flushed scalp.

"There are two of us left," said Lukasz coldly.

It was a lie. But Bieleć didn't need to know about Franciszek. Not now.

"Indeed," agreed the professor, clearly oblivious. "And yet, anthropologically speaking, the Wolf-Lords are an extinct people."

"Keep it up," Lukasz returned coolly, "and I'm going to make you an extinct people."

Bieleć fell silent.

They took another abrupt turn into yet another hallway. For a moment, Lukasz wondered whether, in a different life, he might have ended up in a place like this.

No, he thought. *I'd never have come here.*

Bieleć's lecture might have been more drama than actual substance, but the Unnaturalist had been right about one thing: in no other life would he have left Hala Smoków. If it hadn't been for the Golden Dragon, he'd still be there now, probably choosing a black-haired bride and building a wooden lodge amid the ever-changing hills and howling wolves. Like all of his brothers had done before him, Lukasz hated the Dragon. But secretly, he was glad to have gotten out of the Mountains. Bieleć had gotten it wrong. Lukasz wasn't a stranger. He didn't long for blue hills or wolves or the things his other brothers had wanted; he loved this city. He loved this *world.* When he died, it would be in the shadow of the Miasto Basilica; it would not be under the unforgiving skies of the Moving Mountains.

"It's around this corner," murmured Professor Bieleć. "Take care. Frankly, it's not a very pleasant creature."

Lukasz laughed. The sound echoed down the corridor, and who knew, maybe the Apofys heard it.

"Not many dragons are."

He cracked the knuckles on both hands. Even without his gloves, he wasn't worried. Franciszek would have made him go back and retrieve them. *Not anymore,* he thought, striding ahead of Bieleć. *Never again.* His throat constricted a second time. Better not to think like that.

More dim gaslights reflected off the painted walls, the rows of oaken doors. The end of the hall had been boarded off. On the other side, there was the sound of a bird chirping. Lukasz's hand closed over the sword at his side. The Apofys had eaten four Unnaturalists. There was no way a bird was alive back there.

"It's the Apofys," confirmed Professor Bieleć in a shaky voice. "It practices ventriloquism. Voice-throwing. Most unusual. Likely a technique for distracting prey during hunts." He glanced from the boards to Lukasz, looming above him. "But of course, you knew that?"

"Right," said Lukasz, drawing his sword.

The blade, dark with dried dragon blood, scraped against the scabbard.

"So you've killed one of these?" asked Bieleć hopefully.

It was almost enough to make Lukasz doubt himself. After all, Franciszek was the one with the notebook. Always poring over library books, making notes. Doing the research. But Lukasz knew nothing about this dragon, and he'd done absolutely no preparation.

Not to mention the fact that he'd forgotten his gloves . . .

"Are you sure you want to do this?" asked Professor Bieleć. Lukasz had a flash of insight: an Unnaturalist afraid of harming the last of a species. He just wasn't sure if Bieleć was thinking of him or the dragon.

"I've killed dozens of dragons," said Lukasz. He pointed at the office nearest them. "Do these rooms have adjoining doors?"

Bieleć nodded, swallowing.

Lukasz crossed the threshold. The office held more gas lanterns, these unlit, and several neat stacks of books. He eased open the side door and edged through a second identical office before reentering the hall on the other side of the barricade. This door was slightly ajar, and Lukasz wasn't sure if he was imagining it, but something was rustling out there. Could that be part of the dragon's ven . . . ventri . . . ?

He couldn't remember the word.

Whatever. Lukasz thought of the doubt on Bieleć's face and scowled. *Voice-throwing.*

He weighed his sword in his left hand; he could fight with both, but he preferred his left. The blade didn't glitter. It was dull brown down to the hilt, thoroughly coated in dried dragon blood. Even the sight of the poisoned blade was reassuring. He was good at this.

Lukasz eased the door open with the toe of his boot, pressed his back against the frame, and leaned out into the hallway. The barricade on this side was smeared with soot, and a few boards lay, charred and glowing, on the floor. The dragon had been tearing at it.

Bieleć was watching him through the barricade. He could feel it. He wondered if the professor knew how close he was to getting killed. Literally playing with fire.

"Unnaturalists," he muttered under his breath.

Apart from the barricade, the hallway looked like the others, except that nearly all the lights had been smashed. One lonely lamp still glittered, just above Lukasz's shoulder. The rest was shadow and hazy, warm air. Lukasz froze.

There it was again. The rustle.

Several office doors hung ajar, black smoke spiraling out into the hall. There were holes in the carpet, too, rimmed with glowing red. From these holes, more black smoke trailed up to the ceiling to collect in an inky fog. Giving them a wide berth, Lukasz advanced down the hallway.

God, he loved this.

He moved methodically, checking each office, enjoying the old sense of adventure. This was what he liked. He had to stoop to avoid the black smoke cloud. It was the first time in a long time that he had hunted a dragon without Franciszek's meticulous research. It was a good feeling. It reminded him, for a moment, of that first hunt, in the cathedral, when he had killed the Faustian. There had been that same sense of the unknown.

Lukasz sidestepped a shoe.

The hall seemed to go on forever, getting murkier and smokier with every stride. The dragon chirped. Lukasz caught a flicker of movement. Feathers flashed across the doorframe and disappeared. It chirped again. From the office. Lukasz shot to the wall.

He pressed his back into the doorframe. He took a breath. The dragon chattered, inside the office next to him. On the other side of that papered wall was a real, live Apofys dragon.

He grinned to himself. *Not for long.*

And with that, he lunged around the door.

The office was empty.

There wasn't even a desk. No bookshelf, no chair. No papers. Just a bare carpet and bare walls. The sun streamed through the window, making the room look somehow even emptier. Lukasz frowned.

Another chirp. Somehow still . . . behind him? *In* the office?

Lukasz twisted around.

The other door—!

He had been so distracted by the voice-throwing, he'd forgotten that the offices connected. Now the adjoining door swung open. Silently. It was a terrible, dreamlike suspension. Everything slowed down. Lukasz raised his sword. The dragon took shape.

It was huge, orange, covered in feathers and scales. It had a curved beak and a quizzical, birdy look in its eye. It chirped again. It threw the sound to somewhere behind Lukasz, and he felt himself sweat. It was beating its wings steadily against the doorframe. Its feathers were soft, rasping.

Shhh. Shhh. Shhh.

The dull blade of the sword filled the empty space between them. Lukasz concentrated on his heart rate, forcing it to slow down. Letting it fall into time with the wingbeats. He'd done it on every hunt since the Faustian. It worked every time.

Shhh. Shhh. Shhh.

"Come on, you feathery bastard," he muttered. "Come on."

Time snapped back.

The dragon hurtled out at him. Lukasz swung. It twisted midair and flashed away. Its beak clicked. Flames erupted across the office and consumed the opposite wall. Thick smoke filled the room. It was oily smelling, burning. Lukasz choked, stepped back. His vision blurred. The Apofys chirped on his right. Temporarily blinded, Lukasz swung again.

The beak clicked again. Flames from the left. Heat seared his face. This time, it didn't miss.

Fire engulfed Lukasz's left arm. Yellow flames silhouetted his unprotected hand. The sword trembled and dropped. For a moment, he just stared. At his hand, his fighting hand, burning like a torch at the end of his arm.

Then, pain.

Lukasz screamed. He was on his knees, screaming. Coughing. Tears streaming down his cheeks, dripping off his chin. Black smoke pressed in on him. The only light was his own flaming skin. Pure agony.

The dragon was coming back. He didn't have much time.

Lukasz jerked his arm out of his coat and buried his hand in the flame-resistant material. The smell of burning flesh mixed with the oily smoke. The combination of smell and pain was too much, and he vomited.

You need to get up. But he couldn't. He was kneeling on the floor, gasping, clutching what was left of his arm to his chest. *Get up.* The dragon was coming back. *You have to get up.* He could feel his hand twist and curl in the coat, useless, charred. *Get up.*

Another chirp.

The sound cleared his mind. The chirp had come from the smoke overhead. He needed his sword. Desperate, terrified he might lose another hand, Lukasz scrambled across the room, searching the darkening floor. The smoke pressed in from every side. *Where is the damn sword?* The dragon chirped again, overhead. But there was another sound. Behind him. It was soft. So soft he'd have missed it.

Shhh. Shhh. Shhh.

Missed it if he hadn't been listening. If he hadn't been looking for those wingbeats to slow his heart. To calm him down. It had worked for the Faustian. It was working now.

His hand struck metal.

Shhh. Shhh. Shhh.

His right hand, his last hand, closed around the sword hilt.

Shhh. Shhh. Shhh.

Wingbeats.

He whipped around. He was ready. Wingbeats, not chirping. He wasn't going to fall for the voice-throwing. Not this time.

The dragon dived down from the smoke, all beak and talons.

Lukasz swung.

2

TWO MONTHS LATER

AFTER SEVENTEEN YEARS IN THE forest, Ren knew all the monsters by name.

"*Strzygi,*" she muttered, edging out of the trees. "Why did it have to be strzygi?"

She wasn't sure why she bothered to keep her voice down. They'd smell her long before they heard her.

But for now, the clearing was still.

The trees curled around each other like lovers, tangled overhead like beasts at war. It was as if any sunlight that found its way down here was trapped forever. Heating, baking, turning the grass to mush and giving everything this sweet, earthy smell. Heat caressed her, seeping through her bare skin. It ran damp fingers across the nape of her neck, pressed sticky palms to her cheeks.

Three shapes, shining and red, sprawled on the ground ahead. Ren took a few more cautious steps forward, earth yielding silently under her bare feet. It felt like the trees were watching her.

They probably were.

She moved through enemy territory as silently as a cat.

"It has to be you," she said, mimicking her brother. *"They'll come for a human."*

But Ryś had a point. A strzygoń could smell a human from miles away. Maybe it was human blood. Maybe it was human fear. Such a specific, cowardly scent.

And so here she was: pathetically, nakedly human. Ren was the most powerful, the most respected creature in the whole cursed forest, and she got the pleasure—the *honor*—of being the bait in her big brother's trap.

"Ryś, I'm going to kill you," she growled under her breath.

Somewhere on the edge of the clearing, Ryś laughed. Ren rolled her eyes. Wherever he was, safe in the shadow of trees, he was probably grinning that feline smile. At least he was nearby.

The red shapes were bodies: two men and a woman. Ren cringed as her feet squelched in the bloodied mud.

The dead man still clutched part of a rifle in stiff hands, its steel barrel shorn clear through by monstrous claws. Ren recognized their clothes from the village: dark coats and vests, white shirts, and striped skirts and trousers. Now blood obliterated every color. The strzygi had been feasting on their guts.

Ren snarled. The sound was low, utterly inhuman. It echoed in her chest, cut through the brown half-light. And for a moment—for the briefest moment—even the trees seemed to shiver.

Humans. In her mind, the word sounded like a curse. *Careless, stupid—*

The trees, once so silent, rustled.

Ren stiffened. Ignoring every instinct screaming inside her, she did not move. She blinked, as slow and luxurious as a cat. She felt her vision transform, sliding into familiar angles and shades, as she scanned the trees opposite. The colors had paled, their relative dimness sharpening every movement, every heartbeat in the trees. Everything was still. It was a good thing the humans were dead at her feet. They wouldn't have taken it well: the black-rimmed eyes of a cat, slit pupils and all, shining in the face of a girl.

Ren turned around.

A strzygoń stood before her.

Her eyes may have been animal, but the rest of her was still human. And right down to the human bone, she trembled.

Run, whispered a tiny voice somewhere inside her. *Now.*

Though roughly the size of the human it had once been, the strzygoń looked nothing like the corpses in the clearing. It stood on all fours, joints locked. With the bulging eyes of a goat, oblong pupils in slate gray, it considered her. It put its head to the side, feathery brows jutting over those terrible eyes. It looked almost like an enormous moth, and again, Ren trembled.

Run.

But she was rooted to the spot.

The strzygoń began to pace. It retained all the right joints for a human, but its limbs bent in all the wrong ways.

Ren scraped up every last scrap of courage and forced her face into a grin.

"Still hungry?" She jerked her chin, beckoning it toward her. "Come on, then."

She wasn't sure if it could understand her. It issued a low hiss, feathers ruffling on the lower half of its face. Ren felt her smile falter.

Run, screamed her still-human heart. *Run.*

It took one nauseatingly uncoordinated step toward her. It twitched its head. Almost all the way around, like an owl.

"Oh, yuck," she murmured.

The strzygoń leapt.

Ren fell back. She hissed. And she changed.

Her knees shot to her chest and her spine curled up. Her muscles expanded, snapping into place around her limbs. Power tore across her shoulders. Fur raced over her skin. Her world tilted into focus.

Ren leapt. She met the strzygoń midair. And not as a human.

As a lynx.

Her fangs found its throat before it even had a chance to fully register the transformation. It howled as she drove it into the ground. The strzygoń screamed and lashed out with broken nails. They scraped harmlessly off her thick fur. It kicked with its back legs, but Ren easily pinned them. Its re-formed limbs could not match the strength of her forelegs. She bit down. Hot blood splashed over her face.

The strzygoń slackened. It twitched twice and went still. Ren did not let go right away. Some monsters took more than one kill.

"Not bad, Malutka," said Ryś, sauntering out of the trees. "Really waited for the last second to change, didn't you?"

Ryś was the only one who dared used that pet name. *Malutka,* the little one. And only because he was older.

Ren dropped the strzygoń, still cautious enough to keep a paw on its lifeless corpse.

She grinned. "Keeps it interesting."

"If you ask me," came a second voice, "killing undead owl-people is a little *too* interesting."

A slender black wolf had followed Ren's brother out of the undergrowth. Where both the lynxes were low and muscular, the wolf was long-legged and elegant. He walked with the slightest suggestion of a limp.

Ren smiled back. Her heart was still pounding, but terror had begun to give way to a thrilling kind of light-headedness.

"Come on, they're so easy to kill," she said as scornfully as she could. "I wouldn't mind a real challenge, you know?"

"A real challenge?" asked Czarn. "As in, let's say, taking on a whole pack of these delights, and being wildly outnumbered?"

Ren grinned.

"It would be a pleasure, Czarn."

"Excellent," he said, nodding to the trees opposite.

Ren turned slowly.

The strzygoń hadn't been alone. The rest of its pack paced at the edge of the clearing, hunters weighing their prey. Their limbs moved in unnatural directions. They all had variations on the same face: some with beaks, some without eyes. Some still looked almost human, except for the feathers trailing over their skin, the wicked spikes of their teeth, the insect eyes peering out of their faces.

Czarn shifted his weight to his good paw. Ryś flexed his claws, growling. Ren's stomach knotted and unknotted.

"How many?" she asked.

The strzygi wove in and out of the trees, disappearing and reappearing.

"Nine," counted Ryś.

"Three each," said Czarn, divvying them up.

"Unfair," Ren griped. "I already killed one. *And* I was bait."

"If you're scared," Ryś said, chuckling as the strzygi began to move more purposefully, "then I can take four—"

"I'm not scared—"

"I hate to interrupt," drawled Czarn, always the picture of elegance. "But—"

The strzygi charged.

The animals met the monsters mid-clearing.

The fight was short. And bloody. One of the beakier strzygi managed to take a chunk out of Czarn's ear before the wolf's powerful jaws closed around its throat and severed its head. When all the creatures were dead, the three of them went through the corpses and ripped off the rest of their heads. It was not clean work. By the time they were done, the trees were sprayed with blood, and Ren was drenched from nose to claw.

She wondered how long these strzygi had been a pack. Ren didn't know exactly how it happened, but they often started as humans. She suspected they were the villagers who'd wandered into her forest, got lost, and—unfortunately—survived. The longer they stayed, bathed in the forest's particular kind of evil, the more monstrous they became. A warm breeze riffled the clothes on the humans who had been killed. Next to the strzygi, they looked almost . . . peaceful.

Ren shuddered.

To think these had *all* once been humans. Had once looked a bit like *her*. . . .

Czarn wove through the corpses, tongue lolling over his wet chin. He was tired, and it made his limp more pronounced.

"I'm too old for this," he panted, flopping down.

"You're younger than me," Ryś replied, rolling over and stretching into a lynx-shaped crescent. A shaft of sun braved the thick boughs and shone in, warming his belly. Czarn just smirked and crossed his long black paws. A patch of whitish-gray fur covered his injured foreleg.

"Czarn, Ryś," Ren interrupted. She avoided looking at the dead humans. "We need to bury them."

Czarn and Ryś looked up at the same time.

"They can bury themselves," snorted Ryś. "That's what they get for coming in here."

"I'm serious," said Ren. "They could still turn into strzygi."

Czarn and Ryś exchanged a glance. Recrossing his paws so his scar was hidden, Czarn said, "We don't know that for sure."

"That's the point," replied Ren. "We have no idea how they change. I don't want them waking up tomorrow and then we have to kill them again."

There were too many strzygi these days, and she couldn't run the risk of adding three more to a forest already boiling over.

Ryś looked doubtful.

"Very well," said Czarn at last, getting to his feet. "I will help you."

"Thank you," said Ren, moving aside as he passed her.

Ryś made an annoyed sound but grudgingly joined them.

They dug in silence. Czarn helped Ren tip the bodies into graves. The dense branches trapped the late-afternoon sun, and the work was punishingly hot. Now that the strzygi were dead and her panic had faded, Ren was acutely aware of the heavy warmth in the air.

There were more monsters every day, every night. And not just strzygi. Other, terrible things. *Zmara*, who hung around throats in the night and throttled their victims into a permanent slumber. Rusalki, who dragged humans under the water and wore their skins above it. Nocnica, who drank up any foolish souls sleeping too near their webs. Psotniki, who collected eyeballs in their high-up nests.

And of course, the humans.

They came rarely, probably because what had happened to Czarn—and to the hunter—had lit the fires of fear in their hearts. If the occasional hunters ventured in, someone else usually got to them before Ren did. They died at the claws of strzygi, rusalki, nocnica, psotniki . . . they died at the whims of the forest itself. Tangled in roots, hemmed in by walls of trunks. Captured on trails that circled for miles, yielded no secrets, and eventually, without warning, closed in forever.

Despite everything, this was Ren's forest, and she loved it. But even if she had wanted to leave it, she wasn't sure whether it would let her.

Czarn finished kicking the dirt over the bodies. His black fur was drying into sticky points, and when Ren ran a paw over her own face, she found it was crusted and sticky with blood. The strzygi had left their mark on the surrounding forest, too: bloody scratches in weeping tree trunks, bits of rotting flesh strewn around the perimeter. The trees themselves bent a little lower, the grass a little slimier, the horseflies a little hungrier. The smell of blood was overwhelming in the clearing. It smelled like fury. Anguish. Evil.

It smelled like monsters.

Sweat broke over her shoulders. Suddenly, she didn't want to be in the clearing. Didn't want to be covered in blood. Her power rippled away, and she was human once more.

"Hoping to get eaten, I see," observed Czarn in his lazy voice.

"I'm going for a swim," she said. Blood coated every inch of her body like a second skin. "I need to get this off."

Ryś was already using a dampened paw to wash behind his ears. He gave her a look of supreme disdain.

"*Or*"—he sniffed—"you could just be normal and lick it off."

"Be careful," called Czarn as Ren disappeared into the trees. "There are rusalki in the river!"

"I'll be fine," she called back, already deep in the trees. "Wodnik will be there!"

As Ren got farther from the clearing, the forest changed. Trees unbent, dark trunks lightening to golden brown. Overhead, boughs untangled and welcomed in the sun. Rot yielded to grass and the hushed voices of the last animals brave enough to stay in the forest.

She breathed in the clean, woody air, and with it came a sense of relief. She hadn't realized how tightly wound she was—hadn't noticed the sense of dread hanging over her. It was so constant that she often forgot how heavily it weighed on her. *How much longer?* she asked herself, never daring to speak the words out loud. How much longer could she keep her animals holed up in the castle, keep these last parts of the forest sunny and bright?

She didn't know. The forest had already driven out most of the humans. Now it was coming for them.

The river roared into view. The trees were smooth and straight, covered with thick green moss. Cool light filtered through the tree-tops, and everything smelled fresh and clean and alive. No claw marks on trees. No blood spattering the ground.

No monsters.

Ren glanced over her shoulder, frowning. Nothing had followed her, and the trees were silent. Somewhere, crickets were chirping. But all the same . . .

She hadn't noticed that this part of the forest lay so close to the strzygi's clearing . . . hadn't realized that the river—*her* river—had almost been in the strzygi's path—hadn't realized things were getting so bad so quickly—

Ren forced down the dread. She was catastrophizing. Everything would feel better once she'd gotten the blood off.

Ignoring the wild water, Ren sat on the riverbank and slipped easily into the coolness. The water instantly calmed.

"Thank you, Wodnik," she said across the expanse.

The water spirit didn't reply. The river was still.

Ren smiled and pushed off, swimming for the center of the swell. It was ice-cold and perfect. Even though she was mostly lynx these days, there was still some human left in her. And that human loved the water more than any cat ever would.

As the crusted blood melted off her skin, she began to feel better. Cleaner. Like there wasn't a pile of strzygi corpses and buried villagers a half mile away.

A wave broke over her shoulders.

A new, horrible thought occurred to Ren. The poisoned parts of the forest were expanding—might even have reached this river. A second wave rippled inquisitively across the clear surface. Literally, it seemed, testing the water.

And then a third. This one was high enough to brush her chin as it passed.

Ren's heart skipped a beat. Was there a monster in the water? Something other than Wodnik? One that could hear that skipped beat below the surface. That could see her bare legs, kicking. That . . .

Ren kicked harder. Whatever it was, it touched her ankle. She screamed, floundered—

The voice was as soft as water.

Our queen, it whispered. *We have returned.*

The water began to roil.

Our queen.

Fear released her. She knew these creatures: *nimfy.*

Silver fingertips broke the surface. They tangled her long dark hair. The strands slid down their silvery forearms as the creatures rose from the water. Hollow eyes trained on her, cold fingers played over her lips, her chin, rubbed away the blood. And then Ren was surrounded: one dark-haired girl surrounded by dozens that—it seemed—had been cast in silver.

Our queen. Their voices carried through the water, sank into Ren's skin. *Our queen.* Each one repeated the words. *Our queen. Our queen. Our queen.*

One nimfa pulled away from the others. She clutched Ren's shoulders in icy hands, silver-white webbing glittering between her fingers. She bent and kissed Ren's cheek.

Our queen.

The water churned, and three dozen silent silver bodies slid up from the depths and kissed their queen.

"Welcome home." Ren grinned, hugged their shoulders as they came. The kisses were ice-cold on her cheeks. "You've grown."

Back in the winter, half of these creatures had been just tiny tadpoles. They'd flitted in and out of the bulrushes, too shy for Ren to hold them, always darting back to the safety of Wodnik's arms. Then, as they'd done every spring, the tadpoles disappeared upriver to grow strong and beautiful. For the first time in her life, Ren had feared they might not make it back. They had seemed so fragile, and the evil had not spared the waters.

Ren heard a sudden splash as bubbles appeared near the opposite bank. The brownish rushes trembled. It was so subtle that anyone else might have ignored it completely.

But Ren wasn't anyone else.

"Wodnik," she called. "Is that you?"

From among the bulrushes, a single bulbous eye blinked. Wodnik didn't answer, but a second eye joined the first. He had no eyebrows, just raised scales over vivid yellow eyes. He blinked again.

Ren couldn't help but grin. Typical. She liked Wodnik.

"I wish you'd consider bringing your nimfy to the castle this year," called Ren. A very small nimfa, still a bit more tadpoley than the others, clambered up on her shoulders and began to braid her hair. "We killed some strzygi half a mile from here."

Wodnik blew some bubbles, which sounded suspiciously like "We're fine."

Somewhere, a horse whinnied.

Ren twisted around. She met the questioning eyes of the nimfy. Had she misheard . . . ? The horse whinnied again. The nimfy shrank low in the water, all silver tendrils and hollow eyes.

There were no horses in her forest. Except . . .

"Go," she growled.

The water cleared. No whisper of the slim bones and silver hearts that had been there a second before. The horse whinnied a third time as a hand closed on Ren's shoulder.

Ren whirled around, teeth bared.

But it was only Wodnik. He had risen almost out of the water, that toady face framed by damp rushes instead of hair. He met her gaze, silent. The only sound was a small splash as a fish flopped out from behind his ear.

Wodnik blinked. He took her hand, looked toward the opposite shore.

"No," she whispered back. "Someone has to stay. We don't know what it is."

Wodnik tugged her toward the shelter of the bulrushes.

Run, he seemed to say. *Run now.*

But Ren didn't budge.

"I can smell him," she hissed.

Smoke first. Then horse, which she was expecting. But then: blood and tanned hide and oiled leather. Even if every scent was animal, it was a hideous kind of animal: a patchwork of different creatures. The most gruesome of monsters. Clothed in the bodies of others.

"It's a human."

❧ 3 ❧

IT HAD BEEN TWO MONTHS since the Apofys had burned Lukasz's hand.

He barely remembered most of it, just staggering down the pink-carpeted stairs, coming face-to-face with a dozen reporters, their cameras sparking and billowing smoke. Standing there in a daze, burned arm buried in his black coat, while Damian Bieleć had rushed up to him, shaken his remaining hand, weaseled his way into the photographs.

After that, Lukasz had collapsed. At least, that was what he'd been told.

His next memory was of white hospital walls and a doctor wearing pale blue. They'd kept him knocked out with opium for a full two weeks. *For the pain,* the doctor had explained.

He'd been confused.

For your hand, she'd reminded him, pointing.

He'd looked. He'd remembered. And he'd wept at the sight of it.

Six weeks of nimfy-hair dressings and the best care Miasto

could offer, and it was a horror. Stripped of flesh and burned to the bone, the ends of two fingers had eventually been removed. What remained of the hand had initially been glistening red, and as it had healed—was still healing—it shrank and withered away.

And it was his left hand. . . .

The hand he fought with. The hand he needed. It looked like wax left too close to the flames, melted and then re-formed, molded into some grotesque semblance of a human hand.

Lukasz hated it. He hated looking at it, and he hated anyone else seeing it. The photographs from the Apofys hunt had been bad enough. He'd looked gaunt and dazed in every last one of them. Thank God he'd had the wherewithal to hide the horror at the end of his arm.

He shouldn't have been surprised. Every dragon slayer ended up with some scar sooner or later. And at least it wasn't his face; Michał and Eliasz had had far worse luck than he. Anyway, even if they'd ended up scarred and disfigured, it hadn't mattered. It ended for them the way it ended for all Wolf-Lords: swallowed up by this god-damned forest, devoured by that goddamned dragon. . . . But the dead didn't need to worry about pain. That was the burden of the living.

The light was getting dimmer. The trees crowded closer together. The ground was puddled with pools of brownish, sweet-smelling water. Apart from the buzzing flies and Król crunching on his bit, everything was silent. Maybe the sun was beginning to set.

Or worse: maybe he was lost.

"Whoa, boy." Lukasz drew up Król's reins.

The black horse halted. In the dim light, the bridle's silver antlers almost glowed. Lukasz produced a small leather-bound notebook from his coat pocket. He opened it against Król's neck, flexing what was left of the fingers on his left hand.

He carefully turned the tea-stained pages, wincing as they rustled in the silence. Neat, elegant writing took up most pages, interspersed with the odd hand-drawn map or illustration. Most of them had been drawn by Franciszek—although, before he had disappeared, Jarek had often contributed his illustrations, too. Lukasz smiled at the memory. If Franciszek had been the scholar of the family, then Jarek had definitely been the artist.

Even if Lukasz couldn't read them, Franciszek's neat notes were oddly comforting. Not for the first time, he wished he'd actually paid attention every time his brother had tried to teach him the letters.

"Why did you leave?" he muttered. One of Król's ears swiveled toward him. "Why did you leave, when I needed you?"

He kept turning pages. Franciszek would have known how to kill that Apofys. Franciszek would have taken his time; he'd have disappeared into every library and museum in Miasto, and they'd have taken weeks to do the job, but they'd have done it in the end. Lukasz would have gotten his adventure.

And he'd still have his hand.

But Franciszek had left. Franciszek had done what they'd all done, uttered some nonsense about mountains and going home, and he'd left. He'd said other things, too. Things that made Lukasz's stomach turn over with guilt.

At last he found the page he needed. It was a map of the country, less detailed and elaborate than the one from Bieleć's lecture. No nicely drawn dragons or fancy lettering here. Lukasz considered it for a minute.

He'd ridden north from Miasto, following the half-constructed railway, asking directions from the crews along the way. It must have been a sight for the ages: a Wolf-Lord on an antlered warhorse, cantering alongside the lumbering engines, yelling at the bewildered operator over the noise.

After that, he'd stayed out of the forest for as long as he could. The borders of Kamieńa had been expanding for almost twenty years. Not out of any human intention, but because the forest seemed to be spreading, and with every mile closer he drew, the towns grew emptier. Finally in view of the first trees, he'd spent the night in an abandoned village on its borders. Unseen evils had chattered in the trees and the stars had seemed particularly dark that night, so dark that Lukasz had brought Król indoors and slept in a modest little kitchen, rifle pointed toward the door.

The next morning, he'd entered the forest.

There'd been no one to stop him. Even if Kamieńa wasn't exactly forgotten these days, it was at least ignored. Besides, Welona was an unusual country in that most of its internal borders were unofficial. Ruled centrally from Miasto by King Nikodem and his parliament, Welona was also separated into smaller constituent provinces. Often referred to as kingdoms, these provinces were governed by minor kings—usually the descendants of the great war chieftains of medieval days when the country was constantly at war with itself.

Once upon a time, Hala Smoków had been the country's last truly independent city.

"All right," said Lukasz at last, and Król's other ear swiveled toward him. "East. We'll be in the village by sunset."

If it was still there at all.

Franciszek's map had been drawn based on a seventeen-year-old memory. And the last time Lukasz had been in this forest, he'd been four years old, fleeing down from the Mountains with nine older brothers. He barely remembered any of it.

He and Król started moving again, and still feeling uneasy, Lukasz stowed the notebook once more in his pocket and unslung the rifle from the back of the saddle. Even if he wasn't as good with a sword anymore, he wasn't completely defenseless.

They broke into a small clearing. He had a glimpse of a river before Król whinnied and reared up on his hind legs. Lukasz narrowly avoided being impaled on the silver antlers.

"Damn it, Król," he growled, dragging back on the reins with his good hand. "What is it?"

Król shrieked and reared again.

"Król—" He slipped off the horse's back. He grabbed the bridle, tugging the horse down to him. Król's eyes were rimmed in white, his nostrils flaring. "Król, calm down. There's nothing here—"

Lukasz turned toward the river. He froze. There *was* something there.

No. Not something. *Someone.*

It was a girl. She was almost completely submerged, only her eyes and the top of her head visible over the calm water. Her dark hair was plastered to her skull, and its ends floated on the surface in dark coils. She was utterly silent, staring back.

Her eyes were green.

"Hey," he called across the water. "Are you okay?"

She blinked. Her lashes, long and black, disturbed the surface. When they came up, Lukasz could see every bead of water on them.

"Are you okay?" he asked again. "Can I help you?"

Without thinking, he turned to Król and unfastened a length of rope from the saddle. When he turned back to the river, the girl was almost at the water's edge. He jumped back.

"Damn," he gasped.

She'd moved so swiftly, so silently. And strangely, the water had remained still as glass.

Lukasz could feel monsters in his bones the same way other people could feel the weather, and this was all wrong. Between the still water and the hypnotic lilt of her hair on its surface, everything in him was screaming.

Run.

Her eyes fell to the rope in his hand. Then they flickered back up to his face. The only motion was in her hair, glimmering on the surface with a life of its own. Lukasz knew his monsters, and she burned with enchantment.

And yet here he was . . .

Her eyes were so green.

"It's okay," he said. He lowered the rope to the ground. Then he straightened, holding up both hands, palms out. "I won't hurt you."

Her eyes slid to his hands.

He swallowed. The right was brown, with long fingers and scars across his knuckles. The left was pale and mottled.

She stared.

"Here," he said. He knelt at the water's edge. "It's okay, I won't—"

The girl pulled back her lips. Long incisors and dark gums stared out at him, and the rough tongue of a cat. She hissed, and it was the guttural hiss of a wild animal. Lukasz scrambled backward.

"What the—"

The girl launched herself out of the water. Only she wasn't a girl anymore—

He rolled out of the way just in time for two hundred pounds of fur and muscle to burst out of the river. The lynx skidded on the bank, tearing up the earth, before rounding on him, fangs bared. Lukasz scrambled back to his feet. Król screamed and danced out of the way, but the lynx ignored the horse.

"Listen, I won't—" Lukasz held up both hands.

The creature—whatever it was—hissed. He still had his sword at his side, but the rifle was on Król's saddle—behind the lynx. Lukasz weighed his options. Its tufted ears lay flat to its skull. He could see every muscle tensing, coiling, getting ready to attack. His mind reeled.

What the hell is this?

Even through his panic, even with those bright green eyes boring into his, a very small voice whispered:

Franciszek would know.

The creature snarled. It began to pace.

"Easy—" he started. He held out his hands, aware of his left gravitating to the sword hilt. Better to take his chances—

The lynx went still.

Its pupils narrowed, face turning to the sky, and its ears sprang up. For a split second, Lukasz considered making a dash for Król and the rifle—

A shadow fell.

The smell hit him next. He choked on the scent of scorched hair, burned flesh. The air was hot. The rest of the world fell away, even the creature opposite him, and his heart automatically fell into time with wingbeats.

Thud. Thud. Thud.

Lukasz raised his eyes and met the gaze of the Golden Dragon.

It hovered about thirty feet overhead, its great golden face weaving down from the clouds. Lukasz wasn't an idiot. He knew his dragons. He'd killed more dragons and in a shorter time period than any other slayer in known history. He knew this was different.

It was huge. At least three times bigger than any dragon he'd ever seen. Its antlers branched like a forest, with too many tines to count. Its scales rippled like an ocean of gold, and its claws were chipped, stained with soot. Its eyes were pure black, and when its long jaws opened, a black serpentine tongue slithered out and flicked the air. It also defied species—the antlers and head of a Faustian, the body of a Ływern, the color of a—

No, he thought. *Nothing is gold. Not like that.*

In its own terrible way, it was beautiful.

Wonder hardened into fury. He'd lost nine brothers to this damn dragon, and he wasn't about to miss the opportunity. He still wore his broadsword at his side, and now he considered whether to go for his sword or the rifle, which was still on Król's saddle.

The dragon watched his indecision, and then its jaws curved. It took Lukasz a moment to recognize it as a smile. Then the smile widened and it spat a stream of fire.

Lukasz dived for the ground. He hit the grass, rolled over, and careered toward the edge of the bank. Clawing for a handhold, he had a brief—horrible—swooping sensation before he hit the water.

There was a moment of silence. The river was as cold as ice. He could make out golden light through the rippling surface. Then he found his footing and scrambled upright.

Golden flames flickered over the riverbank, exactly where he had been standing. They spread to the trees beyond, swallowing the branches in golden flames. Lukasz shielded his head as a few feet away, a burning psotnik plummeted from one of the branches and hit the water with a hiss.

He pushed his soaking hair off his forehead.

The water was shallow, barely up to his waist, and his hand went to the sword at his side. The dragon hovered overhead, watching, wings beating. He raised it in his left hand, old blood peeling off the blade.

The dragon watched.

His arm was even weaker, and his fingers were too stiff to bend around the hilt. He could see the blade trembling. He wondered if the dragon could see it, too. He changed it to his right hand. It felt foreign.

"Come on," he whispered. "Come on—"

Lukasz readied for the attack. He didn't have time to get out of the water. Not if it struck. But he was not going to die. Not in the shadow of this monster, and not in this forest.

But the Dragon did not attack. Instead, the slim head retreated back into the sky. And then, while he wondered whether it was dumb enough to fall for the old lighter trick, the Dragon began to lift away. Scarcely believing what he was seeing, Lukasz watched it rise above the trees. Its long throat curved up toward the sky, and a few scales tumbled down to earth as its tail clipped a tree.

The sky was empty.

The flames burned steadily. Lukasz realized suddenly that his heart was pounding. And he knew, looking at that shaking blade, that his left hand was no good. All because of his damn gloves! Lukasz swore and flung the sword onto the bank. It skidded a few inches along the grass, and then lay, even more blood chipping away, useless. He was useless.

He was shaking. Was this what his parents had seen, before they'd died? A black-toothed grin and golden flames? And his brothers . . . ? And Franciszek . . . *Oh God,* he thought. Franciszek. If only he'd listened. If only Franciszek hadn't left. And if only *he* hadn't gone after that damn Apofys.

If only he could still hold a sword.

Lukasz clasped his hands behind his head, trying to catch his breath. The air was hot, filled with the smell of burning trees and the crackle of flames. Around him, the forest burned gold, and more psotniki dropped like fireballs, hissing as they hit the water around him.

It was at that moment that someone touched his shoulder.

"My darling," whispered a musical voice in his ear. "Let me help you."

Lukasz turned and came face-to-face with the girl from the river.

4

FROM THE SHELTER OF THE trees, Ren watched.

The human didn't see her. He was too focused on the Dragon, as it lifted away. Then he flung the sword on the bank, shouted a word Ren didn't recognize. She squinted. She wasn't used to humans, but this one seemed angry. Not realizing how stupid he was being, he took a few dazed steps deeper into the water. Ren had little sympathy, but she thought she recognized this look. Someone reeling after an unexpected escape. And yet . . .

He didn't seem afraid of the Dragon.

Why not?

Ren quelled the growl that rose in her throat. *And why am* I *afraid?*

Logically speaking? Because she was smarter. Because she knew what it had *done*. Because she knew how dangerous the Dragon was. Because all humans were reckless and dangerous and because humans never looked at something without dreaming up a way to kill it.

Why had it let him live?

The river began to move. Ren blinked. Tiny eddies twisted and broke in white crests, as if just below the surface a creature was circling. The river went still.

Then it came.

Water broke smoothly over the female head, eyes fluttering as droplets showered the surface. At first, he didn't notice it. The creature had slick wet hair, deep brown against skin so pale that it glimmered in the steel-blue water. She had sleek features, and when they finally opened, her eyes were green.

The creature straightened, and Ren's heart dropped right out of her chest.

It looked *just* like her—no, it *was* her—it was Ren herself, standing in the water—

A rusalka.

Ren tried not to panic. Rusalki made strzygi look about as sweet-tempered as fawns. She'd heard they took their victims apart piece by piece, molding their skins to their own glistening bodies. Ren swallowed, realizing with a sickening feeling why this rusalka had chosen to resemble her.

The creature laid long-fingered hands on the human's shoulders and whispered in his ear. The human turned to face it.

Reckless, thoughtless fool. Ren hesitated. *Stupid, dangerous creature. But . . . but—*

"STOP!" She galloped out of the trees, over the burning ground. "Get away from it—"

If he heard her, he ignored her. Maybe because she was an animal. Ren shook herself out, unfolding to her full human height.

45

"Get out of there," she shouted. "It's a rusalka—"

Over his shoulder, the rusalka caught her eye. It giggled, and even Ren could hear the music in it. The creature undulated out of the water and pressed itself into him. Bone-white skin against the wet black coat, it entwined those webbed fingers in his hair.

"I am the queen," said Ren, with as much authority as she could. "And I command you to let him go. Now."

She told herself it wasn't out of pity. Or compassion. It was because the dragon had spared his life, and because she needed to know why.

The rusalka giggled again. She wrapped one arm around his neck and pulled herself up to whisper more quiet things in his ear. *No . . .* Ren corrected herself. Not a *she.* An *it.*

Ren could see its fingers flat across his back, gossamer-thin membranes sparkling between them. Maybe it looked like her. Maybe it looked like a dozen other girls. But nothing about that thing, right down to the broken, bloodstained nail, was human.

The light of the fire caught them both in flashing angles, and then the rusalka took its face out of his neck and looked Ren right in the eye.

"Let him go," Ren repeated.

It smiled. Its perfect lips peeled back from stained teeth. They were square, but so chipped and crowded that they looked like fangs. Ren snarled back. She was the queen. She came second to no one.

But the rusalka just laughed. It didn't take its eyes from her as it took his chin in a clawed hand and jerked him to face her. Eyes still locked on Ren, it kissed him. His arms came up, encircling it. And to Ren's disgust, he kissed it back.

It had him. It had him, and it was keeping him. Ren watched, suddenly nauseated, as the rusalka closed its eyes, kissed him like it was starving, and together—forever—they slipped below the water's surface. Water slid over, covered them. The river was still as glass.

Ren swallowed.

She stared into the water. She should leave. She knew that. But the *Dragon* . . . She glanced down at her feet, where the heavy sword lay in the grass. She reached down and touched the blade. Blood came away on her fingertips. And then, before she could react, her fingers began to tingle, and tiny sparks of flame leapt to life and then disappeared.

Ren jumped back, heart racing. She stared at the still water again. *Is that . . . Could it be . . . ?*

She glanced up at the burning trees.

Dragon blood?

It was possible, she realized, that he knew about dragons. And it was possible, she reasoned, that he might even deserve better than death from a rusalka.

I won't hurt you, he'd said.

He didn't just look different. He'd looked at *her* differently. Without fear or anger. He'd looked at her like he wanted to help.

Ren shook her head. No, better not to think about that. She had seen what they'd done to Czarn. The humans called *her* a monster, but they'd been the ones to . . . to do *that* to him.

Ren gritted her teeth.

There was no point in trying to find good in them. Trying to find compassion, or kindness. She needed him alive for the same reason she had needed to bury those humans in the clearing: it was for her forest.

Nothing else.

Ren closed her eyes, took a deep breath, and dived into the water. It was cold. Bone-chillingly cold.

While her eyes adjusted to the dark, she scrabbled blindly, searching for the riverbank, trying to orient herself—

She nearly screamed.

She'd expected mud. What she found was a skull.

She pulled her fingers out of the empty sockets, her vision clearing a little. It was embedded in the riverbank, one of hundreds. The skulls formed rows in the mud. Fishers and water spiders flitted in and out of their evil grins. Bones floated around her, illuminated by shafts of light, shot through the green water.

She peered into the murk. The river seemed to go down forever. Far below, a writhing shape receded rapidly into the depths.

Ren kicked hard and shot down like a missile.

He'd come to his senses. He was trying fight off the rusalka. No longer beautiful, it had turned to a skeleton, draped in slime and bloated flesh. Stringy hairs still clung to its skull. It clawed at his eyes and he flailed like a wounded animal.

Ren grabbed the skeleton's arm and pulled. It reeled, hissing at her, tongue still intact in its toothy mouth. Ren snarled back. She seized the creature by the eye sockets and yanked. The skull came right off the spine. The skeleton went instantly limp. Ren pushed past the bones and grabbed his arm. His eyes were already closing.

Around them, the water began to writhe. Skeletons rose from the depths. They drifted, hissing, baring more broken teeth and bits of tongue. Ren growled, but it didn't carry through the water.

There were too many to fight. It wasn't going to be a battle—just an escape. Hanging on to the human, she kicked as hard as she could. Bony fingers closed on her ankle, jerked them back down.

No. Ren cursed inwardly. She wasn't going to die down here. Not like this.

Ren hissed again. She flexed her free hand, watched it shorten and broaden into an animal's paw. She swiped down at the hand on her ankle.

Ren felt bones splinter under the blow. The rusalka screeched, the sound muffled by the water, and fell away. Its rotten hand scattered into a hundred tiny bones, floating slowly away in the gloom.

On every side, darkness writhed. Another rusalka lunged for Ren, but she hacked at it with her claws. With every blow, more skeletons fell away, bones splintering, empty mouths howling. She gripped the human tight and kicked upward.

Golden light marbled overhead. Her lungs burned. The human was like an anchor on her arm, motionless and silent. A rusalka grabbed her shoulder, but Ren's heavy paw smashed its skull in two. She needed air.

She kicked with all her strength, ignoring the pain in her legs. Her lungs were in agony. She aimed only for that patch of light. She kicked harder, but she barely moved. She watched, in horror, as bubbles streamed from her lips. No—no—not like this—not *for* this—

A hand closed on her shoulder.

With the last of her strength, Ren turned. She felt slow. The world was getting dimmer.

The hand was yellowish-brown, with webbed, thick fingers. Wodnik. He blinked at her. Without a word, he gripped her tight and together they flew upward.

They broke the surface.

Ren gasped, gulping down the fresh forest air. It had begun to rain, and droplets pelted the river surface and bounced off the riverbank. She sputtered up the rank water. The human was heavier than ever, still not moving at all.

Wordlessly, Wodnik took them each in one hand and bore them to the riverbank. He heaved Ren onto the bank, then the human. The man was totally unconscious.

"Wodnik," she gasped, between coughs. "Thank you—"

Wodnik didn't reply. He was already slipping back into the murk, yellow eyes glowing, his toady face as serious as ever. Rain still hammering the water, he blinked once and faded away.

Ren caught her breath. She couldn't even scrub at her eyes properly, she was shaking so hard. She wrapped her arms around her knees and dug in her nails. It took her a few trembling moments to realize that her left hand was still a paw. She'd scratched her own knee, and a thin line of red blood trailed down her shin. She ignored the blood. She held the paw in front of her and flexed each claw, watching them lengthen to fingers. The fur shivered and melted into smooth, rust-smeared skin. She let out a shuddering sigh. Her bloodstained human hand hugged her knees.

Thunder rolled overhead. It shook the trees to their roots, and Ren put her chin on her knees and shook with them.

Beside her, the human stirred at last. He lurched onto his side, spitting out river water. He twitched a bit but fell back into the mud. Then he was motionless again.

The horse was long gone, bolted into the underbrush. Ren looked over at him, cheek resting on her knees, arms drawn up around her. He had one hand over his eyes, and at least he was breathing. She didn't ever want to do that again. Didn't ever want to see the Dragon. Didn't ever want to see a monster like that . . .

She reached out suddenly and touched his hand. Gently, she ran her own long fingers along the sinewy, puckered skin.

A burn.

The old-fashioned sword. The blood that had disappeared in flames. His horse had been decorated with antlers, she realized suddenly. Not just the ones mounted on its forehead; dozens of pairs had hung from the saddle, in precious metal and glass, so that the horse had chimed and glowed with every step.

Ren examined his hand, thinking.

The remaining fingers were so curled under that they looked like claws. The Golden Dragon had antlers.

The human started to pull back the wounded hand. Ren let it go. It fell to his chest, where the thickened, leatherlike skin looked even uglier against the black fabric. He didn't open his eyes. Ren ran a hand over his jacket's silver braid. She'd never seen clothes like this.

She put her hand on his cheek. Spread her fingers, like the rusalka had done. With her thumb, rubbed away the brownish blood. She wasn't sure why. To see how it felt, maybe.

He'd tried to help her. She'd lived in this forest for seventeen years, and no human had ever tried to help her.

His eyelashes were long. He had a notch out of one eyebrow. Ren ran a finger over that, too. Thunder rolled, his eyes flickered, and Ren imagined she could hear his heartbeat over the roar of the rain.

Ren realized suddenly that she had leaned down very close.

She felt a hand on her cheek. She didn't know what was

happening, exactly. But she did know she didn't mind. He was cold from the water, and his palm was rough. Ren wondered whether he was close to smiling, and she could just make out a crooked front tooth, beneath his lips.

His eyes cleared.

Click.

Ren jerked back, as—from nowhere—a flame appeared in his hand. The fire danced, and fear seized her.

What was she thinking? What was she *doing*?

Her teeth lengthened to fangs as she shot back across the bank, silvery legs lashing out, claws catching the grass. She was a lynx. This was a human. A dangerous, cheating, murderous human. And what if the other humans, the villagers and the hunters, found out she'd just *save* them like this. . . .

The flame still in his hand, he scrambled backward. With his other hand, he searched the grass. The blood-encrusted blade sparked in the damp.

Ren circled, snarling.

Click.

The flame went out.

She snarled again.

"What are you?" he whispered.

And before she could change her mind, Ren turned and dashed back into the trees.

❧ TADEUSZ ❧

SEVEN YEARS EARLIER

"YOU COULD HAVE USED THE lighter"—Franciszek gestured to what was left of the cathedral altar—"light it, throw it away—"

Lukasz bit back a curse as Tadeusz wrapped a bandage around his leg. It took every shred of his self-control not to swear at Franciszek. He *knew* that, for God's sake. But Franciszek hadn't been the one trapped alone in a cathedral with a three-hundred-year-old Faustian the size of a house. Back up against the wall, nothing but a few feet of broadsword between him and eternity—

"The dragon will go for the lighter every time," continued Franciszek, oblivious to Lukasz's growing irritation. He could never help himself. "Give you enough time to get away."

They were seated in one of the few remaining pews, shoved up against the side wall. Except for the steady drip of blood on the tile, the cathedral was quiet. After everything, the silence made Lukasz uneasy. He half expected to hear it again. The whisper of scales on stone, the low purr of an ancient engine priming for the kill . . .

Tadeusz yanked the bandage tight.

"God, Tad—!"

"Tsk, tsk." Tadeusz clapped a hand to Lukasz's cheek and pretended to be offended. "This is a church, little brother."

Lukasz pressed his head back against the wall, teeth gritted.

Around them, the pews were splintered, the statues were shattered, and what remained of the choir loft was scattered across the marble floors.

"He did just fine, Fraszko," said Tadeusz, turning to Franciszek and wiping bloody hands on his trousers. "It barely caught him."

"But it *did* catch him," replied Franciszek, adjusting his glasses. "One day," he said, in precisely the kind of voice that made Lukasz want to whack him, "you're going to get yourself in real trouble, Lukasz."

Less than a year separated them. When they'd been younger, Lukasz had loved having a ready-made partner in crime. But that was changing as they got older. Franciszek was a worrier and a know-it-all.

"Don't be a jerk," said Lukasz, "just 'cause your horse doesn't have antlers yet."

Franciszek flinched, and Lukasz instantly regretted his words. No one was more aware of the fact that Franciszek had yet to kill anything.

"Fraszko—" started Lukasz.

"Speaking of which, I'll—uh—collect the antlers and fur," said Franciszek, not looking at the other two brothers—Lukasz seated, Tadeusz rising to his feet. "I don't trust the vultures out there for a minute."

"Fraszko, please—"

But Franciszek was already making his way to the dead dragon.

The Faustian was sprawled across the nave, smoke rising gently from its rapidly tarnishing sides. The reporters had taken all their photographs, Tadeusz practically carrying Lukasz through the smiles. They'd been smart to get their pictures quickly. The Faustian's hide was already spoiling.

Even now, their other brothers circled the perimeter, keeping out anyone stupid enough to come after the hoard in the crypt. Although the dragon had taken up residence almost three centuries before, the cathedral's devoted monks had never left. Worshipping under such a prescient reminder of hellfire, they had since been dubbed the Order of Faustus and were known mainly for their tenacity, their poverty, and their scorched habits.

Perhaps unused to good luck of any kind, the poor monks had been quite overwhelmed by the size of their Faustian's hoard—to the point that they'd given almost the entire trove to the Wolf-Lords (although Tad had gifted them more than enough for them to rebuild their leveled cathedral). Remembering the sight of the treasure, heaped among crypts and naked bones, Lukasz could almost taste the gold.

Or maybe it was just blood.

With a sigh, Tadeusz settled beside Lukasz. Lukasz wriggled back into his trousers, doing his best not to yelp as his knee scraped against the coarse fabric. Scarlet pooled on the floor, streaked the wooden pew. Tad crossed his ankles, extracted a glass flask from his leather vest.

"Shall we drink, little brother?"

Lukasz took the proffered flask. Inside, gold swirled through the clear liquid.

"The good stuff, eh?"

He took a long draw as Tadeusz chuckled again.

"The slayer of the Saint Magdalena Faustian deserves the good stuff," he said as Lukasz passed back the flask. "Even if he is only fourteen."

Of them all, Tadeusz looked the most like their father. Black haired, with the sharp, handsome face of a bird of prey. Usually Tad looked stately. Like the eldest Wolf-Lord, the first heir, the statesman he was supposed to be. But today, his hair was windswept and his beard was singed.

It began to rain. Lightly at first, then crescendoing to a torrent. Under their scrap of roof, the brothers watched it turn into a downpour. The floor ran black with soot, drops thundering off the Faustian's lifeless hide. Just beyond the dead monster's jaws, a pool of Lukasz's blood scattered and washed away.

"Be patient with Fraszko, Luk," said Tad after a moment. "He's only taking care of you."

"He babies me," said Lukasz shortly.

"Let him. You're his only younger brother."

Smoldering and blackened by smoke, painted cherubs leered down from what was left of the ceiling. They seemed faintly malevolent. Demonic, even. Lukasz glanced away. His leg looked skinny, and through the tear in the embroidered fabric, his skin was painted in blood and soot. Franciszek was right. He'd been lucky not to lose it.

Then Tadeusz said, a little thoughtfully, "Fourteen, my God."

The sounds of the other brothers drifted through what was left of the walls: horses whinnying, men shouting, the metallic tinkle of treasure loaded and unloaded. The steady thunder of the rain.

"Here," said Tadeusz. "I wanted to give you this."

Lukasz glanced over. In the gloom, a cross revolved, suspended from Tadeusz's hand. It was small and plain, wrought from silver. Next to all the gold and jewels in the crypt, it looked rather small.

"It was Dad's," said Tadeusz as Lukasz took it. "He gave it to me before . . ."

Tad's voice trailed off.

Lukasz had been four years old when their father had ridden out under the great gates of Hala Smoków. When he did not return, the other Wolf-Lords had gone after him. In service of their chieftain, in pursuit of gold and glory—who knew anymore. It didn't matter. Lukasz barely remembered any of it. Barely remembered the hushed voices. Barely remembered how his mother had wept, lighting the sacred *gromnica* in every corner of the lodge while she prayed.

What he remembered were the *domowiki*. How they had howled, that last night. Wailing under the floorboards, screaming from the rafters. He remembered every door in the lodge slamming shut, the force shaking them like thunder, while he cowered in his bed. He remembered his mother's blessed candles, every last one of them blowing out.

Even then, Franciszek had been the smartest.

When the domowiki cry, he'd whispered in the darkness of their bedroom, *it means the head of the house is dead.*

What do you mean? Lukasz must have asked. He never knew what he remembered and what he just imagined.

He's dead, said Franciszek. *Dad's dead, Lukasz.*

Gone up in golden flames, consumed by golden jaws. Who knew how it had happened. It didn't matter. Domowiki did not lie. Lord

Tadeusz the Elder, Friend of Wolves and Slayer of Dragons, was dead.

The very next morning, their mother sent them away.

Keep your brothers safe, Lukasz had heard her command Tadeusz, amid wood-carved walls and under the glow of dragon bones. *I will kill it and send for you.*

But she never did. Ten years had come and gone, and the brothers did not go back.

"I think," said Tadeusz after another moment, "it is time that I returned to Hala Smoków."

"Why? We were told to stay out." Lukasz looked up sharply. His heart skipped a beat. "Or did you hear—?"

Tadeusz's chin jerked. It was short and compulsive and negated the rest of Lukasz's question.

"Our home is in the Mountains," said Tad. "It is time we returned."

"Why?" repeated Lukasz. "There's no one there. Our parents are dead." He ignored how Tadeusz flinched and continued: "It's been almost ten years. We should build lives out here. We left for a reason, Tadeusz."

"I understand, Lukasz. But I am the eldest. It is time I went back and rebuilt what was once there. We are the last in a tradition of great warriors, and it cannot die with us." Then he added, in a softer voice: "When I have killed the Dragon, I will send for you."

"That's what Mom said."

Tadeusz didn't answer.

Around them, the rain thundered on. Darkness clouded the Faustian's dull scales. Soon its corpse would begin to erode. Flesh darkening, fangs loosening. In a few months, it would be dryness and dust, as fragile as sand castles on a Granica beach. Soon enough, wind would blow the dust from its flawless silver bones.

"It's not our home anymore."

Tadeusz put an arm around his little brother's shoulders.

"For a thousand years, our people have run with wolves and slain dragons. We are heirs to gold and fire, baptized under ice, destined to inherit a tradition as ancient as the hills themselves. Whatever lengths we travel, Lukasz, whatever worlds we visit: we shall be buried in the shadow of the Mountains, beneath the blessings of wolves."

At Tad's words, a chill scuttled over Lukasz's shoulders.

"Shadow of the Mountains, eh?" He rubbed his eyes. "What about ruined churches?"

But Tadeusz did not laugh. He looked like their father in that moment: heavy jawed, serious. Not the kind of man who joked over blasphemy and gold-flecked vodka.

"You are still young, Lukasz," he said. "But one day, you will see."

And then he turned their father's eyes away. Trained them on the silver Faustian, stripped of its antlers and its fur and gathering darkness. Three hundred years of terrible beauty, now so swiftly fading, crumbling to ruin. And when Tadeusz spoke again, his voice carried the growl of wolves, the roar of mountains, and the echoes of ten centuries.

"One day, Lukasz," he whispered, "the Mountains will call you home."

⚚ 5 ⚚

LENGTHENING HER STRIDE TO THE flexible gallop of a predator, Ren sprinted home.

She dashed under the ramparts and tore up the front steps, past twin stone lynx statues. She streaked across the cool, dark entrance hall, vaulting over shards of the fallen chandelier. On the upstairs landing, she rounded a corner, carpet shredding under her claws.

Czarn was waiting for her.

He lay on his belly, high in an alcove opposite a wall of windows. The alcove had previously housed a rather vivid rendering of a witch being drowned. Ren despised the painting on principal, and she and Ryś had deposed it early in childhood.

From his vantage point, Czarn surveyed the forest below.

"That was a long swim," he observed.

He had the kind of voice that could stop a conversation in its tracks: round, slow, a little clipped at the edges.

Ren picked her way across what was left of the shredded canvas. The sky was dull gray, and Czarn looked like just another shadow in the dim light of the hall. His perch was flanked by faded banners in purple and gold, rippling slightly in the chill draft.

"You look quite at home there," said Ren.

She transformed, slowly this time, back to a human. This was always the gentler part of the change. The transition from four legs to two came more easily to her.

"I am very noble," agreed Czarn serenely.

"I meant you're a snob."

Czarn chuckled and watched as Ren used the closer banner to scale the wall to the alcove. She settled next to him, long dirty legs dangling over the edge. As darkness fell, a few sparrows swooped in through a broken window, home to their nest among the golden-wrought deer busts.

"Were you waiting for me?"

"Maybe."

"Why?"

Czarn eased onto his side and kicked out his back legs. He said, as the hall dimmed another shade: "Maybe I was worried."

Ren was about to laugh when she saw the thin stream of black smoke over the trees. It was stark against the low purple rise of the Mountains beyond, already rumbling in the east.

The smoke was coming from the river. The Dragon.

"You saw it?" she asked.

"I did," said Czarn. Then he added, very gently: "Are you all right?"

Ren nodded, staring at her knees. Her human legs looked appallingly skinny here in the dark. She barely spent any time as a human, these days. There was no time for it. No use.

A raccoon family trundled past, probably on their way down to the cellars to curl up in the empty vodka barrels and bicker with the badgers.

Ren swallowed and confessed: "I . . . I saved a human today."

Czarn didn't say anything, but his tail gave an involuntary twitch. He had suffered the most at their hands. He deserved to hate these humans more than anyone else.

Ren couldn't look at him.

"I didn't mean to," she said softly. "I mean, I didn't want to. He came up to the river, and the Golden Dragon—Czarn, it . . . I think he wanted to fight it, but it left. It left him alone."

Still, Czarn didn't say anything. Ren watched the gray sky turn purple, watched the black smoke disappear into darkness. Wondered, for the first time, where that human was now . . .

"He fell into the river," she said. "And a rusalka almost killed him."

Here, Czarn took a sharp breath in.

"I'm sorry, Czarn," she whispered, knotting and unknotting her hands. "I'm so sorry. I just had to know—I was curious. He—he was strange, Czarn. Different from the villagers. There was blood—dried blood that turned to fire—on his sword, and his horse had antlers on its head and—"

"*What?*"

Czarn's voice was sharp.

Ren finally looked up. He was not looking at her with anger or disappointment, but—maybe she was imagining it—*hope*?

"You said his horse had antlers," said Czarn slowly. "Are you sure? On its bridle?"

Ren thought back to the horse on the riverbank, before it had bolted into the trees.

"Yes," said Ren, trying to remember the details. "One pair on its bridle. More on the saddle. There must have been hundreds of them."

Czarn exhaled through his fangs. It brought up a rumbling growl. When he spoke again, his voice was low and heavy, and it hummed in Ren's heart.

"What did he look like? This human?"

Ren shrugged.

"Black hair."

"He may have been wearing a fur vest?" asked Czarn. "And a belt! Wide, made of leather."

"No." Ren shook her head. "He wore all black."

"Long hair? A beard?"

Ren shook her head.

Czarn searched her face.

"Ren, did he have blue eyes?"

"Czarn, I don't know. I was kind of busy killing rusalki," said Ren exasperatedly. "Why does it matter?"

Czarn stood abruptly and leapt down from the alcove. He paced in front of the window, eyes on the floor. His tail twitched, swishing back and forth across the floor, scattering dust. His limp was worse, and guiltily, Ren wondered if he'd hurt himself fighting the strzygi.

When he finally spoke, his voice was deeper than usual, cooler: as if forged by the Mountains in which he had been born.

"We used to say that to enter our Mountains was to die in them," he began. "The cliffs move in tides every night, and never to the same place twice. If you don't get lost in them, then you will be crushed between them. And the dragons. The Mountains were once filled with them. Dragons and wolves. That's all there was, for a very long time. Dragons and wolves."

In that moment, he seemed much older than her. An ancient sort of quality had entered his voice, for he was telling the oldest stories of his world.

"But then came the Wolf-Lords," he whispered. "They were not like other men. They were fearless. They carved out their home up there in the cold, and they killed the dragons. Decorated their lodges with their bones, wore their fur, mounted their antlers on the heads of their horses. And they understood those Mountains."

Ren had never been to the Mountains. They lay well outside the forest boundaries, and she'd only ever seen their low purple shadow against the sky. Sometimes she heard their murmur on the quietest nights. They had always seemed, to her, to carry secrets. Held close to blue-rock chests, whispered in one another's ears.

"I think," continued Czarn, as if reading her thoughts, "it's easier for us animals, being closer to the earth, to understand the Mountains. But the Wolf-Lords . . . they were different."

Czarn's voice had changed again. He paused by the window, glancing out to the Mountains where he'd been born.

"We were brothers," he murmured. "We swore to protect one another from the dragons and the danger, up there in the cold. And for a thousand years, we did. The Wolf-Lords never came down from their wooden lodges. They preferred the cold blue air, preferred the cliffs that moved every night, preferred the dragons."

In that moment, he was far away. Not in a ruined castle of long-dead humans. Not even in her presence. He was in the cold blue

Mountains of his birth, shale underfoot and his father still living, keeping watch over the humans they had clearly loved so well.

"The Wolf-Lords preferred us."

These brothers of wolves. These enemies of dragons. These humans with the tides of the Mountains written in their blood.

"They sound animal," murmured Ren.

"They were," said Czarn, and his voice was heavy. "And in the best of ways."

He misses them, Ren realized.

"What happened to them?" she asked.

"They died." He continued: "Like we all did. They went after the Golden Dragon. They were dragon slayers. It was, in a sense, only natural. But . . ."

Czarn fell silent, taken away by the memory of days long over. She could imagine the scene. Rows of men and heavy mountain horses picking their way through the Mountains, while Czarn's wolves watched them from afar.

"Czarn," Ren whispered. "What are you saying?"

Czarn looked back at her.

"He is a Wolf-Lord, Ren," he said. His ruff lifted on the draft. "The Mountains have called him home."

Huddled under damp sheets in the topmost tower of the castle, Ren couldn't sleep.

She changed to a lynx, then to a human, and back again. Nothing felt comfortable. Human, and the sheets were damp. Lynx, and she thought of *that* human . . .

ALEKSANDRA ROSS

She should not have saved him. She knew that. She should have left him to the rusalki, like countless other souls had been doomed. She should not have hauled him up onto the riverbank; she should not have caused Wodnik the trouble. She should not have put her hands on his face, and she should never have allowed him to do the same.

His eyes *had* been blue, she remembered suddenly.

A Wolf-Lord, she thought, concentrating on the tiny flowers painted along the white walls of the room. Surely if the wolves called them brothers, they could not be terrible? After all, Czarn had more reason than any to hate the humans. And yet he'd spoken of these mountain people with such fondness, even admiration.

Dragon slayers. Could someone really be that terrible, if their mission was to kill terrible monsters?

Ren got up abruptly and crossed the tower floor. It was blackened, one wall completely torn away. It was the highest tower of the castle, the same tower that the Dragon had first attacked, seventeen years ago. Ren knew the stories; she'd chosen this place on purpose. For it was in this tower that the first queen of this forest had been killed.

And it was in this tower that the second queen reigned.

There had once been a balcony, but it had been torn away in the attack. Now Ren stood at the very edge of the floor with a shoulder against sharp stonework. She edged forward until her toes hung over oblivion, and she looked out at the forest she loved. The forest she would die defending.

The forest she might lose.

Every day she saw the change: dark patches of burned branches and rotting trees. Over the river, black smoke still rose from the

66

burning trees. The village was in there, hidden among the trees, its tired spirals of smoke lost in the black sky.

For the first time in a long time, she felt a pang of sympathy for the villagers.

She blamed the Dragon. Every time it came, it made everything worse. It sent the world up in golden flames, laying open huge gashes in the forest floor. Hidden in the underbrush, Ren had once watched how, in the Dragon's wake, a crater had erupted in the forest floor. It had sizzled red at the edges, tree roots writhing down into the expanse.

And then came the strzygi. Climbing out, licking their scorched limbs. Sloughing off their blistered gray skins. Hungry.

How dare it?

How dare the Dragon come like this, letting these monsters into her world. How dare it set fires and open these pits and scar her forest. It was bad enough that it was always there, always hovering over her shoulder, always threatening to burn her world down. But the fact that it *brought* the others in . . .

Ren's throat burned. She was the queen. It was her duty to protect her animals, and she couldn't even do that.

Ren sighed and crossed her arms.

They needed to kill that Dragon. *She* needed to kill that Dragon.

She turned away from the window. As she walked toward the door, she passed the old armoire. Clothes spilled out onto the floor, and she caught sight of pale lace and blue embroidery. *That stupid human,* she thought viciously.

That stupid, blind, selfish creature.

If she'd put on a nice skirt and a shirt, if she'd worn clothes and not fur, if she'd tried *half* as hard as that rusalka had—

He'd never have known the difference. He'd have kissed her, just like he'd kissed that rusalka. He wouldn't have had that fire, he wouldn't have reached for his sword, he wouldn't have—

Ren stopped, hand on the door.

Slowly, she turned back to the long-forgotten clothes.

"YOU WANT TO DO WHAT?"

Spit sprayed from Ryś's lips, and on the other side of the library, cozily ensconced in armchairs, three *vila* began to giggle.

"Keep your voice down," said Czarn mildly. "I don't think the whole castle needs to hear about this."

Ryś rounded on the wolf.

"Did you *know* about this?"

"Absolutely not," said Czarn delicately.

Ryś sputtered, too overcome to even form words. Ren stood in front of him, arms still crossed. She wore a white lace blouse, decorated with flowers embroidered in pale blue and gold, along with a long navy skirt. Both items were very uncomfortable, and she'd struggled more with the buttons than she cared to admit.

"It's insane," added Czarn after a moment. "And brilliant. I'm sorry I didn't think of it."

Ryś only managed to make a hissing sound.

The three of them were standing on the topmost balcony, overlooking the rest of the library. Even in the moonlight, the library was alive. Birds hopped among the tooth-marked shelves, collecting shredded pages and gold leaf for their nests. Bats hung, snuggled together, from the chandeliers overhead.

On the opposite side of the library, on a matching balcony, the vila continued to pick at their nails and chatter in voices better left unheard.

"Czarn says he's a Wolf-Lord, Ryś," said Ren. "That means he's a dragon slayer. He could do it—"

"We're *not* asking a human to slay the Dragon for us," growled Ryś. "End of story."

"Oh my," murmured Czarn. "I believe the bears have gotten into the Unnatural history section."

Ren glanced to where three bear cubs were happily shredding their way through the shelves of the east corner.

"And Ren," said Ryś in a very dangerous voice, "how did you meet this human?"

The timbre of his voice was enough to make a herd of deer glance up, several of whom delicately exited the library.

"I—" Ren unfolded her arms, then refolded them. "I helped him. The rusalki were going to get him."

"*WHAT?*"

The rest of the deer bolted.

"Don't *what* me," retorted Ren. "I'm the queen!"

"No!" shouted Ryś. "You're my little sister!"

Czarn crossed the balcony to stand next to Ren. Then he settled back with his tail wrapped neatly around his feet.

"Trust me, Ryś," said Czarn. "The Wolf-Lords are reasonable men. They are not like other humans. And besides, this one owes a debt to

Ren. She pulled him out of the water."

Ryś puffed himself up like a sphynx and blinked.

"Reasonable?" he repeated. "Reasonable? I'm surprised, Czarn, after what they did to you."

Ren didn't mean to, but her eye flickered down to his paw.

"Perhaps," said Czarn, in a low voice that warded off further questions, "my past might indicate my enthusiasm for this plan has been carefully considered."

"You don't *sound* enthusiastic," pointed out Ryś hotly.

Czarn lowered himself onto his belly and crossed his paws before responding levelly: "This is just my voice."

Ryś leapt off the pedestal. Two hundred pounds of fur and muscle hit hardwood. He stretched, claws cutting scars in the floor. Then he said quietly, "I worry you're asking for trouble, Malutka."

Ren met his eyes.

"You were happy to make me strzygi bait this morning," she said. "Why is this any different?"

He blinked.

"You know this is different, Ren. Strzygi are one thing. Humans are another."

"What about the Dragon?" Ren could hear the edge in her voice. "It's the worst of them all. And this human—this Wolf-Lord—he could kill it, Ryś. He could kill the worst monster this forest has ever seen."

At that moment, a white eagle swooped through the open window and settled on one of the chandeliers. They were solid gold, the chandeliers, and molded into circles of animals that chased each other's tails. Its swinging shadow fell over the three of them, sent smaller shadows of animals dancing over the hardwood.

Ren loved those chandeliers. They reminded her of what her forest had once been. She held on to that dream; she knew, because she couldn't let go of knowing, that one day, her forest would look like that again. One day, she'd stop it. One day they'd drive the evil out.

One day, even the burns would fade.

Ryś looked sad.

"Ren," he said quietly, "don't you see? Of all the monsters to set foot in your forest, by far the most evil has been man."

6

THOUGH THE RAIN HAD LIFTED, it had spoiled the twilight that remained. Lukasz emerged from the trees to find the remaining houses of the village leaning upon one another. Evergreens encroached, glistening and damp. A cat, as gray as the sky, sat in a dim window and watched him with narrow eyes. The streets were empty.

Lukasz would never forget riding through Kamieńa's village as a boy. It had seemed bigger back then. Had terror made it loom larger? Maybe he just had less to fear these days. Less to lose.

Król's halting steps carried them over the soaked, crumbling streets. The houses watched their advance. Lukasz's leg had been aching more than usual since the river.

Stupid, stupid, stupid. Hadn't all those years of fighting dragons taught him *anything*?

Goddamnit, Lukasz, you should know better. He could practically hear Franciszek's voice. *We've been at this for long enough. But no, along comes someone pretty and you forget* everything—

Lukasz shook off the imagined lecture. *No*, he decided. Franciszek had no right to scold him. He'd already done the stupidest thing a man could do, coming back here alone. Besides, he didn't want to linger on what had dragged him underwater.

And he didn't want to linger on what had dragged him out again.

A few shutters creaked as he passed. Shadows moved within, and bizarrely, Lukasz found himself hoping they were human. This damn forest was playing tricks on him. Washing draped like wet wraiths over the clotheslines. The eaves sank, and a few streets ahead, mist wreathed a lonely church steeple. He unhitched his rifle and laid it across his knees, but no one challenged him.

Maybe he was being paranoid. But after the river . . .

As he rode, faces drifted up to the windows, foggy and pale. People stepped out of the shadows. Mothers wore folksy skirts with black vests over billowing white blouses. They balanced their toddlers on the windowsills, pointing at his horse. Or maybe at the Faustian fur on his jacket. Or maybe at the dragon antlers.

Lukasz dismounted, wincing as his bad leg pivoted on the slippery street. A public fountain stood in the middle of what had once been the town square. A scummy angel poured a dribbling stream of water from an even scummier urn. Król turned up his nose.

"Snob," muttered Lukasz.

He took off his gloves and pushed his damp hair off his forehead, tucking it under his cap. He still hadn't dried off properly from the river. He looked around while Król drank, acutely aware of the rifle's weight on his shoulder. It wasn't his imagination; the village was definitely smaller. Evergreens loomed darkly on every side, swallowing the outermost dwellings.

Between the church and an ornate stuccoed building three men were working in the graveyard. Two dug steadily, while a third presided over them, rifle resting on his shoulders and a curved pipe in his mouth. All three had black hats and sandy mustaches.

Lukasz let Król's reins drop and drifted toward the gate.

They wore green-and-orange-striped trousers, long coats, and pointed black boots. Compared with the city, their clothes seemed a hundred years out of date.

For some reason, he remembered Bieleć's comment.

I have a special interest in historical peoples.

Lukasz rested his forearms on the fence. They were digging graves. Three bodies, wrapped in white sheets, were piled next to mounds of dirt. The men paused every now and again to climb out and lean against the tombstones, smoking and chatting.

Lukasz watched, running his good fingers along the burns of his left hand. He hated that hand. Hated how it looked, hated the fact that it trembled if he didn't pay attention, hated that the fingers didn't bend all the way down, hated that he couldn't hold a sword—

He was never going to get used to it. And honestly, he didn't want to.

"A Wolf-Lord in sheep's clothing," said a cool, smooth voice. "An honor indeed."

Lukasz jerked around. On the other side of the fence, the three gravediggers glanced up, then went back to their work.

"Major Koszmar Styczeń," said the newcomer. "Light calvary. Call me Koszmar."

Lukasz wasn't sure if it was an invitation or a command.

Koszmar Styczeń was around his age and wore a formal black tailcoat dripping with gold braid and topped with golden epaulets. He had a shiny black cavalry helmet clasped to his side. Even his appearance was annoying.

Lukasz inclined his head.

"Lukasz Smoków. Brygada Smoka."

The other man clicked his heels together and bowed.

They must have looked ridiculous, standing on the street of a ghost town. And this perfectly polished and turned-out officer, bowing to a soaking-wet, completely disheveled, sorry excuse for a dragon slayer.

"I know a lot about you, Lieutenant," said Koszmar Styczeń.

Lukasz raised an eyebrow. "How exciting for you."

Uninvited, Major Styczeń leaned an elbow on the fence. Lukasz noticed that he wore a seal around his neck: a cast-gold stork and serpent, symbolizing high-ranking officers. He continued, obliviously:

"The youngest of the Brothers Smokówi. At first there were ten, then two. The smallest brigade in Wrony history." He smiled. He had very long teeth, with slightly too much space between them.

"Now, don't get me wrong," said Lukasz at last. "This is my favorite fairy tale. But I have heard it before."

"Of course. How thoughtless of me. You'll forgive me. It's a rare day that one meets a Wolf-Lord." Koszmar replaced the helmet on his head, the vila-hair plume cascading over one shoulder. He glanced over and asked abruptly: "How is your hand, by the way?"

Lukasz felt his jaw tighten.

A group of young women had congregated near the fountain. Their hair was as dull as the stripes on their long skirts, their skin was almost as white as their blouses, and they held thin cigarettes in thin hands. The only things colorful about them were their bloodred boots, vivid against the dull street.

"You'd think they'd never seen Wrony before," observed Koszmar after a moment.

Wrony was the nickname for the royal army. *The Crows.*

"They probably haven't," replied Lukasz.

Warily, he watched as the women moved a little too close to Król for his taste. Sometimes, the antlers proved too great a temptation.

"I've been here for three days," said Koszmar in a thoughtful voice. "No one stared then."

"I'm a Wolf-Lord," Lukasz said without thinking. "People always stare."

Koszmar turned to him, and for an instant, he seemed almost predatory.

"Yes," said Koszmar in a very soft voice. "Yes, they do."

Against the dim haze of the village, Koszmar looked somehow sharper. Only his eyes reflected the gloom around them: pale, gray, and flat.

Lukasz glanced back at the women, unsettled. One of them, maybe a bit younger than he was, was stroking the black horse's neck. Król turned toward her, ears flicking forward, and she produced a carrot from her pocket. Even from across the square, Lukasz could see the horse's eyes light up.

"So," began Koszmar, extracting a pipe from his pocket. It

was an expensive little trinket, carved and inlaid with amber. He puffed a few perfect smoke rings in the gathering gloom and asked, with deliberate casualness: "Lukasz. I suppose you're here for that Golden Dragon?"

God, I wish.

Lukasz curled and uncurled what was left of his fingers. It had taken eight weeks, a trembling blade, and a Golden Dragon, but at least he could start admitting it to himself.

His dragon-slaying days were over.

He shook his head. Koszmar Styczeń watched him closely. His eyes had gone black, and they were set back under brows much darker than his blond hair. It gave his face a hard, closed look.

"Not to point out the *kikimora* behind the stove, but you are a dragon slayer. Possibly the greatest dragon slayer in history." A smile unfurled on Koszmar's face. Then he added: "Lost your nerve, have you?"

Lukasz curled his melted fingers under, out of sight.

"Saw the light, more like it," he replied. "At the end of a very long hallway, and it turned out to be dragon fire. I've retired."

In the heartbeat that followed, Lukasz decided that he had no interest in elaborating, and simply added, "I'm here looking for my brother."

Koszmar's eyes narrowed. Smoke poured out of his nostrils and swirled, as languid as his gaze, toward the sky.

"Your brother?" His brow furrowed. "Which one?"

Lukasz wasn't surprised that Koszmar knew nothing of Franciszek's disappearance. Franciszek didn't like photographs; he was shorter and thinner than the others, and whereas the other nine were instantly recognized as Wolf-Lords wherever they went, Franciszek was often mistaken for a townsman. Besides, he always preferred to remain behind the scenes, to step in when needed, but otherwise, to leave the glory to Lukasz.

Lukasz missed that about him.

"What are they doing?" he asked, changing the subject.

The gravediggers had finished digging, and one at a time, they rolled the bloody, sheet-clad figures over the edges. The bodies made thick, wet sounds as they hit the mud.

Thud.

"Burying the dead," murmured Koszmar.

Thud.

"Lonely way to go," observed Lukasz. He tried not to consider the possibility that more likely than not, at least a few of his brothers had gone in lonelier ways.

Thud.

The gravedigger with the rifle took it off his shoulder and held it ready. One of the men jumped into the grave. He raised the shovel and brought it down, hard.

Lukasz jumped back from the fence. The second man climbed down into the second grave. Brought his shovel down, hard.

"What the *hell*—?"

"They were killed by strzygi," explained Koszmar in a calm voice. "A villager found them buried in the woods today—only they hadn't been dealt with correctly. So they brought them back here to do the thing right. Strzygi victims need to be buried facedown and beheaded. Otherwise they could turn into a strzygoń."

"Who says?" asked Lukasz.

He'd heard of strzygi, but he'd never seen one up close. Dragons were more his wheelhouse.

"Superstition?" Koszmar shrugged. "You'd have to ask that writer on the edge of town. Nasty face. Looks like a regular *gargulec*," he added, without sympathy.

One of the men climbed into the third grave and, lifting the shovel high, severed the head of the last body.

"The poor bastards put up a good fight, though," said Koszmar. Thoughtfully, he ran his fingers through the vila hair where it shimmered on his shoulder. "There were over a dozen dead strzygi in that clearing. Quite impressive, really."

Briefly, Lukasz wondered what took a man like this from Miasto, dragged him here, to the edge of the world. To stare into graves, lean on fences, and make conversation with dying breeds.

"Writer?" Lukasz repeated suddenly. "What writer?"

Koszmar looked at him blankly.

Lukasz's voice came out rougher than he intended. "You called him a gargulec—"

"Oh." Koszmar raised his hands to the darkening sky. His tone did not alter from its soft, controlled elegance. "Rybak, I think? Jakub Rybak? Fancies himself an Unnaturalist, or something of that kind. He lives in one of the ruins on the edge— *Hey!*"

Koszmar broke off as Lukasz lurched back from the fence. *Jakub Rybak.* That name . . . a name six years old, left in a different lifetime, learned in a dark cellar, Lukasz and Henryk crouched in the darkness, a notebook changing hands . . .

Lukasz's burned hand closed on Koszmar's arm, and the elegant Wrony recoiled.

"What—?"

"Take me to him," growled Lukasz.

The girls by the fountain watched them. The men burying the strzygi victims looked up warily, the one hefting his rifle. Lukasz ignored them all. He had eyes only for Koszmar Styczeń, for that wily curve to his mouth, for the sly spark in his eyes. But even caught in the grip of the wolf, Koszmar did not cower.

"Take me to him," said Lukasz hoarsely. "Take me to him *now*."

"Take me to the Dragon," countered Koszmar in a silky voice.

Lukasz shook him hard, once, shoving him back. Koszmar hit the rails of the fence and grinned. Realizing too late what he was doing, Lukasz stumbled back, catching his breath.

Unruffled, Koszmar readjusted his helmet and straightened his cuffs. Lukasz wondered if he was used to people losing their temper with him.

"All right, all right," Koszmar said, smirking as he righted his helmet. "Get your horse. I'll take you to your gargulec."

7

LUKASZ WAS SO PREOCCUPIED THAT he didn't notice the girl.

It came as no surprise to her, for in her eighteen years, she had rarely been noticed. After all, she looked like everyone else: faded, tired, hollowed out, and with just a little bitterness in how her mouth always tended to frown. Of the red-booted girls in the square, she was the only one who had not been smoking.

He and the blond soldier came and took the black horse away. They were so absorbed in their task that they didn't notice that she'd given the horse the only food she had. They didn't notice her fade back into the gray, all dull skin and dull hair and—yet—the most spectacular pair of eyes in the village.

Why should they notice her? No one else did.

So of course they didn't notice her following them.

❊ 8 ❊

REN APPROACHED THE VILLAGE LIKE any animal would: with caution.

She'd insisted on coming alone. Czarn and Ryś were tough, but Ren couldn't risk it. After what had happened to Czarn, she didn't want anyone else getting hurt. Besides, she was the queen. This was her battle. Better to fight it alone.

The last hundred yards of forest were marked by solitary chimneys and crumbling walls, by moss growing over collapsed tables, by books and candleholders and children's toys disintegrating into the mud. Even if she disliked the humans, it had still broken her heart a little bit. She'd found herself wishing, as she crossed the rotten expanse, that they had gotten out in time.

Her careful feet, a little clumsier because they were human, brought her at last to the edge of the village. The remaining houses were circled up like deer against wolves. Orange light spilled from the windows, pooled on the ground.

Forest floor gave way to stone streets, and Ren tugged her cloak over her hair. Trying to brush it out had only made it bigger, and the pale blue hood barely covered it. Woodsmoke drifted between the houses, and she fought down her fear at the smell.

She didn't know where she was going. She didn't even really know what she was looking for. If he was still alive, she reasoned, then he would probably have come here, to the village. These humans seemed so afraid of solitude. They built their homes so close together. Leaned upon one another in the streets, huddled together before tiny fires.

The afternoon rain had faded to fog, and the dampness crept into the fabric of the clothes and made her shiver. She passed a house with a cat on the windowsill. It hissed until she looked back at it with feline lynx eyes, and it fell silent. In the room beyond, a family was sitting down to dinner. They called out to the cat, and it jumped down and stalked across the room. Completely unafraid, it curled up near the fire. Eating, speaking, walking, sleeping . . . they were incapable, she thought disdainfully, of being alone.

She watched, feeling contemptuous—and somehow, a little sad— as one of the children knelt down to pet the cat. Even their animals couldn't be alone. Didn't like being alone. Ren wondered, oddly wistful, what the cat saw in them. Wondered, very briefly, if she was missing something.

She moved silently along the streets. They weren't completely unfamiliar. After all, she hadn't always hated the humans the way she did now. Back when she'd been a child, she'd crept into these streets to look through the windows at night.

And who could blame her? She'd been the only human in a castle of animals. These creatures—these creatures who looked like she had, back then—had fascinated her.

Listening at their windows, she had learned the humans' language. If anyone had ever seen her, they had never bothered her. They'd probably assumed she was just another orphan, cowering in the dark. Little had they known. One day that little girl would grow claws sharp enough to tear a man to pieces, and she would haunt their dreams with glowing eyes and wicked fangs. She would be called queen by the animals, and they . . . they would call her monster.

No fangs tonight, though.

She wondered where she might find him.

Can I help you? he'd asked.

Best to look for his horse, she thought. It had been so distinctive: antlers mounted on its bridle, with hundreds of other, tinier antlers hanging from the saddle. Were they *all* from dragons?

She paused by a small garden filled with purple flowers. She ran two fingers around her lips, thinking.

I won't hurt you, he'd promised.

It made her stomach twist with the same feeling she'd had seeing the cat. She knelt on the damp cobbles, brushing her hand through the flowers. Not twisted in a bad way, exactly . . .

"What are you doing here?"

Ren froze. The voice spoke again.

"Who are you?"

Careful not to move too quickly, Ren looked up. It was a girl, maybe her own age. Her hair and skin were almost identical in color, with freckles scattered over her cheeks. The girl wore very different clothes than the ones Ren had selected: a striped skirt and bright red boots. While Ren wondered if she had chosen the wrong disguise, the girl crouched down.

Ren's heart began to pound.

"I am—" She could hear her harsh, growling accent as she tried to lie. "I am from the village."

The girl had deep hollows under her cheekbones. Purple circles swung, like dark moons, under her eyes.

"You're lying," said the girl, without any anger. "Why are you stealing flowers?"

Fury flared, and before Ren could stop herself, claws burst out of her fingertips.

"I am not stealing!" she snapped.

Pain seared across her palms as the claws cut into them. She bit her lip and forced the claws to slide back. Heart hammering, panic growing, Ren raised her gaze to the other girl.

The girl's eyes had gone wide, but there was no fear in her face.

"You're the monster."

Despite her words, her voice was full of wonder, not insult. Ren wiped her palms on her skirt. She fought the urge to change. To slip back into the dark. She suddenly didn't trust herself. Not around a human.

"I am not a monster," she said.

"I saw what you did to Jakub," said the girl.

Is that the Wolf-Lord's name?

Even the possibility made Ren's anger burn. *Liar.* She'd saved him. Blood thundered in her ears. It took every ounce of her strength to keep her voice level.

"I saved him," she said. "Whatever lies he has been telling. I saved him."

"You ripped his face off!"

Ren froze. Her heart plummeted right into the cobbles. The girl hadn't meant the Wolf-Lord. She'd meant . . .

Then all at once, it was flooding back. The smell of fresh snow, metallic blood. The cold. The sudden warmth of fur. The wet black body heaving in the white. Her best friend, dying.

And the huntsman.

"He deserved it," she whispered.

The girl shook her head. It was short, clipped.

"No one deserves that," she said.

A door banged up the street. Ren's head snapped over. A shadow appeared on a threshold. She felt her eyes transform, drink in the darkness. She caught the silhouette of a man's face, eyes wide. Skin pale.

Then the door banged again, and he disappeared.

"He's seen us," said the girl. "You need to leave."

"I need to find—" Ren began.

The girl cut her off.

"Don't you understand? They'll kill you. You need to go."

Ren turned her eyes to the girl, and they slid from green to gold. Her voice came out as a growl.

"I am not afraid of them."

The shadows of houses bled into the street and formed the shadows of people. A crowd gathered in the darkness, forming a wall against the night. There might have been fifty of them—maybe more. Their voices blended together, and she didn't know their language well enough to understand what they said.

The girl had not moved. They were still crouched by the flowers.

"It's all right," she said, and put a hand on Ren's lace-clad arm. "Stay quiet."

They smelled like fear.

They all did. Ren could smell it sticking in their throats. She could smell it dripping from her skin. The girl smelled most like fear, and Ren could feel it in the hand trembling on her arm. She could hear it in the tightness of her voice. This girl was the most terrified person in the village, and yet she stayed.

"Don't say anything," she whispered. "Let me talk to them—"

The humans crowded around. The murmur of their voices rose to dull thunder. A few began to shout. Metal flashed among them, and Ren shifted backward. They stood in *her* presence, and they thought weapons could save them . . . ? Ren climbed to her feet. Mist clung to her, wreathed the street behind them.

"Please," said the girl. "Please, let me—"

Fear washed over her. Not her fear.

"Please—"

Theirs. Ren began to shake. The fight was struggling to get out. Trying to force its way out of her skin, rip off the humanity. Leap into the frightened, spectral shadows. Ren reined it in. Clenched her teeth and bit it back.

This had been a mistake. The faceless wall of darkness was closing in, suffocating her with fear. As the whispers scuttled out at her, she caught the same word repeated, again and again.

Monster.

Monster.

Monster.

And she didn't mean to. She couldn't help it. It just slipped out from between her teeth: a growl. It was low but loud enough to cut through the whispering. For a moment, silence held the village.

Ren took another step back. If she attacked, she would not be able to stop herself. She would tear through them faster than they'd demolished the strzygi. And she might even kill the Wolf-Lord. . . . She needed to get back to the forest. Escape into the darkness before her human skin was covered with fur and yellow fangs pushed her teeth out of her gums . . .

She shouldn't have come.

"Get out!"

Ren spun around, just as something sailed out of the shadowy crowd. A rock collided with her cheek and stars exploded.

Ren hit the ground. Wet poured down her face and stung her eyes. The word pounded her into the earth.

Monster. Monster. Monster.

Ren hissed. It ripped out of her human throat with animal volume. She lurched to her feet. She was bleeding from a cut below her eye.

She faced them. Felt her teeth ache, her throat close. Here it came.

The crowd roared. The shadows separated into people. Somewhere, the girl was shouting. Ren could barely hear her. She could not see her in the crowd. Blood and tangled hair fell into her eyes.

First came the fangs. Then came the fur.

Then came the fury.

9

THEIR HORSES' HOOFBEATS WERE MUFFLED by ivy, by dead leaves, by a decade-old carpet of scum on the cobblestones. The forest loomed at the far end of the road, swallowing the farthermost houses. The shadows of trees sprouted straight through their roofs, black branches choking their chimneys. If Lukasz had been a more imaginative man, he would have said that the forest was strangling what remained. But he wasn't imaginative. He was a pragmatist right down to the broken bone.

He kept a hand on his rifle. It wasn't as if he'd be using the sword again.

"You know," said Koszmar. He had a very deep voice, with a wild kind of edge under it. "They killed the strzygi. And the strzygi killed them."

It took Lukasz a moment to realize he meant the bodies in the graveyard.

"Was that poetry?" he asked dryly.

"Lukasz," murmured Koszmar. "If the strzygi and those poor souls killed each other . . . who buried them?"

Lukasz didn't answer, but a shiver scuttled over his shoulders.

The sooner he found Franciszek, the better. Hopefully he was still somewhere in the forest, because Lukasz had no interest in revisiting the Mountains. Then he and Franciszek could get the hell out of here and return to Miasto. Franciszek would finally get what he wanted: he could quit hunting dragons, especially now that Lukasz was probably off the job permanently. Besides, they had enough dragon gold in the vaults of the Royal Welona Bank to live in luxury for the rest of their lives.

Koszmar drew up his horse. Near the end of the row, light flickered behind the shutters of one of the houses.

"There—"

Lukasz spurred Król on, urging the horse up the steps to the front door. The wood creaked alarmingly under Król's heavy hooves, but Lukasz ignored it. He unslung the rifle from his shoulder and pounded the door.

"*RYBAK!*"

At the shouting, a nocnica scuttled through the branches overhead, pincers clicking. Lukasz was about to raise his rifle when a white eagle swooped down from the darkness and snatched it off its branch.

"Eugh," said Koszmar.

"RYBAK!" repeated Lukasz. "It's Lukasz Smoków, and you've got a hell of a lot of explaining to do!"

No response. It didn't seem possible. Six years, and he was still alive . . . and he'd *lied*.

Lukasz slid from Król's back and hammered on the door until it danced on its rusty hinges.

"OPEN THE DAMN DOOR, RYBAK."

Behind him, Koszmar dismounted. With two fingers and an expression of exquisite disgust he looped his horse's reins around a slimy horse rail. He cast a doubtful look to the eagle overhead, crunching loudly in the eaves.

Lukasz hammered the door again. *That lying, cheating—*

"RYBAK, OPEN THE DOOR."

No one stirred inside. Lukasz took a step back and stared up at the second floor. The whole house had a precarious lean to it. He cupped his hands around his mouth.

"RYBAK! OPEN UP, YOU FILTHY, STRZYGOŃ-KISSING, *BANNIK*-B—"

"Steady on," interrupted Koszmar languidly. "I wouldn't be rude, if I were you—"

The door swung open.

"*STRZYGOŃ-KISSING?*" boomed a voice from inside.

A figure appeared in the doorway, the top of his head lost in the shadows of the room beyond. All the color drained from Koszmar's face, but Lukasz was too angry to be scared.

"Well, it's about goddamn time," he growled.

"You are very lucky," said Jakub Rybak. One eye glittered in the dimness. His voice was different from how Lukasz remembered it; it was softer. A bit lisping. "If you had broken my door, young Smoków, I would have removed your teeth one by one."

Like the rest of the house, the door was falling to pieces.

"Yeah, right." Lukasz rapped the door, and the top hinge clattered to the floor. "I could huff and puff and blow this shack down."

Every word cracked like a gunshot. Rybak didn't respond. Then he moved out of the black interior and into the damp moonlight. Lukasz retreated a few steps, right into Koszmar.

He wasn't sure Koszmar would have been his first choice, but at least he had someone to back him up. Besides, the noble was a major. Surely that counted for something?

"What do you want, Lukasz Smoków?" asked Rybak.

It took Lukasz a moment to find the words.

Jakub Rybak's beard had grown down to his chest, where it tangled with his long, matted hair. What remained of his face was oddly distorted, with the last shreds of an eyelid fluttering over an empty left socket. His mouth didn't close properly over his teeth. Five gaping scars ran from his left temple to his right jaw.

It was as if an animal had spread out its claws and dealt him a single, raking blow.

"Finished?"

Only then did Lukasz realize he was staring.

Rybak turned and disappeared back into the house. Lukasz glanced back toward Koszmar. He wasn't sure why he did it—maybe because he was so used to seeing Franciszek? Maybe the sight of Rybak's face—the reminder of Henryk, of the basilisk—maybe for a moment, he'd forgotten. Maybe he'd forgotten his brothers couldn't possibly be standing with him.

Maybe he'd forgotten they were dead.

"Go ahead," said Koszmar. "I'll be right behind you."

When Lukasz didn't move, Koszmar twitched open his coat to reveal two expensive revolvers holstered at either side.

"Have a little faith, Lieutenant."

Lukasz unslung the rifle from his shoulder and followed Rybak inside.

Despite the rain and the mist, the interior was dry as bones. The floor buckled and crackled under his feet. It was baking hot, warmed by a fire roaring in the hearth. Beside the fire, oblivious to the heat, the white eagle was now settled on her perch. The air tasted rough. And when Lukasz steadied himself on an overhead beam, he was taken aback by how crisp it felt.

And the parchment.

There was parchment everywhere. Parchment piled on the three-legged table, spread across the windowsills, sitting in stacks in a washbasin caked in brown dust. Covered in spidery ink, sheets of it hung on rows of clotheslines strung across the kitchen. Lukasz was already too tall for the house; he had stoop to almost half his height because of the pages, illuminated and semitranslucent in the firelight.

Quite unnecessarily, in Lukasz's opinion, Jakub Rybak stoked the hearth until the fire roared. He was barefoot, in nothing but trousers, and judging by the smell, he had not washed since Lukasz had last seen him six years ago.

"Welcome," said Rybak, without turning around.

Lukasz did not feel especially welcome.

He glanced sideways at Koszmar, whose hand was on his hip, resting very close to the gun.

"It's, um . . ." Lukasz searched for the right word. The house smelled overwhelmingly of soot and sweat. "It's, um, very . . ."

"Flammable," provided Koszmar.

The loose pages were densely packed with text, all in the same cramped writing. Poorly drawn pictures. Clumsy-looking maps. *Should have asked Jarek,* Lukasz thought. Then: *Did Jarek come here?*

A worse thought:

Did Franciszek come here?

Lukasz looked at Rybak sharply and realized that the single eye was fixed on his burned hand. For a moment, he wondered if there was something there. A bond that went beyond blood and betrayal. After all, ugliness was a lonely state.

Then Rybak asked, "Finally learned to read, have you?"

No. No bond.

"You can't read?" Koszmar looked up from fiddling through some pages on the mantelpiece.

Lukasz ignored him. He told himself that he couldn't care less what Koszmar thought. He'd slain dragons at fourteen years old, for God's sake. Who gave a damn if he couldn't read?

"How did you know that?" he asked as levelly as he could. "How did you know I can't read?"

Rybak tugged a shirt and a coat off a chair. The coat was long and had once been ivory, with black embroidery. Lukasz recognized it.

"Your brother told me," said Rybak.

Koszmar had gone very still and was watching them both intently.

"When was Franciszek here?" Lukasz asked at last.

"Six weeks ago," said Jakub.

Lukasz sank down at the table.

Franciszek had probably sat at this very table mere weeks before. Lukasz ran a hand over his face. Franciszek's spectacles would have been sparkling on the end of his nose and his hair would have been neatly pulled back, and he'd have shared a drink with this one-eyed monstrosity and calmly planned his road through the forest.

Lukasz rested his forehead in one hand and asked, "What did he say?"

"He asked for his notebook back," said Rybak. "It had a map to the Mountains."

Of course, Lukasz realized. Franciszek had been taking notes for as long as he'd been able to write. The bank vault in Miasto was filled with every volume he'd ever filled, going back ten years. Well, every volume except for one.

The one they'd given to Jakub Rybak.

"Notebook?" asked Koszmar, firelight flickering off his uniform as he shifted closer. "What notebook?"

Lukasz lifted his head, using his ruined hand to rub his chin.

"It was the first one Franciszek kept," said Lukasz, without taking his eyes off Rybak. He didn't mention Franciszek's most recent notebook, tucked in his coat pocket. "It had a map of the forest in it. The route we took when we came down from the Mountains in the first place, seventeen years ago."

Rybak watched his burned hand, enraptured. He said, in his soft, lisping voice:

"Your brother was well prepared."

"Of course he was." Lukasz laughed, rubbing his eyes. "He's always prepared."

To a fault, he added silently.

ALEKSANDRA ROSS

He could feel Rybak watching him. Over the crackling fire, the teakettle began to whistle.

"For what it's worth," said Rybak, getting up from the table, "I think that wherever he is, your brother is still alive."

Lukasz watched Rybak pour two dirty cups of tea, and waited for his throat to loosen. If Franciszek had been here, it could only mean that he was at this very moment making his way to the Mountains. And if Franciszek was going back to the Mountains, then Lukasz would follow him.

Behind him, Koszmar peeled himself off the mantelpiece long enough to take a cup of tea. He returned to his perch by the fire, where he idly examined his tea before asking, "Did you make copies of the maps?"

Rybak returned to the table and eased himself into one of the chairs.

"Even if I had, they'd be useless," he said. "The forest is changing too quickly. It is being devoured by evil. The Golden Dragon is burning it down, and from the embers of its fires, new monsters rise. Nawia, nocnica . . . all the unimaginable evils in the world. Every day, new pits open. New things crawl out. The forest itself is growing, swallowing up this village."

Perhaps flirting with destruction, Koszmar shoved aside a few stacks of parchment and lit his pipe. With an elbow on the mantelpiece, he said, "Even if you don't have the map, you could be our guide. You could get us to the Moving Mountains."

Lukasz shot him a questioning glance. Rybak snorted, seeming just as baffled.

"Why would you think that?"

Koszmar's fingers played with the pages on the mantel. There was an exaggerated slowness in how he moved. A lazy kind of elegance that completely escaped Lukasz.

"Only one of us is illiterate, Rybak. You've been writing about this forest. Specifically"—Koszmar put his pipe in his teeth and rifled through a sheaf of papers—"about the monsters. I'm impressed by your level of detail. Eyewitness, I should think."

Lukasz swallowed and rapped his knuckles on the table. When he had time, he promised himself, he'd learn to read.

"That is a manuscript," Rybak replied in a stiff voice. "It is an observational field report on the development of monstrosity in this kingdom. It is not a how-to manual for idiots looking to get drowned by rusalki or—or eaten by strzygi or—"

Koszmar interrupted.

"Or attacked by lynxes?"

Lukasz's heart skipped a beat.

"What?" he asked hoarsely. "What are you talking about?"

He wasn't sure if he had imagined the hands on his cheeks, the wet strands of hair that had flickered across his face. Those green eyes, changing, slipping away, turning to slit pupils and perfect rounds—

"There's a monster in the woods," said Koszmar, striding forward to drop the sheaf of papers in front of Rybak. "Vila, demon, who the hell knows what she is. She preys on humans. Well. *One* human, especially."

Despite the disfigurement, Rybak had an expressive face. And now he was glaring at Koszmar with a look of pure murder.

"She's not a demon," he said at last. "At least, not in the traditional sense. In my opinion."

Koszmar smirked.

"Your *opinion*?"

Lukasz was reeling. She'd pulled him out of the water. Thrown him down on the bank. Dragged him up the grass. She'd come so close—

"What . . ." He hesitated, not quite able to gather his thoughts. "What—what is she?"

"I suspect she was human once," said Rybak. He sat back from the table, hands folded in his lap. "Or, at least, as human as the rest of us. Perhaps something got ahold of her, made her as she is. The strzygi, for example, multiply not by procreation, but by consumption. In the act of devouring a susceptible human, the strzygoń creates its progeny. Perhaps that is how this creature came into being."

Her eyes, above that water. That dark hair, wrapped slick and shiny around her throat. She had been so overwhelmingly human. But then again . . .

"I do not know whether she is better or worse than other monsters," continued Rybak thoughtfully. "But I do think she is more powerful. The forest seems to listen to her. She is, to my knowledge, part human and part lynx. The animals adore her. She has the allegiance of wolves. To them, she is almost . . ." He searched for the right word. Cast his eyes to the ceiling, and after a moment, seemed to pluck the term from the rafters. "She is almost . . . a queen."

"And you know this how?" Lukasz asked, dreading the answer.

Rybak smiled. His mouth didn't move fully on one side, and it looked more like a grimace.

"I met her."

Sympathy flared dully in Lukasz.

Lukasz looked up at Rybak's notes. His last contribution to this doomed kingdom. Volumes of evil, of destruction, all cataloged here in a house just waiting to burn to the ground. *Gargulec.* That was what Koszmar had called him. It had been so conversational. A single person's suffering, summed up in one light-hearted, cruel comparison.

"If she gets in our way," said Koszmar, "we'll kill the evil witch. No problem."

But those hands. Those eyes.

"I do not know," replied Rybak. "I do not know if creatures of her ilk deal in good or evil. I think they deal in survival."

Those teeth.

Lukasz would have replied, but at that moment, a scream split the silence.

Koszmar jumped and knocked a basket of crumpled papers directly into the fire. The blaze surged, casting the whole room in dancing gold and red.

All three rushed to the window, upsetting the eagle. She gave a piercing whistle and shot into the air. Shouting and clattering sounded outside. Beyond the window, yellow light spilled down the cobbles. While Koszmar frantically cleared a tiny space in the dirty glass, the eagle shrieked to high heaven.

"*Ducha!*" called Rybak. The eagle flew to his arm, where she perched, eyes rolling. Jakub stroked her head.

Outside, the shouting got louder. Lukasz put his cap back on, readjusted it on his head.

"What the devil is going on out there?" he demanded.

"Speak of the devil, indeed," murmured Koszmar. He stood a bit out of the direct line of the window, one hand resting lightly on the windowsill. "Or she-devil, shall we say? She's here."

Rybak leaned forward, peering through the dirty glass. Then, after a moment—a moment in which the scars on his face grew stark in the dry, red-tinted heat of the house—he whispered, "God help them. They've cornered her."

❧ HENRYK ❧

"THEY FOUND THE BODY HERE."

Henryk knelt and touched the cellar floor.

The restaurant owner had tried to cover the stains with sawdust, but Lukasz's lantern illuminated a scrap of bloody silk, caught on a nail driven into the wall. It fluttered gently as Henryk got back to his feet.

"She put up a fight," said Lukasz.

"Most people do," replied Henryk, taking the lantern and shining it around the cavernous cellar. "Everything wants to live, Lukasz."

Lining the walls were barrels the size of carriages, dozens of which were splintered to smithereens. Bits of twisted steel loop curled toward the dim ceiling, wrenched free by superhuman claws. Wine dripped steadily in the darkness.

The two brothers continued their search in silence. The nine of them had split up, each taking a different restaurant in the city. Rats scuttled in the corners of this one's cellar, and behind one of the smashed barrels, a toothy creature spat saliva that sizzled straight through the glass on Lukasz's lantern. This dragon—whatever it was—had been keeping to the cellars. They had only been in Szara-woda for a few days, and it had already killed two more people.

Footsteps sounded on the stairs, and both Henryk and Lukasz drew their swords.

"It's just me," said Franciszek, putting up his hands. His face hardened when he saw Lukasz. "Henryk, what is *he* doing here?"

"He's the best," said Henryk simply.

"He's too young!"

"*He* is standing right here," interrupted Lukasz. "Besides, we're practically the same age, Fraszko."

There was a loud crash.

Silent understanding passed between the brothers. Henryk put a finger to his lips, and Franciszek snuffed out his lantern. Lukasz weighed his sword in his hand. He half hoped the dragon would attack—he was starting to wonder if he'd ever get another fight like Saint Magdalena. There was a second tinkling smash, a muttered curse, and then a tiny light flickered behind one of the barrels.

They advanced.

As they rounded the corner, they came upon the flickering light, outlining a person crouched behind a very large wheel of cheese.

It was a man, perhaps a little older than Henryk, wearing dark trousers and boots and a long coat the color of pale honey. It was trimmed in black embroidery, he wore a fine red necktie, and his hair was sandy blond. He was kneeling over a cracked gas lantern, trying, without success, to right the fallen light.

"Who are you?" demanded Henryk. "What are you doing here?"

Even in a whisper, his voice carried.

The man looked up.

"Oh my," he said, apparently unruffled. "I'd heard there were Wolf-Lords in town, but—"

"*Who are you?*"

Henryk's voice echoed off the cellar walls.

The man was unperturbed. He had a square, handsome face and a broken nose. He got to his feet and held out his hand.

"It's an honor to meet you," he said. "My name is Dr. Jakub Rybak. I am an Unnaturalist, with a specialty in anthropomorphic monstrosity."

The three brothers regarded the outstretched hand with suspicion.

"It is a handshake," said Dr. Rybak. "It is what people do when—oh, never mind. It's not important."

Lukasz looked past the polished Unnaturalist to what he'd been examining: a feathery figure, somehow bent up and comprised entirely of elbows. It had bits of red fur hanging off its scaly body, and a beak instead of a nose. All in all, it had a faintly gross, dried-up look to it.

"Strzygoń," said Dr. Jakub Rybak, catching Lukasz's look.

"Bless you," said Lukasz politely.

"Strzygi are monsters, Lukasz," explained Franciszek. "Derived from human victims."

While Lukasz blushed and fumed, Henryk gave Dr. Rybak a long, appraising stare. There was an unathletic slope to the Unnaturalist's shoulders, and the broken lantern did not speak well of his dexterity.

"Right," said Henryk after a moment. He had a near-permanent furrow between his brows, and now it deepened slightly. "Found anything else, have you?"

"Ah, certainly." Dr. Rybak tugged a notebook out of his pocket, flipped through it. "I've found plenty. The crypts of the Miasto Basilica have been particularly bountiful: twenty-six nocnica, four psotniki, copper and silver in great quantities, one wax puppet—"

"No," interrupted Henryk. "I mean here. Have you found anything here? Burn patterns? Flint deposits? The dragon—"

"Not a dragon," corrected Dr. Rybak, holding up a hand. "A *basilisk*. Much, *much* worse. Of an entirely different patrimony from a dragon, and of a very different species. Serpentine morphology. Extreme rarity, and it has the gift of medusaidism." He glanced at Lukasz and Franciszek and explained: "The ability to murder with a single stare."

He looked thrilled.

"I know what medusaidism is," said Franciszek quickly. His eyes shone, even in the darkness. "If you don't mind my asking, Dr. Rybak, what exactly is an Unnaturalist?"

Dr. Rybak beamed.

"A historian and curator of Unnatural objects and creatures," he said. "As I mentioned, I am most interested in anthropomorphics. In other words, monsters of human origin. Like this strzygoń, for instance—" He indicated the desiccated creature on the cellar floor. "Based on the degree of mummification and the comparative beak length, I suspect—"

Another crash.

All four twisted around. Lukasz recognized it as the sound of splintering wood. There was a beat of silence, then the whisper of scales on stone and a low-pitched, shuddering whistle. It was soft, a gentle *eeee* sound in the darkness.

"What the hell?" growled Lukasz.

The thing—the *basilisk?*—exhaled. It was almost like a sigh.

"It's here," said Dr. Rybak. "Put out your lanterns. It's coming for the light."

They smashed the lanterns, glass raining like blades of snow. The cellar plunged into darkness.

"Come on," whispered Dr. Rybak urgently. "We have to move."

The soft, low whine came again. *Eeeeeeee,* it murmured. It whispered straight through Lukasz's skull, echoed in his head. Then it exhaled again.

The cellar was nothing but the dark shadows of barrels, their own panicked breathing. It was no use. The basilisk would be able to smell them. And surely, if it had eyes that could kill, then it had eyes that could also see in darkness?

"We need to hide," whispered Dr. Rybak.

"We need to *kill* it," snarled Henryk.

Lukasz's hand closed on the hilt of his sword.

"You may know your dragons," whispered the Unnaturalist in a cutting voice. "But I know about other monsters. You need to listen to me."

"Henryk, he's right," whispered Franciszek as they huddled behind the nearest barrel. "We can't fight it blind. We don't stand a chance."

"Come *on*—" started Lukasz.

Outside, there was a thudding sound. Lukasz realized, feeling suddenly sick, that it was the sound of serpentine coils hitting the ground. The creature kept hissing.

"We have to hide," commanded Henryk. "All of us—"

"But where—" whispered Franciszek.

Lukasz stood up, trying to look over the barrel, and his shoulder hit metal.

"Damn hinge," he muttered, wincing.

The darkness moved, and Franciszek reached over his head.

"It's not a hinge," he said. "It's a bolt."

He tugged on the metal bolt, and the hissing grew closer. Silently—thank God—the door swung open. Wine rushed out over their boots. The sweet, fermented smell was enough to make Lukasz choke. The rustle of scales on stones grew louder.

"Get in," said Dr. Rybak. "Get in, all of you—"

He was only aware of a hand on his back, and someone had shoved him up, into the barrel.

The door closed behind them. They were plunged into blackness. The remaining wine splashed over their boots, and the tang of fermented fruit was overpowering. It was sticky and warm. He hoped to God he never ended up getting swallowed by a dragon, but if it did come to that, then he was willing to bet this was what it would feel like. Then someone kicked Lukasz right in the bad knee.

"*OW!* Watch it, Henryk—"

"Well, if you'd stayed behind, Lukasz," griped Franciszek, "we'd *all* have more room."

"Don't start—"

"*SHHHH.*"

In the darkness, Lukasz couldn't be sure, but he was fairly certain that the unassuming Unnaturalist had just shushed them.

Outside, the hissing echoed. Something collided hard with the barrel and it rocked in place for a moment. The wood groaned, and the creature outside smashed against it a second time. Wine sloshed up and over them, and the hissing grew deafening. Lukasz wondered if he was about to die in a barrel filled with wine, Wolf-Lords, and one very brave Unnaturalist.

Then it was silent.

Lukasz could hear the Unnaturalist gasping beside him.

"Do we need a light?" whispered Franciszek.

"*No!*" snapped Lukasz. "We might as well be sitting in a kerosene lamp, Fraszko!"

Franciszek must have heard the hysterical edge in Lukasz's voice. His own whisper came back stuttering, apologetic:

"I—I'm sorry—I didn't think—"

"*Quiet,*" whispered Henryk. "I'm not sure it's gone."

They sat silently in the blackness. Lukasz didn't know how long they stayed, huddled in that hot ferment, but he did know that he was never going to drink wine again.

At last, in a cautious whisper, Henryk said, "You must have to write a lot of books, with your job."

It took Lukasz a second to realize that he was talking to Dr. Rybak.

"Yes," said the Unnaturalist.

Even without seeing his face, he sounded very calm. It struck Lukasz that the Dr. Rybak was in his element. Whatever he'd said about being interested in anthropo—anthr— Lukasz gave up on the word. *Monsters from people.* Whatever he'd said about being interested in those types of creatures, there was no denying it: Dr. Rybak knew his monsters better than they did.

"What if you wrote a book about Wolf-Lords?" Henryk was asking. "The first and only book in a thousand years."

Dr. Rybak gave a little chuckle.

"Your people are infamously elusive, my friend."

There was another silence. Lukasz wondered if he was the only one who felt the tension in the air. Henryk spoke again.

"What if we weren't?"

"What are you proposing?" said Dr. Rybak in a shrewd voice. "An exclusive interview? Surely there must be some cost."

"Not an interview," said Henryk. "You see, six months ago, my brother went back to Kamieńa Forest."

Lukasz's throat tightened. They hadn't talked about Tadeusz in months. He'd assumed it was for the same reason: that they were waiting for him to come back, to tell them the Dragon was dead, to say that it was over and they could go home.

"I think he must have . . . gotten lost," Henryk was saying. His voice was heavy. "Because we know the Mountains, and we know dragons. Monsters are another thing entirely. But you . . ."

Henryk's voice trailed away. Lukasz was too stunned to interrupt.

"You need my expertise to get through the forest," finished Dr. Rybak.

"And you would get a book on Wolf-Lords," said Henryk. "And Dr. Rybak, that forest is full of monsters. You could write a hundred more books. You'd be famous."

"Or dead," said Dr. Rybak.

"I give you my word," said Henryk solemnly, "I will not let you die."

"Henryk," interrupted Lukasz, "what are you doing?"

"And you can take my notebook," interjected Franciszek eagerly. "It would help. And when you're done, you could include me as a reference—"

"I can't—" sputtered Rybak. "I couldn't—"

"Come on," murmured Henryk. "What have you got to lose?"

Lukasz was about to argue, when the barrel rocked again. They all fell silent. There was a metallic whisper, and Lukasz knew that one of them—Franciszek or Henryk—had drawn his sword.

The barrel door cracked open. A lantern swung in the opening, temporarily blinding them.

An exceptionally elegant man stood behind the light. He was handsome, except for a mouth almost too wide for his face. Despite the darkness around them, he wore dark glasses.

"I've heard of rats in a barrel," he said. "But I wasn't expecting them to be so big."

"We're Wolf-Lords," said Henryk, extricating himself from their awkward refuge. The wine had soaked through his clothes, and it looked like blood.

The tall man barely moved, except to raise an eyebrow. As he looked at them, the edge of his lip curled.

"If you say so."

Dr. Rybak looked around, his broad face heavy with disappointment. Wine was smeared, like blood, over one cheek.

"It's gone," he said heavily. "We missed it. The basilisk is gone."

And maybe Henryk felt the call to the mountains, like Tadeusz had before him. Or maybe he just missed his older brother. Maybe he was done with being a stranger in faraway lands, and maybe he missed the wolves.

But whatever the reason, the basilisk was gone, and by the next morning so was Henryk. Lukasz did not see him again.

And for the next six years, he did not see Jakub Rybak, either.

❧ 10 ❧

LUKASZ SKIDDED OUT INTO THE road, Koszmar sliding into him.

Light flickered at the cross street, just ahead. It looked like every person in the village had come out to watch.

"Come on." He grabbed Koszmar's sleeve. "We have to stop them—"

The crowd had closed in on her, left no room for escape. They were shuffling nervously, whispering. Lukasz could hear them breathing, he could hear their pounding pulses. Lukasz knew panic, he dealt in panic, and he loved panic—but tonight, for the first time, it scared him.

"Out of the way!" he roared. He shoved his way through the bodies. "Out. *OUT!*"

Behind him, Koszmar was shouting at the villagers. They were too terrified to listen. Stricken as deer. Violent as bears. Lukasz needed them out of the way.

"Get them out," he said over his shoulder to Koszmar. "Get them the hell out of here."

Koszmar's eyes widened. "Oh my *God*."

Lukasz whirled around. The villagers scrambled back, then broke into a stampede. The tide of bodies pressed against him, trying to shove him backward. He had a glimpse of her, just for a moment; her eyes were closed, and then they opened.

Lukasz went still. The crowd parted around him.

Her eyes were green, with huge, luminescent pupils. Ringed with black, almost perfectly circular in the human face. Human lips drew back from four-inch fangs, and the tongue in her human mouth was rough like a wildcat's.

Koszmar was shouting. People kept flooding past Lukasz.

She roared.

It wasn't the sound of a human, but it wasn't anything like a lynx. It split across the street and stopped his heart for a moment. It rushed over the rooftops and it blasted across the trees, and for half a second, Lukasz was sure it must have echoed in the streets of Miasto.

Somehow, he found his voice.

"It's okay," he said, advancing unsteadily. "I don't want to hurt you—"

A lynx stepped smoothly out of the human clothes, the material slipping off its muscled back.

The lynx paced in front of him, hissing. All the same, he could see her in it. Her eyes were riveted to his. She was calming down. He could feel it.

"Listen to me," he said, both hands raised. "Please—"

Before he could finish, he caught movement from the corner of

111

his eye. A lone villager remained, and he had just stooped to the cobbles.

"STOP!" Lukasz roared.

He was too late. The stone sailed out of the darkness and *thunk*ed into the lynx's shoulder. Her head snapped from Lukasz to the villager.

"NO!"

Lukasz and the lynx leapt at the same time. They met midair. By some miracle he caught her forelegs in his hands, kept the claws off his throat. She yowled. A strangled sound, almost like disappointment. Then she changed her focus.

They hit the road, and pain exploded in Lukasz's knee as it bashed off the cobbles. Claws sank through his clothes and raked his skin, teeth gnashing for his throat. She snarled, lines of saliva hanging off her fangs. And she was much, much stronger than he was.

Lukasz caught her by the neck. She thrashed. It took all his strength to keep the slashing teeth off his throat. Every muscle screamed as she threatened to overpower him. The claws tore deeper. The dripping mouth lunged closer. The wicked incisors snatched so close that he felt them scrape his skin.

She was too strong. Lukasz struggled, could feel his arms giving way—

CRACK.

The lynx paused. Then very slowly, as if in a dream, she slumped forward into his chest and rolled off him. Lukasz didn't wait. He scrambled back to his feet, panting.

Lukasz put his hands on his knees and looked between the

unconscious lynx and Koszmar. White-faced and white-knuckled, the major had a shovel clutched in his hands.

Two more people hung back at the edge of the street, but it was otherwise empty.

Lukasz pushed his hair back.

"Did you just hit her with a *shovel*?"

Koszmar hugged the shovel to his chest and said, in a very small voice:

"Well, er . . . you weren't doing very well."

"Yeah, no kidding!" Lukasz gestured to the lynx. "Did you *see* her? Oh God—"

The lynx was changing back. The fur was receding, her limbs lengthening once more. Long dark hair covered the cobblestones, masking her face. Lukasz had a glimpse of one pale, blue-veined shoulder, before he realized—a little too late—that she was completely naked.

He slapped a hand over his eyes.

"Oh my God, now what do we do?"

Lukasz was a far cry from a gentleman. But he owed this girl—this monster, this . . . *queen*? Whatever she was, he thought. He owed her. She'd pulled him out of the river. She'd saved his life. And now . . .

"Don't be a prude," Koszmar was saying somewhere.

There was the sound of fabric rustling over stone. Lukasz could feel blood trickling into his shirt collar, where her teeth had caught his throat.

"We've just got to put her clothes back on," Koszmar was saying. "Besides, not like she's human anyway."

113

Lukasz rocked backward on his heels slightly, uneasy. It wasn't that simple, he wanted to say. It wasn't just about garguleci or monsters or following some unambiguously mapped path to Franciszek and the Mountains. For better or for worse, this girl had saved his life.

"You can open your eyes," said Koszmar. "You're quite the gentleman for being a Wolf-Lord, you know that?"

Lukasz put his hand back on his belt. Koszmar was standing with her supported on his shoulder. Her shirt was on backward and she had a big cut on her cheek. A mask of blood encased the left side of her face.

"Oh my God," he said. "You really brained her."

"Like I said," returned Koszmar. He had recovered himself. With truly astounding elegance, he used his free hand to produce his pipe from his pocket and put it back between his teeth. "You weren't doing very well."

"Right," said Lukasz, looking between the girl and the cavalryman.

"Do you think this is her?" asked Koszmar.

He pushed the dark hair off the girl's face. Dark hair and green eyes. She was definitely the same girl from the water. She'd pulled him out. Or, he thought, with a sudden, sinking feeling: Had she also pulled him in?

Could they be the same . . . ?

"You look like you've seen a ghost," said Koszmar.

"What?"

"Your face," said the Wrony. "What's the matter?"

"Nothing." Lukasz rubbed his eyes. "I'm fine. What were you asking?"

"I said, do you think this is the girl Rybak was talking about? The . . . *queen*."

The way he said it, the word sounded faintly insulting.

Lukasz glanced around. The two remaining villagers had now disappeared. He half expected Rybak to appear at any moment. Then again, Rybak probably hadn't left his personal tinderbox in six years.

"Why does it matter?"

"You want to go to the Mountains, don't you?" asked Koszmar.

"Yes," said Lukasz, before catching himself: "No. *No*. I want to find my brother."

"Who's headed to the Mountains," spelled out Koszmar. He gestured with one hand, as if encouraging a very slow-witted soul to arrive at a very simple conclusion. "And how are we going to get to the Mountains?"

"Rybak—"

"The man can't even organize his damn papers, Lukasz," interrupted Koszmar, instantly impatient. "Can you actually trust him to organize a route to the Mountains?"

"I don't trust you," pointed out Lukasz.

"A wise decision," agreed Koszmar. "But our interests are aligned. You want your brother, I want the Dragon, and regrettably, all roads lead through this forest. And you and I need to make a choice quickly. Those villagers are coming back soon."

He hoisted the unconscious queen a little higher on his shoulder and added, "And *she* isn't getting any lighter."

Król had wandered over and now nosed curiously at the girl. Lukasz wasted a second watching his horse before glancing back at Koszmar.

"What are you saying?"

The moonlight caught Koszmar's long white teeth, and for one ridiculous moment Lukasz couldn't help wondering if he might also turn into an animal.

"Easy," he said. "She takes us."

Lukasz let out a bark of laughter, and Król started.

"She won't help us."

Koszmar took the pipe from his lips, and smoke poured out of his nostrils.

"She might," he said. "With some persuading."

"We're not hurting her," said Lukasz, more sharply than he'd intended.

"My word," breathed Koszmar. "I'm not a monster, Lukasz. I wasn't talking about hurting her. We just need to find out what she wants, and we *tell* her we can help her get it. A good old-fashioned deal, Lukasz. It's how *our* world works."

Lukasz ignored the fact that "our world" seemed to pointedly exclude the Wolf-Lords.

"What if she doesn't want anything?"

"Oh, Lukasz." Koszmar smiled. "Everyone wants something."

Lukasz took off his cap and smoothed his hair back, thinking. He shifted off his bad leg, looked up at the empty houses, put his hands in his pockets. She'd dragged him out of the water. Risked her life for him.

Or had she . . . ?

"Koszmar," he said at last, but he didn't sound very convinced. Not even to himself. "You attacked her."

"She attacked you first."

Lukasz hesitated, put his cap back on. There was some truth to what Koszmar said. Besides, who was to say that this girl wasn't the monster who'd dragged him under the water? Maybe she was just as malevolent as the rest of the creatures out there, and maybe he should just toughen up and do what needed to be done.

Koszmar puffed his pipe, looking smug. Once more smoke rings drifted upward, and once more his embroidered uniform glittered. The girl—the queen—the monster—whatever she was, she dangled limply from his arm. Koszmar took the pipe out of his mouth.

And then he uttered the magic words.

"Come, Lukasz. Do you want to find your brother or not?"

⚡ 11 ⚡

REN WOKE TO PAIN AND the realization that her hands were bound. Fear sparked in her waking mind. Somewhere nearby, a fire crackled. The air was fresh and cool, with a hint of a breeze. Her hair, wet with sweat, stuck to her neck. Her mouth was dry.

"Hallelujah," said a voice overhead. "Sleeping Beauty awakes."

She blinked and opened her eyes.

It was still night, and except for the crackling fire, the forest was still dark.

Two men stood in front of her, one with his arms crossed and the other with his hands in his pockets. Their similar black uniforms only heightened the differences in their looks. On the left stood the Wolf-Lord: even taller up close, the cap pushed back on his head. Dark stubble now covered the lower half of his face.

She didn't know the other man. He had golden hair and eyes that seemed too pale for his face. He watched her with his head tipped slightly to the side.

"She's pretty," he said, over the quiet crackle of the flames. His voice was muted, caressing, and horrible. He added: "Prettier than I expected, at least."

Ren shivered, still vaguely adrift. The Wolf-Lord did not answer.

Then, all at once, it came back: the village, the rocks, the—

Ren sprang to life. Power thrilled down her spine like a wildfire, and her jaws seized up, gathered bone-crushing strength.

The blond one took a step back.

Ren snapped lengthening but still human jaws. White fangs pushed straight out of her gums and shone from her human mouth. Nothing else changed. Something was wrong.

Panic welled up in her throat.

She hissed. Tried to lunge again. Her bare feet scored the earth. Rope cut into her wrists. But the strength was already ebbing away from her mouth, trickling back down her throat. And a half second later, she was human. Fully, stably human.

"Oh, thank God," said the blond man, uttering the words in a chilling kind of mumble. His lips barely moved when he spoke. "Oh, thank God, I really thought that might not work."

Ren smelled it. There was a strange scent to the ropes.

"Go away," said the Wolf-Lord, speaking for the first time. Then he added: "I want to speak to her."

Ren's heart hammered. She fought the urge to cower back into the tree.

Even though the blond man hesitated, he did not argue. He retreated to the campfire and tethered horses. Ren and the Wolf-Lord both watched him move away.

Then the Wolf-Lord looked back at her. He crouched down on

one knee, just out of reach of her now-useless claws. He ran his own hand over his chin, a hungry cast to his eyes, to the curve of his half-open mouth. For a moment, the only sounds were the crackle of the fire and the rustle of his hand over the beginnings of a beard.

Ren began to shake. Her hands were tied and she didn't even have her claws. She had never felt so defenseless. So naked. Fear burned on every inch of her skin. She was certain he could smell it on her.

Ren hated being afraid.

"What have you done to me?" she whispered. It came out as a hollow, rasping sound.

The Wolf-Lord dropped his hand from his chin. Of all things, he grinned. It was a surprisingly nice grin. Ren didn't like that.

"Hit you with a shovel," he said. "Sorry."

"No," Ren growled. She shook her head furiously, hair whipping across her eyes. "This—my change—"

"*Bylica*," he said. "It's an herb that breaks enchantments."

Ren's heart sank. "Untie me," she commanded in her coldest voice.

He pushed his hair out of his face, but a few strands slowly unbent and fell back into his eyes. She decided the smile was less of a smile than it was the sly upcurve of a dog. Maybe that was why she'd thought she liked it.

"You promise not to attack?" he asked.

"No."

He laughed. It occurred to her that his voice had the same musical corners as Czarn's. She shouldn't have been surprised. After all, he was a Wolf-Lord.

"I need your help," he said.

Ren did not answer. Fear was hardening, shifting. He'd called her a monster and soaked the ropes, and Ren was, for the first time in her short and very powerful life, completely helpless.

Fury roiled.

When the soft crackle of the flames was too much, he spoke again.

"I've lost my brother," he continued. His voice was soft and even, as if he was using every ounce of his strength to control it. "He came here to hunt the Golden Dragon, two months ago. Have you seen him?"

They—Mama, Ryś, and the others—were always telling Ren that her heart was too soft for her own good. That she cared too much for the animals. She took too many under her wing. She'd brought home too many baby birds fallen from nests. Too many foxes, paws injured in snares. Too many otters, too many deer, too many squirrels . . .

And maybe, maybe, once upon a time, for the briefest flicker, she could have felt the same way for humans. At the very least, she'd been willing to give *him* the benefit of the doubt. But that was yesterday. Today, she wanted nothing from these cowards.

"I have seen no Wolf-Lords but you," she said.

One of his eyebrows shot up.

"How do you know I'm a Wolf-Lord?" he asked.

"I would not be much of a queen if I did not know."

Ren licked her teeth. Smooth, blunt. Human teeth. She could barely contain her anger. She had *saved* him. She had saved him, and he—*he*—

"You hurt me," she said levelly. "And I am the queen. The fury of the forest will rain down on you."

She would have said more, but her voice was shaking too much to continue.

The Wolf-Lord did not seem particularly concerned. One side of his mouth curved up a little higher than the other.

"Right," he said at last. "I'll watch my back."

Ren snarled. But before she could lash out, a blade pressed against her skin and the ropes fell away. The Wolf-Lord stepped back, faster than an animal. For a moment, Ren was too shocked to react.

She rubbed her wrists.

"Does that help?" he asked.

Even slower, she got to her feet. Her cloak fell off her shoulders.

"No," she replied.

The Wolf-Lord very deliberately put his hands back in his pockets. It looked as if he was shaking slightly.

"My name's Lukasz."

He extended a hand.

Ren looked at it, suddenly remembering the burned flesh of his other hand, now hidden within a glove. She blinked, long and slow. Then she moved her gaze from his hand to his face.

"I do not care," she said.

He withdrew his hand. He stared at her with a horrible soul-stripping gaze, making her skin crawl and stomach curl. He pushed back his cap again, readjusted it on his hair.

"There's a stream down there." He tapped his temple. "You can wash up."

Ren reached up, mirroring him, and encountered matted hair and sticky skin.

"You—"

She tried to lunge, but he stepped out of the way, and she just caught his shoulder. All the same, he stiffened at her touch. Maybe he was afraid she might hurt him. She should change. She should run. Disappear into the darkness, back home, tell everyone the truth about these selfish, violent creatures—

But she didn't.

She didn't stop to think why. She just walked to the river, trailing her fingers over the tree trunks. Whatever he had done to her, she reasoned, he could still kill the Dragon.

It could still work.

"Be honest," he said behind her. His voice was low. "Was it you?"

Ren stood on the riverbank, overlooking the water moving silently just beyond her feet. It was black and tranquil. Her forest was still beautiful. Her forest deserved to be saved.

When she answered, her voice came out clear and unhurried.

"I am always honest."

Then she added, "What are you asking me?"

Ren half turned. He leaned with one shoulder against the tree, a little higher on the embankment. He had his hands in his pockets. Patches of silver embroidery adorned each leg of the trousers, frayed and creased. Then he asked:

"Was it you who dragged me under?"

Moonlight crept out from beyond the trees and caught a silver cross, stark against the brown skin of his chest.

The night rushed in to fill the silence. Fury, silent and simmering, spread through her veins. Ryś had been right, she realized. He'd been right about them. There was no point in asking for help of creatures so ignorant, so closed-minded. So blind that everything looked the same to them. Hadn't he seen the rusalka's webbed fingers? Hadn't he seen its broken teeth? Hadn't he known, she wondered, the difference between her touch and that of a monster?

She had risked her life for someone who couldn't tell the most basic difference between good and evil. She laughed, and it was cold and angry.

"You were dragged in by a rusalka."

He shook his head, pulling a small contraption from his pocket to click it open. *Click, click.* A tiny flame ignited, and he put it to his lips. *Click, click.* It was a small paper cylinder, which glowed red in the darkness.

"She looked a lot like you," he said. The slightest suggestion of a smile stole onto his face as smoke filtered down from his lips.

"Rusalki can take any form they choose," Ren began.

"That's convenient." He laughed. It cut across the darkness. And stung.

"But most often," she continued, "they take the shape of someone the victim already wants."

Even as she said it, her anger was renewed. She hadn't considered the possibility until she'd said it aloud. And even as she thought about it, she remembered how close they'd been, remembered his hand on her face, remembered—

Click, click.

He opened and closed the contraption once more. The flame leapt to life and then died. Then he grinned around the ember between his teeth, and glancing up and down the river, he said:

"That, my friend, is wishful thinking."

She did not like him. Whatever had happened on that riverbank, she did not like him.

"I am not your friend," she said softly. "And rusalki do not lie."

She turned back to the water.

The surface began to shiver. Then it danced. Then it freckled, as if under rain.

Ripples expanded. Silence fell. Fish flashed by, shooting through dangerously shallow waters. Ren's heart quickened. Frogs raced past. On the opposite side of the stream, a family of otters erupted out of the water and frantically gathered their babies onto the bank before disappearing into the shrubs.

Click, click.

An icy blast of wind whipped across the forest, chilled Ren to the bone. For a moment, she was frozen. Her eyes were fixed upstream, waiting. Beyond, the Mountains loomed to the east. Ren spun around. She could just make out the edge of one castle tower in the distance. Mist billowed from the trees and rolled toward them. The water clouded, then became opaque and frozen.

Ren's breath, long and shuddering, hung in front of her like a cloud.

"What the hell was that?"

The Wolf-Lord had straightened up. Around him, the trees flashed blue-white, sparkling with new frost.

Ren backed away from the water.

"We need to go," she said. "They're behind us."

"What?" The Wolf-Lord's hand went to the sword at his side. "What's behind us?"

Ren scrambled up the embankment.

"They've cut us off. I don't know where they came from, they're surrounding us—"

Lukasz grabbed her forearm and hauled her up the rest of the way. He dragged her so close that she knew the mist from his lips smelled like smoke and cinnamon.

"What the hell are they?" he repeated.

The fog thickened around them. It had a bluish shimmer to it—cold, and prickling, and unnatural. Ren snatched her arm back, and as frost and silence descended, she hissed:

"Nawia."

⚔ 12 ⚔

FOR A SECOND, FEAR BOUND them together. For a second, she forgot to be angry.

"We have to go," she choked. "Now—we can't—"

Frost descended.

"Not so fast—" He had a wild look in his eye. "What's going on? What are these—*nawia*?"

The temperature plummeted. The trees bent closer. Filigreed spikes crystalized on the branches overhead, and the stream buckled under the weight of the fog.

"Nawia," she gasped. He looked blank, unafraid. "How do you not know? What kind of fool are you, coming into this forest—?"

Lukasz shook her with one hand, hard.

"Get a grip, Queen," he growled. "What the *hell* are nawia?"

In that growl, all Ren heard was fear. She wrenched backward, but he held her fast. The night roiled. Twisted. Caught in the sawtooth claws of demons, the forest cowered.

"Terrible things," she whispered. "They'll kill us—"

"What *are* they?" he repeated.

Ren felt paralyzed. She'd never seen nawia. Only heard about them from the animals, about the frost that preceded them. Only smelled the trail of blood and rot that followed them. Only had her imagination to fill in the gaps, to feed her fear . . .

"They're terrible," she whispered.

Her voice seemed to catch him. He paled, and his blue eyes darkened. An eerie light surrounded them now. Sharper than moonlight, giving away even less than the darkness. The forest held its breath.

"Lukasz," came a soft, murmuring voice. "What's going on?"

The blond soldier emerged from the trees, as suddenly and as silently as a predator. His eyes went from Ren to Lukasz and then lingered on Lukasz's hands, closed over her shoulders.

Lukasz let go of Ren immediately. He stepped back, and his expression was once again annoying and not entirely hideous.

"She says it's something called nawia," he said. His voice was casual, but Ren watched his hand close on the sword at his side as he added: "Koszmar, I think we should leave."

The blond one—Koszmar—carried two rifles, and now he tossed one toward them. Lukasz snatched it out of the air. Ren jumped at the sudden movement and nearly slid down the embankment.

With a surprisingly gentle hand, Lukasz grabbed her arm to steady her. Koszmar watched that, too.

"Nawia," repeated Koszmar. His pale eyes glowed in the darkness. "What are they?"

"I do not know much about them—"

"Can we trust her?" asked Koszmar, speaking over Ren.

The Wolf-Lord looked down at Ren. His expression changed abruptly. In the strange light, he did not look quite human.

"I would not lie," she said urgently. "I want to live."

Koszmar spoke again. His voice was soft, almost muffled.

"Oh, everything wants to live," he said dismissively, and Lukasz's head snapped toward him. "But you said it yourself. *The fury of the forest will rain down on you.*"

"Come on, Koszmar," said Lukasz. "You said she could help—"

Metal chimed, and Koszmar drew his saber.

"Maybe I was wrong," he whispered. "Because, my darling queen, I do not want to die tonight."

Ren couldn't tell whether the saber was for the nawia or for her, but both possibilities infuriated her. He couldn't defeat a whole slaughter of nawia with one saber.

And he certainly couldn't kill her.

"You *will* die if you keep standing here!" she shouted. "We have to run!"

The supernatural light cut new lines in Koszmar's face, carved the softness out from under his cheekbones.

"Tell me, Queen," he murmured. "Is this the shape of your fury?"

The Wolf-Lord looked between them, wasting valuable time. When he met her eye, Ren knew it was gone. That shared fear. That moment of understanding. It had burned up in strange light and steel and sabers.

Ren rubbed the back of her hand over her mouth.

"Then you two can die," she growled. "But I will not."

Before they could stop her, Ren wrenched herself free of Lukasz's grip. She was aware of both men lunging for her, but she was too fast for them. The gun cracked behind her, and a branch near her head exploded in a spray of splinters.

She heard Lukasz shouting and Koszmar swearing, and she didn't look back.

She ran.

The forest floor was cold, frozen sharp as glass. It tore at her feet with every step. Frost raced alongside her, trunks flashing silver-blue. Ren did not look back. She did not stop. She ignored the gasps, rising like sobs, in her throat.

And then . . . slowly . . . bewitchingly . . .

Something began to sing.

It was soft and haunted. It gathered the sounds of her forest, reshaped them, from the wind whistling through the branches to the violin legs of the crickets. It caught the rustle of leaves on the forest floor. It captured the slither of reptilian skin, the lonely cry of a wolf, the whisper of an unseen river. A thousand coincidental noises, arranged into a semblance of a tune.

A figure stepped into the path.

Ren skidded and crashed into it, and they both hit the ice-cold ground. She leapt back to her feet, snarling. Claws split through her fingertips.

Ren had never seen a nav. This could be one of them.

The other girl climbed to her feet. Ren wondered wildly if it was one of their tricks. After all, wasn't that how the rusalka had tricked the Wolf-Lord? Couldn't this just be another mirage, from the freckles on this girl's blunt nose to the toes of her crimson boots? And yet . . .

That face was too familiar. She recognized those eyes, with the dark circles beneath them. Ren hesitated a moment.

It was the girl from the village.

"Please," begged the girl. "You have to go back."

She had tried to help Ren. She'd tried to protect her. She'd told her to run.

The music swelled around then. It seeped through Ren's skin and rushed through her whole body, and her own wild heartbeat joined the sound.

"Please," echoed the girl. "They will kill him."

The woods grew colder. The beat of the music was moving faster and faster and taking her heart with it—

"What are you talking about?" demanded Ren.

"My friend," said the girl. "After those two soldiers kidnapped you, he tried to follow you. To save you. But they—he—"

While the forest changed and sang around them, the girl's eyes grew wet.

"I don't know what to do," she said desperately. "He saved my life. Please, I can't leave him—"

The frost was growing around them. Ren had to run. She had to get back to the safety of the castle and let these selfish humans answer for their cruelty.

"He should not have come," said Ren harshly. "*You* should not have come."

"Please—"

"No," said Ren coldly. She went to push past the girl. "You humans can fend for yourselves. You are nothing but cruel."

"People make mistakes." The girl's voice rose. "Even you!"

"*I am not people!*" Ren roared, and the trees trembled.

The girl did not cower, and Ren paused. She was taken aback. No human had ever looked on her without fear before. The girl was not finished.

"Just because they say you're a monster," she shot back, "it doesn't mean you have to act like one."

That stung. Stung worse than the herb-soaked ropes, cutting into her wrists. Worse than the cut on her cheek. Worse than that horrible, ignorant word, pounded into her skull.

Monster.

Evil gathered. The trees turned to hoarfrost around them. Brittle, crumbling. Under the claws of the most terrible of monsters, Ren had to choose.

"Fine," growled Ren. "Fine. I will help. But only for you."

The girl followed as she turned on her heel, starting back through the trees. Toward the epicenter of the cold. The heart of the evil. That girl was going to die, thought Ren. That girl was going to die in the frost and the starlight, and it would not be her fault.

All for a human.

"They're near the river," said the girl behind her as they walked. "They have a camp—"

Ren spun around.

"How do you know that?" she demanded. "Were you with them? Are *you* part of this? Are you lying?"

"No!" retorted the girl, "I came to *help* you, but the Wolf-Lord had already let you go."

Ren turned back around to hide her expression. He *had* let her go, hadn't he? He had cut the ropes. . . .

She spoke as they walked, without turning back.

"And they never noticed you?"

"No one notices me."

Ren did not answer. They walked in silence back through the campsite, even though every instinct in Ren screamed against it. Everything in her wanted to run. A thousand unseen hands placed themselves on her shoulders, trying to force her back. Each step was harder than the last, and she was breathing raggedly as the trees became familiar.

They passed the remainder of the campfire. Ren looked around.

"The nawia took them," the girl was saying. "They must have taken them all—"

Ren remembered the glimmer of the saber in the dark. Then she remembered that other time, too—when the snow had been red and Czarn had been hurt. They had hurt Czarn. They had hurt her. She owed them nothing.

The horses shrieked, stamping, still tied to tree branches, showing the whites of their eyes.

"I said I would help your friend," said Ren, and it took a great effort to get the words out. "But not the others."

Is this the shape of your fury?

The girl was going through the soldier's saddlebags, and now she looked up. There was a light burning in her eyes, bright enough to obliterate even the dark circles beneath them.

"There is no *other* here," said the girl. "It's good or evil—us or the nawia. And you're on our side—whether you like it or not."

Ren pressed her lips together.

"I do not like them," she said at last.

Up ahead, a gun went off.

"Neither do I," said the girl grimly. "But they don't deserve to die."

They made their way to the river, the same path Ren and the Wolf-Lord had walked only a few moments before. But now the world felt different. The song surrounded them, enveloped them. Tugged them on with a force equal to the instincts pushing Ren back. On the embankment, one of the rifles lay on the ground. The girl picked it up and held it at the ready. Neither of them said anything. The stream below was covered with a layer of ice. When they walked across it and Ren glanced down at her feet, the fish below gaped up at her, eyes wide.

Go back, they seemed to plead. *Go back, Ren.*

She wished she could.

On the other side of the stream, a hill rose before them. Light radiated over it, silhouetting the edges of branches, softening the harsh crystals of ice around them. It practically glowed with danger, but it was beautiful. Ren climbed the hill, trying not to taste the fear in her throat. When they finally reached the top, her breath caught.

Beside her, the girl had gone very still.

"My God . . . ," she murmured.

Ren licked her lips. It wasn't just her strength or her skill that had made her queen; it was also that she picked her battles, and because she knew when to run. When she finally spoke, her voice was rough with gravel.

"I told you: we should not have come."

Below them, bodies lay among the trees.

Hundreds of them, if not thousands. They stretched as far as the eye could see, piled and heaped on top of each other. They lay on their backs, limbs at odd angles. They draped across roots, hands outstretched, begging for help that had never come. They slumped against trunks, they keeled over, they sank to their knees in final prayers. Even from the top of the hill, Ren could see the gloved fingers clawing at the dirt. The trees, crusted in frost, tried to lean away.

White, spectral figures walked among them.

Nawia.

It was from the nawia, intensely white, that the light emanated. With hands outstretched and fingers longer than their forearms, they walked among the corpses. Of all things, there was love in their faces. Ren's heart went cold. Love in their soft smiles and their dark eyes. Even their song, she realized, was gentle and caressing. She shivered.

A hand closed on Ren's arm, and she nearly transformed on the spot.

"Where are their heads?" whispered the girl.

Among the trees below, the human corpses were headless. Ren watched the nawia wander among them, singing, gazing upon their dead.

"I do not know," said Ren. She swallowed hard. "I don't know anything about these creatures."

"But you're—you're the *queen*."

Perhaps Ren should have been ashamed, but she couldn't be.

There were too many monsters for one queen to keep in check. And every good ruler knows which wars to wage.

Ren would have rather run from a nav than face one.

"Felka," said the girl after a moment.

Ren glanced at her. In contrast to how she had looked at the campsite, here the pale light only made the circles under her eyes darker. It rendered her hair even duller. But when this girl looked Ren in the eye, there was no fear in her face.

"If I'm going to die with you," she said steadily, "then you should know my name."

Ren could feel her fear. But she was a queen, she told herself, and she'd led troops into battle before. She was good at this.

I am best at this.

"My name is Ren," she said. "And we are not going to die."

Below them, she could make out the two soldiers who had captured her, plus a third man who was separated from the others. This third man must have been Felka's friend. From what she could tell, he seemed to be speaking to a nav, this one smaller than the others. Suddenly, she remembered the rusalka, whispering in Lukasz's ear. She went cold all over.

"We will need the soldiers' help," she said, thinking out loud. "We should get them first."

Lukasz and Koszmar were on their knees, surrounded by nawia. Ren wondered, acidly, if they had even put up a fight. She was not especially surprised, but she was disappointed. A part of her—a very small part—had hoped the Wolf-Lord might be capable of more.

"I need to save Jakub!" protested Felka. "You have to get him before the others."

For some reason, the name was familiar. Ren didn't have time to dwell on it.

"You said there are no others," replied Ren firmly. "We cannot take the nawia alone. And look . . ." The small nav had bent toward the third man, holding his hands in hers. Ren didn't know what it meant, but she knew it couldn't be good. "Look, he's safe for now."

"You don't know that—" began Felka.

"He is surrounded on all sides," interrupted Ren. "We need the soldiers' help."

Felka looked furious. Ren knew she would have been equally adamant if Czarn or Ryś had been on the line. She did her best to be reassuring:

"Felka," she said, and the name felt strange on her tongue. "No one is going to die tonight."

Then she turned and started down the hill, hearing Felka behind her. As they slipped down the mulchy hill, the smell became overpowering. Like blood and rot. Ren's bare foot came down on a bone, which broke with a tiny *snap*.

The nawia turned toward them. Up close, they were not nearly so beautiful, with black eyes that took up half of their elongated faces. They looked almost like insects. For a moment, Ren saw her own face reflected in a thousand pairs of black eyes.

"*Move!*" she shouted.

She and Felka broke into a mad dash. The song turned into a scream. The nawia hurtled toward them.

Ren tried to ignore the bodies that she kicked aside as she ran, tried to ignore how the limbs flopped as her feet interrupted their decay. The nawia closed in. Ren was faster, ahead of Felka.

"HEY!" she screamed. "HEY!"

But Lukasz and Koszmar were far gone. One of the nawia was already slipping white arms around Koszmar's neck, his head bent back, staring into her large black eyes. Ren watched the white claws gleam against his pale skin, and she doubled her pace.

A nav cut her off. Ren skidded to a halt just as a hand swiped the air inches from her face. The spidery fingers resembled jointed claws with sawtooth edges. A second nav, this one behind her, lashed out.

Its blow caught her across the ribs. Ren went flying. Her head bashed against a breastplate. She gagged, and yet another nav bore down on her, screaming. Its black mouth loomed, filled with thousands of needlelike teeth.

Panic and fear burned hot, changed. Fury.

Ren hissed.

The nav hesitated.

There it was, the raw, rushing surge she knew so well. Ren fell to her knees as the rush of power bristled in her neck, wrapped around her throat. More nawia joined the first. Ren had no idea where Felka had gone, and she had no time to care. Her hair crawled on her head, raced down her back. Her legs shortened, bent up. Her spine stretched out. Ren climbed to four feet, her clothes slipping off her back.

For a second, no one moved. The nawia surrounded her, close enough that she could hear their claws clicking, like a thousand insects ready to pick the flesh from her bones. Ren could feel her own saliva freezing on her teeth. She could see the frost forming on her fur. She could see her breath, rising like smoke, from her whiskered lips.

And Ren struck.

They crumpled under her claws. They collapsed under her fangs. Blood, silvery and ice-cold, flowed down their bodies and froze on the ground. They were a storm of black eyes and needle teeth, screaming. Dying.

Ren tore her way through them. She threw aside their elegant bodies. She made her way toward Felka, who was swinging a curved sword, red boots dancing in the black.

Ren was impressed. The girl was tougher than she looked.

"Come on," shouted Felka. Silver blood spattered across her striped skirt and bathed the corpses at their feet. "We have to get to the others—"

They were already almost across the field, nearing the two soldiers. Their attack had temporarily distracted the monsters, but the two men lay still amid the dead.

Ren sank her claws into Lukasz's jacket, tried to shake him awake.

"Get up!" she shouted through her animal teeth. "Get up, you fool!"

Ren swiped, claws retracted, across his face. He groaned. She whacked him again.

"Get *up!*"

His eyes began to open. Felka backed up behind Ren, and she could hear the nawia screaming as they fell under the blade. They didn't have much time. Felka couldn't hold them back forever.

"You need to get over this," growled Ren. "Come on—"

He moaned, blinked. But his eyes were glassy and fogged.

Ren growled, shook herself out, and felt her fur recede. She took his rough jaw in the hands of a human and hovered with her face an inch from his. Maybe it was because she was human. Maybe—and her heart skipped a beat—it was because he recognized her. But at that moment, to her complete surprise, his eyes flickered toward her face.

"They are in your head," Ren whispered, leaning close. "You can resist them. You have to keep them out. We need you to save your friend. Keep them out."

He groaned, tried to twist out of her hands. Ren could still hear the nawia's music, but it was no longer beautiful. It was terrible. Skin-crawling. Beside her, Felka was shaking Koszmar by the collar while he woke, swearing dazedly as he tried to shove her away.

The Wolf-Lord also began to struggle, tearing himself from the dream. Their misty breath intertwined, filled the space between them.

"I need you, Lukasz!" she hissed. *"Wake up!"*

His eyes cleared and widened. He reached up, maybe to rub his eyes, but instead his hand hit her bare back.

"You came back—" he managed, while the monsters raged around them.

Ren raised her eyes to the treetops, stretching out her neck until the joints cracked on either side. Fur covered her. Claws pushed against his skin. When she returned his gaze once more, he faced the fangs of a lynx.

"Come on, Wolf-Lord," she said coldly.

Ren stepped off him, turned once more to the monsters.

She heard him get to his feet behind her, drawing his sword. Koszmar was waking up, unholstering the revolvers. Around them the nawia closed in, and Ren swiped and brought one down.

A dozen feet away, the third human knelt among the monsters. He did not look up. But Ren recognized him.

I saw what you did to Jakub, the girl had said. The man grasped the little nav with both hands, speaking to it. *You ripped his face off.*

One eye, five scars. Ren had thought he was dead. She thought she'd killed him.

Jakub.

While Ren hesitated, her eyes flashed to the trees beyond. Shapes moved among the trunks. For a moment, she barely believed her eyes.

It could not be. . . .

The rifle blasted. Ren came back to the present.

The screaming became punctuated as Lukasz fired round after round into the monsters. Ren and the three humans formed a tight circle, while the nawia came at them from every side. Between swings and bites, Ren kept glancing back toward the big human— and at the creatures in the trees behind them.

Ren froze. Her heart pounded in her throat. She had to be wrong—but the creatures in the underbrush were getting closer. Creatures she knew better than anything else . . .

"We're outnumbered," said Koszmar, desperately, behind her.

"Not anymore," murmured Ren.

Czarn and Ryś leapt out from the trees.

❧ 13 ❧

RYŚ AND CZARN FLEW HEADLONG into the nawia, and the humans—apart from Felka—paused. Only Felka's sword flashed in the darkness. Nawia screamed. The night shattered around them.

"What is—?" started Koszmar, the saber wavering temporarily.

Lukasz's voice cut over the screaming nawia. He tossed the rifle aside and drew his sword. "Just keep killing," he said. "They're with her."

A nav shot toward her. Ren sank her teeth into its throat, and it dissolved in a spray of silver. She whirled around.

The man—Jakub—was still speaking to the tiny nav. His remaining eye had gone glassy. The little monster had long, silvery hair and eyes that looked almost human. Oddly, its fingers were delicate. Nothing like the long, sawtooth claws of the rest of the nawia.

"What are you waiting for?" growled Czarn, while Ryś launched himself into the mass of monsters. "Kill it, Ren!"

Czarn's jaws closed around the arm of another nav and bit clean through. The hand hit the earth and twitched, claws scraping in the dirt. Czarn twisted around, muzzle coated in silver blood.

Ren remembered herself. She turned back, teeth bared, and lunged.

"Stop—"

Lukasz flung out an arm and caught her across the throat. The blow knocked the wind clear out of her, and she rounded on him.

"It's going to kill him!" she snarled.

"No." He had a smear of silver blood down one cheek. "Look at it."

The nawia surrounded them. She realized suddenly that the small nav's eyes were those of a child. It smiled and touched what was left of Jakub's face, and for the first time, she recognized the slender fingers as human. Ren's heart dropped into her stomach.

"It's human," said Lukasz, realizing at the same time she did. Then he added, more slowly: "It's still human."

The one-eyed man was weeping.

"What—" she began.

"Oh my God," said Lukasz suddenly. "I've heard of these. Nawia are the souls of unbaptized infants. If they wander in the forest for seven years, then they become . . . these."

"How do you know that?"

Sword gripped in both his hands, he swung at another nav. Beside him, Koszmar fenced rather elegantly with another monster, one of his service revolvers propped against his shoulder.

"My—someone told me, once," stammered Lukasz. "I just remembered. Oh my God, it's a child. Did Rybak have a child?"

Ren lashed out with a paw and severed a nav's arm.

"Who's Rybak?" she demanded.

The ground was silver ice. The trees were silver ice.

It was Felka who answered.

"Yes!" she screamed, while five nawia swarmed her, and Koszmar blasted them away with his revolver. "He had a daughter! She died, five years ago!"

Lukasz looked back at Ren.

"You can't kill her—" he gasped.

The nawia kept attacking. Her mouth tasted bitter with the monsters' smoky blood. Strzygi, rusalki, and now these nawia? It had to stop—it had to stop somewhere—

"I have to!" she burst out.

Lukasz stopped for a split second. Sweat carved lines through the silver smeared up his neck as he turned to her.

"Please," he said. "I'm begging you."

A nav loomed behind him, claws brandished. His name tore itself from her throat.

"LUKASZ!"

He spun around too late. The claws came down. He gave a strangled yell and fell. The nav recoiled, claws over its head, shrieking, and struck again. There was a streak of black, and Czarn leapt past him. The vivid white body fell away. Silver sprayed across them, flecked even Ren's fur.

"Lukasz—"

He was already struggling back to his feet.

"I'm fine," he gasped. He had a hand clamped down on his shoulder, and crimson spilled over the black glove. He stared at Czarn, looking a bit dazed. "I'm fine. Thanks."

It was so cold among the nawia that steam uncurled from his blood.

A few paces ahead, Felka and Koszmar were back-to-back, Koszmar skillfully dancing in and out of the terrible claws. Meanwhile, Ryś was on his own in the middle of the fray, tearing into the heart of them. Enjoying the battle alone. Typical Ryś. Always the daredevil.

"I have an idea," said Lukasz, turning to Ren. He was breathing heavily, hand still tight over his shoulder. "We can save her. I need you, though."

Ren swiped at an encroaching nav. It retreated, hissing. Lukasz swung his sword with both hands and took the head off another one that got too close.

"I'll keep them out of the way," Lukasz was saying. He ripped at his coat, getting the first few buttons undone, and then tore a scrap of bloodstained fabric from his shirt. "Take this."

He held it low enough for her to take it in her teeth.

"What is it?" she said, around the metallic taste of his blood.

"You have to baptize her," he said. "You can do it, as the queen. Literally just say—*I baptize you*, or something. It'll save her. At least, it'll save her soul."

"Bap . . . baptize?" repeated Ren. She had no idea what that meant.

He stepped sideways and put himself between her and the remaining nawia. Czarn crossed the expanse and joined him.

"It will work," Lukasz said over his shoulder. "Trust me."

His shirt and coat were soaked with blood. Koszmar and Felka backed up to join them, their human clothes stark against the crushing white bodies. Six of the living against a thousand who, until this night, had never really died.

Ren turned back to where the man and his dead daughter spoke in their ghost world, serenely unaware of the war being waged around them. The man didn't even blink when Ren, a huge lynx, wound around them. His glassy gaze was fixed on his daughter.

Ren addressed the girl.

"Little one—"

The child turned toward her, face wet with tears. Ren gulped but didn't recoil. Even though she found herself shaking a bit, she nuzzled the child's cheek. It was as cold as steel. Around them, nawia screamed and died.

Ren felt the child's fingers in her fur, and the little nav stroked her ears.

"You cannot stay here," said Ren. And not quite sure why she said it, she added: "Your father loves you."

The little girl withdrew from Ren. She put her arms around her father's neck and held tightly, small shoulders shaking. Ren's throat tightened with tears, and it surprised her. These were *humans*.

"HURRY UP!" roared Lukasz.

Ren still had the cloth in her mouth. Now she dropped it on the ground, a bright square against the bloodstained earth.

"As the queen of this forest, I free you of this world," she whispered, eyes burning as she spoke. "I baptize you, child. You are free. Go home."

The smell of blood and rot receded around her and the shrieks seemed to melt into silence. Ren watched the little girl and her father cry. Then, as if in some terrible nightmare, the death-white child faltered and dissolved. Jakub was alone. Still on his knees, he bent forward until his forehead pressed into the silver-stained earth. Ren knew, without seeing his expression, that he was weeping.

"They're still coming!" shouted Lukasz, tearing her away.

Ren got back to her feet. While the rest of them brought down more monsters, Ren spoke over the screams. Fury filled her voice.

"I am the queen," she said.

A thousand nawia on every side, a thousand silvery monsters, and they put down their claws. Ren hoped she didn't look as shocked as she felt. The nawia closed their lips over needle teeth. They turned their silent faces toward her. *Listening*, she thought. *They are listening to me.*

She wasn't sure how to continue. Still in a frenzy, Koszmar swung once more and a last nav collapsed in spattering silver.

Ren didn't know what to say. She didn't know what she was doing. She only knew this one word, and she hoped it would be enough.

They were mysterious creatures, these humans.

"Go," she said shakily. "Your time here is finished. I . . . I baptize you."

The woods went silent. Lukasz, breathing hard, lowered the sword. Koszmar, trembling, dropped the saber. It clanged against some armor. Ren was overwhelmed by the smell of blood. It almost made her gag.

Some nawia looked upward. Their faces grew shorter and their eyes grew smaller, and suddenly they were as human as the scarred man's daughter.

Others remained, still looking like demons from the depths of her nightmares, but they were silent also. And then, almost as one creature, they seemed to fade away, growing more smoky than solid. A gust of wind blew across the trees, and in a swirl of white smoke, they were gone.

"What did you do?" breathed Koszmar, behind her.

They were alone in a forest of corpses, and it seemed impossible that light had ever touched this place at all.

Lukasz was struggling to catch his breath. He still had one hand clamped over his shoulder. Blood bubbled between his fingers, and under his jacket, his shirt was plastered to his skin. Ren wasn't sure if he noticed. He was looking at her with something near wonder.

"It worked," he breathed. "The baptism. You . . . you *are* a queen."

"Of course I am the queen," returned Ren coolly. "I would not lie."

Koszmar's expression changed, too. He looked at Ren with an unreadable, entirely new expression. Lukasz did not respond. He stuck his sword, point first, into the earth. He took his hand away from the wound and examined his blood-slick glove. Then, looking faintly surprised, he collapsed.

Koszmar turned sharply. Ren was faster. Lukasz's glistening black gloves curled like claws over his chest.

"I am not going to die here," he said thickly.

Koszmar crouched beside them. He lifted back the shirt and coat. They peeled away with thick strings of congealing blood, and Lukasz moaned. Five deep cuts scored his skin over his neck and shoulder, laid open to the gleaming white bone. In the wreckage, the silver cross shone jewel-red.

"Oh," Koszmar was murmuring. "Oh my . . ."

Ren glanced at him. He was looking at Lukasz speculatively, biting his lip. There was nawia blood in his hair; it only brought out the silver in his eyes.

"Aren't you going to do anything?" she demanded.

"Honestly," he murmured, "I don't think I need to."

Ren was about to snap back at him. But then she saw it.

"But how . . . ?" she breathed.

"I know," replied the blond soldier, in a voice filled with wonder. "It's beautiful."

A few inches from where Koszmar's red fingers held back the dripping coat, the impossible was happening. The cuts had begun to narrow. Flesh covered bone. Skin, shimmering wetly with red and a silvery substance, knitted together. Ren swallowed, and Lukasz moaned, and then she was staring at an unwounded, unscarred shoulder, coated in red, human blood.

Lukasz blinked and raised himself on his unwounded elbow.

"What the hell?" he muttered. He ran his hand over the bloodied shoulder, smearing it up his neck and flecking the ground with tiny red droplets.

Lukasz looked up at Ren.

"Did you do this?"

Ren stared back, eyes wide.

"No—" she stammered. "No, I did not touch you—"

"Amazing," murmured Koszmar as he rubbed Lukasz's blood between his fingertips.

Lukasz was still looking at Ren. He searched her lynx face for a moment, but she suspected his human eyes were unused to the expressions of animals'. A wave of heat swept over her. She was suddenly dizzy. It took Ren a moment to name the emotion. *Relief.*

The realization made her stagger backward, in line with Ryś and Czarn. Czarn nuzzled her cheek, his face wet and cold with blood.

"We have to get out of here," he whispered.

"He's right, Malutka," echoed Ryś. "Let's go home."

At long last, the sky began to pale. Ren watched it turn from violet to purple over the treetops, and she could just make out the low shadow of the Mountains in the distance. If the nawia had been terrible, then Ren could only imagine what the Dragon might promise. She'd had her taste of fear. Her forest had surprised her. She'd needed these humans for the nawia. And now, looking at those low dark hills, she knew she needed them for more.

"No," whispered Ren. "We need them."

❧ RAFAŁ ❧

FIVE YEARS EARLIER

"'NAWIA,'" READ FRANCISZEK, USING ONE finger to trace the letters as he went. There was no point; they all looked the same to Lukasz. "'Or nav, in the singular, is a term often referring to lost and restless souls. Nawia encompass a vast array of apparitions, from those of demonic origin (e.g., witches, *upiórs*, strzygi) to pure souls who have died tragic or violent deaths . . .'"

Franciszek looked up.

"Raf!" he hissed. "Stop distracting him!"

"I'm not doing anything," protested Rafał, who had been using a slide rule to catapult spitballs onto unsuspecting library patrons below.

Lukasz snickered, and Franciszek whacked him.

"Ow!"

Ignoring him, Franciszek turned to Rafał.

"My God, Rafał." He cast a nervous glance back at the librarian's desk. "We're *guests* here."

They were spending the autumn in Kwiat, a small town in the

southwest. The buildings were brick, the coffee was good, and the pipes were filled with dragons.

Well, not anymore.

"We're guests of honor." Rafał grinned. "They can't kick us out now."

"They still could," growled Franciszek.

Rafał clutched his heart in mock disappointment, winking at Lukasz. Although, as much as he admired his eldest brother's devil-may-care attitude, Lukasz tended to agree with Franciszek. The people of Kwiat may have been grateful, but if their library was anything to go by, then they were also colossal snobs.

Books lined every wall on the three-story Biblioteka Kwiatów, and there were even shelves built into the vaulted ceilings. These hard-to-reach books were retrieved by special white doves, who otherwise spent their time sitting on their assigned librarians' shoulders and judging the patrons.

Among all this finery, the brothers looked out of place in their Faustian-fur vests and coarse brown trousers. The heavy broadswords on their belts had knocked against the stairs with every step up onto the balcony, and Lukasz had noticed the dirty looks the librarians were shooting in their direction.

"All right," said Franciszek, apparently satisfied that Rafał had been—for the time being—subdued. "Let's try again."

Lukasz groaned.

"'A rare subset of nawia,'" read Franciszek, "'are *mavka*. Of Ukrana origin, mavka have occasionally been sighted in eastern Welona, notably in forests of Kamieńa Kingdom. Mavka are of a particularly violent nature and prey on humans, luring their victims with a beautiful song and subsequently decapitating them.'"

Lukasz stared at the open book on the table. Franciszek had chosen a subject he hoped Lukasz would like: a book of monsters, complete with some delightfully gory illustrations. The current page showed a beautiful woman, dressed all in white with pure black eyes. In the long, spectral fingers of one hand, she held a man.

In the other hand, she held his head.

"'Though typically classified under the larger umbrella of nawia, mavka are unique in the derivation of their souls. If a child dies without a baptism, that child's soul remains trapped in a spiritual wasteland between life and death, bound to the earth. These souls have seven years to obtain a baptism; if they do not, then they are doomed to live forever as mavka. Their baptism may be performed by priests, monarchs, and sea captains and requires the use of a white cloth tossed upon the ground.' Lukasz!"

Lukasz sat bolt upright.

"What?" he said a little too loudly.

On the other side of the room, one of the doves made a cooing noise that sounded suspiciously like *SHHHH*.

"Are you even listening?"

"Of course," lied Lukasz, promising himself not to doze off again.

To celebrate the defeat of the city's Lernęki dragon infestation, Rafał had taken them on a night of revelry that the twins were still sleeping off in their hotel room.

Lukasz rubbed his eyes. "Navs are demons—"

"No," said Franciszek, and he repeated the passage again. "*Nawia* is the plural, Lukasz. Come on, please try. It's only going to get harder the longer you put this off."

They moved on to the next passage, while Rafał wandered away to play with a *dola* scampering in and out of the lowermost shelves. Lukasz gazed longingly at the little catlike creature, comprised mainly of smoke and candlelight, but Franciszek had him trapped.

"'This act is thought to symbolize a severance of their innocence (the white cloth) from earthly attachments (the ground).'" Franciszek looked up. "My God, Rafał, what is that?"

Rafał scooped the dola off the desk. It left four paw-shaped scorch marks in the mahogany and beamed at them, wagging its whole body.

"Come on, Fraszko, he doesn't need this," said Rafał.

"He's right," said Lukasz quickly. "Give up. I'll never learn. I'm not smart like you."

Franciszek gave him a withering look.

"Knowing how to read has nothing to do with being smart, Lukasz," he said. "You're the smartest of all of us. You're the one who got rid of the Lernęki yesterday, remember?"

Lukasz shrugged.

It hadn't been difficult. Kwiat's problem had started when a nobleman had decided that the iridescent little Lernęki would be an impressive addition to the brand-new fountain on his estate. Unfortunately, with construction stalled for a few days, the hapless lord had stored his Lernęki in an available bathtub. The pretty little things had promptly swum down the drains, gone forth into the city's plumbing, and multiplied. Within six months, Lernęki had infested every major water system in the town.

To complicate matters, every cut to a Lernęk caused ten more heads to grow from the wound. The citizens of Kwiat were at their wits' end: their neat little fenced-in trees were dying, merely washing one's hands carried a risk of self-immolation, and worst of all—everyone was beginning to smell.

It had been Lukasz's idea to fill one of the bathhouses' centrally draining baths with wine, lure in the little creatures, and then drop a match and incinerate them all. He'd lost part of an eyebrow in the blaze, but it had been worth it.

"That was different," said Lukasz. "That was dragons."

"But you guessed they would like wine," pointed out Rafał. "Genius."

Lukasz shrugged again. It had been a lucky guess. The Lernęki had been imported from Atena, a country famous for its wine, and even in Kwiat, they seemed to prefer the houses with the biggest wine cellars. But Lukasz had realized something the Lernęki didn't: that Kwiati alcohol was far more powerful—and flammable—than Atenian wine.

"Fraszko," said Rafał abruptly. "Take a break. Come back in twenty minutes or so."

"But—"

"This belongs to someone," said Rafał, handing Franciszek the dola. It began to lick his face. "Probably someone down there. You should return it."

Franciszek fumed, but there was still some hierarchy among the brothers. Even if Rafał was a bit wild and more than a bit irresponsible, he was now the oldest. *Henryk could come back,* Lukasz reminded himself. *Tad could still come back.*

He glanced away, rapped his fingers on the desk.

He watched Franciszek descend the stairs, trying not to smile

ALEKSANDRA ROSS

when the dola pawed at his glasses. Lukasz liked the little creatures; as a rule, they were sweet-tempered and embodied the best of their owners' souls. This one had obviously escaped from some poor sod nodding off downstairs.

"Right," said Rafał, sitting on the desk next to Lukasz. "You should really learn to read, Luk."

Lukasz knew he must have looked surprised. But Rafał looked uncharacteristically serious.

"Franciszek has been a better brother than I have," he said.

"You're more fun," said Lukasz.

Rafał gave a quiet laugh.

After the episode with the basilisk, one reporter had described him as having a poet's eyes and a devil's soul. Personally, Lukasz thought the description belonged in the same pretentious category as book-retrieving pigeons, but it was—he admitted grudgingly—somehow accurate. It was part of Raf's mystery—part of what made him so likable.

Rafał looked down at the book, with its picture of the mavka and her victim.

"I'm the oldest," he said. "I should have taken better care of you."

The words were a shock. Lukasz didn't quite know what to say.

Even after Tad and Henryk had disappeared, Rafał had continuously deferred to their authority. He was twenty-one years old; he did not want to be the eldest. Tad and Henryk were coming back, he'd insist. Until then, they just had to kill dragons, make money, and enjoy themselves.

And so, for a few precious months, they had run wild.

Perhaps that was Raf's secret, Lukasz thought. He had a gift of total and absolute self-destruction, and it was intoxicating. The past year had been the wildest, messiest, most enjoyable twelve months of Lukasz's life: Rafał lay upon the beds of Miasto tattoo parlors, Eryk bought a vodka distillery, and Anzelm drank most of it. In the chaos, no door was closed upon Lukasz. No tavern was too rough. No alcohol too hard. No woman too dangerous. In the spring, they rented out palatial hotel rooms. In the summer, they dined on white-sand beaches in the north. They slept in gutters and stretched out on barroom floors, shrouded in the eternal night of underground taverns. Once, in a grotty little village nicknamed "Skulltown" by the locals, the twins met an upiór in a crypt and almost died.

They were rich. They were handsome. And, as they kept telling themselves, they were happy.

"You know," said Rafał, and Lukasz was horrified to see tears in his brother's eyes, "I have been a terrible brother."

For some reason, Raf had never seemed more unpredictable—more dangerous—than he seemed in that moment.

"You did the best you could," offered Lukasz.

It was a lie. Part of him was tired of hauling Rafał out from the monster's jaws. Tired of how he only seemed happy when he was dragging the rest of them down with him. He was tired of the fact that Rafał wasn't willing to care for them in the same way that Tad and Henryk had cared.

Rafał got to his feet and picked up the book that Franciszek had left open. Lukasz followed. The mavka in the picture stared out at them. At sixteen, Lukasz was already taller than Raf.

"I know how they feel," murmured Rafał.

"I don't understand," Lukasz faltered. "What are you saying, Raf?"

Rafał leaned in, held the book up.

"These monsters. Trapped between two worlds. Doomed to wander. I know how that feels." His eyes were no longer poetic. They were feral. Animal. A thousand years of blood and gore raged behind them. "We're exiles, Lukasz."

"Raf." Lukasz laughed, and it was brittle. "Stop being weird."

A ghostly smile hung on Rafał's lips.

"I don't want to be an exile anymore," he said. He licked his lips. "I want to go home."

"We can't," said Lukasz.

Without answering, Rafał pulled Lukasz close and hugged him. His strength was bone-crushing. Lukasz could feel him shaking. He felt cold, as if he were already dead.

"They're calling me," he whispered. "The Mountains call me back."

The next morning, Rafał was gone.

He left no note. No explanation, beyond his words to Lukasz. He left nothing but foggy nights and disastrous hunts and dark gutters. Nothing but five words. Five words to hold on to, to fear.

The Mountains call me back.

And outside the windows of their hotel room, paid for by the mayor of Kwiat, the snow began to fall.

⚹ 14 ⚹

AS SOON AS LUKASZ WAS back on his feet, they ran.

They ran until Król's black sides ran white with sweat. They ran until the pink sky turned to blue, until the forest grew warm again, until the roots stopped snatching at their heels. Until the evil fell away, until the smell of rot faded. They ran until Lukasz's blood dried to a crust on his skin, until even the pain of the nawia's cuts was barely a memory. They ran until the big black wolf collapsed in the dirt, sides heaving, tongue lolling between white teeth. Eyes blue as a Wolf-Lord's.

Lukasz wished they could run until Rybak stopped weeping. But even after they had slowed their exhausted horses to a walk, his shoulders kept shaking and his single eye produced enough tears for two.

None of them spoke.

Lukasz pulled his cap back over his head and turned in the saddle, trying to get his bearings. It looked like they were heading east, because the queen—whether she realized it or not—was leading them in the direction of the Mountains. But beyond that, he was lost. The trees looked random to him: mostly spruce, interspersed with oaks and Scots pine. Here and there, a linden tree sprouted. There was no order to the forest. No organization. And the natural world, Lukasz knew, tended to make sense.

It was the unnatural that brought chaos.

Lukasz could feel it. He could sense the magic at work here. He always could; it was part of what had made him so good at slaying dragons.

What's your read? Franciszek would ask.

Lukasz would tell him. And without fail, Franciszek would know how to interpret the instinct. How to temper it. How to combine Lukasz's hunches with his research, and then, together, for a short time, they were unstoppable.

Lukasz's hand went to his sword. But even now, the atrophied muscle screamed. Relying on that hand had almost gotten him killed by the nawia. Only the memory of Franciszek's research had saved him.

"Our cat's out of the bag now," said Koszmar in a low voice, drawing up next to him. "Do we trust her?"

Lukasz left the sword alone and instead took the rifle from his shoulder and put it across his knees.

The village girl—Felka—sat behind Koszmar, arms wrapped around his waist. Now she said, "If you don't trust her after last night, then you're a fool."

Koszmar sneered at her over his silver-stained shoulder.

"I wasn't asking you."

They looked different. Something in her dulled eyes. Something in his flattened, hawklike gaze. Horror had etched itself in the lines at their lips. Between their brows. One night among the nawia, and they'd both aged ten years.

Lukasz reminded himself that not everyone had grown up fighting monsters.

"What do you think?" Koszmar asked again, pointedly addressing Lukasz. His voice was very nasal. As flat as his eyes. "Do you trust her?"

Ahead, the queen was leaning over the black wolf. Lukasz had noticed it had a bad limp, and the run had exhausted it. The queen was whispering to the other lynx. As they spoke, the black wolf struggled back to his feet. He held his front paw tucked up under his chest. He wasn't looking at Lukasz, or Koszmar, or the girl on Koszmar's horse.

He was looking at Rybak.

The queen looked up abruptly.

"Set up your camp here," she said. "This part of the forest is safe."

Lukasz tried not to shudder at the human voice issuing from the throat of an animal. If she noticed, she did not show it. She merely watched him with her big lynx eyes, oddly similar to her human ones.

She turned to walk away.

"Hang on—where do you think you're going?" interrupted Koszmar, sounding a little shrill.

The queen looked coldly over her shoulder.

"I am taking my brother and my friend to make sure we have

not been followed. Or would you like to have your eyes gouged out in the night?"

Koszmar swallowed, and at the same time Felka whispered "Psot-niki" under her breath.

The lynx's eyes snapped toward her.

"Felka," she said. "You can come . . . if you like."

Lukasz stared between the lynx and the girl. It was strange, hearing the invitation from the queen. It was almost . . . *shy*?

Felka slid, a little awkwardly, down from Koszmar's saddle. She had a bundle in her arms that looked a lot like the queen's clothes. Lukasz quelled the twitch of jealousy that surfaced, unexpectedly, deep inside him.

Franciszek, he repeated to himself. This was about Franciszek. This was about surviving long enough to find Franciszek. This was not about currying the favor of some feral queen. . . .

Lukasz massaged the fingers of his ruined hand. If it hadn't been for that damn book—if it hadn't been for the fact that Fraszko had tried to teach him—if it hadn't been for that, they'd all be dead.

"Weird pair," observed Koszmar as the girl followed the three animals to the trees and disappeared.

Lukasz shot Koszmar a sidelong glance.

"And we aren't, Kosz?"

A smile flickered over Koszmar's already hardening face. He took his pipe from his black coat and lit it, and the flicker stretched to a full grin around the pipe stem.

"Kosz," he murmured. "I do like that. By the way, nice touch with the nawia—how did you know that a baptism would get rid of them?"

Lukasz took a cigarette from his pocket and lit it. The smell of Faustian smoke filled the clearing. It elicited a visceral sense of loss from him.

"It was in a book, once," he said.

"I thought you couldn't read," said Koszmar, brow wrinkling.

Lukasz didn't answer. He was looking at Rybak. Lukasz had now saved his life on two occasions. A debt was owed, and he was ready to collect.

The queen did not return for several hours.

With the animals gone and Koszmar absorbed in cleaning the nawia blood off his perfect uniform, Lukasz took his time untacking Król and brushing him down. Though it had healed—somehow—his shoulder was still sore from the nav's blow, and it twinged as he lifted the dragon-leather saddle from his horse's back. The antlers chimed. The only lullaby he had ever known.

What the hell was he doing?

He felt oddly light-headed. Nauseated, even. He reached inside his jacket to run his hand over the spot that had healed. He wasn't sure what he expected—a gaping wound, maybe? But the skin was smooth.

Boots crunched beside him.

Lukasz looked up and met Rybak's single, unnerving eye. The Unnaturalist had looked earnest for a moment, but now his brow furrowed.

"You all right, boy?"

Lukasz swallowed against the sudden urge to vomit. He found

himself leaning heavily against Król's side.

"What were you thinking?" he asked. "Coming after us? We could have all been killed."

"With or without me, the mavka would have come for you," said Rybak. "They are the souls of the unbaptized—"

"I know, I know," interrupted Lukasz, and then quoted, almost verbatim: "'They're of a violent nature and prey on humans and lure their victims with their songs and decapitate them.'"

He rubbed his hand over his chin and around the back of his neck, without taking elbows from Król's back.

"How did you know that?" asked Rybak, single eye widening.

Lukasz smiled wryly. "How did *you* know that?" he returned.

Rybak didn't answer, but he pointed up to where a white eagle flitted in and out of the branches. It reminded Lukasz, sickeningly, of the Kwiat library and Rafał.

"You can talk to her?" he asked, suddenly realizing what Rybak was implying.

"Most animals are willing to talk," replied the Unnaturalist. "It's the humans who don't listen."

The underbrush rustled on the other side of the campsite. Even from twenty feet away, Lukasz saw Koszmar's hand go to the rifle in the grass. Then Felka emerged, followed by the queen, who was human once more.

"How could you do this?" Rybak asked Lukasz quietly. "How could you kidnap her?"

The queen sat down cross-legged, flanked by her lynx and her wolf. The wolf flipped over on his back, tail thumping the ground, while the queen rubbed his belly and chatted with the lynx.

"I thought—" began Lukasz.

"No," said Rybak, in that moment sounding very much like Franciszek. "You didn't think."

Lukasz reminded himself, feeling a bit scummy, that there was a debt, and that he needed to collect. *For Franciszek,* he thought, trying to block out the image of Jakub Rybak crying over the little nav.

This is for Franciszek.

"I saved your life last night, Jakub," he said levelly. "That's the second time."

"When was the first?"

"In that cellar in Szarawoda," said Lukasz. When Rybak tried to turn away, Lukasz's hand shot out and grabbed his arm. He added, in a low voice: "You owe me."

Rybak's eye shifted from Lukasz's face to his hand, clenched around his shirtsleeve. Lukasz dropped the arm.

"What do you want?" asked Rybak.

Lukasz remembered the book of demons in Kwiat. He remembered Raf, playing with dola and leading them all to destruction. And then he thought of someone else. Someone with gold-rimmed spectacles and an unfailingly neat uniform and a wildly good heart hidden under its stiff, boring exterior—

Lukasz spoke through gritted teeth.

"Teach me to read."

The nawia had been a close call. Lukasz was lucky he remembered anything at all—was lucky Franciszek had chosen that particular page. But if he had been able to *read* . . . who knew what else he could have learned?

And if he couldn't hunt dragons, what the hell was he going to do with his life?

Rybak inclined his head.

"Very well."

Lukasz watched the Unnaturalist cross the clearing. He was barely the ghost of the man he'd met six years ago. Felka trailed after him, looking a little awkward. She obviously wanted to comfort him. Just as obviously didn't know how to start.

Lukasz propped his Faustian-fur saddle pad against a tree and settled down on the ground. Koszmar was fiddling with his own saddle on the opposite side, his hand never straying far from the saber at his side. He was watching the queen. They stayed close together, strangely fractured. Circling like predators. Watching one another. Keeping tabs on these new, strange partners.

Lukasz needed her.

They didn't have Franciszek's original notebook, the one with the map. Whatever Rybak thought about the forest changing, it would have been better than nothing. As it was, they had no clear path to the Mountains. But this queen had spent years learning about the monsters. She knew this forest. She had told them where to set up camp—she had led them *away* from the mavka. More than that, she had *defeated* them.

She was, against all odds, some kind of queen. The mavka had proved that.

As if feeling his gaze, she looked up. He saw, for the barest second, a flash of gold in her green eyes.

The air thickened with things unsaid.

She got to her feet. She wore only shades of blue. The color of vila. He wondered if it was on purpose. She moved deliberately. No move out of place. No sign of nerves. Lukasz wasn't sure if it was magic or the tutelage of cats, but even covered in dirt and with tangled hair, she looked like royalty.

Lukasz didn't move. Didn't reach for his lighter. Didn't reach for a cigarette. God knew he wanted to, if only for something to do. But she had him, God. She had him, and he didn't want her to know it.

She stood in front of him, looking down, thin arms crossed. Fingernails like claws rested on the torn lace of her shirtsleeves, and her hair had only gotten wilder overnight.

He wasn't quite sure why he said it, but when the silence reached a breaking point, Lukasz offered, "I understand if you hate me."

With great care, she lowered herself to a kneeling position beside him. Lukasz stared warily back. With the unwavering stare of an animal, she took him in her gaze and held him there.

A growl caught the edges of the words, making her voice rasp.

"I do not hate you."

Her long hand reached out and brushed over his shoulder. Her fingers slipped under the edge of his coat, moving it away. Lukasz wondered if she could hear his heart quicken.

"First rusalki. Now nawia," she murmured. She had an odd way of speaking, placing the emphasis on the wrong parts of each word. He could have listened to her mistakes forever. "Where does it end?"

"It ends with my brother."

Still, she did not look up.

"But where is he?" she asked, almost more to herself than to him.

"I'm looking for him," said Lukasz levelly.

"No," she returned. "You are looking for trouble."

She pushed aside the half-opened shirt. He felt her lift the silver cross out of the way. Her nails scraped lightly over his bare skin. He felt her spread out the five fingers, fitting them into where the five cuts from the nawia had been. Her fingers curled in like claws.

"You're not the first one to tell me that," he said, as evenly as he could.

Her perfect face, with those high cheekbones, those thick lashes, fell slightly to the side. Then her eyes flashed to his. He hoped she did not feel his heart stumble under her palm.

"And how has it worked out for you?" she asked. "Looking for trouble?"

He didn't know what made his throat tighten, her or her words. All he knew was that, one way or another, as long as she didn't move, she had him.

"It varies," he said at last.

She smirked. It was soft, almost mischievous. God, she had him. Maybe they were right. Maybe she was a monster. Maybe she only lived in darkness, only in this forest; maybe she bled silver instead of red.

She took her hand away. Lukasz let out a breath and wanted it back.

"I propose a deal," she said.

Her hands were folded in her lap. They looked like the pale translucent hands of a rusalka. And he wanted them back on his skin.

"What deal?" asked Lukasz, still dazed.

Her gaze burned. She had the unshakable calm of a predator at the top of the food chain.

"I am queen. I will take you to the Mountains. You are a dragon slayer. You will slay the Dragon."

He could hardly believe it. Relief flooded through him; for the first time in months, the sense of dread, of responsibility—it all lifted. He could hardly believe his good luck. With her guiding them, they could be in the Mountains in a few days' time. In a week, maybe less . . .

Franciszek.

It felt almost like hope.

Then Lukasz remembered his hand. Shaking when he'd raised it to the Dragon, then betraying him when he'd swung for the nawia. His heart sank. He was finished hunting dragons. Even if he'd wanted to—and he didn't—there was no way he could take down the Golden Dragon. He knew it.

But she didn't.

"All right," he said, holding out his right hand. "Deal."

The queen stared. Distrust flickered in her eyes, reminded him that whatever she was—monster, human—she wasn't anything like him.

"We're going to shake on it," he said. "It's a human custom."

Tentatively, she reached out.

Their fingers touched, and then Lukasz seized her hand and shook it once. It was cold even through the dragon-leather gloves, with sharp, prominent bones. But for some reason, despite the claws and the fangs, it struck Lukasz as being almost fragile.

He was already formulating a plan—hopefully, Franciszek would

ALEKSANDRA ROSS

still be in the forest. They'd follow his most likely route, and with her guiding them, maybe even catch up with him before the Mountains. And then they'd make a break for it. They'd be back in Miasto in under a week, sipping vodka and enjoying their gold. The last two Brothers Smokówi, doing what none had done before them: growing old.

He released her hand. She turned it over, looking dubious.

"It's a promise," he said, irritated with the guilt already stirring in him. "To do what we say."

"No games?" she asked. Her voice was rough and growling.

But she couldn't know. Not when he needed her. Not when he was so close. Lukasz ignored the cold feeling spreading through his chest, replacing that flicker of hope.

He shook his head.

"No games."

She continued to stare at her palm. Then she curled her fingers under and folded the hand back in her lap, still not looking at it. She ran her tongue over her lips. And then she said, in the same hoarse voice:

"My name is Ren."

15

"ONE NIGHT?" REPEATED CZARN IN the morning. "Is that what it takes, Ren? For you to change your mind?"

Ren drew her knees to her chest and wrapped her arms around them. Lukasz had insisted that they try to take the same path as his brother, in the hopes that they might catch up with him on their journey. Ren personally thought the missing Wolf-Lord was lying dead at the bottom of a river somewhere, but she kept the suspicion to herself. She was happy to take whatever route Lukasz wanted. She needed that Dragon dead.

So, together with Czarn and Ryś, she had spent most of the night figuring out how a human might try to get to the Mountains. And at every step, Czarn kept badgering her not to go.

"You can't trust them!" he insisted.

"Drop it, Czarn," she growled.

On the other side of the clearing, the humans had built a fire. They paced back and forth in front of the embers, sipping drinks from tin mugs and watching the sun crest the trees. Ren was cold and hungry, but—whatever Czarn might have thought—she still didn't trust them enough to move to their side of the clearing.

And besides, she did not like fire.

"My God," muttered Ryś, opening one eye. "Make up your mind. Now that Ren's actually made a deal, you're backing out?"

"Did you see those things last night?" growled Czarn. "We—"

"*They* knew how to get rid of them," said Ren, even though she only meant the Wolf-Lord. "We didn't. They could help us, Czarn. Not just with the Dragon, but . . ."

Her voice trailed away, but both Czarn and Ryś knew exactly what she meant.

Without the humans—without Lukasz—they might not have survived the nawia. Whatever that bap—bat— Whatever that *thing* was Ren had done, only the humans had known how to do it. It was the first time that Ren's experience had not been enough. The realization was sobering.

On the other side of the clearing, the Wolf-Lord leaned down to wake Felka, offering her a cup of something hot. She sat up, rubbing her eyes. Ren felt a stab of jealousy as Lukasz lowered himself beside Felka to talk. His eye caught hers across the clearing, and Ren turned quickly back to Czarn.

"Czarn," she said, "they're our best chance. The Wolf-Lord has promised to kill the Dragon."

The black wolf growled. The one-eyed man—Rybak—glanced up nervously.

"I do not trust them," Czarn murmured.

"Come on," groaned Ryś, rolling onto his back and stretching out as far as he could, until he looked like a furrier, toothier crescent moon. "He's a Wolf-Lord, Czarn. You're supposed to like these idiots."

Czarn jerked his slim muzzle toward the one-eyed villager, Rybak. He wore a long cream-colored coat with dark embroidered trousers and boots. The coat had rusty stains, and Ren wondered if it was old blood.

"It's not the Wolf-Lord I mind," said Czarn.

Ren wondered, with a sudden twist, whether it was the same coat he'd been wearing when she attacked him. Even worse, she realized she could not remember.

"You don't need to mind *him*," said Ren. "The man is a wreck. If we'd left him with the nawia, he'd have been happy to die."

Czarn didn't respond at first. At least not out loud. His reply echoed in the silence between them. Was caught in Rybak's mangled face. Trapped in the stained fabric. Screaming, loud and clear, from the scar on his paw.

At last the wolf's lip curled.

"Perhaps you should have let him."

Ren rubbed Ryś's belly, and he purred appreciatively.

She remembered that day very well. Whatever the villagers thought, he was the only human she had ever hurt on purpose. And so what? She wasn't sorry—she couldn't be sorry. She'd *had* to do it. She'd been a child, wandering far from her castle on a snowy day. She'd seen the wolf caught in the trap, and when the hunter had burst out of the trees with his rifle, she'd panicked.

She'd been a *child*. She'd never expected—

Ryś yelped.

Ren snatched back her hand. Her fingers had transformed to claws and scratched him.

"Sorry!" Ren hastily smoothed down his ears. "I'm so sorry—"

Ryś grumbled, licking down the fur on his chest where she'd nicked him.

"You think a little hairball like you could hurt me—"

"We should go back," interrupted Czarn, still harping on the same topic. "We should not help them."

"Oh, get a grip," growled Ryś. "None of us like them. We can kill them if we need to. What we can't kill is that Dragon."

"Ryś is right," said Ren. "It's the lesser of two evils."

Czarn glanced at Ren. His blue eyes lingered on her human clothes.

"Czarn," she said, trying to be reasonable. "Please. I don't understand. You agreed this was a good idea, and now you're just—"

"They hurt you!"

The words exploded in a flash of yellow fangs and pink gums.

On the other side of the clearing, the humans had gone still. Only Lukasz looked unperturbed. He was still sitting with Felka, leaning back against a tree stump. Casually he struck a tiny flame and began to smoke again. He watched Ren, eyes slightly narrowed, dark brows low and thoughtful.

The clearing filled, slowly, with the smell of tobacco smoke. Ren did not like it.

"Oh, Czarn," Ren whispered. She wrapped human arms around his thick neck and pulled him in, burying her face in the soft black fur. "It's okay. I'm okay. I know this didn't start right. But we can finish it."

He relaxed in her arms. She kissed his soft black cheek.

"It'll be okay," she murmured. "We're all going to be okay."

At that moment, a voice sounded above them. Ren took her face out of his fur.

"Hey," said Felka. Her eyes swiveled between Ren and the wild animals. She did not seem especially intimidated. "This is yours."

Felka held out some pale blue fabric, and it took Ren a moment to realize it was the cloak she'd worn to the village.

"It'll get cold at night," she said. "You should hang on to it."

"So we are clear," said Ren, taking the cloak, "I have slept in this forest before."

Felka laughed. It was loud and, it suddenly occurred to Ren, probably the prettiest thing about her.

"I wasn't expecting someone like you to have a sense of humor," she said.

Ren folded the cloak over her arm and returned the girl's gaze.

"What do you mean, 'someone like me'?" growled Ren.

"Well," said Felka matter-of-factly, "you're not like us."

There it was. That little twist—the same twist in the village, seeing that family through their window. Seeing the cat. After all, it wasn't as if the girl was wrong. If anything, Ren agreed. If anything, she was more like the nawia, or even the rusalki—a little bit human, a little bit magic, a little bit . . . wrong. That strange resemblance to humanity, tempered with all the darkness in the world. That same hypnotic fascination.

The same thirst for vengeance.

"I would do it again, you know," she said abruptly.

Felka looked confused.

"I would attack him again," she clarified. "Your one-eyed man. Jakub. Or Rybak. Whatever. But he is not yours, is he? Not really." Ren put her head to the side, thinking. "But for some reason, still you came for him."

At that, even Felka's freckles paled. Her thin mouth opened and closed. "He's been kind to me," she said at last. "You've never lived with people. You wouldn't know how rare that is."

Ren was curious. She waited for the other girl to elaborate, but Felka remained silent. It irritated Ren.

"I don't care," Ren said. "Czarn is my best friend, and he was going to kill him."

She didn't add the rest. That the day she had attacked Jakub had been the first time she had ever transformed. If it had not been for Jakub, she might never have grown claws, or fangs. She might never have grown the armor she needed to fight for her kingdom.

And maybe that made her a monster, but she was not sorry.

"You know," said Felka after a moment, "the villagers think you did this. They think you control the monsters. That you're doing this to us. Because of what you did to Jakub."

Ren stared.

"Is that what you think?" she demanded. "Is that what they say, in the village? That I kill all of you? You are ignorant, arrogant fools. I keep this forest under control. I kill strzygi and rusalki. I warn you all to stay out, and still you come in. I have to protect my animals. I cannot protect you humans, too."

Felka nodded. She looked sad.

"They could have helped you," she said. "But after you hurt Jakub . . . they think the worst of you now."

Ren shrugged. In that moment, she was glad not to be a human. "I do not need the help of creatures who judge so quickly."

"And you don't?" Felka shot back.

Without waiting for an answer, she got up and returned to the humans' side. Koszmar stepped in to cut her off, and they spoke quietly for a moment. Felka was so tiny she made him look like a giant.

Ren watched her. *They could have helped you,* she had said. *They think the worst of you now.* The comment had hurt more than she wanted to admit. Anyway, it wasn't as if she had to be sorry. It wasn't as if she owed them anything.

She'd given up her life to the forest. She'd opened the doors of her castle and spent her days running with wolves and her nights sleeping among lynxes. She'd spent years fighting back the darkness. And it hadn't just been for the animals. It had been for the humans, too. But did they see it?

No, she thought. These humans only saw scars.

Five of them.

They began on their journey, Ren and the animals in the lead.

They moved steadily for most of the morning. The forest was dense and pathless, and the going was slow. They climbed over fallen trees and pushed their way through five-foot-tall weeds and scrub. It was a tricky place. But Ren didn't dare mention that to the humans lest they panic.

Trees tended to move around at random for better patches of sunlight, or better water, or simply for a change of scenery. The waterways liked to change directions spontaneously, just for the thrill of it, and you could never really be sure whether you were up- or downriver.

And now that most of the animals had taken shelter in the castle, there weren't many creatures available to give directions.

The morning lengthened to afternoon, and the trees darkened. They leaned down to watch the little group, and a low whispering filled the quiet.

Ren stopped abruptly. Ryś wandered a few feet up to investigate a root where it writhed and twisted in the forest floor.

"What is it?" asked the Wolf-Lord. It was the first time they'd spoken since they'd set out.

He leaned down from the big black horse to ask. The trees became still, and the low whispering stopped. Ren's whole body prickled. He was smoking, and the gray tendril wound upward into the unmoving branches, where it congealed into a fog.

Ryś sat back on his haunches, put his head to one side, and watched the twisting root.

"This place is not safe," Ren whispered. The trees leaned closer. "We must be careful."

Lukasz glanced sideways at Koszmar. The blond soldier nodded and wordlessly passed one of his revolvers back to Felka, sitting behind him. Lukasz and Jakub took their rifles off their shoulders.

Ren and Czarn exchanged a look. She didn't like guns and she didn't like humans. But she also didn't like the very real possibility of a violent death.

The forest grew tense around them.

"Careful what you say," whispered Ren. "They are listening."

A visible shudder ran through the humans. Up ahead, Ryś sprang back as the root lashed out at him. He puffed up and hissed.

"And put those out," added Ren, pointing at the smoking things that Lukasz and Koszmar had in their teeth.

"Why?" asked Lukasz, glancing upward. "They don't like it?"

Ren gave him a withering glare.

"*I* don't like it," she said.

The two men obeyed.

They moved carefully forward. The trees kept watch, but none of them stirred. Ren loved her forest, even the bad parts, and it broke her heart to see it acting like this. The roots kept snaking out to catch at their ankles, making the horses stumble. Once, a tree branch dropped out of nowhere, straight across the path in front of them. Koszmar shrieked and fired an entire round of bullets into it before realizing it wasn't another monster.

After that, when they'd gotten the horses back under control, Czarn took the lead. Overhead, the branches closed to blackness, and they could no longer see the Mountains. It might have been years since he had come down from their icy slopes, but the big black wolf did not hesitate; he still had the nose for mountain air.

Ren wasn't sure how, but she soon found herself walking next to the Wolf-Lord.

Czarn did not speak often of his cubhood. But Ren knew he had been raised on cold nights and fear, marked by an exodus from a beloved home to a place where the wolves survived, even if they did not quite love it. Ren wondered if, despite his dislike of Jakub and his new distrust for the Wolf-Lord, Czarn longed to see the purple hills.

She wondered if the same was true for this Wolf-Lord.

"How is your shoulder?" she asked as the thought occurred to her.

He grinned down from his saddle, easily enough that Ren knew he was fine. But instead of answering, he said, "Suddenly the queen of the forest is interested in a lowly, savage Wolf-Lord?"

"I never said you were savage," muttered Ren. "I would never say that about someone."

The grin froze. To Ren's immense surprise, he dismounted and landed, flinching slightly, on the earth. Now they were walking beside each other.

"What are you doing?" asked Ren.

"What do you mean?" he replied in an innocent voice.

"Why are you walking with me?"

"Do you want me to leave?" The grin returned.

"If only you'd asked that two days ago."

"Oh really?" He looked surprised, but there was a wicked tilt to the edge of his mouth. "What's changed?"

Ren sputtered.

"No—I—that's not what I meant." Then she drew herself up to her full height, which—annoyingly—was still not as tall as he was. She tipped her chin back and said, in the iciest voice she could manage:

"I do not like you."

Lukasz laughed again.

"I can tell."

Before Ren could retort, there was a loud yelp up ahead. A spidery creature plummeted out of the branches, landing squarely on the black wolf's back. He yelped again and went down on his wounded side.

Nocnica.

Before Ren could transform, a deafening blast echoed beside her. The spidery monster exploded in a spray of brown guts. She reeled, ears ringing, and Lukasz—grinning, the expression completely changed—slammed a new round into the gleaming rifle.

Ren glowered. It hadn't been a fair fight, with guns instead of claws. And yet . . . seeing Czarn struggle back to his feet, unharmed, she was—a very tiny bit—grateful.

"I could have handled it," she snapped.

"I was faster," he said, and shrugged.

Evening fell, and the forest changed again. The branches unknotted to reveal the sky, almost apologetically. The paths were clearer. Roots didn't try to curl around their ankles as they ran. Nothing called down from the treetops. The air was fresh.

And whatever Ren might have thought about the Wolf-Lord, she could not help feeling a small thrill of hope. Even if he was annoying and arrogant, his presence—their deal—meant there was at least a chance that this might work.

As night fell, they stopped amid a collection of closely packed spruce. Jakub went to gather firewood, and Lukasz disappeared with his rifle and returned an hour later with a half dozen dead nocnica in hand.

He tossed the spidery things in a heap by the fire. Their hairy legs twitched.

Koszmar yelped and jumped to his feet.

"What in God's name are those?" he demanded.

"Dinner," said Lukasz. He must have seen Ren's expression, because he added: "Your brother told me you don't eat animals."

Ren hid her surprise. Ryś was nowhere to be seen, probably off doing the things lynxes liked to do on dark nights. Ren made a mental note to tell him off when he got back. It wasn't safe out there. Sooner or later, he was going to get himself killed.

Lukasz leaned down next to Koszmar, and after a small mechanical click, the kindling began to glow. Beside him, Koszmar tugged at the emblem around his neck.

"If you think I'm eating giant spiders—" he began, a little shrilly.

"Fine," interjected Felka easily, sweeping past. "Don't eat them. More for me."

She put her hands to her mouth and waved her fingers like spider pincers. Koszmar almost tripped, stumbling backward.

"Nuh-uh," he stammered as Felka advanced on him with her spider fingers. "No—stop *that*!"

He skirted back out of the way, and Felka gave chase. Lukasz watched, laughing. His fingers snapped at the small contraption in his right hand. *Click, click.* His laughter had a devilish tilt to it.

"It's not funny!" hissed Koszmar, dancing out of Felka's way.

"Don't run too far," warned Lukasz as Koszmar tripped over a saddle. "Or you'll meet the real thing."

Koszmar stopped dead, and Felka crashed into him.

Jakub Rybak returned at that moment with an armful of dry wood. At the sight of him, the beginnings of Ren's good mood evaporated. Czarn looked up from licking his scarred paw. Ren could practically feel the hatred radiating from him.

Leaving Koszmar alone, Felka hauled a pot from the army-issue camp gear. Together, she and Lukasz began carefully preparing what they called a "hunter's stew." Still with an eye on Jakub, Ren listened to Felka's chat about how the dish usually included cabbage and a selection of sausages, but how tonight, the nocnica would replace the usual meats. Across the fire, Koszmar sat staring at their dinner with abject horror.

Ren felt oddly touched that Lukasz had spoken to Ryś. Cared enough—or been wary enough?—to heed her laws. The memory of his heart pounding under her fingertips came back to her.

No games, they had promised. Shaken hands.

It occurred to her that were it not for the Dragon, she might never have met him. And for some strange, irrational reason, the realization lit a glow in her heart.

Lukasz glanced up. Black hair hung messily over one dark eyebrow. His eyes narrowed, and when he smiled, her stomach flipped. The corner of his lip curved upward. His eyes glittered.

Ren looked away.

✖ 16 ✖

FOR THE NEXT THREE DAYS, they moved steadily in the direction of the Mountains. Lukasz kept Franciszek's notebook in his coat pocket, and even just knowing it was there gave him a sense of hope he hadn't felt in weeks.

If anything, during those three days, he was almost happy. The routine of things somehow reminded him of the old days—the first days—before the hotel rooms and the palaces, before the gold and the glory. He liked the wild dark beyond the campfire. He liked the whisper of unseen things. He liked the hunt and the gamble.

He liked, he realized, the company.

Every night, Lukasz and Jakub shared a watch, and Jakub did his best to teach Lukasz his letters. But Franciszek had been right: he had put off learning for a long time, and it had gotten harder while he ignored it.

"Is there somewhere else you would rather be?" asked Jakub.

Lukasz glanced up. The pair of them were seated on a fallen tree, about thirty feet outside the light of the fire. The others were getting ready to sleep for the night, and he and Jakub had an old camp lantern. Strange moths fluttered up to it. They smelled like vinegar and emitted a faint, haunting melody.

"Sorry." Lukasz winced and stretched out his shoulder. "My arm itches."

Jakub Rybak gave him a long, unreadable look.

"They could be venomous, you know," he said. "I think we may be the first people to survive their embrace. If you'd let me have a look—"

"It's fine," said Lukasz, a little more shortly than he'd intended.

"Not to study it," said Jakub gently. "Just to see if I could help."

"It's fine," repeated Lukasz. "Let's just practice, okay?"

Even as he asked, his hand twinged.

Jakub sighed and closed the book.

"Lukasz," he asked, "why do you need to learn this now? I've seen you with that notebook. If you don't need to read it to understand it, why bother learning out here in the middle of nowhere? Why not wait to go back to Miasto and get a real tutor?"

Lukasz hesitated. Behind them, the others were still crowded near the warmth of the fire. Out here, despite its being late summer, the air was chilly. It reminded him, horribly, of the nawia.

"The only reason I knew about the nawia was because Franciszek told me," he said at last. "As long as I'm not reading, who knows how much I'm missing? And besides—"

He paused, and then continued:

"Besides, I'm only good at one thing."

Jakub waited. Made him spell it out.

"I'm only good at hunting dragons," said Lukasz finally. "I don't do anything else. I *can't* do anything else."

The hand twitched again. That weak, traitorous, misshapen, sorry excuse for a hand.

Lukasz didn't tell the truth: That he *knew* he couldn't do it. That he was as good as retired, and if he went back to Miasto and lived like a king, he'd be dead of boredom by the end of the year.

"What if one day, I can't do this anymore?" he asked instead. "What happens then?"

Jakub chuckled. He pushed a few messy blond strands behind his ear.

"Lukasz," he said gently. "I think you'll be hunting dragons for a long time."

Lukasz didn't respond. For a moment, he desperately—irrationally—wanted to tell Jakub the truth. That he'd made a deal with the queen that he could not keep. That he'd lied to find his brother, and he had no intention of sticking around or going after the Golden Dragon. He'd shaken hands and promised no games, and he'd been lying through his teeth.

"I'm worried," said Jakub after a moment.

Lukasz realized he'd been scratching at his shoulder again. Jakub seemed to search for the right words before he said, very uncertainly, "Lukasz, I'm . . . I'm worried she may be the princess."

Lukasz choked.

"Who?"

"Ren," said Jakub.

Lukasz couldn't help it. He laughed.

It took him a moment to realize that the Unnaturalist was being perfectly serious. The forest was black and still around them. And in the darkness, Lukasz remembered the sight of that white castle, looming over the trees. Perfectly preserved, except for its single, charred spire.

"Jakub, the princess died in the tower fire," he said.

The Dragon had devoured the queen, torched the tower, and burned the baby to death in her own crib. Everyone knew that.

But what if . . .

"She died in the fire," he repeated, less certainly.

"Think about it," murmured Jakub. "How old is she? Seventeen? Eighteen? She came from the castle, Lukasz. She can change into a lynx—the official symbol of the Kamieńa crown. I was not sure, at first, but . . . but her name is Ren."

Lukasz felt his brow furrow.

"So?"

Jakub shook his head.

"The queen's name is Ren. The princess—the one who died—her name was *Irena*."

Lukasz was stunned.

"No," he said shakily. "No way. It's impossible. I don't—"

The baptism. Only a queen . . .

"She looks like her mother, Lukasz," continued Jakub. "When I saw her in the village that night, I knew it was her. It couldn't be anyone else. And now you . . . you have kidnapped her. Why do you think I followed you into this forest? I was trying to stop you. Whether you knew it or not, you'd committed treason."

Lukasz held up both hands.

"Wait a second. I tried to help her. Kosz hit her—"

"You didn't stop him."

"So?" demanded Lukasz. "The villagers would have killed her. You saw them. If anything, we did her a favor."

He didn't believe it even as he said it. And from the expression on what was left of Jakub's face, Jakub could tell.

"The queen would have torn that village apart, long before they did her any real harm."

"Fine. So we saved the village. Or what's left of it. And why the hell would you care?"

Jakub closed his one eye for a moment, as if searching for words. Then he said, very carefully: "I set my traps, Lukasz. I went calling the wolves from this forest, and I have paid for it."

Something very cold and very painful rose in Lukasz's throat. He knew that warning well, had heard that warning so many times.

Those words. He thought of the notebook, even now, folded against his heart. He should have learned. . . .

A new possibility seized him. One that could derail their entire venture.

"Well—you're not going to tell her, are you?" He could hear the edge in his voice. "I mean, you don't even know for sure."

Overhead, Jakub's pale eagle settled in the branches. The one-eyed Unnaturalist looked upward, then back at Lukasz. Then he said in a stiff voice, "I am not in the business of emptying another man's snare."

Relief loosened Lukasz's chest. He rolled back his once-wounded shoulder. It still itched like hell.

"All right," he said, before adding, "Thank you."

Jakub shrugged.

"It is not for you. I have no desire to be attacked again."

There was a rustle behind them. Both Jakub and Lukasz whipped around at the same time, rifles primed. A tall, slim figure stood in the darkness. Green eyes flickered in the light from the camp lantern. The moths kept singing, and for some wild, irrational reason, Lukasz wondered if they were singing to her.

Jakub's face split into a smile. Lukasz was less willing to lower the gun.

Had she heard . . . ?

The green eyes flickered from face to face, then to the small book on Jakub's lap. Then she took on more detail: slim cheekbones and a pointed chin. A mouth that seemed to move slower than the rest of her, slow to speak, slow to form the human words.

"What are you doing?" she asked.

For a second time, it struck him: she sounded shy.

He wondered if her shyness was the natural inclination of an animal, or whether it could—just maybe it could—be more. He wondered if she knew that she had him. He wondered if she knew he was already wrapped around those long, inhuman fingers.

He wondered how long he could lie to her.

Lukasz lowered the rifle.

"Reading," said Jakub. "Would you like to join us?"

There was a scuttle overhead and chattering sounds in the trees beyond. Ren froze, eyes suddenly luminescent and feline. Lukasz's hand closed on the rifle.

"What was that?" he asked.

The trees seemed to shift closer together. The blue-gray mist gathered overhead in their branches and trickled down to form a carpet on the forest floor. Between the knee-high fog and the moment of utter silence, it was like they'd been immersed in a nightmarish cloud.

At last, Jakub broke the silence.

"Strzygi," he breathed.

Lukasz glanced around, a chill stealing over his soul.

"Close?" he asked.

No one replied. They held their breath, each one primed. Lukasz could think only of those beaky faces, of the eyes that had once belonged to children, to women, to men. Of the three bodies in three lonely graves. Three shovels, coming down hard.

There was another rustle, and the night cleared.

"They're gone," murmured Ren.

They were quiet for a time. Then Ren whispered in a very soft voice: "Felka told me that when someone disappears in the forest, the villagers blame me."

"Not all the villagers," said Jakub.

Ren smiled, wreathed in mist and woodsy darkness. Lukasz had only ever seen a vila once in his life, and in that moment, she looked very much like one. Then she crept closer and settled on the ground. Lukasz noticed that she chose Jakub's side instead of his. Once again, he felt that irrational stab of jealousy.

"What are they?" she asked. "The strzygi?"

"Lesser demons," said Jakub. "From the same family as upiórs.

Bloodsuckers. Equivalents exist in other countries, I understand. Simply put, they are amalgamations of greed. Creatures created by the consumption of others. In being consumed, the dead find rebirth."

Thinking of another monster, Lukasz asked, "Could—could a living person become a strzygoń? If they were attacked—but not killed?"

"I don't know," he answered. "I'm not sure anyone knows. But we do know that not everyone killed by a strzygoń is destined for the same fate. In fact, statistically speaking, the majority of victims stay dead."

Lukasz fought the urge to rub at his shoulder.

Jakub paused for a moment, and when he continued, it was as if in a rapture. Thinking of Damian Bielec, Lukasz reflected that Jakub would have made a better professor.

"Some believe that strzygi rise from a duality of souls," said the Unnaturalist. "In this belief, most humans have one soul. When that human dies, their soul and body die with them. But—but if by some fluke of nature, a human was to have *two* souls . . ."

He paused before continuing.

"When the human is consumed by the strzygi, the first soul is consumed with them. But in this school of thought, that second soul lives on. Comes to inhabit their new body. And that soul dies more slowly, more painfully. Trapped in the body of a worsening monster."

"That's madness," said Lukasz, suppressing a shudder. "No one has two souls."

"But what if they did?" asked Jakub. "There are old wives' tales of children born with teeth, or with two hearts. These children, the stories say, are those with extra souls."

Jakub shrugged.

"But I think belief in predisposition is too optimistic. Even the theory of souls suggests that we are, in some way or another, guided by twin forces. So perhaps this business of predisposition is simply a lie to help us sleep. Perhaps it is easier to believe some are born evil, rather than admit that predilection exists equally in every one of us."

They were all quiet. The night seemed very heavy.

"I do not like the monsters that were once human," Ren observed thoughtfully. "I think they are the most terrible of all."

"You are a wise queen," said Jakub.

Ren looked at him with sadness.

"But I have been a cruel one."

Lukasz wasn't especially subtle, but even he could tell they weren't talking about strzygi anymore. He'd already pieced the story together from the others: Jakub had gone looking for another creature to research, and Ren had punished him for it. He did not have any interest in reliving that moment with either of them.

"So," said Jakub instead. "Shall we read?"

And suddenly, Lukasz realized that he had even *less* interest in looking like an illiterate fool in front of the queen.

"I have to go," he said abruptly. "Maybe tomorrow."

"But—" began Jakub.

"The strzygi—" warned Ren.

Lukasz got to his feet. His arm was numb, and inside the glove his fingertips were cold. Fear twisted within him.

"See you at camp," he said shortly, and strode away.

Jakub's story had gotten under his skin, as surely as that damn queen had gotten under it. The possibility was horrific. After all, if a strzygi bite could transform a man, what could a nav do . . . ?

He glanced back, but Ren and Jakub were already far behind him. Confident he was alone, Lukasz shrugged off his coat. Maybe he just had a little nick, catching on the seam of his shirt. Maybe, he thought wildly, he'd slept on some kind of poisonous plant. Maybe—

He dragged the shirt down off his shoulder.

The skin was no longer smooth. Five claw marks traced the same lines of the nawia's blow, now bubbling like burns. He ran his fingers over one cut, and a sheet of skin peeled back.

"No," he muttered. *"No, no, no."*

At the touch, pain shot down his arm. Lukasz stumbled back, catching his foot on a root and almost falling.

He'd had his share of scrapes and burns and impalings, and he didn't want to admit it to anyone, but this was worse. Wounds were supposed to heal. Not disappear and reopen and blister and burn. He cringed at the thought. . . . But, then again, what was he supposed to do?

Franciszek was the expert on these things. And Franciszek, God help him, was probably dealing with some monsters of his own at that moment.

This couldn't be happening. Not when things were working out so perfectly. When he had a plan. When he was finally learning to read. When he'd met *her*—

He punched a tree and immediately regretted it. Pain splintered across his knuckles.

"Careful," said a familiar, nasal voice. "I think that one was on our side."

Lukasz swore again.

Koszmar was leaning against a tree a few feet away, smoking. He had one foot crossed in front of the other. He wasn't as much watching Lukasz as he was staring off into space. In fact, he was so quiet and still that between the fog and the dimness, Lukasz had mistaken him for another tree.

"Have you been there the whole time?" he demanded, pulling his coat back on.

The mist gave everything a dreamlike quality as Koszmar turned slowly. He used his tongue to pivot his pipe to the edge of his mouth, and the click of the stem against his teeth echoed in the darkness.

"Yes," he said softly. Then: "Do you need help, Lukasz?"

Lukasz hung back a moment longer. The night played tricks on a man in the best of times; this forest, at this time, was a death trap.

"Oh, come now," said Koszmar in the same soft, almost musical voice. "It's just me."

Lukasz drew level with him. Cautiously, he leaned against a neighboring tree in an identical position, only reversed.

"Got a light?" he asked, casting a wary glance at the alternating blue and black before them. "Left mine by the fire."

From the corner of his eye, he watched Koszmar fish around in his pockets. A languid grin stretched around his pipe.

"Luring you to my vices, am I?" He produced a lighter with amber inlays, and the expensive trinket passed between them, silhouetted by the eerie blue fog. "What a delicious possibility."

Lukasz rolled his eyes, cupping his hands around the cigarette. He promised himself it would be his last. Especially if that girl—Ren—really *was* the princess. He wasn't especially keen to find out what happened to those who disobeyed her rules.

The tip of the cigarette glowed orange in the blue, blue world. Fine tobacco, with a soft peppermint taste.

"We've got a problem," he said in a low voice.

"Did Rybak tell you his theory about her being the princess?"

Lukasz started. For some reason, he'd assumed Jakub would have told him first. In fact, a small part of him was a little insulted that he'd gone to Koszmar before him.

"Felka told me," said Koszmar, as if reading his thoughts. He didn't turn his narrow, angled face. "He tells Felka everything. They used to work together, I think. Odd pair. Don't know what she sees in him." Then he added quickly: "I won't tell the girl if you won't, Lukasz."

His heart sank even as he spoke, but Lukasz said: "Deal."

"So," said Koszmar after a moment. "What's the problem?"

Lukasz stared unseeingly at the endless blue forest, at the mist lazily circumventing them. He kept his eyes on the haunted trees as he tapped some ash on the ground. It was deathly silent.

"I can't do it," said Lukasz at last. He raised his left hand. It looked normal, hidden in the glove. "My hand doesn't work anymore."

It used to be who he was. *Dragon slayer.* And now he was carrying a rifle and making deals with monsters in black forests.

Koszmar gave him a sidelong look. He was all smooth angles and languid smoke rings. Lukasz couldn't quite put his scorched finger on it, but there was something different about him.

"Don't worry," said Koszmar softly. "I will help you."

"How?"

"I can kill the Dragon," said Koszmar. He put his hands in his pockets and the revolvers glittered in the dark. "It's why I came to this godforsaken kingdom in the first place."

Lukasz couldn't help it. He snorted.

"Brought a butterfly net, have you?"

Koszmar's head snapped over. It was almost inhumanly rapid. Lukasz fought the impulse to recoil.

"Don't underestimate me, Lukasz. Butterfly nets don't make majors."

Maybe it was just the tint of strange lights, the sheen of strange silence, or that nagging, gnawing feeling . . .

Lukasz watched from the corner of his eye as smoke poured from the other man's nostrils and drifted away to join the smog.

"All right." He nodded. "I won't underestimate you."

Koszmar smirked.

Then he came off the tree long enough to offer his hand. When he spoke, the single word was slow and lazy and somehow musical. "Deal."

They shook. Then Koszmar put the pipe back in his teeth and Lukasz stamped out the cigarette, and the pair settled back into their original positions, staring out at the silent trees.

"I saw your shoulder," said Koszmar after a moment.

He half turned, chin tilted upward. His mouth was crooked in his face, stretched over his prominent teeth. In the strange light, his blond hair looked almost silver.

"It looks bad." Then he added, jerking his chin over his shoulder: "Saw some *dziurawiec* a half mile back."

"So?"

"Miraculous stuff," Koszmar went on through a stream of smoke. "Just steep it in a bit of vodka, soak your bandages, and there you have it. The perfect cure." He shrugged, more to himself than to Lukasz. "Not bad for a drink either, honestly."

Lukasz didn't answer. It didn't matter which deals they made or what kind of help was offered—the fact was that Lukasz didn't trust Koszmar, and he never would.

He caught Koszmar's eye. The Wrony's pupils were constricted to pinpricks in a sea of gray, and his eyes were rimmed in red.

"Kosz," he said on impulse. "You all right?"

Slowly, Koszmar turned to Lukasz. Smoke poured from his nose, despite the fact that he hadn't taken a draw on the pipe for several minutes.

Lukasz's skin crawled.

"Don't worry," repeated Koszmar. "I can help you."

17

REN WATCHED AS JAKUB SHUFFLED the sheets of paper in his lap before sliding them into a leather sleeve beside him. She had a glimpse of neat block letters and messy handwriting, and although she'd seen enough books in the library to know they were words, she couldn't recognize any of them.

And for some strange reason . . . she *wanted* to.

Jakub's hands shook. She knew he was scared.

"Are you . . ." She hesitated. "Are you . . . feeling better?"

He dropped the last of the papers and scrambled down to his knees to pick them up. He ignored her for a moment. Ren moved from the ground to the fallen tree and knotted her fingers in her lap.

She felt for him. She wasn't sure what exactly. Not yet.

"Jakub," she whispered, "are you going to be all right?"

He looked up.

The magic of the moths and the flickering light brought out the scars. The shredded eyelid flickered over his empty socket, and she noticed, because she was looking at him—really looking at him—head-on for the first time, that his lips did not meet properly anymore.

"My daughter died," he said quietly. "Who would be all right after a thing like that?"

Ren was only half listening. She was mesmerized by his face. Slowly, she registered his words, and she asked:

"How?"

Jakub began gathering up his papers again. There weren't many left, and when he'd finished, he began rearranging them in the leather sleeve.

"Fever," he said. "She was only a few days old, in Szarawoda. My wife died at her birth."

"What's Szarawoda?" asked Ren before she could stop herself.

Jakub returned to sit on the fallen log. He put the sleeve of papers between them, and Ren was grateful for the distance.

"It's a town," he said. "In the southwest."

"Of my forest?"

"Of the country," said Jakub. Then, seeing her expression, he sighed. "Here—"

He took a stick and began to draw in the dirt at their feet. He drew squarish, blob-shaped thing. He drew a big circle on the right side and scraped at it with the stick.

"Your forest is here," he said.

He drew an X at the bottom of the blob with his stick.

"This is Miasto. That's the capital." The stick tapped the north part of the map. "That's Granica, the northernmost port. Everything above it is water." He tapped a spot in the southwest. "That's Szara-woda."

Ren was silent.

The scratched-out area of her forest was so . . . *small*. It was barely an eighth of that giant country, and she had never even seen the whole thing. Lukasz had come from Miasto. . . . She stared between the X and her forest, tried to gauge the distance.

She couldn't. It was beyond comprehension.

"And," she began, hoping she did not sound as ignorant as she felt, "there are . . . humans out there?"

"Ren," said Jakub. "There are humans everywhere."

She didn't dare look at him.

She suddenly felt small and childlike, as if she had never done anything in her life. How on earth could it be, she wondered, that all this existed? That—

"Miasto," began Jakub, filling her embarrassed silence, "is the most beautiful of cities. The houses are tall, with pink and green fronts, and statues on pedestals at every corner. Fifty of these houses surround the Miasto square, and every day, white horses pull carriages full of people to stores and ice-cream parlors and shows. In the center of the square is the Miasto cloth hall, where vendors sell everything—from fabric to guns to toys for children. In the southeast corner is the great Basilica of Saint Barbara, with ceilings fifty feet high."

Ren stared at the map.

In her mind's eye, she saw a country filled with copies of her own castle, full of the sad, angry villagers. It seemed like a terrible place to her. Were there monsters? What had happened to the animals?

Ren couldn't tear her eyes away from the map. No wonder Koszmar treated her like some kind of savage. She must have looked like a barbarian to someone who came from a world this big. She must have seemed like a rat in a hole to them, trapped in here for so long.

"Are you all from out there?" she asked.

"I was born in Miasto," said Jakub. "But I have lived all over the country. I was an Unnaturalist. A scientist studying unusual phenomena. It required that I move around often. Felka is from the village. Koszmar is from God knows where. And Lukasz, as you know, is a Wolf-Lord."

And yet . . .

And yet he had seen all this. He had been everywhere. Ren loved her forest with all her heart, and she'd have been happy to live in it for the rest of her life. But she was also curious. She had always liked to explore. She had always been a little too fearless.

And now, irrationally, she was jealous of these humans.

Then she asked, "Are the humans happy there?"

Jakub smiled, seemed to think for a long moment, and then said: "Few humans are."

Ren nodded. They lapsed into silence.

It was a strange experience, sitting here in the dark with him. With the man she had attacked for doing the most human thing possible, hunting an animal. It was strange to hear about his world, so much more vast than her own. Strange to feel jealous of the person she'd tried to kill.

"I was not going to hurt him, you know," said Jakub suddenly.

At his words, Ren was twelve years old again. Scrambling around in the snow, tearing at the knots of a snare. A black wolf, coated in blood, heaving and whining in the cold.

"You caught him in a snare," she said, without expression.

"Not to hurt him," said Jakub. There was a pleading note in his voice. "I only wanted to study him. To learn."

Ren stared at his shredded mouth, not quite closing over his teeth. She stared at the place where his eye used to be. She looked at those five cuts and realized—with a small twist of guilt—that she would do it again.

"He tried to chew off his foot because of you."

At her words, Jakub's shoulders sank.

"How could you be so cruel?" she asked. "He was suffering. I could hear his cries even with human ears. I could smell his blood even with a human nose. Surely you knew."

"I didn't—"

"You didn't *think*," said Ren. "You saw a wolf. You saw an animal, and it never occurred to you that he might feel the same things as you. The same fear. The same pain. The same instinct to survive, no matter the cost."

Ren remembered how it had felt, turning into a lynx for the first time. How it had felt to lose control. To feel blood between her claws. To be feared.

Ren loved being feared.

"Forgive me," whispered Jakub.

❧

"What are you doing?" asked Ren as she emerged once more at the campsite.

Felka looked up from going through Lukasz's things. Neither Lukasz nor Koszmar had yet returned, and Ren quelled a brief moment of panic. They could look after themselves. Felka lifted an extra coat from the pile, while Król watched them suspiciously.

"Looking for a light," said Felka. She gestured to a lantern on the ground.

Ren folded her arms.

"I do not like flames," she said. "No matter how small."

The other girl shrugged. At length, she extracted the contraption from Lukasz's pocket. It was small, gold, and square. When she held it up, Ren caught a glimpse of an embossed symbol: crossed antlers and a wolf's head.

"There we go," she said triumphantly. She leaned down to the lantern, and with a small *snap* a flame sprang to life.

Ren stepped back too quickly.

The girl watched.

"It's just a lighter." She clicked the contraption a few more times, and the flame died and was resurrected several more times. Ren hated it. "It's totally harmless. Just a little fire, see?"

"There is no such thing as a little fire," said Ren. "Only a fire that has not yet spread."

Felka put down the lighter. The stripes of her skirt looked duller than ever in the flickering light from the lantern.

"Listen," she said. "I shouldn't have said what I did, earlier. It's not your fault people think that about you."

Ren blinked.

"About you being the one killing us," said Felka. "It's not your fault. It's just easier to blame someone, sometimes. You know? I think that's what we do."

"Why did you say it, if you knew you should not?"

"Listen, Ren. It hasn't been easy for us," said Felka. "For the past five years, we've been telling stories of a forest monster who eats people alive. She's what happens to people who leave the village, go looking for trouble. Don't you see? It's a lot easier for us only having to fear one monster. Not the whole forest. Evil with a name is a little less terrifying. The evil that you recognize, that you can avoid— that's an evil you can live with. Surely you can understand that?"

"So you just follow blindly?" asked Ren, a little testily. "Fear the monsters someone else invented? Told you to fear?"

Felka shrugged.

"Don't we all?"

Ryś and Czarn wound back through the trees. Ren could hear them arguing in low, growling voices.

Felka picked up the lantern. She was very small, compared to the rest of the humans. Her wrists, poking out from the lace cuffs, looked fragile. She sat down on the ground.

"Why didn't you leave?" asked Ren.

Felka looked up as Ren sat down beside her.

"What do you mean?" she asked.

"The village," said Ren. "If there was a whole world out there, and if this place is so horrible, why stay? Why not go?"

Felka snorted.

"I couldn't," she said.

"Why not?" asked Ren curiously.

Felka laughed. Ren was not used to the laughter of humans, but it struck her that this had no humor in it.

"I don't have parents, Ren," she said levelly. "I don't have a family. I grew up on the streets, sleeping outside. When I was old enough, I worked as a dancer at the village inn. They gave me these red boots—" She lifted the muddy edge of her skirt, to show the shiny things. "And I danced every night, for five years. It was okay, you know," she said thoughtfully. "We slept in a stable loft. We got two meals a day. It was good. But when I turned fourteen, and everyone knew I was done getting taller and I wasn't getting prettier, the owner fired me."

Ren's brow wrinkled. Felka explained.

"He kicked me out. On the street. I had to find a new way to stay alive, because there were newer, prettier girls to dance."

"So why did you not leave then?" Ren asked.

Felka laughed again.

"You just don't get it, do you?" she said. "Because of *you*. Because of your forest. I had no money to hire someone brave enough to take me, and there were no safe paths. That was when I met Kuba."

Jakub.

"It was after you'd attacked him. Maybe a year or two. He was alone in his house at the edge of town. He used to walk past me, see me begging on the street. That was when he still had to go outside. To get food, to go to the tavern. People would stare." Felka's eyes misted. "They would point. The kids would stop playing when he walked by, just to look at his face."

She looked down at her hands. The forest had gone quiet around them.

"They called him gargulec. Gargoyle."

Ren suddenly felt very awkward.

Casting around for something to do, if only to distract herself, she began poking through the Wolf-Lord's things. The fur at the collar of his coat was oddly warm, despite the chill around them. It smelled like him, she realized. Like gunpowder and the strange, spiced smoke of dragons.

"One day," said Felka, "I asked him for a job. I knew he was an Unnaturalist. I could read. A girl had taught me at the inn. And . . ." Felka's eyes were very wet. "He let me transcribe his manuscripts. I lived in his attic, and sometimes I would go out and buy us food. Then I would go out and buy more paper. And ink, and—"

Ren picked a small leather journal out of Lukasz's things and turned it over in her hands. Her throat felt strangely tight. She did not like the feeling.

"And eventually," said Felka, "he stopped going out. He stayed and wrote, and I helped."

Ren began to flip through the book's pages. They were filled with writing, with drawings, with bits of paper and different colored inks.

"I'm sorry," she said softly.

Felka smiled. Ren couldn't see anything behind it.

"Don't be," Felka said. "I was happy."

Ren smiled back.

"What the *hell* do you think you're doing?"

Ren looked up just as the notebook was snatched from her hands. Above her, Lukasz swung the rifle off his shoulder a little too violently. Ren leapt to her feet. Koszmar and Jakub appeared from the trees.

Beside her, Felka scrambled upright.

"We were just—" Ren stammered. "The lighter—"

"*YOU WERE WHAT?*" he roared.

In that moment, Ren almost changed. She felt the fury thrill through her, felt it her best response to every kind of fear—

"Lukasz," said Koszmar, grabbing his shoulder. "Luk, calm down. There are strzygi—"

Lukasz threw Koszmar off, flinging him back as if he weighed nothing. The blond soldier slammed into Jakub, who barely caught him.

Ren bit back the urge to transform. Jakub was watching everything with his one eye. And for the first time, she did not quite trust herself with those claws.

Lukasz was snarling, his slightly crooked teeth gleaming in the darkness. His shirt was torn where the nawia had gotten him, and the fur trim of his coat was still sticky with blood. For a terrible moment, he looked like the dead, newly risen.

"Who the hell do you think you are?" he demanded. His voice echoed like a roar around the clearing. "You think you have a right to—?"

Ryś and Czarn began to growl, circling.

Lukasz lifted the rifle and held it ready. The barrel glittered in the firelight as it swung toward the animals.

"Go ahead," Lukasz warned. "I'll shoot."

Panic flooded through Ren, while Czarn's lips pulled back from yellow fangs. Felka lunged for Lukasz, but Jakub jerked her back across the embers. Coals scattered, and the earth glowed. Ryś hissed as sparks singed his fur. Koszmar pulled a revolver from the back of his belt and took aim.

"Put down the gun!" shouted Jakub from across the embers. "Put it down, Lukasz!"

Lukasz cocked the rifle without breaking his gaze from Ren, and the sound echoed like a gunshot. Ren's heart caught in her throat. Everything was falling apart.

Every fragile deal. Every uncertain conversation. Every new, terribly delicate friendship.

Felka held up both her hands. Palms out. Like Lukasz had done only the night before.

"We're sorry," she said. "Lukasz, please. We're sorry."

Ren didn't know what to do.

"Put the gun down, Luk," said Jakub, beside Felka. "This isn't you. This isn't you doing this. It's this place. The forest is preying on our minds."

Lukasz's eyes flickered to the Unnaturalist. Ren let out a breath.

Then his eyes were back on hers. He looked insane. Sweat trickled down his forehead, lit in a dull shine on his throat, darkening with the shadow of a beard. The whole clearing tasted like panic. The coals sizzled in the silence, embers scattered across the black ground.

Ren noticed, with a terrible sickening twist, that his eyes seemed to have gone darker since the afternoon. Or was it her imagination? And what was more, under his collar, she could just make out the edge of a blistering cut—

Click.

Lukasz uncocked the rifle and lowered it. Everyone in the clearing let out a breath. Then he looked at Ren and lifted the book. It trembled in his shaking hand.

"Not everything in this forest belongs to you," he said harshly. "Don't forget it."

Ren swallowed. She couldn't speak.

She just nodded.

She waited until he had turned away, until everyone was breathing a little easier, until the coals were raked once more into the fire. She waited until no one was looking at her anymore. She waited until the agony in her hands had dulled to a steady throb.

And only then did she uncurl her hands and wait for the claws to recede, slipping back into her fingertips, leaving behind human palms, already running red with blood.

❧ 18 ❧

THAT NIGHT, LUKASZ DREAMED THAT he was lying on the ground by the fire, covered by his coat. He dreamed that he was not alone, that Ren was beside him, curled against his chest. He dreamed that the fire lit her hair in the most perfect golden glow, that she had never looked more like some glass-skinned, magic-eyed creature of myth. She had slept, in his dream. She had slept, and been beautiful and warm and real, and he had prayed for it to come true.

And then the cuts in his shoulder opened wide.

He felt them twisting, tearing. He felt the skin tear apart and the bones shatter. He screamed, but Ren was not there.

Through the haze of pain and horror came Jakub's voice.

. . . multiply not by procreation, but by consumption . . .

Even as he writhed on the ground, he realized that the campsite was empty. He was totally alone. His blood poured over the ground, more blood than any human should have contained, enough blood to drown the fire in a hiss of steam.

When he looked down at his shoulder, the wounds yawned even

wider. Sawtooth claws pushed out of the wound, pulling apart his skin, and the monster within struggled to be born.

Lukasz screamed.

. . . in the act of devouring a susceptible human . . .

And still, Jakub Rybak's voice drowned him out.

. . . creates its progeny.

🌿 MICHAŁ & ELIASZ 🌿

FOUR YEARS EARLIER

"FINALLY," SAID FRANCISZEK, CLOSING HIS book as Lukasz shut the door behind him. "Where have you been? It's been hours—"

Lukasz pulled off his gloves.

"Killed a Ływern under the king's castle," he said, grinning. He dropped the gloves on their room's sideboard. "Would you believe how the last idiots tried to do the job? They left a sheep stuffed with sulfur outside its lair, and—"

He stopped dead.

The twins were sitting on straw pallets of their tavern room. Franciszek sat on the wide windowsill, twilight behind him, his book closed in his lap. Eryk, second-eldest of the remaining brothers, was painstakingly stitching a gash in Michał's skull. Eliasz held a bloody rag to his mouth.

Both glowered.

"Oh my God," said Lukasz, unbuckling his sword. "Are you all right?"

Michał turned toward him. A veiny, mottled bruise covered half his head. Eryk had shaved down the black hair over the wound and was now placing tiny, perfect stitches in Michał's scalp.

"No," he said in a lisping voice. "We're idioths."

"Oh my God," said Lukasz, this time much quieter.

It was winter. Outside the window, the buildings of Miasto stood out against the sky, in pink and yellow and blue. Snow covered their roofs, and more snow fell behind Franciszek. Their room had the cozy smell of woodsmoke from the fire burning in the hearth; it had the warm, rich smell of evergreens, draped along the mantelpiece and the available sills.

The sound of laughter and music drifted up through the floorboards, which were speckled with blood.

"Why?" asked Lukasz. "Why would you do something so stupid?"

"That's how Skuba defeated the Wawel dragon," said Franciszek from the windowsill. He folded his hands across his chest. "I thought—"

"But this wasn't the Wawel dragon!" exploded Lukasz. "This was an Anglan Ływern! Didn't you look at it? It just needed to be killed, fair and square, no tricks—"

"Lukath." Eliasz shook his head warningly.

Lukasz sat down on the empty bed. When Eliasz took the rag away from his mouth, a few broken white stubs glittered in the dark. He was missing most of his teeth. Lukasz suppressed a cringe and glanced sideways at Franciszek.

His older brother looked pale and drawn.

"Sorry," said Lukasz awkwardly. "It's not your fault. It was a good idea."

Franciszek swallowed. His eyes were a bit shiny.

"I made a mistake," he said. "Ływerni have formative memory. It may have known the story of the Wawel dragon and figured it out."

Lukasz nodded.

"You couldn't have known," he said.

Franciszek didn't look convinced.

"There," said Eryk, stepping back. "All done. Best stitches I've ever done. Come and admire, Lukasz."

Michał reached up and gingerly touched the side of his head. Lukasz stared at the gash beneath the black stitches. It twisted like a serpent, animated by its venom, undulating and iridescent on the left side of his skull.

He made a face.

"Is that . . . normal?" He glanced at Franciszek. Usually eager to share, Franciszek was avoiding his eye.

Instead, it was Eryk who answered. He did not look especially concerned, but then again, this was Eryk. He did not rattle easily.

"Strange things leave strange wounds."

"Will it get worse?" pressed Lukasz.

"It's done, Lukasz. We can't do anything about it now." Michał shrugged. "Now go get us some vodka. We need to celebrate your victory."

The truth was, Lukasz didn't want to look at those injuries a moment longer than he had to. He didn't know what was worse: Eliasz's missing teeth, which might disfigure him, or Michał's poisoned wound, which could very well kill him.

Lukasz descended the tavern stairs. He'd been lucky with the

Faustian. One clean impaling, and he had a neat little scar above his knee that had healed well and didn't look . . . well, didn't look like *that*.

Lukasz pushed past the spectators to descend the staircase to the ground floor. The main attraction was a raised boxing ring in the middle of the tavern, and the rest of the building had been designed around it, with the upper floors opening onto the center. Balcony after balcony, the spectators rained beer and gold upon the prize-fighters, taking and making bets, everything lit with an enormous wooden chandelier, swaying and dripping hot wax on them all.

When he'd finally pushed through the crowd, Lukasz ordered five vodkas from a bartender so tiny he could barely see over the counter. He waited for the drinks, regretting his fur vest. The tavern was hot.

"That your brother?"

Lukasz turned away from the bar.

The man had blond hair and a single premature line between his long eyes. He wore a black uniform that seemed to give off its own shine, despite the dirty light. And everything was covered with golden embroidery: collar, cuffs, even the hem of the spectacular greatcoat. His black cavalry trousers were trimmed in more gold embroidery, and his black boots had golden tassels.

In that moment he struck Lukasz, raised on empty roads and in black caves, as the most elegant person he had ever seen.

The man spoke again.

"Never seen Wrony before?"

Despite his smile, his voice verged on aggressive. Lukasz tapped the emblem stitched, rather badly, to his linen shirtsleeve. They'd been knighted the year before by King Nikodem. The Brygada Smoka was an official brigade of the king's army.

"I am Wrony," returned Lukasz. He heard his accent rumble.

The soldier raised his brows over silver eyes and took the pipe out of his mouth.

"If you say so," he said idly.

Then he shifted gracefully against the pillar, put his hands in his pockets. Lukasz hated himself for it, but he envied that practiced air.

Then, the elegant Wrony gestured to the throng of people.

"You scare them, you know."

Lukasz's grip tightened on the broadsword, the dragon blood flaking a bit at his hip. His eyes raked the room.

"They going to give us trouble?"

When the Wrony didn't answer, Lukasz glanced back at him. Even gleaming with the heat of the tavern, he looked inescapably aristocratic.

"They wouldn't know how," said the soldier in a lazy voice.

Looking back at the crowded room, it was as if he were seeing them for the first time. Three of his brothers were at the bar, the light lost in their dull leather vests, bringing out the dirt in the pale fur collars. Eryk descended the stairs, light glancing off his sweaty hair, illuminating the blood smeared across one cheek. The crowd parted like water. The conversation quieted. Even the chandelier seemed to dim.

For a moment, Lukasz could see it. Fear. It was thick. And then he realized suddenly the soldier in front of him wasn't afraid of them.

"What's your name?" he asked.

The soldier smiled. It was slow, lazy, and too cold to warm his eyes.

"Seweryn," he said.

"Lukasz," said Eryk, approaching. "Let me help. Hey—why didn't you order pierogi? I'm starved—"

Lukasz was quiet as they gathered their drinks and ordered their food. Eryk clearly *was* starving, because he asked for mushroom, rabbit, and onion, and three orders of Rusz-style pierogi, which were filled with potatoes and cheese and fried instead of boiled. They also ordered kielbasa and bigos, and barszcz for Eliasz.

And for the first time, Lukasz saw Eryk the way *they* must have seen him. Streaked with blood and sweat, smelling like mountain air and savagery.

They carried their food back upstairs and settled in.

"Who was that soldier you were talking to?" asked Eryk, diving into a plate of pierogi. He had some cream on the end of his nose that he still hadn't noticed. Lukasz watched him without eating, and Eryk continued: "He looked like one of those peacocks from the botanical gardens."

Michał guffawed and then winced.

"No one," muttered Lukasz, picking at the kielbasa.

"Don't trutht him," cautioned Eliasz.

"I don't," rejoined Lukasz.

For some reason, he found himself thinking of the Kwiat library. Raf playing with the dola and the librarians shooting them dirty looks. Now he suddenly wondered if it hadn't been disdain at all.

Had it been fear?

"Listen," said Michał. "This is a lot. Being one of us. Being you. Killing that Faustian, being famous. Now you've killed the Ływern, too. People are going to try to change you. Just don't forget who you are, all right? Don't forget you're a Wolf-Lord."

In Kwiat, they'd given them money, but they hadn't invited them into their homes. The king had given them a commission, but he hadn't offered them the famous black Wrony coats.

"They're scared of us," said Lukasz. "They think we're animals."

Eliasz took a sip of vodka and winced. He wiped his mouth on the back of his hand and returned to his barszcz.

"Who cares what they think?" asked Michał, sounding incredulous. "Lukasz, it doesn't matter."

A bronze dragon skull hung on the far wall of the room. It had probably once belonged to a minor Faustian. The Wolf-Lords had collected bones, he suddenly remembered. Lashed them into monstrous decorations, hung the halls of Hala Smoków in the corpses of their kills.

How are we not savage?

"The Mountainth are our home," said Eliasz. "Thooner or later, we have to go back."

We're exiles, Raf had said.

He'd seen it, in Rafał's eyes. He'd seen how much his brother had missed Hala Smoków. Missed the Mountains they all talked about. Missed the wolves. Missed the wooden lodges and solitude. Missed their home.

Lukasz put down his plate.

But it was not his home. He'd cut his teeth on broadswords and he'd tracked dragons by smoke alone. He had been raised by the road, by the hunt, and by that magic kind of desperation, unique to strangers stranded in hostile words.

Lukasz looked from face to face. The candlelight flickered between them. From scar to missing teeth. From half-shaved head to bloody beard. Lukasz memorized them in the half-light.

"Don't do it," he said. "Please, don't do it. Don't go back."

The others were silent.

"It's our duty," said Michał heavily. "We don't belong here. We owe it to our people."

"What about your brothers?" demanded Lukasz. "What about us? You can't keep leaving. What happens when we're all dead—?"

"Lukasz—" started Eryk.

"We won't die," interrupted Eliasz.

"We survived a Ływern," said Michał.

"Only after it practically killed both of you!" protested Lukasz. "Come on, we could stay here. If you'd just try—"

Michał looked sad. The purple cut undulated and twisted in the shadows.

"Don't go," whispered Lukasz. "Please."

"They're calling," said Michał. "I'm sorry."

If you were sorry, you wouldn't go.

"You've been hurt," said Lukasz. "Anything could happen."

"More of a reathon to go." Eliasz shrugged. "Anything could happen."

19

"DO YOU SMELL THAT?" ASKED Ren, wrapping her cloak tightly against the cold.

Felka passed her one of the tin mugs of coffee.

"Smell what?"

"Smoke," she said. *And dew,* she thought. And that particular smell—a smell she knew too well—of damp leaves burning. High above them, green boughs blocked out the sky.

Felka shook her head.

"I don't smell anything."

Morning mist, thin and low to the ground, clung to the edges of the campsite. Lukasz was gone, and Jakub was still asleep. Ren sniffed again. She was sure she was right. She suddenly wondered whether what she had assumed was mist might actually be smoke.

"Cold?" asked Koszmar, emerging from the trees.

It took her a moment to realize he was addressing Felka.

"I'm fine," said the girl flatly. Ren could see the goose bumps on her skin.

"Your lips are blue," Koszmar pointed out.

As he sauntered past his horse, he tugged some fabric from under the saddle. It was another black greatcoat, almost identical to the one he wore. This one was fancier, decorated in extra gold braid and edged in black fur. He held it out.

"I do not want it," said Felka in the same flat voice.

"Please," said Koszmar. It was as if he couldn't hold Felka's gaze. His eyes drifted toward the trees, then back to her. As if it cost him a great effort, he repeated: "Please. Just take it."

"No," said Felka.

Koszmar held the coat out a moment longer, then dropped his arm. He crossed back to the other side of the fire and dropped it in a heap. When he looked up, he asked, in an entirely different voice:

"Why are you here, anyway?"

Felka stiffened. Ren could feel it. But she could also still smell the smoke, and now she wasn't sure whether it was her imagination, but she could almost hear something, too.

"I was born," Felka was saying. Her eyes flickered, without humor. "Unfortunately."

Ren began to move toward the edge of the trees. Behind her, Koszmar picked up the tin mug. Turned it over in long, elegant fingers.

"No, no," he was saying, in that soft, slightly rushed voice of his. "I mean, why are you *here*? What interest could someone like you *possibly* have in the Dragon?"

Even half paying attention, Ren caught the tone. Insult.

A shape moved in the trees. Ren transformed her eyes. The shape was gone . . . if it had ever been there at all. All the same, she got to her feet. She couldn't be too careful. There could be anything out here.

Behind her, Felka said: "Who said I was interested in the Dragon?"

"I'll be right back," Ren said over her shoulder as she stepped into the trees.

The forest was cool. Moss, damp and coarse, carpeted the trees and the ground. Her bare feet sank into the cool green, and except for the distant chirrup of crickets, the forest was silent. She kept glancing over her shoulder, trying to keep her bearings. Overhead, Jakub's eagle—Ducha—flitted between the trees.

Ren suppressed a shudder, glad of the company.

As she walked, a wall of smooth white rolled into view. She laid a cautious hand against the side and nearly gasped. The surface was knotted and rough under her palms, and familiar. A tree. It had fallen in the forest, but its trunk was so tall and wide that it had almost looked like an enormous, curved wall.

Ren changed course, walking beside it, fingers trailing along the bark. Ducha dutifully followed. As she went farther, the trunk began to expand and then split into roots, still half-embedded in the forest floor.

Partially uprooted, the fibers that remained tendriled out to her like a many-headed monster. A faint scuttling noise emanated from the other side of the trunk. There was also the sound of someone smacking.

Like a moth to a candle, Ren approached the tree. Its skeletal roots ran directly into the ground, forming a tiny jungle of bare, twisting fibers.

Other than the smacking sound, the forest was silent.

Keeping close to the desiccated bark, Ren crept toward the sound. What was left of the tree overhung a kind of mossy embankment, the forest stretching onward below it. Ren lowered herself to her belly and crept up to the edge.

She froze.

Strzygi.

They dug around in the clearing, chattering. A wagon lay on its side, surrounding by a half dozen skeletons. The strzygi tore through them, clawing at their clothes. Chewing on their bones. They picked. They snuffled. They feasted.

A hand—a *claw?*—closed on Ren's shoulder.

Her attacker slammed against her, propelled her into the ground. Her elbow struck a rock, and she twisted around, hands flashing into claws. A hand clamped over her mouth. Ren felt her teeth change, and she bit down.

Lukasz swore. Loudly.

Below them, the strzygi went still.

Ren froze. Lukasz ducked his head and froze. It brought them very close together.

"You—"

"*You* bit me," he interrupted. She could tell he was trying not to smile. It annoyed her.

His knee was still digging painfully into her side, but she barely noticed. She was wondering, the strzygi dangerously far from her mind, how he had lost that tiny notch of eyebrow. Quite unnecessarily, he put a finger to his lips. Ren was already looking at them.

For a moment, they were both silent and so close that she could hear every ragged breath.

Then, when the silence stretched and Ren not only heard every breath but felt it as well, he raised his head to look over the embankment. The rising sun caught the edge of his profile, haloing his hair and cutting him out in black and gold.

Ren's heart skipped a beat, and she considered it a personal failure.

"What the hell are you doing?" she whispered angrily. More angry at herself than him, but that wasn't any of his business.

She noticed that the crunching sounds had resumed in the clearing below them.

"Purple uniforms," he murmured, unhurried. He pulled back from the ledge and slid down beside her. "Those bodies are from the Kamieńa king's army. They've been there for years."

Ren watched him check his rifle. The light seemed to follow him when he looked back at her. It suited him, she realized. The half-light, the shadow. The flames.

No wonder he hunted dragons, when the fire fit him so well.

Wait. *Flames?*

"Lukasz!" she whispered.

"It's fine, they won't—"

"Lukasz!" she shouted.

The trees began to shudder. The morning mist melted away. Sunlight filtered through the membranes of its unfurled wings, and the pine needles rained down on them.

And the Dragon descended.

Lukasz swore. He pulled the rifle off his shoulder, but Ren shoved him into the tangled roots.

"Quick—" she gasped. "Hide!"

They scrambled into the cover of the tree. The earth smelled sweet and rotten. There was barely enough room for the two of them. Beside her, Lukasz flipped on his back and searched the gnarled underside of the tree, as if expecting the Dragon to tear it aside at any moment. Insects crawled over her fingers and down her neck, and Ren fought the urge to shriek. The whole forest shook with each wingbeat, and Ren didn't know whether the rushing in her ears was its wings or her heart.

"Go—" she whispered. "Let's go—"

They wriggled through the tangled tree roots, in the space between the trunk and the forest floor. Ren hoped that they weren't sharing their hiding place with any nocnica. Up ahead, between the roots, she could make out the green of the forest.

"Oh God," whispered Lukasz.

Still concealed under the trunk, they had reached the edge of the embankment. Hidden from the Dragon, they were looking down into the clearing below.

The pale shapes of strzygi lurched among the skeletons, hanks of reddish hair catching the glow of the Dragon's scales. At first, they ignored it. They devoured indiscriminately. Crunching the brittle bones of the long dead. Tearing at mummified flesh. Insatiable. Irredeemable.

"Ren," said Lukasz, very close to her ear. "Look."

The earth at the center of the strzygi began to tremble. It shook. The strzygi looked down, finally distracted from their feasting, and then they looked up. They raised inhuman noses to the sky. Oblong eyes rolled.

Ren wondered, in that moment, if something in them—if that

small bit that was still human—knew what was coming. Perhaps some of them were not yet lost. Perhaps some small hope still hummed in those twisted veins, still lingered in those darkening hearts. Perhaps that sudden fear, that flash of self-preservation, that universal instinct to survive, was enough.

Enough to make them human, one last time. And maybe—just maybe—in that last moment, they remembered. Maybe they remembered what it had been like, gathering around tables. Building fires against the night. How it had felt: to smile, to sing, to sigh. To love. Perhaps they remembered, in that last moment, what it had been like to be human.

The silence filled with flames.

Gold lit up the dawn. A comet of fire shot from the Dragon's black jaws, caught the tops of the trees. Flames raced down, blackening trunks. Blazing yellow devoured the killing field. It burned away the purple. It charred away the corpses. It lit, like fiery brands, the dozens of strzygi screaming, twisting, melting into oblivion.

One last screaming heartbeat of humanity.

Lukasz grabbed her arm.

"We need to go back—"

"We need to *kill* it," she snapped. "That was the deal—"

Lukasz shook his head.

"I don't have my sword," he said. Ren couldn't quite read his expression. "You can't kill a dragon without a blood-coated blade. It poisons it. We're better off watching, figuring out what we're dealing with—"

"I want it dead!" she screamed.

Somewhere above them, the Dragon roared. She clapped a hand

over her mouth, horrified. Lukasz glared at her.

"Trust me," he hissed. "Now is not the time."

Ren looked back down at the strzygi. They were charring away, only a few of them still screaming. A pit opened up, earth crumbling away in its center, ringed with orange flames and twisting roots. It gaped wide in the forest floor.

"The pit," breathed Ren. "It's making more. It's making more monsters."

"But it just killed them all," said Lukasz, brow furrowed.

"Lukasz, don't you see?" she whispered. "It doesn't care."

He didn't answer as they eased back from the ledge. The trees were silent, except for the crackling flames. Ren was half afraid one of the roots might tap her on the shoulder.

Or worse.

"We should stay here," she said quietly, "until we're sure it's gone."

Beside her, Lukasz nodded. He had dark circles under his eyes. Suddenly, without any warning, Ren wanted to touch him. To run her hands over his face, to feel the rasp of that sharp jaw under her hands. To let him know, whatever had happened, it was going to be all right. To say she hadn't meant to pry—

No. She was being stupid and weak, and—

"Don't grab me again," she said.

He raised his gloved hand. A few wet drops glittered on the torn leather.

"Don't bite me again."

"I'm serious," snapped Ren. "I'm not just some animal you can push around."

He wiped the blood on his pant leg and didn't look at her as he answered.

"I don't think you're an animal, Ren."

"And—" Ren stopped, then decided she did not want to process his words. "I'm not some monster, either."

He didn't look at her. His face was half-hidden in shadows, which darkened his brows and turned his eyes to liquid dark. For some reason, that suited him, too.

"I don't think you're a monster," he said.

Then he added quietly, "And I never did."

For a moment, silence yawned between them. There had been too much silence between the two of them. Too many moments without words. Without explanation. Ren didn't realize it, but she licked her lips. Too many false starts.

He snapped the lighter open and closed, the flame bursting to life and dying. Over and over. The *click, click* was as rhythmic as a dragon's wingbeats. His expression was dark. Haunted.

Click, click.

"How did you know that?" she asked. "About the nawia?"

"Know what?" asked Lukasz.

The lighter clicked on and off. *Click, click.*

"That they needed to be . . ." She could not remember the word. "Sent away."

He paused before he answered.

"They weren't ordinary nawia," he said. "They were something called mavka. If a child dies before it is baptized, then its soul wanders for seven years. If the seven years pass without a baptism, that child becomes a mavka. They are doomed to wander the forests for-ever."

Ren blinked.

"How do you know that?" she asked.

Click.

"My brother told me."

"The brother you are looking for?" she asked.

"Yes," he said.

"And what is a baptism?" she asked.

When he turned around to her, Ren saw the surprise in his face.

"It happens in a church." He tugged the silver cross out of his jacket and showed it to her. "Like a church. You know—people go on Sundays, tell their sins. Listen to sermons. God is watching. Hell is waiting. All that."

Ren thought hard.

"I know some gods," she said at last. "Like water gods. Some say that Wodnik is just the ghost of a drowned boy, but he's a kind of god, too. He rules over the river." She paused. "You know, this forest probably has a god, too."

Lukasz was listening with his mouth slightly open. Then he put the cross back in his jacket and said, "Those are the small gods. But there were real gods before, mighty ones—gods of crops, goddesses of hunting and death—"

"I don't think I like a hunting goddess," Ren said, frowning.

"Neither did the early Christians," said Lukasz dryly. "They drove out the old gods. Replaced them with their new one. Absorbed every old pagan custom—including things like getting rid of mavka.

The baptism—it's part of the new religion."

Ren sniffed.

"Well, I haven't seen your new god around here."

Lukasz shrugged and said in the same dry voice, "Well, I doubt He's in Miasto, either."

Ren couldn't tell if it was a joke. If it was, she didn't understand it.

"What's a baptism?" she asked instead.

"Like a christening," he said. "When you're born, someone gives you a name. They take you to a church and they say a Mass, and they give you a name. It means that you're part of the Church. That if you die, you'll go to heaven, not to hell."

Ren frowned.

"I do not understand."

"My parents baptized me Lukasz," he said. "Kosz's called him Koszmar. And yours—" He stopped abruptly.

The surprise melted to something else. Ren waited. And then he asked heavily:

"Someone named you, didn't they?"

She wasn't sure if it was her imagination, but he looked suddenly older. His eyes had sunken back and darkened, nearly black. He looked sad.

"Do you ever miss them?" he asked when she did not answer.

Ren blinked.

"What?"

"Do you ever miss them? Your family?"

Ren blinked again.

"I've only been away from them for a few days."

"I meant—" He made a gesture with his hands that somehow struck Ren as being helpless. He was still wearing his gloves. "I meant your real family."

"My real family is at the castle," she said.

"I mean—"

"I know what you mean," she interrupted. "My parents are lynxes. They loved me when I was a human. They loved me as a lynx. They love me even though I am different from them, and they never cared where I came from." Her voice came out brittle, with an undercurrent of a growl. "My family—my lynxes—they chose to love me, when no one else would."

He gave her a very strange, unreadable look. Ren wished he would just say what he was thinking out loud. But that was not the way of these humans. They kept their thoughts close to themselves. They lied.

Lukasz crawled back toward the opening over the embankment of dead strzygi. He examined the sky and the forest floor carefully before he returned.

"The Dragon's gone," he said. "But something is moving in that pit. We need to find the others and get out of here."

✢ 20 ✢

THE DRAGON CIRCLED OVERHEAD. IT watched the strzygi burn, and it watched the pit open. Then it watched the girl and the Wolf-Lord crawl out from their pathetic hiding place and return to their little group.

The Dragon watched them.

It had expected more. It had expected her to fight—to burst out from under that tree, to challenge it for the forest. The Dragon smiled to itself. Wasn't that why the girl was coming—to test it?

The girl's mother had fought. Bravely. The Dragon wouldn't soon forget that day, seventeen years ago, when the pair of them had gone up in golden flames. No one had been able to stop it that day. No one could stop it now.

Not even this little princess.

It wondered if she knew how reckless she was being. After all the effort that had been taken to hide her, here she was, burning like a torch in the forest. Surrounding herself with all that humanity . . .

It had been all too easy to find her. They had a particular scent, those humans: like blood and sweat, like greed and pride. Like hope.

And one of them . . .

The Dragon took another breath, just to be sure.

One of them smelled like death.

⚜ 21 ⚜

THEY RODE NORTHEAST, CIRCUMVENTING THE dead strzygi, and around them, the forest darkened.

They agreed they would cover more ground on horseback, and Felka quickly partnered up with Jakub. When Koszmar didn't volunteer to take Ren, she ended up with Lukasz. She didn't completely hate it. Besides, she had noticed that the silver-eyed soldier preferred being on his own.

The branches had closed overhead, sky and sun disappearing behind tangled boughs. The dampness was lit only by the eerie glow of the antlers on Lukasz's horse and by the Dragon's flames. Golden fire crowned the blackened branches, licking lazily at the blistered trunks. It didn't spread at all, just burned steadily. Silently. Dreamlike.

The air was hazy with heat, shimmering. Blurring. Everything was red, warm, and dull, a hundred alternating shades of crimson. It was hot. Ren could already feel sweat beading on her forehead. It was silent. Owls didn't call. Wolves didn't cry. Crickets didn't chirp.

The silence was broken by their hoofbeats and by Felka's and Jakub's quiet voices. Czarn loped beside them, still favoring his paw, and Ryś trotted ahead, trying—without success—to sneak up on Ducha.

This world was bloodstained and empty.

Click, click.

The lighter clicked on and off in the silence.

On impulse, Ren slid her hands up Lukasz's chest. He half turned, and she could just make out the edge of his shadowed jaw as she tugged herself high enough to murmur, by his ear: "I forgive you for shouting."

She felt his heart pound faster. His hair brushed her cheek. It was coarser than she had expected, like someone had cut it off in a hurry and never paid attention to it since. And then he said: "I forgive you for going through my stuff."

Ren bristled.

"Well, I *don't* forgive you for hitting me."

She had never noticed his eyelashes were quite so dark as he grinned. "Me neither."

Ren wondered, for the first time, if they were starting again. Right, this time.

On they went, flames burning silently on every side. In the midafternoon, Lukasz's horse—Król—threw a shoe. Their group stopped while Lukasz hammered a new one into place.

Ren moved on to scout out the path ahead with Ryś and Czarn. The smoke had thickened, now weighing down the branches like dusky red snow. Gauzy drifts floated down to the ground and sparked.

The haze was so dense that Ren could barely see in front of her. Czarn was panting.

Shapes materialized from the smoke. Four wine-colored bundles huddled on the ground while birds circled above them. They swooped down, pecking, taking flight again.

Storks.

"Czarn," she whispered. "Do you see that?"

"Hard to miss," interjected Ryś. "You should change, Ren."

"Don't order me around in my forest," snapped Ren, but her heart wasn't in it.

"I don't know if this is still your forest," whispered her brother.

The little group advanced on the shapes and the birds. Czarn barked, flinging strings of saliva across the forest. The sound was deafening in the silence. The storks barely stirred. Ryś growled.

The closest stork, a shock of white in the red, turned to them. There wasn't any fear in its beady black eyes.

Czarn fell back and growled. The shapes on the ground had taken on terrifyingly familiar forms. From the trees, Ducha screeched.

Almost lazily, the storks spread their wings. They sailed up to disappear into the smoke overhead. The flames had begun to expand, moving out of the periphery of Ren's vision. They cast the bodies in flickering, red-orange light.

Ren reeled. The flames were taller than she was, her vision rippling with heat. The warmth was crushing. Ren felt her hair growing heavy and wet, pressing along her neck. Then she looked down and screamed.

Five bodies lay on the ground. And Ren knew them: Jakub, Koszmar, Felka, Lukasz. . . .

Tree roots entwined them. One black root snaked out of Jakub's empty eye socket, ran down his cheek, burrowed into the skin. Tiny, spidery roots twisted out of his open mouth, like black veins, running down his chin and encasing his throat.

In spidery fingers, they forced open Koszmar's mouth and surged down his lifeless throat. Another one, as thick around as the Dragon's tail, curled lazily around his legs. Next to him, five cuts scored Lukasz's body. Something wriggled beneath his skin, bubbling, slithering. Ren almost screamed as black, twisted fingers started to force their way out of the open wounds.

No. She sank to her knees. *No, not—*

BANG.

A shot echoed across the forest.

Ren staggered and spun around. It was . . . *Lukasz?* Alive and well, he stood five feet behind her, still silhouetted in red smoke. He lowered his rifle.

"What's going on—?" she choked.

The others materialized behind Lukasz. Also alive. She twisted around, looked back at the bodies. The roots pulsed like blood vessels.

"Stay back, Ren," said Jakub, somewhere behind her. "It's an illusion."

Ren suddenly registered that Lukasz had shot his own corpse. A bullet hole yawned in its chest, and through the hole, a red-rimmed eye blinked. Fingers emerged once more, wriggling free of the body's chest.

Lukasz—the real Lukasz—fired two more shots in quick succession. The corpse danced on the ground. Deep within it, something began to howl.

Koszmar used the hilt of his saber to knock away Lukasz's rifle.

"Don't waste bullets," he ordered. "We don't know what's out there."

Ren wasn't listening.

"It's some kind of warning," murmured Jakub. Despite the situation, there was an undercurrent of excitement in his voice. "Notice that the only corpses here are human. None of the animals are represented. . . ."

Ren was moving toward the last body. She couldn't stay away. It was impossible. It pulled her in. One stork remained, ignoring her and picking at its back. Even facedown, Ren recognized the body. The flames closed in as she knelt down. There was no room for fear. Only cold, bone-chilling realization.

Her hand, blue in all the red, reached out and closed on the shoulder. She turned the body over.

Ren met her own dead eyes.

There were no roots. Nothing black pushing out of her eyes, creeping out of her throat. The dead version of her looked just like her. Only its color was faded, lips going white, eyes filming over. Even the darkness seemed to drain from her hair.

She was dead.

Someone touched her shoulder, and Ren whipped around, fangs bared.

"Hey—" Lukasz jumped back. Her hair, wild and sweaty, fell in her eyes. "It's okay. It's a trick. We'll be all right—"

A roar split the forest. It blasted across the trees and blew out the flames. The horses reeled.

Probably instinctively, Lukasz grabbed her shoulder and dragged her in. For a moment they were close, so close that Ren could see the tiniest nick of a scar on the underside of his jaw, and then he looked up and away from her.

"What the hell is that?" he shouted.

The shout reverberated in his chest.

The earth shook. The trees trembled, branches raining down on them. Another jarring tremor. The horses reeled again. A third tremor.

Are those—?

"Those are footsteps!" bellowed Czarn.

"Is it a giant?" stammered Koszmar. He spun around, brandishing his saber.

"I AM NO GIANT," boomed a voice far above them.

Lukasz didn't let Ren go, and she was glad. She wrapped her fingers in the collar of his shirt, stared up at the sky overhead. Her eyes raked the trees. She was so focused on the world overhead that she never noticed that the bodies at their feet had disappeared.

The booming voice continued, and the forest shook once.

"I AM A GOD."

❧ 22 ❧

NOW THAT THE VOICE WAS joined by a body, Lukasz realized that the giant—or the god, or whatever it was—was a bear. It stood as tall as the trees as it stepped toward them, each of its claws the length of Król's body.

Ren's hand tightened and she pulled herself closer to him. It irritated him how easily she distracted him, how her tangled hair warmed his skin wherever it touched, how every time she was there, he wasn't thinking, and then she whispered to him, "Aren't you going to do anything?"

"Didn't realize I was allowed to," he muttered back. "Isn't it *your* forest?"

Ren released him, jostling his wounded shoulder as she let go. It sent a stab of pain down his arm.

Jakub's and Koszmar's horses kept backing up into one another. Ryś was hissing. Czarn was barking. But Lukasz wasn't panicking. He was still focused on where her hand had landed on his shoulder to push him away, and that was exactly the kind of thinking that was

240

about to get him killed.

"WHO DARES DISTURB MY WOOD," boomed the bear. With each word, its eyes blazed more furiously.

Felka was brandishing one of Koszmar's revolvers. Lukasz had a feeling that of all of them, she was the only one who wasn't scared. Well, he wasn't scared either, but that was because he was being stupid. Felka was actually being brave.

"I am the queen of these woods!" Ren shouted, almost deafening him.

Where her touch distracted him, that shout always brought him back. It usually meant someone—*he*—was risking evisceration.

"Ren." He grabbed her arm, but she wrenched away. "What are you—?"

Ren ignored him.

"I was raised on the courage of lynxes and the wits of the wolves," she screamed. "I have faced the monsters of hell and I am not afraid of you!"

Lukasz might not have been the toothiest psotnik in the rafters, but even he knew that threatening this thing—whatever it was—was not a good idea. And he wasn't sure what he expected to come next, but it certainly wasn't . . .

The bear guffawed.

. . . *laughter?*

The trees shook and birds scattered. Then somewhere, someone snapped their fingers.

And all of a sudden, the bear began to shrink. Its shoulders narrowed and its snout shortened and then it was slender instead of heavy, winnowing down by the second. A moment later, the creature—for there was no way it could possibly be a bear—disappeared into the trees.

Lukasz could hear Ren breathing hard.

"Why did you *yell* at it?" he exploded. "Ren, it said it was a bloody god, for Christ's sake—"

"Oh, I'm sorry," retorted Ren. "Did you want to hit it with a shovel?"

"Come on, you two—" started Koszmar.

The trees rustled, and a tiny man emerged from the bushes. Reflexively, Lukasz dragged back on Król's reins.

Not a man. Whatever it was, it was barely waist high and nearly covered in thick brown hair. It had a long gray-brown beard that trailed on the ground and a bright blue cap pulled low over a pair of enormous, fuzzy ears. An uncomfortably big club trailed from one furry hand.

"What's the matter?" growled the little creature.

As he shuffled toward them, his beard swept up a generous quantity of bugs. Lukasz stifled a gag as a spider skittered up his arm and crawled into one long, tufted ear.

The little creature asked gruffly: "Never seen a forest god before?"

Lukasz couldn't help it. He laughed.

The club swung with terrifying dexterity, and then the little creature was pointing it straight at him.

"Watch it, boy," he snapped. "Or I'll knock that pretty head of yours clear off, understood?"

Lukasz heard Ren giggle.

"I came to see her," said the little man. His voice abruptly changed. It had a silky, wheedling quality to it. "The queen."

Ren stopped giggling.

The creature sank to one knee and swept the cap off his head. A few mice fell out and dashed away across the path. Ryś followed them with hungry eyes but thankfully stayed put.

Then, to Lukasz's shock—and minor horror—Ren smiled. With her odd, liquid grace, she slipped forward to kneel in front of the creature. His escaped mice came back and began playing in the folds of her skirt.

"Stay on this path, and you will never the leave the woods alive," said the creature in a soft voice. "The trees are encircling you. They are holding hands and singing sweet nightmares into your minds."

Lukasz suddenly remembered his dream from the night before.

Then the creature added gently: "Did you see the storks?"

"Who are you?" murmured Ren.

Lukasz wasn't quite sure what he was witnessing, but instinct told him not to interrupt. One of the mice crawled up on Ren's shoulder and examined her intently.

"*I* am Leszy—" began the little man, before breaking off.

Looking slightly confused, he inserted a long finger in his ear and wiggled it.

"Itchy-scratchy," he muttered, wiggling furiously, momentarily forgetting them. "Itchy-scratchy, really quite nasty—"

Lukasz remembered the spider and winced.

Koszmar had sidled up beside him, and now he muttered, "What the hell's a Leszy?"

"The Leszy is the protector of these woods," interjected Jakub in a low voice. "He is both god and spirit, shape-shifter and trickster."

"I thought *she* was the protector of the woods," said Koszmar, nodding toward Ren.

The queen straightened up, the Leszy's mice now gathered in her arms. Far from being suspicious of the little god, she looked calm. Almost serene. Before Lukasz could look away, she glanced toward him. And even then, her face softened. He barely recognized her as she raised her cupped palms to show him her tiny charges. They scampered out of her hands up to her shoulders, playing in her hair and squeaking at each other. She looked, he realized, happier than he'd ever seen her before.

Despite the very real possibility of being clubbed to death by a tiny madman, Lukasz couldn't help finding Ren and her mice oddly charming.

"Leszy is different," Jakub was explaining. "He is an ancient shape-shifter. He's very wise and very powerful."

The so-called Very Wise and Very Powerful himself had at last extracted the spider from his ear by one long hairy leg. With exquisite care, he deposited it on the ground.

"Doesn't make sense to me," muttered Koszmar. "Why now? We've been in the woods for days."

"Me neither," agreed Lukasz, feeling a little off-kilter. "We're missing something here."

"Your brains, perhaps?" suggested the Leszy in a snide voice.

With a strangely nimble gait for someone so round, the Leszy danced up to Jakub, who looked confused. All the same, the Unnaturalist knelt down. The Leszy leaned in so close that his slightly animal nose almost touched Jakub's mostly incomplete one. Then, while the Unnaturalist remained as still as death, the Leszy put a knobbly hand on his face and pulled it down, gently tracing the scars.

He smiled.

"Well done, my queen," he whispered.

He had a strange mouth. His upper lip was parted down the middle, curving up on either edge. The mouth of a cat, covered in fine fur.

Ren looked up sharply—almost guiltily.

Before any of them could reply, the Leszy leapt up and danced away. He flashed up the hill adjoining them, disappearing in and out of the trees. With his fur the exact color of the bark, he was practically invisible in the underbrush—

"Well? Come on, you lot! Come on!"

He reappeared, dancing among the trees. He hopped from one hairy foot to another like an impatient, slightly ugly child.

"Follow the god!" he trilled. "Follow the trickster! The saints know where I'll take you, but the gods will it will be good! Follow the god, follow the god!"

Ren glanced back at Lukasz, and he had the sudden conviction that she was looking for his agreement. For some ridiculous reason, the possibility made him happy.

"You can't be serious," he started.

Koszmar had gone very pale.

"We should go," murmured Felka.

Beside her, Jakub nodded.

"I think we can trust him."

The Leszy's bandy legs had already taken him far ahead. He whistled for them and called back:

"Follow the god!"

And with that, they were scrambling up the hill, leaving the path, and disappearing into the heart of the woods.

Despite being such an ungainly little creature, the Leszy took the forest at a dead sprint. The trees flashed in and out. The red mist began to fade. The golden flames trailed away.

Then, all of a sudden, the little god skidded to a stop.

"We're there!" he cried. "We did a few laps on the way, but we're here now!"

Lukasz nearly tripped right over him. Ren went face-first into a bush, and Felka simply collapsed in the middle of the path. Koszmar staggered off a few feet and was sick in the trees. Czarn and Ryś seemed completely fine, and although Lukasz wasn't exactly sure what animal laughter sounded like, he was fairly certain they were making fun of Koszmar.

"We're there!" trilled the Leszy. "We're there, we're there, quick as a hare, led by a bear, and we're there, we're there, we're there!"

Birds were singing. Squirrels chattered overhead. It looked like a normal, only moderately enchanted forest. Even Lukasz's shoulder hurt less. He breathed a sigh of relief.

"And where is *there* exactly?" panted Koszmar, emerging from the trees and patting his lips with a handkerchief.

The Leszy dropped the club and clapped his hands together, capering around in a circle.

"Come, come!" He beckoned with a crooked finger. "All will be well, just follow the trickster. Follow the god. Follow the Leszy!"

Felka groaned but otherwise stayed silent.

The Leszy rapped his furry knuckles on a nearby tree root. Then he swung his club back onto his shoulder so violently that he almost whacked Jakub in the face.

"Honey!" called the Leszy, also apparently to no one in particular. "Honey, I'm home! I brought guests!" Then he rounded on Koszmar. "And if you're sick on the carpet, I'll turn you into a mouse."

Perhaps already sounding a little mouselike, Koszmar only managed to squeak in reply. Ren glanced down at her mice, looking faintly horrified.

The tree blurred. The earth shifted and shook, and suddenly— Lukasz doubted whether anything could shock him anymore—roots began to break through the dirt, curling and undulating like enormous serpents. The whole tree leaned backward, and a hole yawned beneath it.

The Leszy trotted up to the hole and looked back at them.

"Come on, come on! Bring your horse of course, of course. Bring your horse!" he hooted to himself, and looked delighted. "I made a rhyme, did you hear that? Come, come, let's fill your tum!"

Lukasz had already decided that the little creature was completely mad. Now he was also wondering if he was completely dangerous.

If Ren was thinking the same thing, then she didn't show it. In fact, she was the first to the tree roots. The Leszy dropped his club and clapped his hands again, beaming.

"So brave, my queen! Always the first! Nothing to fear, my dear, my dear. Follow me!"

Lukasz seriously doubted that. But Ren had already disappeared.

"What if he kills us?" whispered Koszmar. He gasped. "What if he *eats* us?"

"Don't get my hopes up," muttered Felka.

As Lukasz descended through the roots, he encountered a set of smooth dirt steps. Up ahead, he could just see the outline of Ren's tangled hair, her pale hand trailing along the wall.

"Ren," he whispered.

She slowed, half turned.

"Yes."

"The monsters came from below ground."

Ren looked up at him over her shoulder, and he didn't want her to turn away. He didn't want to lose her. Not after they'd just started again.

"I know."

"Doesn't that worry you?"

She paused, held up their little procession for a moment, and stood on her toes to whisper in his ear. She was going to have to stop doing that, or there was going to be trouble.

"You have to trust someone, sometime."

She grinned. It was a pretty, twisted little thing.

"But this . . . god?" he asked.

They began to move downward again. He knew he was grinning

like an idiot, and he didn't care. He could hear the others catching up. Ren turned back to him, walking backward. She wrinkled her nose.

"I trusted you, didn't I?"

Her teeth flashed, and he knew she was smiling. Then she twirled back around to follow the Leszy.

Lukasz followed, his heart sinking. He'd promised her no games; he wanted to start again. And here he was, telling lie after lie. He didn't want this to end. And he knew it couldn't end well.

The ground leveled out, a new passage stretching before them. Roots curled outward and encircled thick yellow candles. The whole tunnel was cast in flickering brown-gold light. Their shadows played across the walls, spectral and distorted.

"Come in, come in," called the Leszy, long lost in the darkness ahead. "Your timing is impeccable. We're just about to sit down to dinner."

They emerged in an enormous cavern. The far wall formed a kind of earthen castle facade: columns rose from grassy floor to dirt ceiling, each thirty feet high. Stained-glass windows twinkled down on them, set alight by the tree-root chandeliers.

Club swinging, the Leszy burst from the grass in a shower of dandelion fronds.

"Welcome!"

Ren yelped and jumped back into Lukasz.

"Oh dear," said the little monster. He looked Ren up and down. "Oh dear, you look simply *awful.*"

"Well—"

As Ren started a retort that would probably get them all killed, the ceiling rumbled. Cracks raced over the dirt. Then suddenly, the night sky stretched over them like a sparkling navy blanket.

"My apologies for the noise," said the Leszy carelessly. "It takes the trees some effort to move for me. Now, up! We shall celebrate. You are on a quest! Most of you will probably die," he added thoughtfully. He tapped his club against his lip. Then he grinned at them: "So this may very well be your last celebration."

And with that, animals flooded into the cavern. Squirrels raced down the walls, foxes wound between the slender legs of the deer, and badgers trudged patiently along behind the crowd. They were everywhere. Lukasz couldn't tell where they'd come from. Maybe they'd come from everywhere.

"He's been hiding them here," said Ryś suddenly.

Lukasz watched as Ren exchange a glance with her brother. The mice scrambled down her skirt and disappeared into the grass.

Realization dawned on him.

This was why she needed to kill that Dragon. For the coyotes that played with the foxes; for the rabbits thumping their feet in time with birdsong; for the yips and growls; and underneath it all, for that quiet, eerie music of all the magic things in the forest.

She was putting her life on the line for them. And he'd *lied* to get what he wanted— *No.* No, he reminded himself. He'd promised himself, years ago, that he'd do anything for his brothers. And here he was. This was about Franciszek.

This wasn't about pretty girls or lynxes or queens who happened to be both.

The Leszy began to circle them, taking exaggeratedly large

steps, tsk-tsking quite audibly. As he walked, he swung his club thoughtfully, and more than once, Koszmar had to duck to avoid decapitation.

"Really quite awful," the Leszy muttered. Lukasz realized he was focused on Ren. "Not good at all. . . . She has to look like a queen. . . . No, no, this won't do at all. . . ."

The Leszy snapped his fingers.

The dandelions exploded like fireworks. For a moment, Ren disappeared in a cloud of fronds. Lukasz's hand went to his rifle. Then the leaves settled, and they all stared.

The ill-fitting shirt and stained skirt were gone. Eyes wide, Ren ran her hands up her new dress, its bodice formed by interwoven feathers. She picked at the billowing sleeves, gathered into tight golden cuffs at her wrists. She turned, the light skirt swirling, betraying the ghostly shadow of her legs.

"Eagle feathers for courage," the Leszy whispered, clearly enraptured by his own handiwork. "Spider silk for strength."

Ren reached up and touched her hair. She was crowned in golden antlers, threaded purple blossoms. The purple flowers were everywhere, spilling over her gorgeously dark hair, falling down her back.

"Dragon antlers for the fight," said the Leszy. Then his voice changed, no longer playful. "And wildflowers for love."

Ren did not look impressed.

"Get it off," she said. Her shy little smile had turned to murder on her lips. *"Get it off!"*

The Leszy looked surprised. Then sly.

"But my queen," he wheedled, "this is how a queen should dress. This is how a queen should rule."

"I don't care." Ren had begun clawing at the sleeves billowing over her wrists. "It's not mine. I want my clothes back—I swear to the monsters and gods, change it or *I'll* change—"

The Leszy rolled his eyes back too far, so far that the full green swiveled away and only white showed. And when the green rolled back, it was shot through with red. Lukasz's hand tightened on his rifle.

"Very well," said the god at last.

Another snap of his fingers and Ren was back in her old shirt and skirt. Her hair remained untangled and shiny.

"Don't know why you did that," observed Koszmar. "You looked quite—"

"Shut up, Kosz," Lukasz cut in.

"Come," said the Leszy. "Let me introduce my family."

A lawn stretched ahead of them, with a wooden table in the middle. A hundred miniature versions of the Leszy crowded around it, each with a slightly shorter beard and a slightly smaller stomach. They stood on their chairs, screaming at each other at the top of their lungs. One little Leszy was quiet, but only because he was focused on inserting a noodle up his nose.

The little Leszys squalled, and food flew thick and fast over their tiny heads. Another Leszy, identical to their guide, was running up and down the length of the table, pausing periodically to wallop the little Leszys with a chicken leg.

"This is my family," declared the Leszy proudly. "That is my wife, the lovely Leszachka." The bearded Leszy paused in walloping the little Leszys. She took a bite out of the chicken leg by way of greeting. "And these pint-sized delights are my children, the Leshonki."

The Leshonki leapt up and down on their chairs and beat their chests with tiny fists. A hundred tiny clubs swung through the air. A hundred tiny voices whooped.

Leszy chuckled proudly and snapped his fingers.

The table transformed. Tureens refilled with soup, plates of potatoes and pierogi rattled as they appeared, and three enormous pork roasts landed on the table with a thud. Babka, chocolate puddings, and angel wing pastries materialized from one end of the table to the other, along with baskets of oranges and whole bushels of grapes.

The Leshonki sat down with their clubs on the floor and their hands folded in their laps. Seamlessly, they morphed from eight dozen miniature monsters into eight dozen perfect sons. They looked princely with their pressed shirts and clean faces, even though one of them still had a noodle up his nose.

Leszachka also disappeared in a burst of flames. Lukasz heard Felka gasp as the fire cleared to reveal a ten-foot-tall woman with black hair and a deep green gown, relaxed at the far end of the table. Empty chairs, wrought of gold with cushions of purple velvet, sprang out from either side of the table.

"Come, friends," said the Leszy, seating himself at the head of the table and tossing his club over his shoulder. "Let us eat and be merry."

As he threw away his club, the Leszy grew tall. He stepped down off the chair to seat himself in it. Only he was no longer the Leszy, but a kingly man with gray-brown hair and a beard and lines at the corner of his eyes. Like his wife, he was ten feet tall.

"We must put on our dinner attire for you," he said with a wink, and gestured to the newly appeared chairs. Without his bandy legs and potbelly, he had a somewhat less insane air about him.

It made Lukasz trust him less.

He lowered himself gingerly into a chair next to Jakub, leaning the rifle against one gilded arm. Jakub glanced sideways at him, and Lukasz wondered if the Unnaturalist was equally suspicious.

What could this . . . *god* want?

Across the table, Ren collapsed into a couch-sized chair, Ryś and Czarn curling up on either side of her. Her hands fell to her brother's head, and with a furrowed brow, she ran her fingers over his ears. On her other side, Koszmar was seated next to a little Leshonki who immediately poked him in the ribs.

"Ow!" yelped Koszmar. He shoved the little Leshonki, and a half dozen chairs toppled like dominoes.

"Koszmar," cautioned Jakub.

Koszmar folded his arms.

"He started it," he sulked.

The little Leshonki resurfaced from under the table, grinning evilly.

Meanwhile, the rest of the Leszy's children began to serve the guests. On either side, everyone ate feverishly, while still more feverishly the Leshonki refilled their plates. Lukasz kept farther back from the table than the others, one ankle crossed over his knee.

He watched very carefully before he even took a bite. He wished Franciszek were there. Franciszek would have read about this creature. He would have known what to do.

"So," began the Leszy, gesturing expansively. "What brings you into my forest?"

"We're on our way to the Moving Mountains," said Ren. "To slay the Golden Dragon."

Lukasz watched the Leszy drench a piece of chocolate cake in gravy and devour the whole thing with relish.

"The Dragon, my, my," chortled the Leszy. "Selected quite the beastie, haven't you? Wouldn't you be better off starting at home? I hear your little village is under siege at the moment, by the way. The strzygi have proved, ah, territorial."

Both Jakub and Felka looked up in alarm. Ren's expression did not change.

"The humans can defend themselves," she said. "They have managed well enough for seventeen years."

The Leszy smirked and steepled his fingers.

"Have they?"

Some grease ran down his wrist and stained his sleeve. His nose began to quiver, and then he snuffled at the wrist like some kind of animal. When Ren didn't answer, he continued, "What about your castle?" He pushed back the sleeve and licked his forearm from elbow to fingertip. Lukasz tried not to gag. "Strzygi are nothing if not persistent. Those walls won't hold forever."

This time, Ren swallowed. Then she said: "Cut off the head, and the body will die."

The Leszy paused mid-lick, then chuckled.

"Wise little queen," he said. "Single-minded."

Lukasz glanced at Ren. Her eyes met his, and his stomach flipped. But when he smiled, her eyes flickered away. He kept his good arm around the back of Jakub's chair, did his best to look relaxed.

"You look very familiar," said the Leszy suddenly, pointing at Lukasz with a whole roast duck. "Have I killed you before?"

Lukasz didn't answer immediately. He wasn't sure what the little creature was getting at. He wasn't sure he wanted to know.

Then the Leszy laughed maniacally, as if he had told a particularly clever joke, and began applying plum jelly to the duck. He stuffed the whole thing into his mouth, bones and all.

"I think I would remember that," said Lukasz slowly.

The Leszy crunched down and then grinned, revealing unnaturally sharp teeth. They were full of shredded duck.

"Rightly so, Wolf-Lord," he said, "rightly so. Off to slay the Dragon, are we? Mountains are calling, are they?"

Lukasz's blood froze. He was aware of silence falling over the table. He was aware of his own heart beating in his ears. When he answered, it was in a deliberately casual voice:

"I'm just trying to find my brother, Leszy."

The Leszy selected an orange and began to peel it with long yellow fingernails.

"Which one?" he asked.

Lukasz felt his jaw twitch. The Leszy speared an orange segment with one vile claw and popped it in his mouth. As the yellow teeth worked on the orange, Lukasz found himself fascinated with the rivulet of juice running from the corner of the creature's abnormal mouth.

"You'll forgive my confusion," said the Leszy into the silence. "For nine have gone before you." He gestured with an orange piece, speared on his fingernail. "I did like Rafał, though, I must say. Delightful man. Could've drunk me under the table, that one."

For a moment, Lukasz was numb. He was aware of everyone watching him.

"Really," he said at last. Flatly.

"Yes, I believe that was Rafał," said the Leszy. He rocked back in his chair and clasped his hands over his belly. He seemed to enjoy the moment. "He had nice eyes, your brother. Quite dreamy. Michał and Eliasz were quite lovely as well. A bit more the strong and silent type, aren't they?"

Lukasz choked.

"Where—what—"

"Oh, I sent them on their way," said the Leszy airily. "To the Mountains, as they wished."

"To the Dragon?"

"Yes," said the Leszy, maddeningly enigmatic.

"Did they make it?"

"To the Mountains? Yes," said the Leszy. He grinned, mouth so wide it almost touched his ears. "Back again? No."

Ren interrupted.

"Please," she said, leaning forward. "Please, Leszy. We're going to the Mountains, too. Lukasz is going to help me kill that Dragon. I need to save my forest." She glanced around, as if searching for inspiration. "It's your forest, too. Surely you understand. If we don't do something, it's going to destroy us all—"

The Leszy cut her off, eyes narrowed.

"Don't go. The Dragon will kill you."

"The Dragon is *killing my forest!*"

As Ren and the Leszy began to shout, Jakub leaned in suddenly.

"Give him your cross," whispered the Unnaturalist.

"What?" asked Lukasz.

He was still too stunned by the revelation that his brothers had met the Leszy. Had Franciszek met the Leszy? *Is he still here?*

"A cross will bind the Leszy," whispered Jakub. "You'll be able to ask one question."

That was all he needed to hear. It was all he needed.

He jerked Tadeusz's cross from around his neck. For a moment, it was suspended over the table, revolving slowly in the light. Its movement had an almost hypnotic effect on the table. Even Ren and the Leszy stopped arguing.

The Leszy licked his lips. His tongue was long and forked. He began to shrink, his clothes transforming piece by piece into his thick coat of fur.

The question was on the tip of his tongue.

Where is my brother? No, he should be more specific: *Where is Franciszek?* No. It would have to be perfect, with a tricky little creature like this. No loopholes.

How can I bring Franciszek safely back to Miasto?

There. That was perfect.

Lukasz leaned forward and caught a glimpse of Ren's face. Her eyes shone with tears of frustration.

"How—" he started, and then hating himself, changed tack. "How do we kill the Golden Dragon?"

Silence fell on the table. Lukasz could hardly believe himself. One flash of green eyes, and he'd wasted his question.

The Leszy's gaze glittered. It was almost as if he knew what Lukasz had meant to ask. Then his voice seemed to tear itself, as if against his will, from his throat.

"There is a glass sword in Hala Smoków," he whispered at last. His eyes were bloodshot, swirling. "The Dragon can only be killed by a sword made of glass. The sword must be carried up the Glass Mountain, where the Dragon has made its lair. It must be killed *on* the Mountain itself."

Then the absurd creature shot forward and yanked the cross so hard that Lukasz nearly slammed into the table. Briefly, the volatile little face was very close to his own. Then the Leszy tossed the cross away. He settled back in his chair, cackling obscenely.

"A myth," said Lukasz, sitting back. He could hear his own accent growing thicker. "A thousand years of Wolf-Lords have searched for the Glass Mountain. It does not exist."

"How typical of a human," sighed the Leszy. He mimicked Lukasz's accent to perfection. "*I cannot find it, therefore it does not exist.* Of course it exists," he continued sharply. "The Glass Mountain is the perfect lair. The walls are too smooth to climb, but perfect for tumbling down. The Dragon breathes fire, and the knights fall down." He began to sing. "Fire! Fire! The knights fall down. Fire! Fire! The knights fall—"

He leaned backward until his neck bent at an unnatural angle, and he spat a stream of flame into the air. Then he turned back to them, grinning. His voice fell to a whisper. "—down."

He likes it, thought Lukasz. *He likes to see humans fail and die and disappear.*

Lukasz could not bring himself to look at Ren. He couldn't believe what he'd done. His chance—his one foolproof chance to find Franciszek—and he'd blown it away on a pair of pretty eyes and a couple of tears.

"You've made me tell secrets," said the Leszy. He turned the cross over in his knobbly fingers, catching it on his cracked nails. "Like spilling secrets, do you? You know," he added with an evil glint, "I can spill secrets, too."

Then the wretched little thing turned to Ren.

"Did either of these pretty boys tell you their secret, Ren?" he asked.

Lukasz stood up so fast that he knocked his chair over.

"Don't you dare—" he started.

The Leszy smiled sweetly. He looped the cross around his chest, running his vile fingers back and forth over the metal.

"Or should I call you Irena?" asked the Leszy. His eyes flashed, and Lukasz, with a jolt, noticed that they had turned back to green.

"Perhaps even . . . *Princess* Irena?"

23

REN COULD NOT MOVE. SHE could hear herself breathing. She could hear her heart beating. She couldn't hear them talking. They were talking, all at once.

He wasn't. He was quiet.

He was looking at her. But he was quiet.

No, she thought, feeling dazed. No, her lynxes were her parents. It had just taken her *longer* to act like one—to look like one—it had just taken until she'd been twelve, and no one had ever thought it strange that she could change between the two. So maybe she'd always had just a little bit more magic than Rys—the forest did strange things, the magic was unpredictable . . . no one had ever thought—*she* had never thought—it was because . . .

A human?

A weak, pathetic, helpless human? *Like them?*

No. Her eyes darted around the table. *Not like them.*

They were villagers. They were soldiers. They were Wolf-Lords. And she was not a queen at all . . . she was . . .

A princess?

Ren's stomach dropped through the earth.

She was *a princess?*

Her mind was a blur. Disappointment welled up in her. And even then, even frozen at the Leszy's table, she wasn't quite sure if she was disappointed in her own origin, or in the fact that he had lied.

"Is it true?" she whispered.

Silence fell over the table.

Lukasz met her gaze.

"We didn't know for sure," he said.

Ren nodded.

Very slowly, she rose from the table. Czarn and Ryś stood with her. Claws pushed out of her fingertips and dug into the table, where her long human hands rested. Two of the Leshonki made little *eek* sounds and slipped under the tablecloth. The wolf and the lynx pulled their lips back and growled at every human and monster at the table.

It occurred to Ren, for the first time, that she didn't know which of those things she was.

"No games," she said quietly.

She saw Lukasz swallow, but his expression was unchanged.

"No games," she repeated. "You promised to do what you said. You asked me to forgive you."

Tears started in her eyes.

She could feel them brimming, spilling over. She didn't care. It wasn't fair. She should have seen this coming. This man shared blood with the creatures who had thrown rocks at her. With everyone who had happily laid the sins of the forest at her feet. With every bloodthirsty, rotten-hearted, selfish human who had come before him.

With her.

"You shook my hand," she said, and her voice trembled.

Lukasz's gaze wavered. Then it came back to her. His dark brows were still raised a little too far over hollowed-out eyes. The hungry gleam had intensified. Ren instinctively knew that all the enchanted lanterns in the world couldn't have taken the darkness out of that face.

"I had to," he said. "I had to find my brother."

Ren blinked.

"What difference would it have made?"

He opened his mouth, as if to speak, but it seemed that he could not find the words. Ren watched, feeling her eyelashes growing wet and sticky.

"I see," she said at last. "You thought that if I found out, I would leave. You thought I would be so upset, I would break my promise to you."

She looked up to the open sky, took a breath, and met his gaze again.

"You thought . . ." She paused and wiped the tears out of her eyes. "You thought I would act like you."

"I'll do anything for my brothers," he said, unapologetic. "Anything."

Ren laughed, and the sound was brittle. It had a hysterical edge to it.

"Well, if this is how you treated them," she said, "then I'm not surprised they left you."

She instantly knew she had gone too far. Lukasz dragged in a harsh, rattling breath. Ren had never seen such fury in his eyes. They were practically black. Then he laughed. The sound was cold and dark and Ren could hardly believe she'd ever liked his laugh before.

"You need me to kill that Dragon," he said at last. "Tread carefully, Princess."

Before Ren could stop him, he turned and walked away.

"If you think this changes anything," said Ryś, pacing the grass, "then you're crazy."

"It changes everything," protested Ren. "I'm *human*, Ryś. My parents were—"

"Your parents are lynxes," interrupted Czarn.

The three of them had gathered on one side of the field, and the humans had grouped themselves away on the other side. Only now, even as she looked across the expanse, Ren wondered if she was in the wrong group.

The Leszy had dismissed them after the disaster at the dinner table. They'd left the food to his animals, and the raccoons had been quick to gather the leftovers in their bandit hands.

"You don't understand," said Ren, wrapping her arms around her knees and rocking back and forth. "This—this doesn't make any sense. Why would my parents have left me in the castle?"

"You don't know they did," protested Czarn. "Maybe they thought you were dead."

"And why do I have *claws*?" she insisted. "If I'm human, why—"

"Maybe the forest changed you." Czarn shrugged. "Maybe you got the magic you needed to survive. Maybe you aren't completely human—"

"Ren," interrupted Ryś. "Ren, it doesn't matter."

How could he say that? How could he say that after they'd spent seventeen years together? She'd saved Czarn from a human hunter. They'd made the unofficial promise to hate humans forever. They had hunted monsters, and hadn't Ren said it herself?

I do not like the monsters that were once human, she'd said to Jakub. *I think they are the most terrible of all.*

"Ren." Ryś bumped his furry face against her shoulder and purred. "Ren, it doesn't matter."

"It does," she whispered.

"Do you know what our parents said?" he asked her, purring. "They brought you to me when I was just a cub, and they said: *Ryś, this is your sister.*"

Ren knew she was being sappy, but that made her wipe away a tear.

He'd been so against asking the help of the humans. He now knew her provenance and had dismissed it in four words.

"You are my sister," he said. "You are always going to be my sister. That's all that matters."

There was a small cough above them, and Ren looked up. Felka was standing over her, and behind her, Koszmar and Jakub lurked nervously. Lukasz was not with them. He'd disappeared into one of the Leszy's tunnels, probably to lick his wounds.

Ren tried not to miss him.

"May I sit down?" Felka asked. She cut a very awkward curtsy.

Ren rubbed her hand across her cheek.

"Why are you doing that?"

Felka blushed.

"Well, I—"

"I'm a queen, not a princess," she said a little hoarsely. "I'm what I always was."

But that wasn't true. Now she was a human. She watched the three of them sit down. She had always taken a very special kind of pride in being different from them. She'd ranked herself equivalent to the vila, the rusalka—even the nawia. A *good* equivalent, opposing their evil, but equivalent nonetheless.

But now . . .

"Did you know?" she asked.

Felka shook her head. Felka, maybe, was her only friend. It hurt. She'd thought Lukasz was her friend, too.

"I suppose . . ." Ren gave a small shrug. "I suppose I'm more human than I thought."

"With all due respect," said Jakub with a smile, "I've never met a human with your . . ."

He struggled to find the right word.

"Dentition," supplied Koszmar.

"Lukasz was right. We did suspect," said Jakub, ignoring Koszmar and seating himself. "Forgive us."

"Still," said Koszmar, lowering himself to the grass, only to do an awkward half-standing crab scuttle when Ryś growled at him. He tried to salvage some of his dignity, adding: "You shouldn't have said those things to Lukasz."

Czarn folded his elegant paws and watched the blond soldier through narrowed blue eyes. He said:

"You shouldn't have lied."

Koszmar frowned. "I don't like it when *they* talk," he said to Ren.

"Now you know how we feel about you," muttered Felka under her breath.

"Please, Ren," said Jakub, ignoring Koszmar. "You have to see it from Lukasz's perspective, too. He's desperate to find his brother."

"If he's even still *alive*," said Ren without thinking.

Silence fell over the group, and Ren knew that she was the first to voice what everyone else had been thinking. His skull could have been set in the riverbank, doomed to watch an eternity of souls have their skin stripped away. His eyes could have been staring, petrified, out of the recesses of a psotnik nest. His headless, black-coated body could have been piled somewhere, rotting away, in the field of the mavka.

He could be at the bottom of the Glass Mountain, consumed by golden flames.

He could be a strzygoń.

"Don't tell Lukasz that," said Koszmar, and tried to laugh, but no one joined in.

Ren was angry with these humans, and she was angriest with Lukasz. But it made no difference to the tiny part of her heart that broke at the thought that his family might be gone. In Ren's experience, everything wanted to live, and nothing wanted to be alone.

It was Felka who changed the subject.

"How do you think he knew?" she asked. "The Leszy, I mean."

"He's the god of this forest," said Jakub. "Traditionally, the kings of this kingdom have asked for the forest's blessing at the baptism of their children. Perhaps the king called upon him for . . . yours."

Lukasz's words came back: *Someone named you, didn't they?*

"I'd never heard of a Leszy before today," said Ren, squashing the memory.

"I can assure you he exists," said Koszmar.

Ren rounded on him, but Ryś intervened.

"Listen," he said. "Nothing's changed, all right? We still need to get to that Mountain and kill that Dragon. And last time I checked, we need the Wolf-Lord to do that."

He turned to Ren.

"You need to get to that Mountain, Ren. You need to get that Wolf-Lord, find that sword, and kill that Dragon."

Ren watched the animals playing in the grass.

"I am angry with him," she said quietly.

"Good," said Ryś. "But he owes you. He promised."

For a long time, they were quiet. Three humans, two animals, and someone who lay in between. Someone who had been left to die in a crib seventeen years ago. Someone who had been abandoned and who had been called a monster, and who now held the fate of a forest in her hands.

⚜ 24 ⚜

FAR BELOW, LUKASZ WANDERED THE dark tunnels of the Leszy's cave. He was furious with Ren. He would have loved to confront her. Shout at her. Shout that she knew nothing of his brothers, of his people, of his world. But he didn't. Firstly, he was pretty sure that Ren could have killed him—even drenched in bylica with her hands tied behind her back.

Secondly, she was right.

If this is how you treated them, then I'm not surprised they left you.

If only she knew how cruel he'd been to Franciszek. For seventeen years his brother had taken care of him, and for seventeen years, Lukasz had resented it. He couldn't blame Franciszek for leaving. Not when he had spent most of his life being mad at him.

Ren. Irena. Once the princess. Now the queen. Jakub had been right all along, and Lukasz had convinced them all to lie. . . .

And then he heard it.

A dull clanging rang through the tunnel, like someone banging metal on metal.

He knew he should turn back, but light flickered at the end of the passage. It seemed to pull him forward. He suddenly felt groundless. It was as if darkness and earth had sealed out the rest of the world. There was magic here. Thick, dark, dangerous magic.

Lukasz hesitated at the tunnel's end. His shadow flickered on the wall behind him.

It was a forge.

Glass sheets hung from the walls, shimmering in a dark rainbow. Curling in the heat, enormous scrolls of parchment lay strewn across workbenches. At the far end, a forge the size of a house glowed like the gates of hell. And in the center stood a little shadow. A little shadow with bandy legs and a cap that dragged on the ground.

The Leszy danced from coals to anvil, gripping huge iron rods, bending them with superhuman strength. Lukasz watched him stab a particularly unwieldy rod into the forge. The metal rapidly changed color: purple, red, orange with a heart of vivid yellow. . . .

The hammer banged on. Steady as a heartbeat, dangerous as dragon wings.

The Leszy stopped suddenly. His shadowed face turned toward the door, and Lukasz caught the gleam of animal eyes.

"Come out, come out, wherever you are," trilled the Leszy. "I see you, I smell you, come out, come out."

Lukasz emerged warily from the black, moving into the glow of the forge. The heat was unbearable. The Leszy licked his lips.

"You smell like death," he said.

He had hammered his piece of iron into a curve. It took Lukasz a moment to recognize what he was creating—the iron frame for stained glass windows. It struck Lukasz as an odd choice for a forest god in an underground castle.

But Lukasz didn't say that out loud. Instead, he willed himself to appear relaxed, and he leaned against the worktable and crossed his arms to hide how they shook.

"I got attacked by mavka."

"Tut-tut," chided the Leszy. He abandoned the rod in the forge and stood, bandy legs apart, skinny wrists poised against his round middle. "Clumsy, aren't you?"

Lukasz shrugged. The Leszy thrust a new rod into the forge, humming. Purple, red, orange . . .

For some reason, Lukasz flinched as the orange gave way to yellow. It glowed, sizzled. Looked, for a moment, like those burning pits. And like those pits, Lukasz imagined, it could burn down the world. He spoke, still staring.

"Will I make it to the Glass Mountain?"

"I thought you were looking for your brother," said the Leszy snidely, without looking up. "Not the Dragon."

Lukasz didn't answer. The Leszy was right, of course. He was only going as far as Franciszek. He wasn't even capable of fighting a Dragon. Even if he'd wanted to help her.

Which he didn't, he reminded himself.

The Leszy hammered in silence for a moment. Then he said, in a voice that had entirely lost its musical quality, "I find it very interesting, you know."

Lukasz didn't move. He stayed still, a tense outline in the yellow light.

"Find what interesting." Lukasz spoke flatly. Despite the heat, the Leszy's abrupt change of tone chilled him to the bone.

"You have an appetite for monsters"—the Leszy licked his lips and then they curved upward, enough to make Lukasz's skin crawl—"and they for you."

Lukasz shrugged. It was a short gesture. He meant it to be casual, but it was cut off by a spasm of pain. He put his hand on his belt, considered how to answer.

"I suppose," he said.

The Leszy grinned again.

"Just remember, this is my forest," he cautioned. His face, still partially obscured with shadow, looked like a nightmare where the light touched it. "It's mine." And then the Leszy's tone became dangerous. "Don't think you can keep it for yourself."

He paused again, and then his voice dropped an octave and made Lukasz's blood run cold.

"*Any* of it."

✤ 25 ✤

THE LESHONKI WOKE THEM EARLY the next morning, whooping and hollering as they tugged them back to the dining table. Breakfast comprised heaping dishes of literally every food Lukasz could imagine, but he could barely eat a bite. Across the table, Ren avoided his eye and talked to Jakub and Koszmar. It left him furious, and he couldn't decide whether it was with her, with the Leszy, or with himself.

He decided it was all three.

After that, with predictably chaotic glee, the Leszy led them through the tunnels. The little god enjoyed dancing far ahead and disappearing, leaving them to flounder in the dark. He found it especially hilarious to then surprise them—either by plummeting from the ceiling like a psotnik or by popping out of the ground—usually snatching off Koszmar's helmet or pulling Król's tail. Once—very bravely, thought Lukasz—he even snuck up on Ren.

Unfortunately, Lukasz was in her line of fire on that one and almost lost an eye to her claws. More disturbingly, she seemed genuinely disappointed to have missed. All in all, he was grateful when they finally erupted, around midday, into the open.

Only it was not open at all, but dark and poisoned. Black slime dripped from the surrounding trees, and horseflies the size of hummingbirds droned in the shadows. A few feet away, Koszmar stepped in something syrupy black and cursed like a sailor while Felka and Jakub dragged him back out of the sticky pool.

Leszy checked on them one last time, ensuring they were adequately supplied with provisions, bad couplets, and sarcastic remarks. Then, as abruptly as he had appeared, he simply melted back into the forest.

"What happened?" demanded Koszmar, whirling around and nearly tripping into the black goo again. "Where's the little devil?"

But the forest was watchful, pathless, and empty. It was mostly a testament to his unease, but Lukasz almost missed the little madman.

Lukasz left Felka to reassure Koszmar and wandered over to where Ren was adjusting the girth on Król's saddle. She gave him the kind of look that would have caused a less courageous, more sensible man to retreat.

Lukasz was neither.

"What do you want?" she demanded.

"Ren, I—"

A few feet away, Ducha took a direct nosedive from the treetops and tackled a psotnik to the ground. The creature hissed as it died, like air escaping a bellows.

Felka sidestepped the dying monster and joined Ren at Król's saddle. Lukasz wondered if she was intentionally running interference.

"Ren, do you ever get the feeling," she said, pointedly excluding Lukasz, "that this forest isn't on your side?"

Then she bent out of sight, buckling a saddlebag to the saddle. When she reappeared, she clarified: "Like, do you ever worry it might not be worth saving?"

Ren looked at her. Then she looked at Lukasz.

"Well," she said coolly, "I *am* regretting a few things I've saved."

Lukasz knew he deserved that.

Still, he leaned down, and he wasn't sure if it was his imagination, but Ren's hand went still on the saddle. It might be his only chance. He could tell her the truth. He could tell her about his hand. He could tell her that it was all for Franciszek.

But he didn't.

"Forgive me, Ren," he said quietly.

He wished they could start again. He wished he hadn't lied. He wished there weren't nine dead brothers and a Dragon standing between them. He wished he hadn't pulled out that lighter on the riverbank, and he wished she hadn't run.

He wished she had been the one to kiss him.

Their breath hung in the air between them, then mixed, and finally, drifted up to join the fog overhead.

"If you keep asking me that," she said, "one day, I'll stop saying yes."

The day went quickly. Ren gave Felka her clothes, transformed into a lynx, and walked most of the way with Czarn and Ryś. She was avoiding him, and Lukasz knew it. Even when they set up camp, in the trees just beyond the river, she avoided him. She curled up between Felka and her animals, but he saw her watching him, one green eye open and accusatory.

Lukasz gave up. He left the camp to join Koszmar at the river. When he got there, the blond Wrony was nowhere to be found, and he took a moment to reexamine the wound on his shoulder. The cuts had fully reopened, and their edges were purple. They wouldn't stop bleeding.

Lukasz knelt at the river's edge. He used one hand to scoop the dark water over his shoulder. He couldn't stop thinking of Michał and Eliasz.

He wondered if the Leszy was right. He wondered if he was going to die out here, like he'd promised himself he wouldn't. Burning his hand had been one thing; it had been ugly, but it had only ended his career.

But this . . . this might end his life.

He scooped the dark water over his shoulder. The blood ran thick and black down into the quiet river, and he half feared it would draw trouble to the surface.

Franciszek, he thought, flexing his arm and watching the cuts shiver in the moonlight. *Franciszek, I am sorry.*

In the darkness behind, steps sounded.

Lukasz jumped to his feet, rifle ready.

"Down, boy," murmured Koszmar, palm raised. He indicated a bundle wrapped in a sheet under his other arm. "And after I nearly died at the hands of that rodentous god for you."

Lukasz lowered the rifle, feeling his hands shake.

"I don't think that's a word," he said.

Koszmar laughed. It echoed in the quiet forest.

"As if you would know," he said, without venom.

The Leszy had said they would reach the Mountains by the following evening, and Lukasz had half a mind to set out tonight. Maybe this forest was Ren's, and maybe she loved it, but it scared the hell out of him.

Koszmar's eyes lingered on the wounded shoulder. Lukasz knew the cuts had opened wider. Thick, dark blood oozed down his skin and was staining his shirt. When Koszmar lifted his eyes back to Lukasz's, they gave nothing away.

"Come on," he said, lowering himself to the ground. "Let's fix that."

Lukasz's heart sank.

You smell like death.

"It's getting worse," he said.

Koszmar shook his head.

"We don't die here, Lukasz. Not like this. We die on that Mountain, or we don't die at all."

His words hit home. It was, for a moment, almost like having one of his brothers back. Wasn't that how they'd always talked? In absolutes and on scales of epic proportions? He'd said he wouldn't die out here. He'd promised himself he wouldn't. Then again, his track record in keeping promises wasn't exactly pristine.

He sank down next to Koszmar, who had already bent over the cloth-wrapped package. In the dim light, Lukasz could make out a small square of wax the color of spun honey, dotted with bits of something dark. It smelled starchy and a little foul.

"What the hell is that?" asked Lukasz, more aggressively than he intended.

"Don't turn up your nose," replied Koszmar idly. "It's *żywokost*. Dziurawiec would have taken weeks to prepare, and I think we both know you don't have that long if this goes on."

Lukasz didn't answer, but it was the second bleak assessment of his longevity in as many days, and he was not especially keen to dwell on it. Koszmar didn't notice and kept talking.

"Besides, this was all our hairy little friend had growing in that little rathole of his. And you know what they say about beggars and choosers. Just a harmless little herb, boiled down in some fat and honey. It'll do the trick."

The żywokost came apart in sticky strings as Koszmar applied it to several strips of bandage. It seemed overwhelmingly gross to Lukasz, but he took off his shirt.

"You have a strange set of skills for a major," he observed.

With an expert hand, Koszmar positioned the żywokost over the wound. The bandages hissed as they touched the cuts, sending waves of searing pain down Lukasz's arm and radiating up his throat.

"I was a medic," said Koszmar simply.

It still burned like hell.

"Didn't know medics could be majors," said Lukasz through gritted teeth.

"Well." Koszmar began to smile. "I also killed a lot of people."

There was a pause while he finished tying the bandages. He used knots Lukasz didn't recognize, fingers flying over the fabric.

"Hurt?" he asked.

"Like the devil."

A slow, satisfied smile curved over Koszmar's pale face.

"Good," he said. "It's working."

Koszmar watched as Lukasz moved his arm experimentally. The pain was subsiding, and he had done a good job with binding it up. Lukasz could move his shoulder easily—easily enough to swing a sword, if it really came down to it.

Lukasz pulled his shirt over his head.

Suddenly, Koszmar's head snapped away. His eyes were trained in the darkness beyond the river. Lukasz followed his gaze. A wall of trees stared back. There was nothing there. *Or . . . ?*

"You hear something?" he asked, hand already moving to the rifle.

"No," said Koszmar, but he continued to stare across the river.

The trees crowded together on the opposite bank, and Lukasz felt like they were being watched. He couldn't shake the memory of the red mist, and the dragon's quiet golden flames.

This forest felt alive. Not just its animals, its trees, its underbrush—but the earth itself, the air, the dark sky overhead. Even in stillness, it seethed. A silent heartbeat pulsed in the air, and he wondered if Koszmar, too, could feel it.

It's alive, he thought. *It's alive, it's watching, it's—*

"She likes you," said Koszmar suddenly.

Lukasz didn't answer.

"Ren," said Koszmar. He began putting away his supplies. "She cares about you."

Lukasz laughed. It sounded tired, even to him. The forest leaned in.

"I think she wants to kill me," he said.

Koszmar chuckled. It was soft. The human sound broke up the forest's heartbeat, occluded that strange, vital thrum around them.

"Well." He kept his eyes across the riverbank. A half smile slipped over his face. "If she didn't like you so much, then maybe she would."

They might have been strangers talking nonsense in a pub somewhere. Not two soldiers in the service of monsters and queens.

"You know," continued Koszmar, as if a thought had just occurred to him, "I would stay."

"Here? In the forest?"

Koszmar nodded, eyes unfocused in the distance. He leaned forward and rested his elbows on his bent knees. His uniform was still spotless: from the sparkling emblem at his throat to the toes of his tasseled boots. But something else had changed.

"I like this forest," he said. "I would stay."

Lukasz got to his feet after Koszmar left. He slung his rifle over his shoulder and was about to turn back to the camp. But for some reason, he lingered. Perhaps that hypnotic, eerie heartbeat. Perhaps that overall sense of vitality, of things watching and life burning. Perhaps it was the evil. Here, it lay thick enough to taste.

Evil so powerful, so dense, webbing the ground and soaking into the soil. Evil trickling through tree roots and nestling under tree bark. Evil had twitched the tree branches and it had scraped and burrowed and whispered, and in its own way, evil had breathed life into these things.

He couldn't understand why Ren would sacrifice so much to save this. He looked down at his hand, hidden in its glove. He had to tell her. Maybe she'd understand. Maybe she'd see that hand and she'd realize why he couldn't do it, and maybe—for what felt like the thousandth time—maybe she'd forgive him.

Or maybe she wouldn't.

Calling wolves, are you? Franciszek would have said. *Asking for trouble, are you?*

The gloom shifted. Lukasz twisted around. The trees behind him rustled, the wind whistled, and then all the sounds and ever-changing shadows came together, and as if made from the darkness itself, she took shape.

She hung back a moment.

She was looking at him the same way she had once looked at him on another riverbank: cautious, curious, nothing cold, nothing closed off. Eyes full of the things that kept making them start things they couldn't finish. Things better left unsaid. Better left ignored.

She had him. She had him forever.

She moved closer, and despite the dark sky, it was as if she had a light all her own. Still she was coiled, ready to spring away, cautious as always. Wary of what lay ahead.

"Me too," she whispered, breaking through his thoughts.

He toyed with the lighter in his hand. His voice was hoarse.

"You too what?"

Her eyes glittered, a little glassy, and then she looked down. She spoke again.

"I've also been told I go looking for trouble."

Lukasz laughed. He put the lighter back in his pocket. Part of him wondered if she'd read his mind. But she hadn't; it was just her. She understood animals; she understood him.

"You know, humans have a saying for that," he said. He repeated the old phrase, a phrase first learned as a child, now seared into his memory forever: *"Don't call the wolf from the forest."*

Ren thought about it for a moment.

"I don't really understand."

"Don't ask the wolf to leave his home and come eat your livestock," said Lukasz. "Don't go looking for trouble."

Ren nodded.

There was a heartbeat's pause.

"Did you come here to say something?" he asked into the silence.

She shot toward him. Faster than he could react. Faster than he could pull away. Not that he would have. God, he never would.

Her hands found his collar, pulled him to her. Her lips on his jaw. Warmth, pressure, and then her smooth cheek slid past his rough one. And while he listened to his own heart pounding, her lips on his ear. Her voice, soft and beautiful and animal, rasping straight into his soul.

"No."

She let go. He staggered. She took a step back. He reeled.

Her eyes were like pools of glittering darkness, marooned in a bone-white face. The kind of beautiful specter that lured a person into shadows, into nightmares.

She didn't say anything else.

Instead she kept retreating, while Lukasz stood, stunned. And suddenly, like mist off a river at night, she became indistinct, almost nebulous. And suddenly his fantasy that she was a specter, a monster, a vila, a witch . . . it all became much more reasonable than the alternative. Because she was not human. She had melted, she had shifted, and she had simply faded away. *You have an appetite for monsters.* She never actually moved, was just accompanied by all the secret sounds of the river. And then Lukasz was looking at black trees and he could barely believe there had ever been anyone there at all.

And they for you.

⚔ ERYK ⚔

THREE YEARS EARLIER

LUKASZ AND JAREK MET THE other three brothers just under the eaves of the mayor's house. They looked imposing, army caps pulled low on their foreheads, fur-collared greatcoats slick with rain.

Now that he was the oldest brother, Eryk was in charge. Certainly the most lupine of them all, he had always been fond of the bottle and the beautiful things that winked at handsome men from smoky shadows.

Now he checked a silver pocket watch before stowing it in his coat.

"Two minutes to spare," he said. "Cutting it close."

"They wanted photographs," said Lukasz, out of breath.

Eryk raised an eyebrow.

"Well, if they'd wanted good ones, they should have asked Anzelm," he said before striding up the front steps to knock on the door.

Anzelm rolled his eyes, but they all knew Eryk was right. Anzelm was the handsomest of the Wolf-Lords.

The five of them had just slain a pair of Tannimi scuttling shipping boats in Granica Harbor. The mayor's house loomed overhead, in white stone with arched, blue-tinted windows. The Granica flag flew from the topmost floor, and the second story was flanked by statues of mermaids.

The door swung open, and a maid curtsied.

"You still smell like fish," murmured Franciszek as they filed inside.

"We smell like courage," replied Lukasz.

The mayor of Granica was a powerful man. His city controlled the import of goods; his city welcomed the drab ships of the west and gorgeous ships of the east; his city weighed and measured the cargoes with cranes; his city produced the most capable of engineers and the wickedest of privateers; his city shipped out the great salt blocks that kept the Miasto nobility draped in jewels and lace.

And the mayor was jealous of the Wolf-Lords. They were near the ages of his own disappointing sons. According to the Granica gossips, the mayor had looked into five dark faces and five pairs of sharp blue eyes, and he had envied them. Resented them.

And so, under his direction, the celebratory dinner, held in the opulence of amber-paneled rooms in the gatehouse's upper floors, took an unexpected turn. Between the soup and the entrées, the mayor clapped his hands. Double doors opened at the end of the amber room, and his attendants entered. Lukasz froze, midway through a generous glass of vodka.

Noises of awe and fear echoed in the sparkling room.

The mayor's attendants carried a cage of amber. Candlelight glanced off the carvings at its crown, caught the herbs trailing down the delicate bars. Linden tree leaves lined the bottom of the cage. Lukasz assumed they were merely decoration. And inside, of all things—

"Is that a vila?" he murmured to Franciszek.

At the head of the table, the mayor smiled. His two sons watched, eyes narrowed.

Lukasz was riveted on her, whatever she was. Her blue-white hair swept the bottom of the cage. Her arms were wrapped around shaking knees. Her face was bent away from them. Her shoulders trembled. In the stifling heat of the room, she emitted a chilly kind of glow. She was light, she was monochrome, she was beauty.

She was fear.

Thick enough to taste. Bitter enough to choke on.

"A challenge." The mayor steepled his fingers, blew smoke rings at the ceiling. "It would seem that a common dragon is no match for a Wolf-Lord. Why not something a little more . . . *sophisticated*?"

Nervous laughter around the table. None from the brothers. Eryk spoke.

"We're supposed to kill her?"

The laughter died. One of his sons, thin and blond, pushed back his chair and left the room. The mayor ignored him and gestured to the cage:

"If you can resist her."

Eryk stood up. He'd already lain in the arms of all the beautiful things in the world. He'd had everything, was invincible to anything. The vila didn't stand a chance. He circled the table, and very slowly, he crouched down before the cage.

He whispered something to her. She lifted her head.

Lukasz put down his glass.

A ripple of awe raced through the guests. She wasn't just beautiful. She was enrapturing. None of them knew it, but even as they looked, her eyes were slipping into a different shape for each of them. For some, they were big and innocent. For others, narrow and sly. Her lips bent and unbent a dozen times, her hair flowing into a thick straight mane, then back into gentle waves. And if it was what they wanted, then she stopped being a woman at all. None saw what the others saw; they saw only what they wanted. What they needed. In that moment, she was all things to all people.

Afterward, Lukasz wondered what Eryk had seen.

He unlatched the cage. The vila trembled, weakened. Afraid. She knew, probably. Knew that he was invincible. He alone impervious. In his own way, Eryk had her enchanted. He leaned inside, put his arms around her, and drew her out.

To Lukasz's surprise, she came willingly.

Her long arms wrapped around his neck, and she buried her face in his shoulder. A sheet of silver-blue hair fell over the black of his uniform. As her face disappeared from sight, the enchantment evaporated. The room let out a breath. Cutlery tinkled, gowns rustled, and voices sounded.

"What are you doing?" asked the mayor.

Eryk ignored him, crossing to the window. The vila had wrapped her legs around his hips, tightened her arms around his neck. He unlatched the window, flung it open. Black sky and cold air rushed in, almost snuffed out the candles. Still, she clung to him. Looked helpless. Nothing like the powerful spirits Lukasz had always secretly dreamed of meeting on a dark and lonely road.

"I said—" The mayor got to his feet. His voice had gotten dangerously low. *What are you doing?*

The vila looked up.

The room went still again. Maybe they were under her spell. Or under Eryk's. He was too lupine, too magnetic. He carried his own magic in his hypnotic eyes. Pulled you in. Didn't let you go. And when he spoke next, it was in a voice so harsh and so thickly accented that even Lukasz barely understood him.

"I don't hunt things in cages."

"That's a vila," sputtered the mayor. "Vermin."

Eryk leaned back, enough that she turned that gorgeous face—a face Lukasz wanted back—to him. He smoothed down her hair. Lukasz had never seen him look like that. He looked sad, wistful. He looked like a boy. He looked like every moment thus far had led to what he saw in the face of that wraith.

"Everything wants to live," he whispered.

"Don't you bloody dare—" began the mayor.

Eryk did not answer. The vila was growing mistier at the edges, pieces of her floating away on the wind. He stared at her, and she at him. They were entangled, enraptured. She had Eryk, only Eryk, in her spell. Or maybe he had her.

"She's calling," whispered Eryk. "She's calling me home."

And suddenly, Lukasz knew what he meant to do. And deep down, he knew what Eryk saw in her.

And then he was gone.

Taken away by wind and night and the vila's magic. The window was a gaping black square in a wall of amber and gold. Eryk's words hung over them. Danced in the amber-tinted shadows overhead, settled in their hair. Lodged in their hearts.

She's calling me home.

Lukasz never saw Eryk again.

26

LUKASZ STILL HADN'T COME BACK. Koszmar settled on the other side of their tiny fire, propped up on one elbow. The others were fast asleep, full of the Leszy's food and the hope of reaching the Mountains.

For a while, it was just Ren and Koszmar.

As the darkness pressed in, he appeared brighter: hair so luminescent it seemed to glow. Sparkling eyes, as pale and icy as a vila's skin. Long blond eyelashes. Face no longer a muddy tan, but corpse-pale, with an undertone of gold. Immersed in the darkness surrounding them, he burned with light.

"Do you think he's going to be all right?" asked Ren.

She'd been shocked by the sight of Lukasz down at the river. In just a few days, he'd aged ten years.

"I used some żywokost on it," said Koszmar over the fire. "It should help with the healing. We can try bylica if that doesn't work."

Ren tried to smile. She couldn't stand the thought of Lukasz in pain. She wondered if that was a weakness. And if it was, she suddenly realized, then she didn't care.

"Thank you," she said. "You . . . I wasn't expecting . . ."

Koszmar looked up.

"Me to help?" he murmured. "You wouldn't be the first."

Ren flushed. "I was trying to be nice."

Koszmar put his pipe between his teeth with a *click*, which echoed in the darkness. His hawkish face softened.

"I know," he said. Then he added, "I suppose I am, too."

Ren wondered suddenly if Koszmar was as unsure around the others as she was. It seemed unbelievable that humans could be uncomfortable with their own kind. But all the same . . .

"How did you meet Lukasz?" she asked.

"In the village," he said softly. "The day we met you."

Ren's eyes widened.

"I thought you knew him before," she said.

Koszmar laughed. It was hard to believe she had ever thought him silly. Since beginning their journey, he seemed more angular. A little more uncompromising. Somehow, not unhandsome.

"No, no," he said. "Lukasz is too famous for me. All the Wolf-Lords are—were. I'm a nobody."

It was hard to imagine anyone as glossy as Koszmar being a nobody. He practically dripped gold.

"What do you mean?" asked Ren.

Koszmar grinned at her.

"I was born in a town called Granica, on the northern shores," he said. "Ever heard of it?"

Ren shook her head. Koszmar laughed again and examined his perfect hands.

"No, of course you wouldn't. You've never left this place. You'd like Granica, I think," he added. For once there was no sarcasm in his voice. No pretense. "The beaches are white sand. There's a pink hotel on one of them, with a pier that reaches into the middle of the ocean. The mayor's house has entire rooms made of amber. The houses are all different colors. But ours was white." He closed his eyes. "It smells like the sea."

It was odd that someone who so obviously loved the colors of his old world now dressed only in the same black uniform. The thought filled her with an inexplicable sadness.

"Granica has the biggest port in this country," he continued. "The mayor collects taxes from every merchant ship that sails through that port. He decides on all the fashions of this country— on what silks the fine ladies will wear, on what spices the cooks will love, on what designs will be in vogue for the next thirty years."

"Those seem like silly things," said Ren frankly.

Koszmar chuckled.

"They are, Ren," he said. "But they're the things that humans care about. In my world—Lukasz's world—it isn't about who has the sharpest claws or the strongest jaws. It's about who has money. And the mayor of Granica has the most of it. He is the most power-ful man in this country. Probably even more powerful than King Nikodem."

"You humans are very strange," said Ren.

"We are," Koszmar agreed.

Ren had never seen him like this. She wondered what could have come over him.

"So you come from this city?" Ren struggled around the word. *"Granica?"*

"Oh, it's far worse, I'm afraid," murmured Koszmar. "The mayor is my father."

Maybe, she realized, he behaved this way because she was both queen and princess. And because, as he had just made very clear, Koszmar understood the value of such things.

"Your father?" she echoed. "Really?"

Koszmar smirked. It was a very different smile from Lukasz's. Lukasz had the kind of smile that felt special, just for you. Lukasz pulled you in, turned you in circles, left the world a little brighter when he let you go.

Koszmar just made you cold.

"Certainly," he said. "I was the second son of the mayor of Granica. Don't look like that. I was never anything special. Seweryn, my older brother, is far more lovely than I. He is handsomer, smarter, taller. He is a general in the Wrony. He is a drunk and a gambler, too, but one day, he will be the mayor of Granica."

Ren digested this for a moment. "You mean . . . you don't like your brother?"

Over the heat of their small fire, he blurred and blended with the trees behind. Glowing, obscured by the smoke from his pipe.

"Ren, darling," he said, smirking, "I *loathe* my brother."

Ren thought of Ryś, snoozing gently on her other side. She couldn't imagine loathing Ryś, or Czarn, or anyone in her castle. Even Lukasz was risking life and limb for his brother. It seemed very sad that Koszmar didn't feel the same way. For some reason, it made her like him more. Perhaps it wasn't his fault, that he could be so mean. And anyway, she'd forgiven Jakub for trapping Czarn, and whether she liked it or not, she knew she'd eventually forgive Lukasz.

Surely she could forgive Koszmar for being unhappy?

As if he read her thoughts, he laughed quietly. Ren looked up.

"Who would have thought?" he muttered. "A monster and a failure, searching our souls in a place like this."

Ren smiled, even though she did not find it remotely funny.

"And why shouldn't we?" she asked. She tried to keep her voice light. She couldn't bear the thought of making him any sadder. "According to Jakub, we have so many souls, after all."

"Ah yes," he whispered. "The duality of souls. What a beautiful thought. To think any one of us could be a monster."

"But Jakub doesn't believe in second souls," said Ren thoughtfully. "He thinks that saying someone is predisposed to evil is just making excuses for their poor character."

"Maybe," said Koszmar. "But it doesn't make it untrue."

"Perhaps you're right."

Ducha swooped suddenly overhead, and Ren ducked. Koszmar didn't even flinch. Only looked up, a strange, lazy admiration in his eyes.

"The eagle told Felka that things are worse in the village," he said after a moment.

"I know," said Ren, remembering the Leszy's comments. "We need to get to that Mountain."

They both fell silent. Ducha landed near Koszmar, and to Ren's surprise, he stroked her sleek head. He smiled at the eagle. Or at the forest. She wasn't sure.

The forest liked Koszmar. In a strange, luminous way, it suited him.

It entwined its dark fingers in his light hair, it settled in the crook of his arm in the twilight, and with him in it, it sang with life. His skin had faded to gray and his hair had diluted to silver. He practically glowed. Sitting here, in the darkening firelight, Ren felt like an intruder on their quiet understanding.

Koszmar hadn't belonged in Granica. He hadn't belonged in Miasto. But here . . . but here he had changed. Become handsome, braver, perhaps even . . . *kinder*? Perhaps here was where he could belong. Perhaps here was a place he could love as much as she did. Enough to live out his days here.

She'd welcome him, she realized. Like any lost bird, any cranky badger. She'd let him stay, if he wanted. And, as she drifted off to sleep, Ren had the sudden conviction that he would like that, too.

⚔ 27 ⚔

A SHOTGUN BLAST JOLTED LUKASZ out of sleep, left him cold on the ground.

He came to slowly, pushing himself to his elbows, vision not yet clear. He was vaguely aware of movement, of screaming, of scaly bodies and blast after shattering blast as rifle fire tore through the night. He ran a hand over his eyes. What was happening . . . ?

Sharp claws dug into his shirt, dragged him upright. The creature pushed its face into his.

"What the—"

Lukasz tried to scramble back, but the strzygoń sank its claws deeper. Yellowish drool coated what was left of its face. Its nose had lengthened into a beak. Scraps of embroidered cloth hung from its shoulders, but that was the last human thing about it.

"Get off—"

He swore, tried to reach for his gun. But the strzygoń had enough humanity left to recognize the gesture. Claws sank into his forearm, and it snarled.

Another blast. The creature exploded in a spray of blood and legs.

Lukasz shook off what was left of it. There was a scrape on his forearm, but he was otherwise unharmed. *Thank God,* he thought. He scrambled to his feet.

Strzygi vaulted across the campfire, scattering the coals. Jakub had his shotgun, blasting them away and reloading as fast as he could. Felka stood beside him, one of Koszmar's revolvers in her hand. There were too many of them. They lurched, screeching and slavering. They swarmed in flashes of dirty red hair and gray, peeling bodies. Czarn and Ryś leapt among them, snatching them out of the air, dragging them to the ground. The strzygi were all claws, all jaws, all dark rolling eyes and echoes of this last, horrible bit of humanity.

Across the seething mass, Lukasz saw Ren.

She had his rifle, and now she threw it up to her shoulder and fired again. The blast scattered a horde of strzygi clustered over Koszmar. A single hand emerged from the throng, twisting, convulsing in the earth.

"Lukasz!" Ren hefted a second rifle. Koszmar's. "Catch!"

It sailed over the swarming strzygi and Lukasz snatched it out of the air. He slammed a round into the barrel, took aim, and fired.

The monster on Koszmar exploded.

"We'll hold them off," she shouted. "Get Koszmar."

Lukasz nodded.

He advanced over the congealing strzygi, blasting aside anything that got in his way. Koszmar was trying to get away. Lukasz could see the hand curling and uncurling, nails grasping. Fingers twisting. Shot after shot scattered the monsters. He blasted them back, their bony legs flailing. But there were always more. They just came back. Swarmed over the Wrony again. Devouring him.

"Come on, you little bastards," he growled, advancing. Shot after shot. "Come on."

Now that he was closer, he could see why Koszmar had been swarmed. A blistering pit, newly erupted, simmered beside the blond Wrony—it was still rimmed in red, still billowing tarry black smoke. Purple-black roots uncoiled from the darkness. Body after scaly body, the strzygi clambered out.

He raised the rifle for another shot.

Click. Nothing.

"Damn!" He squeezed the trigger again.

Click.

He was out of bullets. And the strzygi were still feeding, chewing away at that poor idiot's soul. There was no time. They were insatiable.

Lukasz swung the rifle like a club. The swarming bodies went flying. With every blow, he ignored the screaming protest from his wounded shoulder. He swung with all his strength. It wasn't enough. God, there were too many of them—

Fur flashed. Ryś. The big lynx tore into the strzygi.

"You okay?" asked Lukasz, between blows with the rifle.

More of an arm appeared. For the first time, the pristine black coat had been marred. Smeared with blood.

"Enjoying this, honestly." Ryś caught a strzygoń in his teeth and flung it into a tree. He was soaked with blood, but his eyes burned. "You?"

Lukasz didn't respond.

Long silver hair appeared. It was smashed into the earth. It took

Lukasz a sickening moment to realize it was all that remained of the vila-hair helmet.

Koszmar's face appeared. He was whiter than a mavka, streaked with his own blood. A gash yawned in one high-boned cheek. He whimpered, thrashed. For a moment, the strzygi receded.

Ryś whooped in triumph. Lukasz dropped the rifle, hauled Koszmar up. Somewhere, Ren was reloading and firing into the monsters like a clockwork machine. A warm feeling flashed in him, more than admiration. But he didn't have time to analyze the feeling. Because Koszmar looked like he might be dead, and—

"Kosz." He shook him. "Kosz, *damn it*. Get a grip—"

The cut in Koszmar's cheek was so deep that it revealed his blood-streaked teeth. The gray eyes flickered.

"Oh hell," muttered the Wrony. He stumbled, wincing. Put a hand to his torn-apart face and flinched. "My *face*—"

"It's fine," lied Lukasz. He glanced at Ryś, who was sniffing at the undulating roots by the pit. He looked up and nodded vigorously. "It's fine, it's not that bad, Kosz, I swear—*Ryś, watch out!*"

He was too late.

The temporary lull had left Ryś alone by the pit. But under the onslaught by the opposite side of the campsite, the strzygi had—with a chilling kind of organization—switched their target.

Ryś looked up.

His pupils dilated as he saw the tide change. Lukasz dropped Koszmar. While the Wrony fell dazedly to his knees, Lukasz swung the rifle with his screaming shoulder. A single blow swept three strzygi back into the pit.

He could hear the others shouting. Jakub paused to reload.

The strzygi came. They pushed straight past Lukasz, didn't even break stride when the rifle sent them flying. It was no use. There were too many of them. Ryś saw them coming. His ears flattened, and he crouched down.

Terror registered, starkly, on his face.

"Ryś!" Lukasz roared. "RYŚ!"

Lukasz threw aside the rifle, drew his sword. But it was too late. The strzygi covered Ryś.

The pit loomed. Smoking. It looked like a yawning, starving mouth. The lynx was being borne back, back . . .

"RYŚ!"

Entirely covered, the lynx was a mass of seething bodies. His head surfaced like he was drowning. Then he was gone again. Lukasz slashed and hacked, ignored the agony in his shoulder. The mass of strzygi pushed him back. Back to the pit. Ryś yowled.

Sweat poured down Lukasz's forehead.

"HANG ON!"

Lukasz flung aside the bodies. Fought his way to the edge of the pit. Without thinking, he flung himself flat on the ground. Roots curled over his arm. He tore his hand free. More strzygi barreled toward him.

Ryś screamed again. The others shouted. Lukasz was deaf to everything else.

A paw shot out of the pit. Claws dug into his leather glove. Lukasz's hand closed around the foreleg. Ryś was completely covered by the monsters. Movement flickered beside him, and when he looked over,

Ren had thrown herself on her stomach next to him.

"RYŚ!" she screamed. "RYŚ, HOLD ON!"

A yowl. It was strangled. Lukasz threw down another arm, grasped the foreleg with his other hand. Long fingers wrapped around his gloves. Ren was practically falling into the pit.

"You're okay." Lukasz's voice cracked. "I've got you—"

He had no idea what was going on down there, below the lip of the crater. What was happening to that poor lynx, hidden under the strzygi. Lukasz didn't want to know.

Ryś let out a piercing scream, and Lukasz heard himself shouting: "NO—"

The claws extended suddenly. Five toes spasming, every tendon straining under the fur. Ren was screaming, fingers scrambling. The claws tore free of Lukasz's glove. Ryś screamed again. Lukasz grabbed frantically.

Fur slipped through his gloves. His hands closed around nothing. *"Ryś!"*

Ren lunged down the pit. Lukasz grabbed her shirt, dragged her back. She thrashed against him, and he threw his arm over her shoulder. She shrieked and tried to throw him off, but he held her fast, pressed her into the ground.

"Ren, he's gone—"

"Let me go!" She was screaming. Changing so rapidly from human to lynx and back again that he feared she would get away. He didn't let go.

He kept her pinned to the ground, watched the blood from his shoulder trickling down the back of her neck. Watched it staining her shirt. The pit burned below them, from red then to maroon.

Cooling, to depthless black. It reminded him, sickeningly, of the Leszy's forge. Everything went still. Roots hung lifelessly. Darkness stretched down forever.

Ren stopped screaming. She stopped changing.

She lay flat and human and broken, hands over her face, sobbing.

Ryś was gone.

❧ 28 ❧

SHE HAD A MOMENT.

A moment of numbness, of horror. Of Lukasz holding her down, the only thing keeping her from diving down there herself, finishing them off. Bringing him back. A wild flashing moment when she considered every possibility, every single scenario where Ryś wasn't gone, wasn't gone, wasn't gone, wasn't *gone*—

Thud.

Ren's heart slammed into her chest.

Thud.

Lukasz swore.

Thud.

Then they were both on their feet, Lukasz weighing the sword in his hand. She'd been so distracted that she hadn't realized a battle was still raging behind them.

Jakub, Felka, and Czarn had kept the strzygi away from her and Lukasz. Done her, she realized, the same kindness they had done Jakub among the mavka. Now Jakub had the firewood hatchet and was wildly hacking in every direction. Felka kept firing and reloading Koszmar's revolver. Czarn fought with tears in his eyes. On the other side of the clearing, Koszmar had drawn his saber, surrounded by strzygi.

A shadow fell across the trees.

Ren crushed everything in her that wanted to scream and cry. She held up the rifle.

The sky disappeared, replaced by a sparkling gold canopy. The sun blazed through the membranous wings of the Golden Dragon. It circled once. And then, even through the screaming monsters and the sickening thuds of Koszmar's blade, through Lukasz's heavy breathing, even through a sound that she realized was her own sobbing, she knew what was about to happen.

The Dragon had come to join the fight.

Ren dragged Lukasz back as a stream of gold shot across the clearing and fire lit up the world.

The strzygi twisted upward, deciding whether to feast or to burn. The first wave of flames incinerated a dozen of them, left the rest to stumble, still burning, around the clearing. Fed by flesh, the fire flared higher.

The others reeled. As the flames closed in, she saw Felka drop the spent revolver to yank Jakub away from the blaze. She dragged back on Lukasz's arm. His face was livid in the golden light, his eyes almost black.

"We have to go," she gasped. "Get Koszmar—"

"KOSZ!" he was already shouting. "KOSZMAR!"

But the fire had separated them from the blond Wrony. If

Koszmar had heard them, then he didn't show it. He just hacked away at the monsters around him, still attacking despite their already charring limbs.

The Dragon roared again, shot out a second jet of flames. By luck alone, it lit the trees behind them, lighting the roots around the pit and barely missing them. Heat broke over Ren's back.

"Koszmar!" she screamed. *"Kosz!"*

Through the dancing curtain of fire, the Wrony looked up. Even through the haze of heat, Ren saw his expression change. She watched realization dawn.

"KOSZMAR!" yelled Felka. "COME ON!"

Koszmar moved slowly. He looked up at the Dragon. Blood covered one side of his face, and for the first time since Ren had known him, his hair was a mess. He had his cavalry saber in one hand, his remaining revolver in the other. He was still for a moment, staring upward into the gold. Then he turned back at them. His image shivered with heat. He smiled, and his mouth moved. It was too loud to hear him over the shrieking, but Ren could read one word on his lips.

It seemed like the same secret voice of the nimfy. A quiet monosyllable of enchantment, a two-decade game of cat and mouse, summed up in a single syllable.

Run.

And Ren knew.

"NO!" Lukasz shouted. "NO, KOSZ, DON'T—"

He didn't listen. Koszmar never listened. He only did what he wanted. He only did what suited him. He was cruel and mean. He was arrogant and angry and sad, and worst of all, he was Ren's friend.

"NO!" shouted Ren. "Koszmar!"

The revolver rose. A shot sounded. And behind the flames, Koszmar fell.

"*NO!*" Felka was screaming. "*NO!*"

Lukasz dragged on her arm. Pulled her back, but Ren was screaming, crying. She would have run right through those flames. She would have dived back down that pit. She would have done anything, she would have burned, she would have taken on the Dragon at that moment, with nothing but her claws, if it only meant—

"Ren," said Lukasz, pulling her almost off her feet. "Ren, he's dead."

And they left Koszmar to burn amid the dying strzygi, and they ran.

How long had he been dead? Hours? Who knew. It was still night.

The longest night of her life. They'd caught the horses on the way from the clearing, Ren still sobbing. Felka and Jakub had been white-faced and silent. Ren could not look at Czarn.

Lukasz was the only one who kept it together. He moved mechanically. Efficiently. Like he'd run from flames and left behind the dead, and like it was all so familiar, so easy for him now, like he'd been doing it his whole life. And of course, as Ren knew, he had.

She owed Lukasz her life. If it hadn't been for him, she would have died back there in the clearing—twice, once for her brother and then again for Koszmar, and her poor brother—

They stopped when the horses could go no farther.

Czarn had tried to stop her. Ren couldn't look at him. It was all a blur. All a terrible, horrible blur.

She left them. She left them and went to the water. Because the water kept you safe from flames. Because water was where this had started. Because she had always loved the water, and because she'd always been happy in it, and because despite the rusalki and their horrible skulls, she chose to believe that nothing bad could happen in water.

She didn't know how long she sat there, cold in the shallows. Watching her skirts float in the black. The river was up to her chest; her arms were wrapped around her knees. She wondered if she was cold. She couldn't feel it.

Footsteps sounded behind her. She recognized them. Slightly uneven. The limp he thought he hid.

Lukasz waded into the shallows, and Ren wiped the tears off her cheeks.

"Don't," she said, keeping her face down. "You'll get wet."

It began to rain, a thousand tiny bullets hitting the smooth river surface. Lukasz lowered himself down next to her.

"I'll get wet anyway."

The rain crescendoed to a murmur. It enveloped them in the blackness, the trees blurring. In that moment, they were alone in the world: a wet black uniform and a wet blue wraith.

He didn't look at her. But he asked, "Are you going to be okay?"

Ren's throat felt stretched to the breaking point. He'd called her Malutka. He'd been the only creature alive who'd known how small she could feel. In the entire forest, the only one who saw her as a sister first and a queen second. His claws opening. His fur slipping through her hands. Her human hands.

Ren pressed her fingers under her eyes, tried desperately to hide the tears. Lukasz pretended not to notice.

"Are you okay?" she asked instead of answering him.

Was she asking about her brother, or about his? She didn't care.

It didn't matter. They were all dead. His and hers. Ten of them. Dead and gone. Not even buried. Just lost, lost forever.

How was she going to tell Mama?

That thought brought the tears.

They slid down her cheeks, dripped off her chin, dotted her soaked, shaking body. Got lost in the rain. Ren covered her face with her hands. They transformed into lynx paws. She raked her claws through her hair.

When Lukasz finally spoke again, his voice was low and hollow. "I let go."

The monsters swarming like ants over her older brother, her wildest brother, the brother who had followed her and who had loved her and who had hated her plan but who had defended her to the death.

"No." She swallowed against the pain in her throat. "He let go. He knew." She swallowed again, hard. "He knew he couldn't get away."

Like Koszmar. They had both known.

Ren let out a ragged sob. Clamped her half-lynx hands tight over her mouth. Wished he wasn't there to see her cry. She hadn't always been like this. So on the edge that she feared the moments when anyone asked her how she was holding it together, because she knew that one day she wouldn't, that everything would fall apart.

"I . . ." Lukasz's voice cracked. "I don't know what you need me to tell you."

The water, now dancing with rain, began to roil. Ren watched, somehow distant, as the river came to life. Long silver bodies, long silver hair. Long beautiful fingers and sleek beautiful faces, nimfy twisting in every direction.

Lukasz stiffened beside her.

To him, water meant monsters. To her . . .

Deceptively human, with those lithe bodies. But beneath the river algae clinging to their scales, they were anything but: all magical bones and sparkling organs and hearts and minds that changed on a whim and picked favorites. Loved and lived and drowned with the same reckless abandon. There was nothing human at all under that sparsely scaled, silver skin. Quiet creatures. Simple creatures. Magical, only playing at humanity, in love with this dark, murderous world.

Creatures like her.

"Tell me it's going to be okay," she whispered.

His voice didn't crack again. It was hollow, deep. It echoed in her soul.

"I can't." Then: "I don't know if it's going to be okay."

The uniform put an arm around the shoulders of the wraith.

And Ren, who had never been comforted by a human in her life, let him pull her in. Leaned against his shoulder, rested her cheek against the rough angle of his jaw.

"I know," she whispered, feeling selfish. "I know."

They didn't speak again. Instead they watched as the nimfy shivered and twisted and undulated through the rain and the darkness and the sorrow of an evil forest.

✦ 29 ✦

WATER ABOVE THEM, WATER ENVELOPING them, the strzygi long gone and Lukasz shoulder to shoulder with the creature he admired, the creature he loved, the creature he feared he might devour.

In the end, Koszmar had been the braver man. He'd seen what was waiting for him: an eternity of slow transformation, of gradually forgetting, of peeling skin and yellowed teeth. It could have ended in monstrosity or humanity, and Koszmar had done the brave thing. He'd chosen how to die. He hadn't relied on the Dragon to kill him. He hadn't left anything to chance.

He'd pressed the gun into the underside of his jaw, squeezed the trigger, and chosen death.

He'd chosen humanity.

Lukasz wrapped his arm tighter around Ren.

Now was not the time to tell her what was happening to him. Not when she was hurting like this. She didn't need to know about the monsters he imagined were under his skin, seething. Writhing. Clamoring to get out. She didn't need to know that he was afraid: afraid he was not as brave as Koszmar. Afraid that when the moment came, he didn't know how he would choose. Didn't know if he could end it, choose death as a man. Wondered, instead, if he would hang on until his dying breath—whatever throat it tore itself from. Maybe he'd cling to those last heartbeats, caught up in the universal, obsessive instinct to survive. Maybe, oh God, *probably*, he'd go out sputtering and slobbering, a monster desperate to live.

Lukasz shuddered. He hoped she didn't feel it.

Or—he let that last bit of hope have a moment—or maybe he'd survive. Maybe this was just a passing fever. Maybe the Leszy was wrong, maybe mavka were nothing like strzygi, maybe he'd laugh about this in a week, in a month—

She wept. She placed her hands flat against her cheeks, spreading them out over her eyes.

"I don't know what you need me to tell you," he said at last.

"Tell me it's going to be okay," she whispered. And her voice cracked.

Maye it was because of the strzygi. Because Ryś was gone. Because Koszmar had been brave enough to die and let them run, and because Lukasz didn't know if he could do the same. But whatever the reason, all Lukasz wanted was to pull her in. To pry her hands away. To finish what they both knew had started on a rotten riverbank in a different lifetime, before he had known how much he cared.

But he didn't pull her in. He didn't finish it. He couldn't. Not now. Not like this.

"I can't," he said. "I don't know if it's going to be okay."

"I know." Her voice caught. "I know."

She cried quietly, settling her cold wet hair under his chin. And he didn't get used to having her in his arms, and he didn't say anything else, and he didn't make promises he couldn't keep.

Years ago, he had stood in the shadow of dead brothers and sworn not to die, not like this, not out here, not in the service of guilt and ghosts and a Golden Dragon. But tonight his mind was burned, his veins were black, his arms were full with the creature he loved, and tonight at least, he was still human.

For the first time in twenty-one years, Lukasz prayed for death.

⚜ 30 ⚜

THE SKY TURNED GRAY WITH dawn. The horses stood in the rain, grazing on moss. Lukasz's saddle glimmered in the damp dark green. Koszmar's saddle was plain black leather, with a *W* inside a crown embossed on the skirt. Czarn, maybe seeking the company of animals, lay at their feet.

Felka felt terrible for him. Her eyes burned. She felt terrible for all of them.

They had all lost someone. All of them, from Ren to Lukasz to Jakub.

Why are you here? Koszmar had asked, smirking.

I was born, she'd said sarcastically. *Unfortunately.*

She had never appreciated it before, but there were advantages to being alone. Felka was eighteen years old, and she had never lost anyone in her life. Not that she had ever *had* anyone in her life, either. But there were worse things than being alone.

Please, he'd said. *Just take it.*

Felka wiped at her cheeks. This was worse than being alone.

She wrapped Koszmar's Wrony greatcoat around her shivering shoulders. She wished she'd kept his gun. Somehow, a weapon seemed more representative of who he'd been.

"Where is the queen?" asked Jakub.

He rose from across the glowing coals and brought her a mug of coffee.

"With Lukasz," said Felka, adding: "You're bleeding."

Jakub had a cut above his remaining eye, and there was blood crusted down his cheek. He rubbed ineffectively at it for a moment, before Felka raised her arm and—feeling mechanical—used the damp sleeve to wipe it away.

"Thank you," he said.

Felka smiled, then looked down at her coffee.

For a moment, neither of them knew what to say.

A twig snapped. Jakub's hand closed on the hatchet. Felka twisted around. But it was only Ren, materializing from the trees. She was soaking wet, her hair plastered to her neck and shoulders. Between the wet hair and the shadows under her cheekbones, she looked less like a terrible queen and more like the drowned heroine of some tragic fairy tale.

Czarn did not stir.

"Here." Felka removed her coat and wrapped it around Ren. Then she put the coffee in Ren's hands, and behind her, Jakub began making a second pot. "Sit down."

She did not ask if Ren was okay. She knew she wasn't. None of them were.

Ren's eyes were rimmed in red. Her lashes were stuck together.

She looked different, thought Felka. She wasn't sure how, but she looked different.

At last, Czarn rose. He padded across the campsite and laid his head across her knees. Ren gave this sad, twisted sort of smile that threatened to break into tears, and put a hand on his head. He sighed, and Felka missed being alone.

Jakub brought more coffee and handed one mug to Felka. Moving a little stiffly, he sat down next to Ren. The dawn paled to a lighter shade of gray. Over Ren's shoulder, Felka noticed Lukasz returning. He, too, was soaking wet. His easy, slightly uneven stride took him to Król's side, and he unhitched the rifle from the saddle. He looked better than she did.

Then again, he'd been on hunts before. He'd lost brothers before.

"What was her name?" asked Ren at last.

No one spoke.

"Your daughter," Ren repeated. "What was her name?"

Lukasz was still standing near Król, one arm crooked over his saddle. He weighed his rifle in his other hand, tossing and catching it slightly. He looked restless.

"Anja," said Jakub softly.

Ren twisted her human fingers together. Then, suddenly, she took his hand and squeezed it. Felka noticed that even though her hand was dirty, with broken nails, it was still so elegant that it made Jakub's look coarse and heavy.

"It was the worst week," he said. His voice became blurred at the edges. "But it was the best week. My wife died at her birth. Six days later, my daughter followed."

Felka's eyes prickled. She wished she could put her arms around him. Let him weep. She wished she could bring Anja back. She wished none of this had ever happened. She wished, for a moment, she was still alone.

It was unfair, she thought. She wished she was still alone; she wished they had never met; she never wanted to leave any of them again. Unfair that if you loved people, you had to feel this way.

"I want you all to go back," Ren said.

Czarn lifted his head. Felka and Jakub fell silent. Lukasz sauntered over, rifle in hand.

"I don't—" Ren gulped and looked down at her hands. "I don't want anyone else getting hurt."

Her voice cracked on the last syllable.

Czarn spoke.

"Ren," he said. "We love you. We knew this when we came with you. We all did."

Ren smoothed down the fur of his ruff. She smiled at him, and she looked very pale.

"I know," she said. "But I am also worried about the forest. And . . ." She swallowed, and Felka thought that what she said next took great effort: "And the village. I know Ducha said that things are worse. And the Leszy did, too."

There was a beat of silence before Lukasz said, "Ren's right. You should all go back. We'll—we'll go on to the Mountains."

They were quiet. Felka could feel their indecision. She knew it was Jakub's dream to see the Moving Mountains, to walk the varnished halls of Hala Smoków. His fascination was what had led him to make that deal with the Brothers Smokówi six years ago. His fascination with them had cost him his face five years ago. Felka knew he wanted to go on.

She wanted to go on, too.

Not just because Jakub was her friend. But also because Ren was her friend: possibly, ridiculously, her *best* friend. She wanted to be here. She wanted to help.

Czarn got to his feet. The damp had made his fur spiky, and it was pushed up over one of his forelegs, revealing a pink, mottled scar under the white fur. Felka realized, suddenly, that he must want to go on just as much as they did. The Mountains were his home more than any of them.

But he said, "I'll go back, Ren."

It never ceased to unsettle Felka, hearing the animals speak. She knew it shouldn't have surprised her, for she'd heard Jakub talking to Ducha enough times.

"But Czarn, your Mountains—" Ren said.

"Ren," he said, shaking his head, "please. Let me do this for you."

"I will go with him," added Jakub. "Back to the village. I will warn the villagers."

Felka watched Ren. Even in such a short time, losing her brother had changed her. She *did* look different.

"My daughter was so alone, for so long," Jakub was saying. His voice was dry. "You saved her from being alone forever."

Felka felt suddenly selfish. She couldn't believe she'd ever wished to be alone.

She glanced between Ren and Lukasz. There was something new between them—she could feel it. They'd all lost friends and brothers the night before. And yet, despite all their deals and agreements, today was the first time that the pair of them actually looked like partners.

Now Lukasz glanced at Ren. Felka had never seen him look at her like that. With concern and hope, and more . . .

And Ren said, in a very small voice, to all of them:

"Thank you."

Then Ren hugged Jakub. She turned to Felka, looking as shy as she had that day in the village. Felka felt her eyes get wet.

Felka didn't want to leave. She didn't want to leave her friend alone. She didn't want to be alone. But it was what Ren needed. And for the first time since she'd met him, Felka trusted Lukasz. She couldn't help feeling that somehow, when it came to Ren, he would do the right thing.

"I'll go back," she said at last. "Ren, be careful."

Ren smiled, and only because she didn't know what else to do, Felka put her arms around the queen's neck, and she hugged her only friend goodbye.

ANZELM

TWO YEARS EARLIER

ANZELM WAS A HARD MAN to dislike. For one thing, he was certainly too beautiful for a dragon slayer. Alone among the ten, you could almost believe that Anzelm belonged in the vaulted white ballrooms of Miasto and Granica.

He always swept people up in his beauty, in the way his eyes sparkled, in his unfailing good manners, his unerring kindness. While Lukasz gambled with thieves, Anzelm memorized the placement of table cutlery. While Lukasz posed for photographs with increasingly impressive dragon kills, Anzelm perfected the season's most fashionable polonaise. While Lukasz gave interviews peppered with a charming number of curse words, Anzelm guest lectured for the uniwersytet's department of medicine.

And although Lukasz didn't realize it until afterward, Anzelm was also in love.

It happened in Saint Klemens Hospital, where Jarek was getting his arm stitched up after a run-in with a very nasty bannik.

"I'd've been fine," slurred Jarek, who had been given a lot of pain medication. He gestured, dripping blood on the floor. "If 'e 'ad just 'eld shtill—"

Anzelm had procured a suture tray and was trying to teach Lukasz how to stitch a wound.

"Will it shcar?" muttered Jarek.

Anzelm clapped him on his shoulder.

"Only if Lukasz keeps pulling those knots too tight."

Lukasz rolled his eyes, but he made sure the next suture was loose enough. As Anzelm had taught him, he took care not to let the skin pucker under the thread's tension. He actually kind of liked suturing. For someone who couldn't write like Franciszek or draw like Jarek, he was pretty good with his hands.

Thinking of his brother, he wondered where Franciszek was. Either asleep or studying, most likely. Lately, he was researching each new job with an increasing obsessiveness. It was bad enough that he'd delay their jobs for weeks, insisting that he had to wait on a loan of rare books, that he had to study the curve of this particular tooth, that he had not yet finished analyzing the schematics for a given lair—

"Didn't have schematics for the Faustian," Lukasz would mutter.

"And now you have a limp," Fraszko would retort.

Then Anzelm would chime in, across the gilded hotel rooms, the expensive coffee clubs. "*Relax*, Fraszko," he'd say, laughing. "We all know *this* isn't the dragon that'll kill us."

Franciszek's mouth would get thin. His eyes would cloud and he would look like an ancient warrior chieftain. Not the kind of man who smoked good cigarettes and preferred purchasing journals to buying guns.

Anzelm loved telling stories of the Mountains. Lukasz often wondered how much was memorized and how much was invented. But it was part of his charm.

Anzelm's favorite story was the story of Lukasz's birth.

How proud their father must have been, he would say, to lift his tenth son from his crib of golden bones! His father, the Lord of the Moving Mountains, had taken the black-haired boy in his arms and carried him from room to room, through the entire wooden lodge of the Wolf-Lords. In an ancient truce, Kamieńa's villagers had brought the stone down from the Mountains to build their king's castle; in exchange, the Wolf-Lords had carried the wood up from the forest to build their city.

Anzelm told them how their father had moved Lukasz's tiny fingers over the wood carvings that spoke of their history and shown the baby the dragon antlers on the walls. And in the Mountains above, the wolves—for there were still wolves among the cliffs then—peered down from between the purple rocks and saw Hala Smoków, the city of Wolf-Lords, alight with gold and music.

There is another, they had said in the dark hills. *A tenth Wolf-Lord is born.*

"Lukasz," said Anzelm presently, "divide the cut in half with each suture. Don't go end to end. Otherwise it won't line up."

"It won' line up!" slurred Jarek, from the bed.

Lukasz looked guiltily at his rather crooked sutures.

Then Anzelm spoke, as he always did, about how their father took this youngest son—his last son—out to the great wooden verandas of the lodge. There they were swept up in wind and in snow and in starless nights, and he had shown his son the blue slopes of the Mountains and the silver-crested peaks of their world.

Today, Anzelm left out part of the story, but Lukasz had heard it enough times that he knew the words by heart. Not that he remembered them being said by his father. But his brothers had been fathers to him, and Miasto's paved roads had been his mountain paths.

Outside these Mountains, their father had said, *they fear us. Outside these Mountains, they warn their children not to call wolves from the forest.*

But this is not a forest, my son.

And we are the wolves.

Anzelm did not say this part out loud. But Lukasz, counting stitches, said it to himself.

Then his older brother settled against the windowsill, cradling an imaginary baby in his arms, and Lukasz tried not to laugh. But Anzelm had very few faults. Lukasz could forgive his melodrama.

"*Listen close, my Lukasz,*" said Anzelm. "That's what our father said. *If ever you are lost, or alone, or frightened, remember that this is your home. These Mountains will always call you back.*"

He pushed himself off the window and inspected Lukasz's handiwork.

"Excellent. Perfect skin alignment. Well done."

Then Anzelm returned to lean heroically on the windowsill, one hand on his hip and the other on the frame, and it was as if he were looking at the hills themselves, not the dirty streets below.

"Shrouded in blackness and keeping away from the light," he whispered, "the wolves howled their congratulations to the Lord of the Moving Mountains."

Then Anzelm gathered up the tray to take it back to the supply area. He left Lukasz alone, sitting with Jarek on the wrought-iron bed, sunlight streaming through the high window.

And then Lukasz heard them.

"One of the men from the Mountains."

It was a girl, a few years older than him, who spoke.

Lukasz stood up and listened at the door. He couldn't quite see into the hallway.

"Yes, well," answered another person's voice. "Don't get too attached."

"But Ola—"

"Agatka, what did I tell you?" whispered the other voice. "Our father will never allow it. Flirt with him all you like, but it will never happen."

"Ola!"

"They're savages," snapped the first voice.

Lukasz went very still. Surely they weren't . . . ?

But the etiquette book on his brother's nightstand . . . ? And the guest lectures? The polonaises? They couldn't . . . they couldn't really think—Lukasz's mind turned cartwheels, and in a kind of delirium of shock, it silently screamed:

The dinner forks, for God's sake!

"Savages, do you understand me?" repeated the voice. "They drink human blood in those Mountains. They made deals with demons to keep their hold on them. Agatka, we won't have you mixed up in it."

They moved away. It was the first time that Lukasz realized, no matter what praise they received, that he and his brothers stood apart. They would never truly belong—never be accepted—among this world of paved roads and elegant parties. Not even Anzelm. Outside, the carriages rolled on in the street, clattering below and breaking over Lukasz's ears like a thunderstorm.

It was a long time before Lukasz realized that he didn't want to belong.

He never found out what happened, exactly. But Agatka must have told Anzelm what her sister had said. Or maybe what she really thought of him herself. Lukasz wasn't sure. But a few days later, he saw Anzelm chatting with Agatka outside the hospital. While Lukasz watched from across the square, he tucked her arm in his, and together they ducked into an ice-cream parlor. Fifteen minutes later, Agatka came back.

Anzelm did not.

⚜ 31 ⚜

REN AND LUKASZ REACHED THE Mountains by the evening of the next day.

The trees thinned around them, then disappeared. Ren had never seen a world without trees. Never seen a sky so big. Unfiltered by the forest and reflected off the glittering peaks, the sun almost blinded her. Everything was barer, sharper, somehow harsher. The air was ice-cold and clear, filled with the rush of wind and the scent of snow.

Ahead, they faced a gorge a mile wide, extending parallel with the forest in both directions. Beyond its vastness, the Mountains rose from a mist of snow and fog. Purple and blue and gray, they formed an unending vertical wall. Ren had never felt smaller.

She spared one last glance behind, absurdly sad to be leaving the dark. The forest—*her* forest—stretched behind them, smooth tree trunks fading to brown murk. She knew she was lying to herself, but from out here, it looked safer in there. In there, the world knew her name.

Out here, she was just another heartbeat in the silence.

These Mountains didn't care if she was the queen. Didn't care if she'd lost her brother. Didn't care if the world was under attack. These Mountains had been here for thousands of years, and neither queen nor monsters had ever stopped their tides.

When she looked back, she caught Lukasz's eye. He must have been feeling worse, because he'd asked her to take Król's reins. There were dark circles under his eyes. Shadow and beard darkened his jaws, pooled beneath his cheekbones.

"What?" he asked wearily.

It was the first time either of them had spoken since the morning.

"Nothing," she murmured. Her voice sounded pathetically small in the vastness.

She didn't like how their words echoed in the silence. Didn't like how the air made them somehow louder. It was too empty here. So unlike her forest, always cramped and wild and ready to close in. Except for the rush of wind, the cliff was silent.

"How do we get across?" she asked at last.

"There's a bridge up ahead."

He motioned for Ren to direct Król along the path of the gorge.

As he leaned forward, she felt his chest against her shoulder, the rough edge of his jaw against her cheek. It was as if they were in the river again, and again he was refusing to say the things she needed to hear.

But he hadn't said those things then, and he didn't say them now. Ren noticed, with an uneasy feeling, that he smelled like blood.

The promised bridge appeared first as a shadow, outlined by

the sunlit clouds. It gathered detail as they got closer, supported by giant arched columns that extended downward to disappear into the cottony gray clouds.

The bridge was moving.

Scaly creatures undulated over the stone rails, like enormous snakes. They coiled in perfect, hypnotic rhythm. As they neared, the creatures gave a deep, guttural hiss.

No, Ren thought. *Not . . .*

Dragons uncurled around the bridge. There were two of them, with faces that were equal parts serpentine and equine. Sets of antlers, each with at least thirty tines, crested their heads. Thick silver fur ringed their necks like manes, only to merge into scales on their backs. Glittering feathered wings unfurled from their long snake-like bodies.

Ren wanted to disappear behind Lukasz. Run back into the forest. Never come back here. To this. They reminded her, horribly, of the Dragon.

They reminded her of Ryś.

"It's okay," said Lukasz behind her. "They're statues."

At his words, Ren could make out a grainy edge to their fur and wings. And they weren't merely the color of the stone bridge; they were part of the bridge itself. The Faustians beat their wings against the sky. Slowly, they began to descend. Their coils hit the stone with clouds of dust.

"What now?" she whispered.

"I'm a Wolf-Lord," said Lukasz. "They'll let us through."

But his horse trembled as the Faustians wove around them.

Scales slid over the cliff edge, and the two dragons intertwined themselves like braided hair, until Ren and Lukasz were surrounded by a heaving wall.

They couldn't go back.

Lukasz clicked at Król.

"Let's go, boy."

Król trotted, then broke into a canter. Dust exploded under his hooves. The air bit down in sharp blasts from the rocky slopes. Snow scattered. They thundered onto the cliffside beyond the gorge. Ren looked back only once, and the bridge twisted and hissed after them.

"The sun is setting," said Lukasz. "We haven't got much time."

The hills climbed steadily upward, transforming to low trees and brush. Squat firs rose from the rocky earth, and a thin layer of dust coated every surface. The air was oppressive, silent. Ren couldn't see any animals. The narrow path wound ever upward, twisting away through the high rock walls. The Mountains blocked out most of the sky, edges glowing with the setting sun.

Ryś would have loved this, she realized. The climbing. The cold, the adventure—

No.

She couldn't think about that now. It was too final. She thought of Lukasz, of Franciszek. Even if he was dead—and Ren wondered if he was—it was easier to think of him as missing. It was easier to accept things that way. Ease into the newness. Ease into the aloneness.

Ren blinked back tears as up into the Mountains they rode.

❧

Lukasz watched as night fell like a veil of smoke.

They walked long after the darkness; Ren heard the dull crunch of stone moving around them. But Lukasz had been born here and Lukasz knew the way, and their trek did not waver. Their path did not fall away.

It was only after what felt like hours that they chose a wide ledge for the campsite. There was a cliffside behind them, and a view of the Mountains below. Even in all the open space, darkness enveloped them. It filled the gaps between the more distant peaks and tethered itself to the edge of every horizon. With it came a chill wind strong enough to rattle the shale and cut right to their bones.

"No fire," he said, lifting the saddle from Król's back. "The smoke might attract the Dragon."

Ren turned to him, arms crossed tight across her chest. She nodded. The movement was sharp and forced, and immediately she looked away. It took him a moment to recognize the disappointment in her red-rimmed eyes.

"Are you cold?" he asked.

He unhooked his formal jacket from Król's saddle. It was like the ragged one he wore, only clean and lined with silver fur. It was meant to be slung over one shoulder and secured with a chain. He couldn't remember the last time he had worn it. Maybe when Franciszek had still been ali—still in Miasto.

Ren didn't move. The jacket hung between them, just another bit of black in the night.

At last she turned.

"Thank you," she whispered.

The jacket passed from hand to hand, and when she slipped it over the pale shoulders of her blouse, she almost disappeared into darkness. Lukasz blinked. His mind was playing tricks on him.

They settled with their backs against Król's warm side.

Lukasz had a sudden, almost visceral sensation of familiarity, and although part of him held back, his memory stretched and searched, and suddenly, suddenly he had it: night, in these Mountains. Sitting in the front of the saddle, someone behind him, holding him tight. The same chill air. The same endless sky. And instead of silence, the soft, keening cry of wolves.

"It's so quiet," whispered Ren, shattering his thoughts.

"There used to be wolves," he murmured.

He wasn't sure if it was his imagination or his weakening mind, but it seemed that Ren shifted closer to him.

"I don't like it out here," she said, in the same soft voice. This time he knew it wasn't his imagination, because she put her head on his shoulder.

"Neither do I," he managed.

Ren slipped her arm through his and moved closer. She asked, "Isn't this your home?"

He took a long time to answer. And in that time, he had the same haunted, sick feeling. In that time, he remembered glowing windows and light-kissed snow. He remembered climbing steep stone steps. Warm hardwood under bare feet. A hand, which had seemed so much bigger than his own, reaching up to break a small carved dragon off a mantelpiece.

"No."

To Ren's surprise, Lukasz put his arm around her. When they had first met, she'd always been struck by how quick he was to laugh. Now, when he glanced at her, it was hard to believe he'd ever smiled at all.

The closeness gave her courage. Made her wonder whether all those other starts had been enough.

"Tell me about your brother," she said.

"Franciszek?"

Click, click. He had the lighter in hand again.

"That's a nice name," said Ren.

There was a long pause.

"I had nine brothers," said Lukasz at last. "Franciszek was—is—the last."

He said it matter-of-factly, then became quiet again.

"Nine?" she asked. "What happened to them?"

When he answered, his voice was round and soft, more like Czarn's than ever.

"The Dragon."

Ren couldn't help thinking of Ryś. She was trying not to, but he kept coming back to her. Poor, dear, adventurous, irresponsible Ryś.

"How do you do it?" she asked suddenly.

"Do what?"

The stone was so empty. The world was so cold.

"Move on," she whispered.

To her surprise, Lukasz's arm tightened. She turned to look up at him. He was very close, and he smelled like blood. She felt the words on her lips.

"I don't."

In that moment, Ren wanted him closer. She wanted his other arm around her. His words on her lips weren't enough. She wanted more than that. And maybe he did, too, she realized, seeing how dark and shiny his eyes had gotten. Feeling how he pulled her that much closer. His other hand had found her hair, and he smelled like blood and smoke and—

The ground buckled. Król leapt to his feet.

Lukasz swore and jerked Ren out from under the flailing hooves. She scrambled out of the way. For a second, the ground was still.

"What is that—?" she gasped.

Lukasz pushed his cap back on his head. He looked momentarily stunned.

"It's—it's a—"

There was a deafening rumble. It came from below them, from the very depths of the Mountains.

"It's—a tide," he managed.

The earth shook again, so violently that it threw Lukasz down to his knees. Ren slammed back into the rocks. The crags shuddered overhead. Król dodged out of the way as a horse-sized chunk of rock shattered on the ground.

Lukasz was still swearing somewhere. The earth lurched on all sides; rocks hurtled past them. A wave shook the ground. The three of them tumbled off the path and through the rocks, borne along on a current of stone and shale.

Then it stopped. Everything was still.

Ren was on her back, coughing up dust. Król was getting gingerly to his feet. Shale tumbled past them.

The sky was rapidly lightening. Behind them, the slopes continued to move. Rock crunched on rock. The jagged peaks rose and fell. But here, for some reason, the earth stayed still.

Lukasz crawled to his knees, flexing his wounded shoulder, tugging his cap out from under a rock. Then his eyes focused in the distance, and he froze. His black coat was gray with dust. Slowly his hands went to his hair, pushed it back. All the color drained from his dust-streaked face.

"Oh my God," he said.

Ren turned slowly, followed his gaze.

The sun had finished rising, and its light came out from behind the Mountains, glanced off smooth stone walls in pink and orange. But it also caught the glitter of golden antlers on a wooden gate. It lit on thatched roofs and glinted off polished walls; it wound through cobblestone streets and gleamed off windows in the distance.

Hala Smoków.

✦ 32 ✦

WIND TEASED THEIR HAIR, RUSHED over the bare streets. As they approached, Ren could make out intricate carvings of wolves and dragons along the gate, encircled with antlers and vines of wildflowers. The wood shone as if lit from within, deep and red, topped with snow but somehow pristine and unweathered. Above the gate, hanging from silver chains, was a dragon skull.

Beyond, a cobblestone road led up the hillside, with the town built around it into the rocks. Wooden houses with thatched roofs stared at them from either side, marching upward to a large house at the top of the village. This one was set back into the mountainside, made of the same red wood but supported on stone arches.

It was all so different from Ren's castle. From the village. There, there had been a sense of disuse. Of things left to rot. The same was not true of this place. No, this town had the same permanence as the rest of the mountains. It had that same pristine emptiness, and Ren was instantly, acutely aware of the fact that everyone who had once lived here was now dead.

Beside her, Lukasz's eyes were glassy.

Almost everyone.

"Welcome home," she said weakly, before she realized what she was saying. He'd told her himself: this wasn't his home. Not anymore. The words sounded brittle in the cold as they fell between them and shattered.

Lukasz ran a hand through his hair.

"We should go up to the lodge," he said. His voice was very rough. "We need to find that sword."

This time, Ren didn't answer, and they began the long trek up the cobblestone street.

The town was perfectly preserved. Bridles hung from pegs, boots stood outside doorways, axes lay half buried in woodpiles. Beneath open shutters, the windows still had glass. Nothing broken, nothing destroyed.

The sound of their footsteps was deafening. The Mountains had turned their ears toward Hala Smoków, listening.

"My God—" started Lukasz.

Ren followed his gaze, jumped violently.

A figure had appeared in one of the doorways. He wore pale trousers with green and black embroidery, with a loose-fitting shirt and leather vest. A leather belt, almost a foot wide, encircled his waist. He looked so different from Lukasz and Koszmar, with their neat black uniforms. But like Lukasz, he was very tall, with long black hair and tanned skin.

Lukasz swallowed beside her.

"A domowik," he murmured.

At the words, a foxy kind of smile lit up the domowik's face. It leaned with a forearm against the top of the doorframe. With a furry hand, it took off its round black hat, then inclined its head. Two small horns pointed out of the long black hair.

When Lukasz spoke, it was with an odd, dreamlike quality, as if he was suddenly remembering things that he had forgotten long ago.

"They wailed every night," he murmured. "None of us slept. All the candles went out. We couldn't keep them lighted. It was only afterward that we realized they were trying to warn us . . . to tell us . . ."

Even without his smile, his mouth remained crooked, dragging down on one edge. He looked hungry. He always looked hungry.

"They're good spirits," he said. "They take care of the house. They live under floorboards. They guard the family."

The domowik turned and disappeared back into the doorway. A long fluffy tail poked out the back of his trousers.

More and more domowiki appeared in the doorways as they made their way up to the lodge. They came out of their stables and stood in their yards. They were ghostly, silent. Black boots, white dresses. Green and red embroidered flowers. Red ribbons trailed from their thick black hair, and more long ribbons hung from their vests and skirts.

Ren thought they were more like specters than actual creatures. And if not specters, then at least spectators. Watching over the lives that had once started and ended here, within these wooden gates. Silent guardians, hanging in the rafters, peering out from under stairs that creaked at night. It was sad, she thought. They had watched this town end.

And now this.

Ren glanced at Lukasz. Next to the domowiki, he looked even more haggard than ever. She could only imagine what kind of memories attacked him, staring into the faces of so many long-gone souls.

Or worse: maybe there were no memories.

They mounted the steps to the lodge, dwarfed by the stone arches, by the windows and verandas. As on the gate, intricate carvings covered the woodwork. Lukasz paused at the top of the steps, ran a gloved hand over the red-gold wood. The whole of Hala Smoków was still, save for their own breathing and steadily pounding hearts. The sun broke over them, shone pale pink and gold on the snowdrifts clustered between the hand-carved railings.

"I was born here," he whispered.

Perhaps it was the color of the wood or the unexpected warmth of the sun, but Ren said, "It's beautiful." Then she surprised herself by adding: "It's the most beautiful place I've ever seen."

She meant it.

Lukasz put his other hand on the railing. He had his back to her, looking down at the town. The domowiki had turned toward them. Ren's heart quickened again. They were so solid, substantial. No black misty smoke here. No skeletal transformations. They were like her.

He spoke again.

"I had forgotten it."

They found the lodge's single, immense door was already ajar. Every fresh gust of wind brought a fine sugaring of snow into the gloom beyond. Inside, with the absence of sight and sound, her sense of smell sharpened. There were the usual human things: fresh chopped wood, frost, and mildew. But she also smelled the things only animals could smell: cobwebs and old dust, gold and tears, and permeating it all, the overwhelming, bitter smell of grief.

The hall was octagonal, with each side vaulting into a doorway bordered with carvings. The walls were horizontal planks of the same red wood, topped with antlered skulls in silver and copper.

Dragons, thought Ren.

Without hesitating, Lukasz led the way under one of the arched doorways. Ren was impressed that he remembered the lodge so well. They moved deeper into the red-wood halls.

"I can't believe it's so warm," she murmured, pressing a hand against a carving of a dragon.

"The wood is enchanted," Lukasz replied over his shoulder. "It gives heat in the winter."

Lanterns hung from hooks overhead. Everywhere, the walls bore the same horizontal wood paneling and carvings. Rows of dragon skulls gleamed down, glowing with the same eerie silver and copper as Król's saddle and bridle. They were the only sources of light in the long dark passages.

"Are these skulls—?"

"Real silver?" finished Lukasz. His teeth caught the bare gleam. "Yes. All dragons have skeletons made of precious metal. The thirst for riches is literally in their bones."

They climbed an intricately carved staircase with spaces between the steps. They walked down a hall with one side entirely made of windows. They came at last to another octagonal chamber. Here, six of the eight sides were also windows. The deep blue Mountains shifted below them, crowned with snow. They stretched away in every direction.

A chair and a desk had been pushed up against one of the windows. The furniture was as ornately carved as the walls. The desktop was invisible under the clutter of papers and strange instruments. A miniature silver dragon curled around a candle stub, and by the window, a telescope stood on jointed brass legs.

There were no dragon skulls here.

"Your father's chamber?" she guessed, looking around.

"Yes," said Lukasz. With each step, tornadoes of dust whirled in the dawn.

Lukasz pulled the chair out from under the desk. Shoved it aside with a bang.

The desk edges were inlaid with gold rulers, marking set distances along each side. Pencils and inkwells dotted the top border, along with compasses, small knives, and a dozen other instruments Ren could not recognize. But everything paled in comparison to the charts that Lukasz now pulled apart.

Writing danced like spiders, drawings sprawled over every edge: of fangs and lolling beasts, of precious metals and wild horses. The maps were gridded with marked squares, inked with mountain ranges and caves. Maps built into books, with translucent pages that, when laid over one another, showed how the Mountains changed over weeks, months, and even years. Maps dedicated exclusively to the lairs of dragons, maps that charted the migrations of beasts, maps that connected the dots of treasure troves and mines for precious metals. There were maps of winds and maps of wolves, maps of avalanches, and more than anything, maps of dragons.

Lukasz's long gloved fingers flickered expertly across the drawings. Ren imagined that she could see the lines reflected in his blue eyes. For all his talk, he looked like he belonged.

He cares, she realized. Even if it wasn't home, exactly. *He cares about this place.*

He ran his hand over his chin, down his throat, and around the back of his neck.

"Is this Glass Mountain on these?" she asked into the yellow, dusty silence.

In answer, Lukasz slid a piece of parchment into view.

It was a mountain. The sides were not smooth, like Ren had expected. Instead, the illustrator had drawn a tangled mass of knights, kings, horses, and banners. All together, they formed a vaguely mountain-like shape. Their limbs intertwined and their faces formed silent screams. Atop this towering, peaked pile of humanity perched a dragon in golden ink.

Next to it, someone had drawn a map.

Ren shuddered.

"It's awful," she said.

He glanced down at her. The sun caught under his cheekbones. Ren found she barely recognized this new stranger, born once up here in these wooden halls and now reborn in the glow of the dragon skulls.

"At least it's still here," he was saying. "I thought Franciszek might have taken it—"

He stopped. Suddenly, he raised his hand, as if to run it through his hair, but knocked an inkpot off the desk. It shattered on the floor, and faded, red-brown liquid oozed across the hardwood.

Ren knew what he was thinking. If Franciszek *had* come here, then he certainly would have taken the maps. And if the maps were still here, that could only mean . . .

Ren's heart sank.

Without being fully aware of what she was doing, she put her hand on his arm. She wasn't surprised, exactly. She had suspected this. She hadn't said it out loud because it had seemed cruel, and because he didn't seem to want to hear it, but there was no getting around it anymore.

Franciszek was dead.

Lukasz moved away from her touch. He turned to face the window, running his hands through his hair, smoothing it down around his neck. With his back still turned, he said:

"They'll be glad."

His voice was steady; his hands didn't shake again.

Ren blinked. "What?"

He turned back around. He looked way too calm. Looked like he'd been doing this for far too long. Saying goodbye, closing doors, moving on.

"They'll be glad that we're dead."

A bed occupied one side of the room, heaped with knitted blankets and furs. Lukasz crossed the room and sank down, his head in his hands. A little unsure, Ren settled next to him. She didn't know what to say.

"Who will be glad?" she asked at last.

When Lukasz finally answered, it was to say more words than she'd ever heard from him at once. She let him talk. She was used to the silence of animals, but she was learning that these humans needed more.

Besides, she liked how he talked.

She liked him.

"Everyone," he said hollowly. "The aristocrats. The Unnaturalists. Even those wretches in the villages and towns. They hear *Wolf-Lord*, they think we're dogs."

He smiled, not quite at her. Not quite at anything. He looked gaunt and old, but he had nine dead brothers, and Ren wondered how he had ever been able to smile at all.

"When they heard my brother could read?" he murmured. "They were shocked. They wanted him to do demonstrations. For *science*. They study us in their universities. You know that? Put our swords and our carvings and our dragon antlers on display. They slap on a few plaques. They tell everyone about the once-great, now-extinct, savage people who couldn't be dragged into this age with the rest of you." His voice had gotten very harsh. "They were right."

The rest of you.

It was strange, being folded in the rest of them.

She wasn't sure why she did it, but she took his gloved hand in

341

hers. Her fingers intertwined with his. White in black, speckled with sun and shadows. He was wrong. She wasn't like them. She wasn't like the animals. She wasn't like any of them.

"I'm sorry," she whispered.

She wondered how it would feel to touch his other hand.

"Why?" He laughed bitterly. "It's not your fault."

"It doesn't matter," Ren said. "No one should feel that alone. It just isn't right."

He turned away.

"I had nine brothers," he said. "I was never alone."

Then she did what she'd been wanting to do almost since she met him. She smoothed back his hair, which was coarser than it looked. Then she ran a hand over the stubbled edge of his jaw. She loved his face. She loved that crooked tooth.

Ren wondered, suddenly, if she loved more than that.

He got to his feet, and Ren's hand fell away. She wondered if she'd gone too far. She looked down at her hands.

"You should sleep," he said roughly, above her, not looking at her. "We walked most of the night."

"So should you," she replied softly.

Still, he didn't look at her.

"No," he murmured, more to himself than to her. "It just reminds me of death."

❧ 33 ❧

I AM GOING TO DIE, thought Lukasz.

He had never thought it would end here. With him in his father's chair, Ren curled up in his father's bed. She was finally sleeping, and he was too terrified to even close his eyes.

Click, click.

He ran his fingers over the lighter casing. He watched its tiny flame spring to life. He watched it snuff out. Was that how it would end for him? A tiny *click, click*, and then utter black? Or would he go out like Koszmar, on a single word and a shot in the darkness?

He didn't think so. His exit would be graceless. He already knew that. He clung to life like a dog. He always had.

Everything wants to live, Henryk had said once.

And by God, Lukasz wanted to live.

His good hand covered his eyes. They grew hot, his vision swimming. The warmth brimmed, threatened to spill over. He rubbed the tears away, looked up to the view beyond the window, now a bit blurry. Dawn had broken, and the Mountains ground to a halt.

Sun streamed through the foggy glass, illuminating dust and pink carpet. Rosy hills stared back from six sides, the very same hills that had once stared back at his father. He shivered.

Lukasz wanted to live.

There was a rustle in the doorway.

He leapt to his feet. Then, swaying for a moment, he half forgot what he was doing. His eyes went to Ren, still fast asleep.

God, she was perfect. She deserved a forest free of monsters. She deserved a kingdom free of that Dragon. She'd lost so much already. A crown, a family, now her forest . . . It wasn't fair that she'd lost a brother.

It wasn't fair that she kept forgiving him.

But she wouldn't forgive him this time. He had one last promise to break. Hard to believe that when he'd first lied to her, he'd thought his hand would be his downfall. And now he wouldn't just lose his career. He wouldn't just lose her.

Lukasz wished he could live.

Someone moved beyond the doorway. Just as he returned to his senses, a man moved out of the hall and into the warming dawn.

Lukasz's heart stopped. It couldn't be . . . not after all this time . . .

The mavka venom must have been eating away at him from the inside. For a wild moment, he wondered: Was he dying? Was he already dead? Was this how it ended, among ghosts in a ghost town, doomed to an eternity in these purple hills?

"*. . . Dad?*"

The man in the doorway had a black beard, and he wore his gray-black hair long, in the more traditional style of the Wolf-Lords.

He wore a Faustian-fur cloak over Dewclaw chain mail. A scabbard hung from his leather belt. No sword.

"How did you—?" Lukasz had to stop and start over. He was horrified by how hoarse his voice sounded. "You're—I can't believe you're alive—"

His father had Tad's deep-set eyes and beaky nose. He had Lukasz's feline mouth. He had Rafał's jaw. In his father, Lukasz could see each of his brothers, he could see fireflies, see his parents dancing, see nights warmed with dragon fur and enchantment, and it took him a moment to realize he wasn't seeing. For the first time in a long time, he was remembering—

The tears came. Spilled over.

"I am not he," said the figure.

His voice was harsh and hollow, as if it had been dragged from a great distance away. He looked strangely dusty, tinted with gray. It was almost like he had been covered with a misty veil.

Lukasz realized why.

The creature was covered in cobwebs. They trailed on the ground, hung between its spread fingers. Suspended on a thread, a spider dangled from one elbow. And its hands were covered in thick silver fur.

Lukasz rubbed the tears off his cheeks and, feeling stupider than ever, said, "You're the domowik."

The creature bowed, revealing two silver horns in its long hair. Its movements were stiff, as if its bones had not moved in years. At its feet, insects scattered across the carpet.

The domowik regarded him seriously, while another spider

scuttled across its shoulders.

"You smell like death," it said.

Lukasz rubbed the back of his neck. It was unnerving, looking into the eyes of his dead father, ensconced in this dusty, creaking body.

"You're not the first person to tell me that."

The domowik blinked slowly. The gesture was overpoweringly reminiscent of Ren.

"I am not a person," it said.

"Right," said Lukasz, not quite sure how to respond.

The domowik seemed to freeze in position every time it moved. It had none of the spark of life that lay beneath human movement. None of the heartbeat, none of the pulse. It moved, stopped. Became a statue. He supposed that was what happened when you spent twenty years alone under the floorboards.

"Not long now," it said.

Lukasz's mouth went dry.

"Please," he said. "Where—how—what happened to my brother?"

The domowik became very still, statuesque once more.

"You could have asked the Leszy this question," said the domowik. "But instead you asked how to kill the Dragon. Nine brothers before you sat at that table. None of them asked that question."

Lukasz tried to smile, but it turned into a grimace.

"None of them had a cross, as far as I remember."

"For a man who has insisted he does not want to kill the Dragon," said the domowik, "you have sacrificed much in its pursuit."

"How did you know that?"

"I am the guardian of this household," said the domowik. "I know you very well."

Lukasz bit his lip, looked away for a moment. Nine brothers gone. Up in smoke, fading into memory, getting darker and fainter and threatening to disappear for good. And soon . . . soon he would join them.

His eyes flickered to Ren, still deeply asleep on the bed. In fact, she looked so still, so perfect, that he half wondered if the domowik had placed some enchantment on her.

Even if Lukasz didn't survive, it didn't mean she had to die with him. It didn't mean her forest had to die. And the domowik was right; he had asked the Leszy to help her, when he could have very easily asked it to help him.

He'd promised. He'd shaken hands.

"Just because I die," he said, "it doesn't mean the Dragon can't be slain."

In a way, he thought, it would be easier. It would all be easier. Ren could fight her Dragon, avenge her brother, return to her beloved forest. And he could join his brothers. As a human. Not as anything else.

"I will show her the sword," said the domowik at last.

"What about the Mountain?" asked Lukasz.

Downy with dust, the domowik's eyelashes flickered. Its expression was unreadable, but Lukasz was aware of his shoulder pulsing, twisting. He could feel the poison at work. Feel it in his skull, pounding through his heart.

Then the domowik spoke.

"There was one who may help," said the domowik. "She is more ancient than any of these hills. She is more terrible than any of their demons. She alone wields the power of life or death over that

Dragon. Her price will be great."

"I'll pay it," said Lukasz.

The domowik looked unfathomably sad. "It will be your life, Lukasz."

For some reason, this hit harder. It was one thing to go kicking and screaming; it was another to lie down and die.

Or maybe a small part of him had thought—had hoped—that he might one day return here, he might one day catch fireflies, he might one day spin a dark-haired queen around the great stone kitchens while children watched them from the stairs. Maybe, he realized suddenly, that part of him had not been very small at all.

A thousand years of Wolf-Lords, and this was how it ended?

Lukasz sank onto the bed. Ren stirred, gave a small, very feline stretch. He rested his hand, the ruined one, on her hair. He had thought he was used to it. Thought he was used to the melted flesh. The missing nails. The end of his index finger was completely gone. Charred right off.

Maybe he had been dying for a long time.

"I am not afraid of death," he said.

"It is not the death that inspires fear," said the domowik, said the ancient creature, the guardian of households, the last echo of humanity in a death-swept town.

"It is the dying."

❧ 34 ❧

KOSZMAR WOKE.

Slowly. Numb at first, with only the vaguest awareness. Shapes merged and fluttered in the dim. It smelled like fire, like charred meat. Someone was moaning. Retching. It took him a moment to realize it was him.

Then came the pain.

Everywhere. Moaning turned to screams. His face—oh Christ, his face—

Koszmar writhed on the ground. It began to come back. He clutched at his face, his eye. Oh God, no—

The bullet had missed his brain. It hadn't been enough to kill him, only to blow off half his jaw. His fingers explored the congealed, damp mess of his left side. His eye was gone.

Oh God, he was still alive. The words came back. Words he'd blocked out. Words from the first time he had ever seen Lukasz, in his father's gatehouse, while the vile old man had goaded them to kill a vila—

Everything wants to live.

Koszmar moaned, writhed, struggled to his feet.

Koszmar wanted to live.

⚜ 35 ⚜

BELOW THE GLASS WALLS OF the hallway, twilight turned the snow-crested mountains to lilac. Ren pressed a hand against the glass, watched her breath turn to fog. Behind her, the row of golden skulls reflected comets of dying light and warmed her shoulders.

This wasn't just abandoned. It had never really been discovered.

She wasn't sure what she had expected from the Wolf-Lords, but it hadn't been this. She had grown up amid ruined finery; she had slept under the breathtaking carvings of the library, pulled moth-eaten gowns from crumbling wardrobes. She had lived in a castle of queens and nobles, and despite what Lukasz had told her, she had somehow expected a more savage place.

Perhaps it wasn't fair of her. But she was glad to be wrong.

Her eyes moved, slowly, to the black cuff of Lukasz's jacket and her dirty hand beneath it. Less than two weeks ago, she had stood at the castle windows in her own hallway, looked out at her forest. Back then, she could have wept for powerlessness.

Today, she was closer to killing the Dragon than anyone else had been in seventeen years. They could do it. She knew it. She had a Wolf-Lord's skill and the Leszy's advice, and all she needed now was that sword. . . .

A reflection flickered in the window. Ren turned, feeling the hairs on her neck prickle. She could have sworn she'd seen a figure in the arched doorway at the end of the hall.

She'd left the other rifle in the tower with Lukasz. When she'd woken earlier in the evening, he'd been fast asleep in the desk chair. She hadn't been able to bring herself to wake him. And besides, she'd assumed they were safe here.

Carefully, she crept down the hallway. The dragon skulls watched her with empty eyes. The doorway opened onto a second hallway, this one lined with carved chairs. The light was dim, and dust gently drifted down from the ceiling.

Ren glanced up, but the rafters were empty.

When she looked down again, she started.

The seat of one of the chairs had opened, revealing a concealed cupboard. She turned, but nothing flitted out of the shadows. No more dust fell from the ceiling. She glanced up and down the hall. It was deserted. She crept toward the chair.

A dress lay folded in the opened cupboard. Seventeen years of dust had dulled the colors; its skirt was decorated in green and pink flowers, cascading down from the waist to gather at the hem. Trying to ignore how dirty her nails looked against the white cotton, Ren lifted the dress out. There was white lace at the cuffs, and the vest was pale yellow.

Would it be wrong?

The skulls watched with hollow eyes. It wasn't like there was anyone left to care. Or even notice. She started to unlace the bodice and then stopped. Though human, her fingernails were so long that they looked like claws. Even without the fur, they were still the hands of a monster. She didn't belong in clothes like that. Neatly, she replaced them in the drawer in the seat.

And even if she had been born a human, she wasn't one now.

This was not her world. These were not her clothes. She had been left to evil woods and evil monsters. And she had survived. Lukasz had seen cities she could only dream about; he had met people she would never see. He had lived in a world like this one, where the streets were whole and the darkness had not yet crept in.

She stood up, and a faint, foggy version of her looked out of the window.

Power shivered through her gums, and Ren opened her lips. The girl in the window had blurry teeth, long and wicked. Ren knew they were yellow, with black speckles in the gums. Ren blinked, and even in the warped glass, she saw pupils big as moons.

Ren blinked again, closed her lips, and when she opened her eyes, she was human again.

Or at least, she looked like one.

There was the sound of tinkling glass. Ren whipped around. A furry tail disappeared around the corner at the end of the hallway. She raced after it.

She skidded to a stop at the next juncture, only to see the tail disappear around the next corner. She chased it down. On and on, she sprinted down halls that were alternately pitch-black or lit by candelabras that burst into flame as she passed. In one hall, the entire wall formed a window. In another, both walls were taken up by bookshelves.

At last, she skidded into the biggest room yet.

Panting, Ren took stock of her surroundings. It was completely empty, ringed with more carved chairs. Chevron-shaped stripes of light and dark wood decorated the floor. The walls were adorned with carvings and amber inlays, topped with dragon skulls and lanterns of dragon bones. There were no windows, but overhead, the ceiling was glass. Beyond it, the moon looked lonely in an endless sky.

A chandelier the size of one of her castle towers hung from its center. It was wrought from dragon bones—not just the skulls, but the rib cages and the femurs, held together by unseen chains, and probably by magic.

A hearth took up the opposite wall.

Ren crossed the great hall under the glow of dragon bones and the stars of ten centuries. The hearth was empty, without any wood or kindling. A tiny figurine was balanced on the otherwise empty mantelpiece. Ren picked it up; it was only two or three inches tall, carved from wood.

It was a dragon.

Then she looked from the dragon to the hearth, overflowing with soot. Thoughtfully, she replaced the figurine on the mantel.

There is a glass sword in Hala Smoków, the Leszy had said.

Before she could change her mind, she plunged her hands into the cinders. Spiders tumbled down the chimney and insects swarmed over her hands. Her fingers touched metal. Heart soaring, she pulled. The hilt slid out of the ash. Except it was lighter than she had expected.

No—

Ren wanted to cry.

"Ren—"

She turned and saw Lukasz, somehow looking even worse than before. When she spoke, her voice caught. "It's broken."

The silver hilt resembled the jaws of a dragon, as if the blade should have issued from its open mouth. But where there should have been a blade, the dragon's jaws were shut tight. It wasn't even a sword. Just a silver hilt.

Lukasz didn't say anything. He just crossed the hall, and Ren held out the empty hilt.

"I can't believe it," she said, unable to keep the catch out of her voice. "It's a trick. A cruel, mean trick. We shouldn't have listened to the Leszy—"

He took the sword from her outstretched hand. Ren broke off.

As his bare hand touched the hilt, it changed. Black tarnish melted away, and the hilt glowed silver. The dragon's closed mouth began to shiver. The jaws trembled. Then they yawned, opened wide, and a column of light shot from the broken hilt.

The light hardened.

In his burned hand, Lukasz held the glass sword. Its blade was whole. It issued the same creepy light as the skeletons, pure and thick with magic. Lukasz turned the sword over. The light caught his face, illuminated excitement and wonder. Then it dulled, like cooling iron.

"And this can kill it?" whispered Ren.

Lukasz glanced back at her without lowering the blade. For a moment, he looked terrible. All hard angles and predator eyes. He grinned wolfishly, teeth not quite coming together.

Then he laughed. The sound echoed off the wooden walls and danced down the hallways. Ren saw only his dark brows, that one stubborn piece of hair, and that perfect, slightly crooked front tooth.

"A thousand years of Wolf-Lords." He flicked down the blade and offered her the sword, its blade full and forged of glass. "And you put us all to shame."

Ren hesitated. She took it from him, surprised by how heavy it felt in her hand. Lukasz turned away to rummage through one of the hidden cupboards.

"What do you mean?" she asked. She felt like an imposter. This was his sword. It had come to life for him—

"Here," he said, returning with a belt and scabbard.

"Lukasz, what—?"

He looped it over her shoulders, across her body. He pulled her very close as he buckled it over her black coat. He looked down at her from his great height, and Ren almost pulled him closer.

"What are you doing?" she asked instead. "Don't you need this—?"

"Ren," he said. "It's your sword. In case—you're the queen, Ren. You've gotten us through everything. You should do this. You *need* to do this."

He was still smiling, but his voice had an urgent undercurrent. Ren didn't quite understand. She wasn't a Wolf-Lord. This was the Golden Dragon—

But when she put a hand over his, Lukasz just stepped back.

"With that sword," he tried to joke, "you look like a queen."

He tried to move away, but Ren grabbed his hand.

"I have always looked like a queen," she said, pulling him closer. She found the buckle on the belt, readjusted it so the sword lay comfortably against her hip. Then added, "I am just not the queen you expected."

And suddenly, he was so close that if Ren had moved even the slightest bit, their lips would have touched. Ren could feel her own heart taking her away, could feel him giving in. And it was going to happen. There was nothing she could do about it.

"You're nothing like I expected," he murmured.

She almost moved forward. But Lukasz twisted away suddenly, eyes trained on the door.

"Stop," he said. "Someone's here."

⚹ JAREK ⚹

ONE YEAR EARLIER

IT CAME AS NO SURPRISE that the last three brothers received invitations to the Royal Exhibition of the Unnatural. Lukasz figured he had Jarek to thank for that.

Because the thing was, Jarek was good at pretending.

Early on, when there had never been enough food, Jarek had pretended he wasn't hungry. Whenever they were invited to some fine party or elegant soiree, he pretended to be flattered.

And he also pretended he liked hunting dragons.

Jarek's pretending made him easygoing and likable. His shyness and kindness made him all things to all people. He was also less threatening, taller than Franciszek but shorter than Lukasz, with a haunted kind of handsomeness that the young ladies of Miasto found romantic. He was, although it baffled him, wildly popular.

The night of the exhibition, the three brothers descended the four hundred steps that led into the belly of the Wieczna Salt Mine. From there, they walked the mineral-crusted passageways and entered the great salt ballrooms. Salt chandeliers hung from the ceilings. Bas-reliefs in salt lined the sparkling gray walls.

And overhead, monsters.

It was, after all, an exhibit.

Dragon skeletons rotated slowly, like obscene mobiles with iridescent silk stretched between the bones of their unfurled wings. Banniks, stuffed with sawdust, were arranged with their arms cranked back, hurling invisible rocks at their enemies. Common things, like psotniki and nocnica, were interspersed among the rarer beasts. Their curator, Professor Damian Bieleć, held court beneath them.

The professor had chosen the salt mine especially. Lukasz supposed there was a kind of thrill in admiring demons next to hell.

"Monstrosity is relative," Lukasz overheard him saying. "For some of these creatures, evil is simply a way of life. Take this strzygoń . . ."

The Unnaturalist gestured to a silver-gray monstrosity revolving slowly overhead. It had been killed in the moment of its birth: the new strzygoń emerging from the torso of its human vessel. The gray bulging eyes stared down at them. Lukasz turned his head to the side for a better view.

The sight took him back to the cellars of Szarawoda, looking at another strzygoń, at another scholar of monsters. . . .

"These creatures are a miracle of survival," Professor Bieleć was saying. "For the survival of their species is based, most unusually, on the consumption of others. . . ."

"Close your mouth," Lukasz muttered, catching up with Jarek. "You look like a fish."

Jarek, who had been staring up at the revolving dragons, started and almost dropped his glass.

"Where's your date gotten to?" asked Lukasz.

In the sallow lighting of the salt mine, Jarek looked even more romantically haggard than usual.

Franciszek approached. They formed an island of black and legend in the center of the chamber.

"Turned out she didn't want me," Jarek was answering, returning his empty glass to the tray of a passing waiter. "Just my gold."

"The women you fall for," said Franciszek. "I'm not surprised."

"Thank you," replied Jarek mildly. "And here I was hoping she wanted me for my wickedly good looks."

Jarek always carried a small wooden dragon with him. When they'd been boys, he'd broken it off one of the wall carvings at Hala Smoków. It was tiny, whittled of varnished wood, and now he turned it thoughtfully in his hands.

"Youth is temporary," said Franciszek wisely. "Gold is forever."

Lukasz snorted.

"It certainly is not," he muttered.

"Maybe not the way you spend it," rejoined Franciszek sweetly.

Lukasz was twenty, bored, and a little tipsy. He lit a cigarette, which Franciszek immediately snatched out of his teeth, hissing: "You can't smoke in here!"

Lukasz jerked back. Franciszek crumpled the cigarette in the cupped palms of a stuffed bannik.

Jarek flipped the tiny dragon nervously between his fingers, watching them.

"Jarek," Lukasz heard his older brother saying. "Did you see the sculptures in the next chamber? I think you'd be quite interested in them—"

They left Lukasz to drain his glass, hunt down another. Damian Bieleć was still lecturing some attendees, now standing next to a wooden model of a small cabin supported by a chicken leg.

This is how he makes money, thought Lukasz. *This is how he makes friends.*

Fake monsters. Fake thrills. Jarek was too mild to notice. Franciszek was so damn excited about being included. Lukasz was the only one who saw the invitation for what it really was. He and his brothers weren't guests, for God's sake.

They were part of the exhibit.

"Jarek," growled Franciszek through gritted teeth. "Why is he still drinking?"

Lukasz glanced up, dazed. Realized that he was sitting alone, in a deserted passageway. Someone, somewhere, was screaming.

"Do you hear someone screaming?" he asked, but both brothers ignored him.

"He's twenty, little brother," said Jarek. Lukasz noticed that Jarek was just as drunk as he was.

Strange, he thought. Usually, Jarek didn't drink at all.

"C'mon," Jarek muttered. "Let him have some fun."

At that moment, the youngest of the Wolf-Lords was violently sick in the mineshaft.

"The—king—is—here—" growled Franciszek.

"I saw," said Jarek with unexpected venom. "Tell me, did he ask you to read for him?" He ruffled Franciszek's hair. "Such a lovely party trick. I say we take bets. We'll make a killing; that lot out there is sure to bet against you—"

"Shut up," hissed Franciszek. "You just have to ruin everything, don't you? We're being honored tonight, you ungrateful—"

Jarek's voice was deadly calm. Lukasz had finished being sick and was now sprawled on the cavern floor, moaning.

"Finish that thought, little brother," said Jarek. "I dare you."

For a moment, the pair of them stood silently in the dark vault. In their sparkling black uniforms, clean-shaven and not covered in soot and blood for once, they almost looked like Wrony.

When Franciszek didn't answer, Jarek's mouth stayed flat and cold.

"I didn't think so," he said, without an ounce of triumph.

He straightened up with Lukasz half draped over his shoulders. Jarek fit in with the Miasto citizens. He'd always been the best pretender. But neither gold spectacles nor books could hide the dogged look in Franciszek's eyes, the way his mouth hung crookedly, like Lukasz's did. If anything, the effort Franciszek took to fit in had made him stand out even more.

"Just take him back to the hotel," said Franciszek at last.

"You even talk like one of them now," Jarek said, smirking. "No accent."

Mock applause from Jarek. Lukasz tried to join in, only succeeded in slapping his own face. Franciszek's gaze was flat. Sober. Cold.

"Just go."

And they did. And although Lukasz did not remember how or

when it had happened, Jarek had somehow gotten him back to the hotel, because he woke up there the next morning. The front page of the newspaper had a picture of the exhibition. The three brothers flanked the tiny Damian Bieleć, four glasses raised, four smiles. Two of the brothers had crooked front teeth.

They looked happy. Looking at those three, thought Lukasz, no one would have ever guessed they were pretending.

But by then, Jarek, who had always pretended not to care, was long gone.

❧ 36 ❧

REN AND LUKASZ TWISTED AROUND at the same time.

It took her eyes—human eyes—a moment to adjust to the darkness beyond the arches of the hall. The human vision didn't bother her, like it would have once upon a time. She wondered if that was weakness, and if it was, she wondered why she didn't care.

But then her eyesight sharpened, slowly and with some squinting, as human eyes sometimes require, and a girl moved into the blue starlight. Ren sensed—almost felt—Lukasz stand a little straighter. The girl wore a dress almost exactly like the one Ren had left behind in the hallway, with green embroidery and ribbons in her braids, all white and lace and long black hair. She held a violin in one hand and a bow in the other.

A film of dust grayed the long black hair. Gauzy threads trailed from delicate eyelashes, whispered across the bow of her mouth. Ren let her eyes slip into their familiar feline acuity, and she realized, with a sharp jolt of fear, that the girl was covered in cobwebs.

She stepped back, stiffly, into Lukasz.

His hand closed on her shoulder.

"It's okay," he murmured as his lips brushed her ear and sent a second, very different jolt though her. "Look."

And Ren, unsure whether she used her lynx eyes or her human ones, noticed the dark horns uncurling from her hair and the fluffy tail swishing across the floor behind her.

At the same time, it dawned on her who had led her to the glass sword: a domowik.

The girl smiled. Then she put the bow to the violin, and she played.

The melody was soft. The instrument was out of tune. But all the same, the notes sailed through the empty room and hung in the air. Deep. Confident. A melody of such shape and such magic that Ren knew it was one she would never forget: not in a year, not in a hundred years, not if the Golden Dragon bore down on them now and burned these halls down around them.

The girl approached. Her heels echoed on the hardwood. She came close, the somber melody filling up every inch of the room, and even though she passed mere inches from Ren's face, Ren realized the girl had no scent, beyond the resin of the strings. No sound, beyond the song. No life, beyond the dark, unmisted light burning in those sharp blue eyes.

"I think," said Lukasz, in a gravelly voice that brought the world— for the barest moment—back into focus, "she wants us to dance."

"I can't dance," whispered Ren, slowly revolving to watch the girl move past.

Her turn brought her very close to Lukasz. Close enough to know that he smelled like horse and blood and a dozen varieties and intensities of smoke. Close enough to know the quiet rasp in the back of his throat when he tried to hold back a cough. Close enough to know that there was nothing hazy, nothing deathly, nothing cobwebbed or misty about him: he was hard angles and bright colors and flashing lights and *Why*, she realized, *he is the last man alive in this world.*

"Yeah," he said. "But I can."

"Since when?"

"Since I was fifteen." He grinned, slipping a hand around her waist. "I'll tell you about it sometime."

And Ren knew, with a tiny, worried feeling, that she would like that. It also scared her that there might not be a next time. That when this was over, if they both survived, he'd disappear to Miasto. He'd be with Franciszek or he'd be alone, but he wouldn't stay here. And she'd fade back to her forest, and it would be like they'd never met.

But she would always know. She would remember. . . .

Without quite realizing what she was doing, Ren took his burned hand in hers. The leathered skin felt strange and foreign against hers. She wondered if he could feel anything at all through that scarring. Then she put a hand on his shoulder, and he flinched.

They were close enough that his messy hair brushed her cheek when she leaned forward.

"You're falling apart," she whispered.

His lip twitched. He leaned down and whispered by her ear: "It's part of my charm."

Their first steps were unsteady. Lukasz seemed to know the way, but Ren felt awkward rather than confident. This was different than running or pouncing. She had been built for battle and trained in war; she had no understanding of things like music and careful steps and keeping time with another person depending on her.

The domowik's song echoed around them. The creature drifted with them, slowing the tune when Ren stumbled. But when she got the steps right, the creature smiled a ghostly, hollow kind of smile. The song became thin, only a few notes, as Ren managed to follow Lukasz's scuffed boots across the floor.

The melody returned. Powerful and confident, and somehow no longer out of tune. It found Ren, and caught her, and held her—like the thrill of a chase, the power of an attack. Ren felt it. Her steps were surer. She knew where Lukasz stepped before he even moved. Around them, the music swelled and doubled in volume.

For the first time, she looked up from her feet. A second domowik appeared on the other side of the hall, smiling at the two of them. Like the first, she had long black hair and white clothes, and she, too, had a violin. Her strings answered the first domowik's notes, and circling one another, they played back and forth across the expanse. Music surrounded them.

She could hardly believe it. Lukasz sped up, and she followed easily. They whirled across the hardwood, dust billowing under their feet and eddying under the stars. As they spun, Ren caught glimpses of more domowiki: they emerged from the doorways with instruments, they crept out of corners, and one soot-faced creature even clambered headfirst out of the fireplace.

The song swelled around them, and the hall exploded to life.

A thousand unlit candles burst into flame at the same time. Fifty domowiki couples came spinning out of doorways, all in white, catching Ren and Lukasz as they twirled across the floor. Flowered skirts flickered against white trousers, black boots tapped the floor, and near-human hands clapped in time. The fire roared. The crest over the mantel glittered. Music enveloped them. They never missed a note.

Above, the chandelier blazed like a sun in the night sky.

Ren and Lukasz were covered in blood and dirt. Their clothes were torn. They were the only black coats in a sea of white. But Lukasz was grinning like a devil, and suddenly, the waxiness was gone. Perhaps it was pure magic; perhaps it was the music. Ren didn't know how and she didn't care why, but she danced as she had never danced before, and she knew she would never dance again. It was as if the two of them had raced backward twenty years and nothing evil had ever happened in these Mountains.

Beyond them, the domowiki danced the traditional dances of Hala Smoków. The skirts spun out and the white jackets danced on their owners' shoulders. Hands clapped, feet tapped, and over it all, the two violins sang to them. But Ren was blind to anything beyond him, smiling at her. For under those silver bones, among those forgotten heartbeats, beneath that bewitching spell, even then, Ren felt like they were the only people left alive.

And in that moment, in that place: they were.

✣ 37 ✣

THE FOREST WAS MOVING.

Half blind, Koszmar crawled, searching for his saber. He would not die. He would not die. Not like this. Not out here. His hand found the hilt, and he staggered to his feet. The trees, still smoking, shifted in his vision. Golden flames licked lazily at the earth. Twisted, melted corpses stretched in every direction, and the air was filled with a low mewling sound. It was angry, whining.

Koszmar almost collapsed. Everything hurt. But he was going to live. *I am going to live.*

The movement took shape. Elbows and knees. Bald heads and long scaly arms. Hanks of gray fur. They broke from the shadows of trees, crawled out from beneath the branches. And then from the pit they came, swarming up, up, up from the bottom of the world, climbing like ants upon each other's backs, breaking the surface.

Yellow eyes. Needle-sharp fangs. Hungry.

Hungry.

Strzygi.

❧ 38 ❧

REN AND LUKASZ DANCED UNTIL the hall grew empty and the night wore on, the domowiki vanishing once more to their shadows and thresholds. Ren didn't notice. The unseen music played on and she couldn't look away from him. They danced until the chandelier dimmed and the sky glowed pink overhead, until Ren finally tripped, until Lukasz tried to catch her. He fell, too. They were on the hardwood. Laughing, gasping. A mess of swords and black jackets and dust.

"I'm sorry," she said, laughing.

He still had his burned hand on her shoulder, and she reached up to hold it. The skin felt thick under her fingertips, like dry leather and sinew.

Lukasz pulled his hand back.

"Sorry," he stammered. "It's ugly—"

Ren pushed back her sleeves and held up her own hands. Her fingernails lengthened. Tawny fur raced up her forearms and shuddered to a stop under the sleeves of the jacket.

"It's who we are," she said.

His smile faltered. Ren moved her gaze to the dust, swirling gently back to earth around them. He ran his disfigured hand up her arm absently, and she couldn't tell whether he was looking at her or at his scar.

Ren reached up and touched his serious brow, then let her hand, human once more, trail down his rough cheek and neck to rest on his shoulder. He flinched as she strayed over the wounds of the mavka, but when she tried to pull away, he reached up and closed his own scarred hand over hers.

"Why do you want me to kill the Dragon?" she asked.

His expression changed. In a split second, it became unreadable and hard. He got to his feet.

"The sun is up," he said. "We should go."

Ren followed. She was inexplicably embarrassed. She folded her arms.

"Where?" she asked. "Did you find the way to the Mountain?"

He backed away, avoiding her eye.

"If we go now," he said, "we'll make it by nightfall."

Ren's hand closed on the hilt of the glass sword. Seventeen years of horror. Seventeen years of hiding in a dark castle, running from golden flames, fighting a war that seemed unwinnable.

Seventeen years, and they could end it today.

❧ 39 ❧

LUKASZ AND REN PASSED UNDER the wooden gate, its dragon skull swaying gently in the breeze. For seventeen years, it had swayed exactly like this, over an empty town. Any—or all—or none—of his brothers might have come here. In another world, he might even have lived here.

Not that it mattered anymore. Not that any of it mattered.

He was getting sicker. For the first time, he couldn't climb on Król's back alone, and the big horse knelt down to help him get astride. Ren watched without speaking. He had never seen her look so unguarded. Her slyness was gone, and he could read her so easily now. Everything seemed written so clearly in those sharp green eyes and that perfect, thin curve of her mouth—

In that other life, he realized, he would not have met her.

They started up the new path, with new mountains surrounding them and Król easily finding his way through the foothills. Behind them, Hala Smoków was empty, except for the occasional snowdrift that swirled in on the silent wind, dusted the hollow streets, and disappeared again.

Up in the lodge, the halls would still be warm. It would have been good to die in those halls. It would not have been lonely, to lie down among the ghosts, domowiki watching from the rafters. To leave the only body in that hollow town. Something at least substantial, more than those poor domowiki, so fragile that one day a sharp blast of wind might come down and obliterate them for good.

They trekked upward for most of the day. Król was tireless, but Lukasz was not. He tried not to speak, only telling Ren where to direct Król when a fork arose in the path. The Mountains watched them. Lukasz could feel them. They were as alive, as watchful, as her forest. They were like a living thing. Waiting for nightfall.

He would have liked to die in Hala Smoków.

We shall be buried in the shadow of the Mountains, Tadeusz had once told him. *Beneath the blessings of wolves.*

In that other life, he would have died there. He would have walked those warm hallways in dragon fur and leather, arguing with his brothers, fighting with his father. He would have learned to chart the Mountains properly. He would have learned to read. The Wolf-Lords would have lived on for a thousand more years, oblivious to what the world thought of them.

He would not have met her.

No one outside of these Mountains would have known his name. No whispers. No rumors. His knee wouldn't hurt all the damn time. He wouldn't be as good with a rifle. His picture would never have appeared in a Miasto newspaper, the Saint Magdalena Faustian would still be devouring milkmaids, Michał and Eliasz would still be handsome, and the rest of them would still be alive—

And he would not have met her.

"I can smell smoke," said Ren suddenly. "There is someone here."

I know, he thought, but he suddenly felt too tired to answer aloud.

They had reached a meadowed valley, squarely between two mountains. There was no snow here. Instead, purple flowers carpeted the grass, and the air was filled with the smell of baking bread. In the distance, a log cabin seemed to await them. Smoke curled from its chimney, washing fluttered in the wind, and the sound of barking dogs echoed faintly in the valley.

Ren slipped easily off Król's back. She put a hand on Lukasz's knee and looked from him to the cabin. Lukasz had never seen her look like that. He loved her. It was one of the last times he would look at her, and he loved her.

"Don't get off," she was saying. "If you fall, I can't get you back up there."

It was the first time either of them had admitted how sick he was. He wondered if she was afraid. He used to be afraid, but now he was just tired. The meadow began to blur at the edges. She stayed at the center.

I love you, he thought.

Ren started to lead Król down the hill. The grass was waist high, without a path. As if by magic, the purple flowers floated out of their way. As they neared the cabin, he could make out a quaint little fence surrounding it.

This was how it would end. It had been worth it. He had met her.

The cabin blurred. The ground lurched. For a moment, Lukasz

thought it was a tide, and suddenly he hit the ground. Pain exploded through his shoulder.

"Lukasz!" Strong hands grabbed at him. "Lukasz, please! Get up—we're almost there—"

He realized he had fallen off Król. Strange, he thought, while the grass danced and Ren's face faded in and out of focus above him. Strange, he didn't remember falling. . . .

"Lukasz," she shrieked, "*please!*"

That got him, and he struggled up. He felt Ren drag his arm over her shoulders. He was warm. As warm as he'd been at Hala Smoków. Things were dimmer. He stumbled again. He wished he could help her.

He could hear Ren panting as she half carried him, half dragged him toward the cabin.

"We're close, Lukasz," she said. "We can rest here, before we go on. It's a cabin. It has two windows and a thatched roof. It looks warm, Lukasz. It's getting windy—Oh, there's even a little fence, Lukasz. And dogs. Do you hear the dogs? We're almost at the gate—"

Ren gasped. She let go of him, and Lukasz hit the ground.

She grabbed his collar. He groaned as his head lolled back, and her voice came out gravelly, close to his face.

"*Where are we?*"

Lukasz forced himself to open his eyes.

"She'll help you," he said hoarsely.

They were in the right spot. They *had* to be in the right spot. The domowik had told him—

Lukasz blinked, tried to orient himself. His surroundings were momentarily clear, lines shimmering out of darkness, and he caught a glimpse of the fence, twenty feet away.

"You said we were going to the Mountain!" She was practically shouting, shaking him.

"No," he said. "I said we would be *here* by nightfall."

He could see why Ren hadn't been afraid of the fence from far away. Even this close, even knowing what he knew, it took him a moment to believe what he was seeing. The fence was made of bones. They were stained red and lashed together with tendons. Crows battered against them, sharp beaks tearing at the remaining flesh. Each post was topped with a human skull. They were crushed in at the back, red candles burning amid broken bone.

"What?" she breathed. "You lied? Where are we?"

She was beautiful. From the slanted green eyes right down to the broken nails at the ends of her dirty hands. She was beautiful.

"I promised," he managed. "I promised to get you to that Mountain."

"This isn't the Mountain!"

"She'll help you."

In another life, she could have been his. In another life, he would not have met her.

"You—you should have told me." It took him a moment—a precious moment—to realize she was trying not to cry. "We could have found a way. We could have fixed this."

Her hands were on his face, sliding down his jaw. *She knows now,* he thought. The hands stayed on his face, running over every line, like she was going to memorize him if it killed her. *She knows what is going to happen.*

"We shook hands," he said, then stopped to catch his breath. He had never seen eyes so dark and sad. "We said no games."

"Lukasz."

A blast of wind lashed across the field. It was so strong that it tore the words from his throat, tore up the grass around them. Ren ducked over him, and several bones tore free of the horrible fence. Dandelions and purple blossoms spun past. The crows scattered overhead. They hit the cabin with dull thuds, and feathers rained down on them.

Then it stopped.

Everything went still.

The wind died, the crows cawed overhead. The gruesome cabin loomed over them. Somewhere above him, Ren was panting.

Then came a sound like someone ripping up an enormous weed. The earth shivered beneath them. Shadows rearranged in the sky. It took him a moment to realize: *the cabin was moving.*

Lukasz turned his head, just enough to make out a blurry outline. The cabin began to rock back and forth.

It lurched violently, and a single, scaly foot poked out from underneath. He heard Ren gasp. The foot clawed at the ground with three gigantic talons. The house heaved once more, sailed into the air, where it blocked out most of the sky. What was left of the sky was purple behind it, lit by a glowing moon and filled with swooping crows.

Too tired to be scared, Lukasz watched the cabin bend over them, peering down with murky, spotted windows.

"The last of the Wolf-Lords," said a voice somewhere above him. "What an unexpected pleasure."

❧ 40 ❧

LET HIM LIVE, REN PRAYED.

She straightened. Lukasz half lay on the ground, moaning. His eyes had sunk back and his gray skin gleamed with sweat. His hands curled above his chest, black with blood.

Let him live. Please.

Reluctant to take her eyes off him, Ren turned around. The cabin watched them, tilted slightly to the side on its leg, like a gigantic, inquisitive magpie.

Ren towered over the old woman. Loosened skin bagged over every pointy bone in her face. Her chin protruded and her nose drooped, and it was long and crooked and covered from bridge to tip with sores and warts and other things Ren didn't want to think about.

Ren could hardly believe it had come to this. Stranded in the Mountains with Lukasz dying beside her, facing—

"Hello, Baba Jaga," she said.

The Baba Jaga wore beautiful clothes: a black-and-red-striped skirt, a heavily embroidered black vest, and a soft white blouse sweetly gathered at her puckered neck. What little hair she had left was covered by an embroidered black kerchief.

"Who are you, little girl?" asked the Baba Jaga.

"My name is Ren," said Ren.

The Baba Jaga emitted a guttural laugh. She had a basket under one arm, filled with what looked horribly like slabs of meat. Her arms were bloodred to the elbows.

"I did not ask your name," she said. "I asked who you are."

Anger flared dully in Ren. Ryś was dead. Lukasz was dying. Her forest, his town, these Mountains—it all lay crushed under black claws, and this woman *dared* ask who she was? Dared mock her?

Ren's fury burned. But when she spoke, her voice was quiet.

"I was born in a place where the sun never set and the monsters stayed out of sight," she said. "Where the birds sang and the walls were whole. Then came the Dragon, and the flowers died and the branches closed overhead and I became queen of the woods."

The Baba Jaga smiled. Her teeth were abnormally long and blunt, yellow covered with red-brown stains. The chicken cabin tilted to the other side, and even though Ren didn't dare take her eyes off the Baba Jaga, she could have sworn the windows *blinked*.

"Bold words from a small queen," murmured the Baba Jaga at last. "Especially as I hold your lives in my hands."

"Not for long," offered up Lukasz from the grass.

The old woman grinned down at him. He was still lying in the grass, his hand clasped over his wounded shoulder. She took in the blood smeared over his skin. The sweat on his cheekbones, the damp hair across his forehead. The longer she looked, the hungrier her expression became.

"You smell like death," she said, as if relishing the idea.

"Why does everyone keep saying that?" he muttered under his breath.

Ren stared from Lukasz to the Baba Jaga.

"Mavka, was it?" asked the Baba Jaga. "You're Wrony. You should have known better—"

"Not like I did this on purpose."

Black blood dripped from between his fingers.

"And yet," said the Baba Jaga, "you came *here* on purpose."

"The domowik from Hala Smoków said you would help."

Ren blinked. She hadn't heard any domowik say that.

"I would never help a mere human," said the Baba Jaga. "Especially not some pretty, arrogant man who thinks he can kiss rusalki and mavka and walk away. You have charmed one monster too many, Lukasz Smoków. I will not help you."

"I didn't kiss any mavka," he said, struggling to sit upright. He held his shoulder so tightly that his knuckles had gone white. "And this isn't asking for help. This is offering to trade."

He coughed again. Blood, thick and black, trickled down his chin.

A shiny tongue protruded from the Baba Jaga's mouth and ran around the edge of her lips.

"NO!" shouted Ren, suddenly realizing what he meant to do. She stepped between them, kneeling in front of Lukasz. "No! You can't do this—"

She took his face in her hands and shook him. She wasn't even upset. She was just angry.

"You promised to take me to that Mountain! You *promised* to kill the Dragon!"

Lukasz shook his head.

"I can't, Ren," he said. "Not like this. But you . . ."

The sky began to darken. Ren smelled the old blood in the Baba Jaga's basket and tasted the fear in the back of her throat.

"What about Franciszek?" she snarled. "He could still be alive. You can't give up on him—not like this—"

"He's dead, Ren," said Lukasz bluntly. "They're all dead."

She didn't want him to die.

She felt the sword at her side, and she realized abruptly why he had insisted that she take it.

"I have the sword," she said suddenly. Inspiration struck, and she repeated it louder. "I have the glass sword."

"Ren!"

With surprising speed, Lukasz lurched to his feet. At the same time, the Baba Jaga's wrinkles rearranged themselves into an expression that could be loosely described as speculative.

Ren drew the sword. Lukasz groaned. Silver blue lit up the twilight. The chicken cabin leaned over their shoulders for a closer look.

"The sword for his life," said Ren. "You could kill the Dragon. Take back these Mountains as your own. And the forest, if you want it."

In the glow, the Baba Jaga's eyes grew in her face and became as livid as coals, and all sounds receded except for Lukasz's ragged breathing. Like a moth to flame, the Baba Jaga inched forward. But instead of taking the sword, the Baba Jaga reached out a long, gnarled finger and traced it down Ren's cheek.

"You would give up your forest?" she asked. "For a *man*?"

"My forest can live a little longer," said Ren. "He can't."

The old woman cackled again.

She turned away without answering. As she did, the candles on the fence posts came to life. Flames leapt high in the air. A rivulet of wax slipped, with agonizing slowness, from the empty eye socket of the closest skull.

"Come inside," said the Baba Jaga.

The chicken leg slowly bent, lowering the cabin back to earth. The wind picked up, formed itself into the shape of hounds. Their jowls flapped and long strings of saliva hung from their fangs, and they barked happily at the Baba Jaga. When Ren reached out to touch a hound, her hand passed through gray-black smoke. Only their jaws appeared solid—yellow fangs in pink gums, snapping and slavering in midair.

Ren took one of Lukasz's arms over her shoulders. He was burning hot with fever.

"I can't believe you offered to let her keep the sword," he muttered.

"I can't believe you offered to let her *eat* you," retorted Ren.

The Baba Jaga produced a yellow key from her cloak, and the lock stretched into a toothy mouth. Ren took a step back. The mouth closed on the key and chewed until the door swung open. Ren knew it was too late to run.

An iron stove took up the entirety of one corner, with an open door and a blazing fire within. Next to it stood a huge wooden table, where a pair of bodiless hands feverishly chopped a mountain of vegetables. A second pair scooped them up and tossed them in a pot. A laundry basket floated by, held up by more disembodied hands. They set the basket down on the kitchen table and began adding to the dozens of clotheslines swaying in the breeze from outside.

Ren wasn't really sure what she had expected. Not this.

"Bring him here," commanded the Baba Jaga, shooing a set of snapping jaws off a giant bed, which took up a whole wall.

Lukasz collapsed. He looked half dead already.

Please let him live.

"What can we do?" Ren hung anxiously over the Baba Jaga's shoulder. "We have to do something—"

A cough cut her off, and blackish blood trickled from the corner of his mouth. His teeth were smeared with it.

Ren twisted a strand of hair between her fingertips, while the Baba Jaga bustled around the other side of the table to the stove.

"Please, Lukasz," she whispered, settling next to him. "Please don't die—"

She took his hand in hers. It was the burned one, with its missing fingertips and scar, and Ren realized that it was one of her favorite things about him. It all felt so surreal. She half believed she might wake up and it would all be all right. They'd still be back at Hala Smoków.

Please let him live.

She leaned down and kissed his cheek. His stubble was rough on her lips. His lashes flickered with the effort of keeping his eyes open.

The Baba Jaga returned with a tea tray, which she set on the nightstand. On it sat a single teacup filled with amber liquid. Ren stared. The Baba Jaga spoke.

"He must drink."

Lukasz managed to get up on one elbow, and Ren helped him lift the teacup. He choked and swore. Then he lay back and coughed and twitched some more.

"Cider," explained the Baba Jaga over her shoulder as she stumped back to the kitchen. "Now we wait."

The bodiless hands fastened an apron around the old woman's waist. Brandishing a meat cleaver the size of a badger, she called out to Ren:

"Come, little one, and eat."

The cleaver lowered to the kitchen table, hacking at some doomed onions.

Ren had to duck under the clotheslines to reach the kitchen. The laundry was in all shapes and sizes.

The Baba Jaga set a bowl of steaming stew on the table before her. Then she cut Ren a generous piece of bread and slathered it with butter. Ren glanced back at the clotheslines, wondering why the Baba Jaga could possibly need so many outfits.

Realization dawned at almost the exact same time that the Baba Jaga spoke: "I made stew."

She had killed—had she *eaten*—?

"It's only vegetables," she cackled, looking at Ren's expression and the untouched bowl. "I know you have sensitive tastes."

Ren was starving. She started with the bread, just as soft and perfect as the bread from the Leszy's table. The Baba Jaga cut a second piece, and Ren devoured that, too. The stew was delicious. It reminded her of the forest. When Lukasz and Jakub had made hunter's stew of nocnica, and Felka had chased Koszmar around the fire, and when Ren hadn't trusted them and the woods hadn't seemed so dark.

She put down the spoon, feeling tears in her eyes.

Poor Koszmar, she thought. Poor Koszmar, who had been so mean and so unhappy and still, somehow, had shot himself so that they could live.

"Will he be all right?" she asked.

The Baba Jaga raised her eyebrows. Actually, as she did not have any eyebrows left, she raised the mottled skin above her eyes. The effect was rather gross.

"We are two queens alone in the world and meeting for the first time," said the Baba Jaga. "Let us speak of something other than men."

"It's not like that—" Ren started hotly.

"These humans," said the Baba Jaga, ignoring her. "These humans are all the same. So desperate to live. So desperate to make deals. *Help me survive,* they ask. *Help me get to the Mountain,* they say. *Save my beloved,* they beg. So desperate for mercy, these humans."

The Baba Jaga paused.

"Do you know what I do?" she asked.

Ren glanced toward the clothes.

"You . . . eat them?" Ren hazarded.

The Baba Jaga chuckled and cut her another piece of bread.

"I eat them," she confirmed.

"But you didn't eat us," said Ren.

"Because you, my dearest, are not human at all."

"I know."

She didn't act like one. She didn't feel like one.

Maybe it was the humans' fault, for forcing her into the creature she had become. For keeping their doorsteps dark, for throwing rocks. They'd called her a monster, they'd blamed every human death in that forest on her. They'd feared her so much they'd made her a legend—and they'd almost made her believe it. Maybe it was the humans' fault, and they'd made her what she was: all broken nails and sharp tongue.

Or maybe, thought Ren, it was the monsters' fault, for cutting her off, fencing her in. Forcing her to fight for that forest, day in and day out. Or maybe, she thought suddenly, it was the king and queen's fault, for leaving her alone in the world.

Or maybe it was just her fault.

She'd attacked Jakub. She'd failed Ryś. Koszmar was dead. In her absence, the strzygi had closed in on the village, and she'd almost ignored it, in this obsession with the Dragon. The whole damn forest was going up in flames, and all she'd done was make it burn faster. It was her fault. It fell on her shoulders. And hers alone.

Her voice came out clipped, broken up with emotion.

"I have been a bad queen," she said.

When she raised her gaze, she thought she saw pity in the Baba Jaga's eyes.

"You have fought monsters for seventeen years," said the old woman.

Ren shook her head. She was aware of the bodiless hands tending to the washing, of Lukasz's shape on the bed. She was aware of guilt. Pouring through every vein, burning hot and bright.

"I have failed," said Ren.

"We have all failed," said the Baba Jaga. "They are too numerous. Do you really think they've confined themselves to your queendom? They are running amok, and you are the only one to have stood in their way. What have the humans done? They have hidden themselves. They have given up. In the cities, they have thrown up their hands. Oh, they write articles and they write books and they even occasionally discuss it in their parliaments. But they've sealed off this place. Called it *forgotten*, but only because they have chosen to forget it. While the humans of this world have hidden, and you have fought."

Perhaps she was right, thought Ren. It was certainly easier to accept. To think of the humans as complacent, enamored of denial. To say they drew lines in the sand, these humans, and never stepped beyond them. She remembered what Lukasz had said: *I don't think you're an animal.* Then: *I don't think you're a monster.*

And I never did.

He hadn't called her animal. Monster. Even human. He hadn't drawn lines for her, and he'd never asked her to stay within them.

"You and I must help each other," said the Baba Jaga into the silence. She pushed some stringy hair back under her cap. "We are the same. Neither quite human nor quite monster. Powerful beyond all reason."

Ren felt a flash of familiarity. Another in the wilderness;

another alone with dark things.

Someone who, unlike her, had never known a Lukasz.

"*They* call us monsters," said Ren.

Ren remembered what Jakub had said about predilections to evil. She remembered the mobs of strzygi, all once human, all thronging together on the hunt. How they died was not so very different, she realized, from how they had lived. So fragile, so changeable. So easily influenced. *Monster.* How quick the villagers were to attack. *You killed them.* How quick they were to judge. They saw Ren, they saw the Baba Jaga, and then they threw back their heads and howled *monster* to the moon.

Ren had once said that of her monsters, she feared the ones who had been human most of all. She'd always assumed it was because she secretly feared a fate like theirs. Now a new thought occurred. Perhaps they had not transformed after all. Just realized what had always been in their souls.

"Of all the monsters to have set foot in your forest," said the Baba Jaga, "by far the most evil has been man."

And then the words came back to Ren, from another lifetime.

"My brother said that," she said sharply. "Where did you hear that?"

The Baba Jaga smiled a bone-chilling smile.

"My home is more than Mountains, Little Queen," she said.

Ren was quiet for a moment. Ryś had said that days ago, fighting strzygi on the outskirts of the village. Before any of this. Before they'd really known their humans. Jakub, who—despite everything—had turned out to be one of the kindest, gentlest souls Ren had ever known. Felka, so sharp and smart and quick to love. Koszmar, at once desperately unlikable and so desperate to be liked; Koszmar whom they had all disliked, whom none of them had wanted; Koszmar, who in the end had given up everything for them.

Poor, dear Koszmar, she thought.

Perhaps he'd been the best of them.

"You're wrong," said Ren suddenly.

The Baba Jaga gave her a piercing gaze.

"You're wrong," she repeated. "I mean, you're right. It's true. They are selfish. When they want something, they don't care who they hurt."

She thought of Jakub, so obsessed with his research that he didn't care who he hurt. She thought of Lukasz, kidnapping her for his brother.

"But the humans," continued Ren, and the Baba Jaga's expression turned piercing. "I like them. Perhaps they can be cruel, but they can also be kind. I think of Jak—of one of my friends. He respected my forest; he loved it. He never wanted to hurt it—only understand it."

Jakub had ventured out into the forest to *save* her. Patiently, kindly, he had shared his knowledge with her. He had grieved for Ryś with the same sorrow as his daughter. He had given up the only things he cared for: his daughter, to save them from the mavka; his dream of the Mountains, to go back to the village that feared him.

Ren thought of Felka, who had welcomed her from the moment she had set foot in the village. Felka had never called her a monster, she had brought back her clothes, she had been sharp and funny and loyal and good.

Of Koszmar, who had died to save them.

Of Lukasz, who had given up everything—his family, his legacy, his life . . . everything, for her.

"The monsters of our world," began Ren slowly, "like rusalki and strzygi—they choose the side of hell, and they never change. But these humans—" Ren thought of her friends. Her perfect, terrible friends. "These humans commit terrible evils and they beg forgiveness. They have such a capacity to change, Baba Jaga . . . and I think that is their real magic. They hold such darkness, these humans, but they still choose the light. Of all the things I love about them, I love this best."

The Baba Jaga's expression had changed. She watched Ren with softening eyes. The hands had paused in the background.

"Sometimes," said Ren quietly, "I think they are the last lights burning in this world."

⚔ 41 ⚔

THE STRZYGI CIRCLED. STRINGS OF saliva hung from their mouths.

Koszmar had fought monsters before. He had walked away from family, from honor, from fortune. He had battled dark things in dark places. And he could win.

He almost did.

But his arm trembled. He hurt. He hesitated. The first strzygoń leapt, and without his eye, Koszmar misjudged the distance. It sank its teeth into his arm, and he howled. Too quickly, he went down. Beneath him, the earth seemed to buckle. He hacked at the strzygoń until it fell away. He was on his back. The trees leaned down to watch.

Doggedly, Koszmar got back on his feet. The strzygi snarled.

They snapped around his ankles, and the saber was too heavy. He dropped it, clawed at them with his bare hands. They leapt on his back, tore at his hair, at his shoulders. Koszmar screamed. He searched for his saber. His mind was a mess. He could not think clearly. His arm, he realized slowly, had disappeared under the seething gray bodies. *He* was disappearing.

Koszmar wanted to live. They dragged him down. He wanted to live. They bit down. He'd give anything to live. They tore in. He'd give anything.

Please.

Blood poured out.

Please let me live.

❧ FRANCISZEK ❧

TWO MONTHS EARLIER

FRANCISZEK AND LUKASZ SAT ON the stone sarcophagus, watching the sun rise and sharing a bottle of vodka.

"An Apofys," said Franciszek. He put down the newspaper and poured himself another glass. "I've never heard of one of those before."

Dawn broke gently across the spires of King Nikodem's castle, where just five years before, the Brygada Smoka had been born. They sat in the cemetery, still under the shadow of the Miasto Basilica, while overhead, the city's clay and copper roofs blazed red-gold.

"Apparently it got into the taxidermy collection," Lukasz said.

Having watched Raf tumble down that particular slippery slope, Lukasz didn't drink in the morning. But Franciszek had been at the library all night, and he had spent the evening betting on the boxing rings, so technically speaking, Lukasz considered this the day's end.

"So?"

Franciszek was looking at him, waiting for an answer.

"Now it has a belly full of sawdust," said Lukasz casually. He poured himself a drink. "Should make a unique challenge."

He waited for his brother to take the bait. Mysterious dragon breed and extra danger? Franciszek should have loved planning that one out.

Franciszek only nodded. Sunlight glinted off his gold glasses. But all he said was "How astute."

Lukasz didn't respond. A few morning drunks passed the cemetery gates, caught sight of the antlered horses. They crowded to the iron, pointing and shouting. Lukasz saluted. Franciszek watched him thoughtfully.

"So," said Lukasz, turning back to his brother, "about this Apofys."

Franciszek's lip twitched. Everyone had always compared Lukasz with Rafał, but he and Franciszek had the exact same, slightly crooked mouth. In fact, if Franciszek had taken off his glasses and grown half a foot, they might have passed for twins.

"You know," said Franciszek, as if he didn't hear, "you're too smart for this job."

Lukasz laughed.

"Yeah right."

The fireflies were still out. They rose gently from the blue-green dew, flickering among the dull headstones. They came slowly at first, one or two whispers of light in the long wet grass. Then they came faster, nearly rising out of the earth, winking and blinking like little candle flames, a thousand glittering ghost lights in the dark green.

"Dad loved them," said Franciszek suddenly. "Do you remember?"

"No."

But Lukasz was lying.

He did remember. Maybe even better than Franciszek did. His mother, leaning against the washbasins in the vast kitchens of Hala Smoków, because she had been born a commoner and she'd never really gotten the knack of aristocracy. Her black hair, shining red in the lights of the fires. Chatting with the servants, affectionately cursing the kikimora behind the stove.

His father, stamping through the kitchen doors, tossing aside his sword and shaking the dragon soot out of his black hair. The door swinging on its hinges, the wolves howling beyond, the long winding roads of Hala Smoków peppered with the lights from its houses.

"Close the door," his mother had said, shooing Tadeusz away with a rag. "You'll let the bugs in, and then we'll never sleep—"

"Let them come!" his father had yelled, seizing his mother by the waist and spinning her around the kitchen.

"They'll keep us up, Tad!"

She would fall into his arms.

"You can never have too much light!"

And then the two of them would waltz across the stone floors, fireflies drifting like a thousand candle flames. Lukasz had been, in those moments, perfectly happy.

Now he lit a cigarette in the cool damp.

"You know what our problem is?" asked Lukasz.

Franciszek smiled wryly.

"Surely not the vodka."

"No," agreed Lukasz. "Definitely not the vodka."

For a moment, he lost his train of thought. Then it came back, fragile as the mist lifting off the headstones.

"Our problem is," he said, with great effort. He fished in his pockets for his lighter. "Is that we always go on about dragons, and wolves, and living in the Mountains for a thousand years. They assume we're ancient and outdated because that's how we act."

A shadow passed over Franciszek's face, but he produced a small gold lighter and handed it to Lukasz.

"We tried to belong," he said in a hollow voice.

Lukasz cupped the lighter around the cigarette.

"We didn't try very hard," he said.

"Maybe they wouldn't let us."

"Maybe we were making excuses."

When he tried to give the lighter back, Franciszek negated the gesture with a small shake of his head.

"Your need is greater than mine," he said, smiling.

The older and the younger. One who still remembered those blue hills and who knew what it felt like to belong. The other, who barely remembered and who, until this second, had never cared.

"I'm sorry, Lukasz," said Franciszek, after a moment. "I have always been hard on you. You were my favorite—maybe that's why I was so protective of you." He smiled sadly. "Even if I know you don't like me much."

"I like you!" Lukasz protested. "You're my brother, for God's sake."

Franciszek smiled, without anger.

"But I'm not your favorite."

"That's not true," protested Lukasz, but it sounded weak even to him.

He loved Franciszek—he really did—but his brother had always been so serious. Berating him for the tattoo he'd gotten after Rafał left. Constantly drilling lessons into him: reading and table manners and dancing and how to be polite to the fine ladies and gentlemen on the street.

You won't be hunting dragons forever, Franciszek would always say. *You need to know how to do something else.*

Lukasz had ignored him. He'd avoided him and tagged along with the twins or gone hunting with Eryk.

"It's all right," said Franciszek. "I understand."

Franciszek was the best of them all: not brutal like the twins, not perfectly heroic like Anzelm. Just unfailingly honest, and good, and kind. Lukasz wondered what they had done to deserve a brother like Franciszek.

"No," said Lukasz. "No, Fraszko. I love you. You're my brother. Let's just—let's get this Apofys, and then—"

Franciszek interrupted.

"Don't you understand?" He turned to Lukasz. Behind his glasses, his eyes were circled in blue. He was close to Lukasz's age, but he looked older than twenty-one. "I'm not coming. I'm going back."

Lukasz was a Wolf-Lord. He had killed dragons. He was on the side of Mountains and wolves and the kinds of legends that didn't die quietly in the darkness. But still, his eyes filled with tears.

"No," he said. "No, Fraszko, you can't—"

"I remember the path," said his brother, speaking over him. "I remember the way home. I don't want to die hunting Apofi or ferreting Lernęki out of storm drains. I want to see the Mountains again."

"You will—" started Lukasz.

"When?" asked Franciszek sharply.

Lukasz opened his mouth, but no answer came out. He didn't have an answer, he realized. He was never going back to those damn Mountains, and Franciszek knew it.

His brother smiled tiredly.

"See?" he said. "You've always belonged out here."

"Don't do this," begged Lukasz, and his voice cracked. "Just listen to me for once, Fraszko."

Franciszek looked away.

"You'll be happier without me," he said. "I won't be bothering you. Besides—" He nodded to where the drunks had crowded the gate. The street was bare now, but Lukasz could hear the sounds of shops opening and carriages rattling. "They love you here, Lukasz. They want your picture in the newspapers—they want you at their parties. You'll be fine."

"You're my brother," said Lukasz.

My last brother.

Franciszek didn't answer. If Lukasz had been upset before, then now he was angry.

"You're just going back because it's easier," he accused. "It's easier thinking you have to go back—doing what all our brothers did before. This is the hard thing, Franciszek. Staying out here. Making new lives."

Franciszek shook his head.

"The Mountains call me—"

"Don't be stupid," snapped Lukasz. "They're Mountains, for God's sake; they don't call anyone. And what are you going to do when you get there? Die alone in Hala Smoków? Kill the Dragon?"

Franciszek went still as stone, and he slid off the sarcophagus. Lukasz leapt down and grabbed his arm.

"You can't be serious," said Lukasz. "Honestly, Franciszek. Tell me you're not going after that Dragon."

Franciszek rounded on him.

"You don't think I could?"

"You've never killed anything!" exploded Lukasz.

Franciszek's face closed. A few strands of hair had come free around his face, and instead of looking wild, he looked like some kind of tragic poet. Lukasz knew he had crossed a line, but he also didn't care. Then Franciszek, with blue eyes hard behind his gold glasses, said:

"Just watch me."

And then Franciszek Smoków turned and walked away, disappearing through the gate, among the fireflies and vanishing fog.

❧ 42 ❧

"I WAS AWFUL TO HIM," said Lukasz.

Ren was settled on the edge of the bed, one dirty foot tucked up beneath her. He spoke without meeting her eye.

"For seventeen years, Franciszek tried to take care of me. And I was so damn awful." He had one hand over his gray face, hair pushed back, chin tilted up to the ceiling. Her leg was pressed warmly alongside his. "Sometimes, I think that if I'd just been nicer—if I'd been more patient—maybe he'd have stayed. Maybe he wouldn't have felt so . . . so homesick. Maybe he wouldn't have come back."

The mavka wound was stark on his bare shoulder. Its edges were curled, with purple-black blood crusting his arm and chest. It was smeared all the way up to his neck, blending with the lowermost edges of his beard. He had a mark in ink on the other shoulder: crossed antlers, a wolf's head, and three words. Ren fought the urge to trace them with her finger. "Maybe he'd still be alive," Lukasz said.

Ren heard herself swallow.

"It's not your fault," she said. "He was always going to come back here. You all were. There was never any escaping it. You're a good person. You're kind and brave and funny—"

Ren suddenly realized what she was saying and felt herself blushing. She broke off as Lukasz pushed his hand off his face and back behind his head. He stared at her, mouth falling a little open and crooked as usual, teeth still smeared with blood.

Ren focused on the tear in the knee of his trousers, and finished, in a very soft voice:

"You're one of the best people I know."

He tilted his head to the side. The effect was overwhelmingly canine, and Ren had never loved him more.

"Ren," he said seriously, "I'm one of the only people you know."

The cabin was quiet, except for the muffled *clink* of plates in the washbasin. From the kitchen, a pair of hands floated up and deposited a bowl of steaming water on the side table. Then they floated serenely back to assist the other hands with washing dishes.

"Wait," said Ren, watching them. "Aren't they going to help?"

Lukasz followed her gaze.

"I don't think so," he said. He jerked his chin to the water. "Come on. I can't do it with my arm."

"No way," said Ren, shuddering. "I can't do that."

"Sure you can, it's easy."

"No!" Ren was horrified. "It—it will hurt!"

"Yes: me." He pointed at his chest. "Not you."

"I don't . . ." Ren struggled for an excuse. "I don't know how! Ask the Baba Jaga."

He held up his good hand.

"No way I'm letting that old hag near my medium-rare flesh," he said. "One look at me and her 'hunter's stew' is going to get a hell of a lot more literal."

He had clearly offended the bodiless hands, one of which began making rude gestures from the kitchen.

"Keep your voice down," hissed Ren. "You're going to get us both eaten. Fine. *Fine*, I'll do it. But you have to tell me how."

"All right. Thank you." He nodded to the side table. "It's easier if you do it one stitch at a time, cutting the thread. Here—"

He picked up the pair of scissors.

"Don't tie the knot until after you've gotten through the skin on both sides of the cut. And don't tie it too tight, or else the scar will be hideous."

"Oh yes, pretty scars, of course," said Ren dryly, threading the needle without any difficulty. The thread had been stiffened with wax.

"Women love scars," he said.

"We both know you like monsters better."

"I do," he said quietly.

This time, the blush didn't make it all the way to her face. But Ren could still feel it dangerously close to her throat. She concentrated on keeping the blush at bay, focused on the task at hand: each cut started above his shoulder blade and wrapped down over his collarbone. The last twisted around his arm, at the very point of his shoulder.

"I'll try." She bit her lip and nervously steadied herself with her left hand flat against his chest. He settled back with his eyes closed, teeth gritted. "All right, I'm going to do this."

"It'll be fine— *OW!* You're not supposed to stab me again!"

Applause from the hands in the kitchen.

"That's why I didn't want to do this!" snapped Ren.

On the next try, she wasn't quite as terrible. He didn't yelp, at any rate. It turned her stomach, advancing the needle on either side of the wound, then tugging the cut edges together and tying the black thread in a careful knot. She placed the knots as he had instructed her, starting in the very center of each wound, continuously dividing each stretch in half with a new stitch. Segmenting them into the smallest possible sections. She repeated her stitch-and-knot process over and over, falling into a rhythm. Three cuts. Too many stitches to count. A seemingly endless supply of thread. A second needle when the first got too dull. And then a third. His hand fell back over his eyes as she stitched. He had angled his chin away from her, and his jaw spasmed, almost imperceptibly, with every entry of the needle.

"Sorry," Ren said, and for some reason, she found herself hoping that he knew that she was sorry for everything.

"Just keep going," he replied. It sounded like his teeth were gritted.

It was an age before she finished. He hadn't made a sound, but Ren could see sweat beading on his neck. She took the cloth from the water and carefully wiped off a week's worth of dried, poisonous blood. Realizing she was finished, he heaved a sigh of relief and turned back to her, his hand falling away from his face.

Their eyes met for a moment. He was still a little gray-looking, still a little sunken. But he looked like himself. A little wild. Trying not to smile. That single piece of hair, uncurling in its stubborn perfect way, falling slowly over one arched eyebrow.

She still had the needle and thread in her hand, and all at once, she was seized by the urgent need to set them down on the table. She wasn't sure why. Probably because her heart had suddenly sped up. Because she was acutely aware of her leg next to his. Because the cabin had abruptly gotten warm, and she was deaf to the sound of the hands working in the kitchen. Blind to everything but him.

Ren had to lean past Lukasz to put back the needle and thread.

He didn't move out of her way, and for a moment, they were very close. So close that she knew her hair brushed across his unwounded shoulder. She could feel his breath on her cheekbone. Her heart pounded.

He spoke, quietly, a hair's breadth away, near her ear.

"Ren," he said. "I've only ever loved nine people."

He shifted against her leg, sat up. They were even closer, and Ren was finding it hard to breathe. Then he added: "You're the tenth."

"I am not people," she whispered.

He laughed.

"True," he said. "You're better than we are."

Her eyes met his. She felt them changing, felt her vision clearing, dimming. He didn't flinch. He didn't care that her eyes were changing from human to lynx and back again. She might have lived the rest of her life as a lynx, had it not been for him. Hard to believe she might never have met him. She might not have met him, without dragons to kill and brothers to avenge—

I am animal.

Cautiously, her hands moved to take his face between them. His beard was prickly in her palms, and she spread her fingers, like she'd once seen the rusalka do. Fur shimmered into light on her forearms, disappeared. Her fingernails sharpened, resting gently against his skin. He did not care. He just looked every bit as mesmerized as he'd looked that first day, on that first riverbank.

I am monster.

Lukasz barely moved. No words, just the slightest tilt of his head. A fraction of an inch, and Ren followed. Their lips touched. Ren's heart somersaulted, started pounding in her ears. His hands found her face, the left a little different from the right, still perfect. Lukasz angled his jaw and kissed her.

Then his good arm wrapped around her back, held her so close that his heart slammed in time against hers. He tasted like blood and smoke and that first day on the river.

I am human.

"I have never loved a person," she whispered. "You are the first."

And Lukasz kissed her.

❧ 43 ❧

BY THE TIME LUKASZ WOKE, Ren was gone. It took him a moment to remember where he was, looking around the little cabin. It was empty, except for the bodiless hands, and lit with the characteristic soft purple of early morning in the Mountains. He had a sudden flash of memory, of waking to this same light as a little boy, in one of the bedrooms of Hala Smoków.

Lukasz sat up. Ren's jacket—his other Wrony jacket—lay in a heap on the other side of the bed. He swung his legs over the side, flexing the wounded shoulder. Ren had done a good job with the stitches.

And anyway, at least his tattoo—safe on his other arm—was still intact. Wherever he was now, Franciszek was probably still hating it. The thought made his stomach twist.

"Thanks," said Lukasz aloud as a pair of hands floated up and placed a cup of black coffee on the nightstand. Clearly still offended, they ignored him.

He flexed the fingers of his left hand. They didn't feel any different. Still in contracture. Still weak. If he'd hoped the cider would

DON'T CALL THE WOLF

make a difference, then he'd been wrong.

He got to his feet, gingerly stretched out his knee. That, too, was still sore. He saw that someone had left out a clean shirt and washed most of the blood out of his jacket. Lukasz dressed stiffly and picked up his rifle. He weighed it for a moment in his right hand, and then he left it propped against the wall.

As he moved, he caught sight of movement beyond the window.

More bodiless hands moved through the purple-flowered lawn, unpinning the washing from clotheslines. The Baba Jaga sat at a spinning wheel made of human bones and spun yarn from a basket in Ren's lap. A gigantic golden apple tree unfurled above them, sparkling against the lightening sky.

That damn domowik. He wondered if the old relic had known he would live. Maybe it had known this would happen, that the old hag would take one look at Ren's haunting heart of gold and fall for her, just like the rest of them had.

He couldn't help grinning at the sight. Ren could settle in anywhere, and she'd belong. She'd always acted like she didn't understand them, but she was the only one they'd all loved. Even Koszmar, the prickly little bastard.

He took another sip of coffee, leaned against the window. At the same time, the Baba Jaga and Ren rose from the spinning wheel. As they approached the cabin, Lukasz noticed that the old woman had given Ren new clothes. They were dressed alike now: black vests over white shirts, with black-and-red-striped skirts.

Ren carried the basket, chattering away. He could see the Baba Jaga smiling. Lukasz could have run out and kissed Ren again right there.

"He deserves it," Ren was saying as they pushed open the door. "He's suffered."

"You are too kind to these humans," the Baba Jaga answered.

The canine jaws followed them in, panting and barking happily. They kept snuffling at Ren's hands, because every animal and monster loved Ren, too.

"Maybe," said Ren, putting the basket of wool down on the kitchen table. "But we all need kindness, Baba Jaga."

They both looked up and noticed Lukasz. Ren beamed.

"Ah, all better, aren't we?" asked the Baba Jaga.

Ren moved around the table to pour a cup of coffee and stood a little too close. It took everything in Lukasz to focus on the Baba Jaga instead.

"Handsome devil, isn't he?" added the old woman, addressing Ren. Then she crossed to them and ran a gnarled hand down Lukasz's cheek. She leaned in and whispered, "If you ever hurt this dear girl, I will find you and eviscerate you."

Lukasz grinned down at her.

"Don't worry."

The Baba Jaga cackled.

"I'm not the one who should be worried."

Ren cocked an eyebrow, as if to say, *She's right.* The Baba Jaga lifted two satchels from the kitchen table. She passed one to Ren and Lukasz took the other.

"It's a straight walk northeast to the Mountain," said the old woman. "You will find it by evening. It is surrounded by a valley and several hills. Both the valley and the hills are fixed points. They will not move with the tides. Go carefully, for now you tread on bones."

Ren nodded, looking solemn. She let Lukasz help her into the extra Wrony coat.

"Take care," said the Baba Jaga. "And Ren—"

Lukasz realized, suddenly, that it was the first time she had used Ren's name.

"—are you sure you would not like to change your wish?"

Lukasz glanced between them. *Wish?* Since when had the Baba Jaga granted wishes? He would have to ask Ren about it later.

"No, Baba Jaga," said Ren, in her soft, hoarse voice. "I want this."

They left Król in the Baba Jaga's meadow, promising to return for him once their battle was over. Together, they trekked upward through the hills until the little cabin and the purple fields were far behind them.

As the sun dipped lower in the sky, they broke from cool pathways into a ring of pink-tinted peaks. The Mountains rumbled around them, but their path stayed still. It took Lukasz a moment to realize that they must have reached the enclosure of fixed foothills. He and Ren paused to rest on a ledge, and Lukasz put his arm around her shoulders as they admired the view.

It was amazing. After this, he would never appreciate another sunset the same way. Beneath them, and crested with snow, the Mountains rolled like waves. A family of mountain goats dashed out between the peaks below and began to climb. As the twilight deepened, the cliffs roiled and the goats danced from ledge to moving ledge. The noise was deafening, like thunder in a summer shower, with the goats bleating below. He realized, suddenly, that they were laughing. They were *playing*.

"It's so beautiful," murmured Ren.

Lukasz glanced down at her as the wind tugged at her hair and she pushed it back. The human clothes only heightened that odd, magical quality that clung to her. Then she smiled. The sly smile, the quiet one, the one that rarely graced those downturned, flawless lips.

He leaned down and kissed her. She ran a hand over his cheek, through his hair. Maybe he should have felt guilty that so many tragedies had conspired to lead to this. But he didn't. He didn't care.

He would do it all again, because she loved him.

"We should go," she said, pulling away. "The sun is almost gone."

They kept on through the hills, now transforming to violet. Then the path led them through a narrow passageway of rock, so tight that they had to stoop and walk single file, and when they emerged, they were in the valley of the Glass Mountain.

Beside him, Ren gasped.

The last of the sun glanced off the Mountains surrounding them. At the other end of the valley, miles away, rose a mountain of shimmering glass. It was so tall that its peak was lost in the clouds overhead. It caught the twilight in orange, yellow, pink, and purple. The sunset ricocheted off its faceted edges, as if the Mountain could not bear to let go of the dying light.

"My God," murmured Lukasz.

But he wasn't looking at the Mountain. He was looking at the armor.

The valley was full of armor. Golden breastplates heaped against gauntlets. Pools of chain mail sparkled like mirrors. Amid the wreckage lay horses' faceguards, broadswords, shields, charred carts with broken axles and missing wheels. Pennants flew from hundreds of pikes, rising at odd angles from the ground. The wind had whipped them ragged and their colors had long ago been faded by sun and rain, but Lukasz could still make out their emblems: bears, eagles, lynxes, and even the wolf's head of Hala Smoków.

Somewhere out there, beneath a pennant of gold and purple, lay the empty armor of Ren's father. Somewhere out there was the sword that his own father had once carried. Somewhere out there lay leather vests and broadswords, black uniforms and antlered bridles. Somewhere out there lay all that remained of nine brothers.

Lukasz pushed back his hair. Ren put a hand on his arm. He put that arm around her and pulled her into his side.

They had made it. They were at the foot of the Glass Mountain.

That was when Lukasz saw them.

❧ 44 ❧

"WHAT IS IT?" ASKED REN as he stooped suddenly to the ground.

When Lukasz straightened back up, his heart was pounding. He didn't trust himself to talk. Ren was speaking in the background.

"Lukasz," she repeated. "What is that?"

Two wire rims, two pieces of cracked glass inside.

He looked up, numb. Ren's eyes went wide. Then his heart dropped right to the bottom of the Mountain, and he swayed so sharply that Ren grabbed his arm again.

As if she read his expression, she turned slowly around.

Someone had appeared behind them, inching out from behind the pink rocks. Now that person squinted at them, as if he had trouble seeing through the rapidly gathering twilight.

He looked so different Lukasz might not have recognized him.

His long black hair fell loose over his shoulders, merging seamlessly with an equally tangled beard. He was smaller than Lukasz remembered, or at least thinner. No longer obscured by glasses, his eyes had dark circles under them. There was a gaunt, hungry look in them. It was a face he'd tried so hard to make a scholar's, one that belonged so obviously to a Wolf-Lord.

The best, the smartest, the kindest of them all.

"Lukasz?" whispered his brother.

When Lukasz finally found his voice, it ached.

"*Franciszek.*"

❧ 45 ❧

KOSZMAR WOKE.

He curled his fingers under, tasted blood. He blinked. The sun had risen behind the trees, and the light was too bright. With what was left of his arm, he shielded his eyes. He was faintly aware of ribs protruding, like fingers, from his torn chest. The light was unbearable. The hum of crickets was unreasonably loud. Something pounded on the ground beside him, and it took him a moment to realize it was his own eviscerated heart.

Koszmar screamed.

The protruding ribs began to move. Wriggle. Then they twisted and tore and stretched, and Koszmar screamed into the empty forest. *No,* whispered a small part of him. A small part not yet dead. *Not like this—*

He had been broken. Undone. Remade. Left to die. The ribs kept moving, clawing, and in another moment, Koszmar realized they weren't ribs at all.

They were fingers.

Koszmar screamed.

The fingers tore free. The world danced on stars of pain. Koszmar's heart pounded wildly in the dirt, and his skin ran slick with blood, and he screamed, he screamed, he screamed. His single remaining eye rolled, looking for flames, seeing only darkness. He screamed until the fingers inside him tore his lungs out, his voice out. And then, without his lungs, he screamed in silence.

These were his last moments. If he had hoped they would be heroic, would be selfless, would be good—

And then, Koszmar Styczeń, who had wanted so much to live, was dead.

The hands kept clawing. They kept tearing.

Only the fingers moved. They pushed farther from his broken rib cage, sliding into hands, then forearms. Then a chest and shoulders emerged, tearing the ribs wide. A head unfurled, with hair congealed in clots. Slick rivers of blood coated naked spine. Yellow fat dripped from bare skin. In quivering loops, entrails fell from its body as it straightened. Slowly, stiffly, gingerly. A new colt, learning to walk. It turned its head from side to side: it saw, it heard, it smelled.

It had struggled, being born.

Then the second soul of Koszmar Styczeń stepped out of his corpse and into the mad, dark world.

46

THE LAST TWO BROTHERS EMBRACED each other.

They spoke so rapidly and in such thick Mountain accents that it was like an entirely new language altogether. Ren only caught a few words, too few to pick out an actual sentence.

At last, they broke apart, and Lukasz introduced his brother to Ren. She smiled uncertainly.

"This is Ren," said Lukasz. "She's the queen of the forest."

Franciszek held out a hand, and Ren shook it.

As Franciszek led them up the mountainside, Lukasz told him their story. About the Apofys, and about his hand, which he offered to his brother for inspection. Franciszek turned it over, examining the missing fingers.

"It's healed remarkably well," he said with interest. "Did you get photographs of the healing process? Now, what do you suppose—?"

Then he stopped and said, "I'm sorry, I didn't mean—"

Lukasz held it up, as if in peace.

"It's all right," he said. "It's not as good as it was. I think . . ." He

DON'T CALL THE WOLF

hesitated. "I may have to fight right-handed now."

Franciszek chuckled.

"You're better with your bad hand than most soldiers are with their good ones."

While they talked, Ren looked at the place Franciszek had been living for the past two months. There was a campfire and a few goatskins spread out on the rough stone. Two leather-bound notebooks stood next to a small pile of spade-shaped pieces of gold.

Ren picked one up, turned it over in her hands.

"What's this?" she interrupted.

"Dragon scale," said Franciszek. "They're all over. Sheds worse than a cat, this Dragon. Interestingly"—he glanced at Lukasz—"they don't disintegrate."

Lukasz raised an eyebrow as he took one of the scales. He looked at Ren.

"There's a saying among dragon slayers. *Bones, horns, and fur.* Everything else—scales, teeth, claws—degenerates when it falls from a dragon."

Ren ran an experimental finger over the edge of the scale. It was razor-sharp, drawing a tiny drop of blood. She was about to respond when a twig snapped behind them.

"Did you hear that?" she asked sharply.

Both Lukasz and Franciszek looked up.

"Hear what?"

Ren turned. The path, hemmed in by hillside and rock, was empty.

"I just—I thought I heard . . . never mind. It's all right."

The brothers continued to sort through the provisions the Baba Jaga had given them, Lukasz continuing to tell their story. Ren returned her attention to them slowly. She still felt uneasy. She could have sworn she had heard, in addition to the snapping twig, a soft, faint mewling sound. It reminded her, unsettlingly, of strzygi.

No. She dismissed the thought. There were no strzygi in the Mountains. Her mind was playing tricks on her.

They settled by the fire. The crackling flames made Ren uneasy, but Lukasz put his arm around her, and for all her claws and battles, she found it strangely comforting. She was glad that he did most of the talking. She leaned into the curve of his arm, examining Franciszek closely. He was shorter than Lukasz—perhaps even shorter than she was—and a little slighter. He was also a little more fox-like than Lukasz, with a slightly pointed jaw and hungry eyes. And yet . . . they bore one another a strange resemblance.

She couldn't help wondering: *What is he doing here?* Had he really been sitting in these Mountains for two months? Watching the Dragon come and go, watching the sun rise and fall on that armor? Why hadn't he turned back?

Why hasn't he tried to kill it?

It annoyed Ren. Franciszek had left his little brother alone, when Lukasz had needed him. And Lukasz had believed the worst—almost *died* trying to get him back. Despite all his talk of protecting his little brother, Franciszek had let Lukasz suffer for two long months.

And what had he been doing in that time?

Then the conversation shifted to others. To stories of their other, lost brothers. Ren couldn't keep track of all their names. Their oldest brother, who looked like their father; the wild twins; the one named Eryk, who'd risked his life to save a vila. She thought she'd have liked the brothers. Stories of palace balls, of beautiful cities, of salt mines and dragons with gorgeous names, like Lernęki and basilisks and Ływerni and Tannimi . . .

Ren could almost imagine it: round tables, packed together and piled high with crystal glasses. The women would be beautiful, in fantastic gowns—though what those gowns might have looked like, she wasn't quite sure. In her mind's eye, ten versions of Lukasz threaded through the crowd. Wolves on the prowl. They might as well have been Czarn and his clan, taking a victory lap in the shadows of a ballroom instead of atop castle ramparts.

These places seemed impossible to Ren. They were filled with humans, with laughter. With roads that were still paved, with kings who still lived. With ten brothers, strangers stranded an eternity from these hills.

One day, she thought, she would like to visit them.

"Lukasz," said Franciszek, when Lukasz had finished their story and they fell into silence. "Our brothers' clothes are in that valley."

The sky had long since faded to darkness. The mountain air was cold and fresh. In the distance, the Glass Mountain had begun to glow an eerie blue color.

Lukasz became quiet for a second. His black brows were very heavy over his eyes. He picked at the tear in his trousers, and when he spoke, the single syllable sounded strangled:

"And?"

"Just uniforms," said Franciszek helplessly. "And swords. Nothing else. I don't know where they've gone. If they're dead or alive, or if the Dragon—"

To Ren's shock—and horror—Franciszek burst into tears. Great wracking sobs like thunder, huge for such a slight man, shaking the whole Mountain.

Lukasz sat up immediately.

"Fraszko, what is it?" he asked.

He crossed to the other side of the fire, and Ren watched them through the haze of heat. It reminded her of all the nights that had come before. He reminded her, terribly, that Ryś was dead.

Lukasz was still talking, ineffectively. "It's all right—"

"It's not—it's not that," sobbed Franciszek. "I've failed you."

Through the shimmering heat, Ren saw Lukasz draw back.

"*What?*" he said incredulously. "What are you on about?"

"I shouldn't have left you," said Franciszek brokenly. "You were right all along, Lukasz. I came back because it seemed easier than staying out there. And now that I'm here, Lukasz—I'm so scared. I can't do it. After finding their uniforms, their swords—" He looked suddenly at his little brother. "Lukasz, I can't do it."

Ren was completely frozen. She didn't want to be here.

"I'm a coward."

"No," said Lukasz helplessly. "No, you aren't, Franciszek—you are brave—"

Ren wanted to leave, but she was rooted to the spot.

"I just can't," said Franciszek, still sobbing. "I just can't do it. I can't go any farther."

"That's because we're a team, Fraszko," said Lukasz. He put an arm around his brother's shoulders. "You do the planning. I do the killing. It's how we work. We can't do it separately. Just like with the Apofys. I didn't plan. I *can't* plan. Not without you."

Franciszek had put his head in his hands. Lukasz put his arms around his brother, the younger comforting the older. She'd never seen him like this: not with Koszmar, not with Jakub.

Maybe with her, once, in a black river in the rain . . .

"You did it this time," said Franciszek at last, in a muffled voice.

Lukasz laughed. He didn't take his arm from around Franciszek.

"No, I didn't," he said. "I needed help from everyone. I asked another soldier. I asked Jakub. Ren—" He looked at Ren suddenly, meeting her eye. She realized, too late, that she had been staring, and blushed. Lukasz kept talking as if he hadn't noticed. "Ren's saved my life so many times. I should have died days ago, Fraszko. I didn't do this on my own."

Ren reflected that even in that river Lukasz hadn't said what she needed to hear. But now—now he seemed to be saying the right things to Franciszek.

"Listen," said Lukasz. "You were right all along. I was stupid. I was irresponsible. I was a jerk—"

"I never thought that," interrupted Franciszek, gulping a bit. He looked totally bewildered. "I didn't leave because of that."

Lukasz's eyebrows shot up. Then they came down again, and even though he didn't say anything, Ren knew she was watching him finally forgive himself.

"Let's just go back to Miasto," said Franciszek at last. "Let's live out our days in peace and forget about this Dragon. Forget about the monsters, Lukasz. All of them. It's like I always said—don't go looking for trouble. Don't go calling the wolf. We've had enough nightmares for one lifetime." Franciszek broke off, looking desperate.

Lukasz put his elbows on his knees and ran his right hand over his burn.

Ren's heart began to quicken. She wouldn't have blamed him if he broke the deal now. She understood, and she wouldn't have hated him. This wasn't his fight. Not anymore.

"I can't," said Lukasz, in the same low voice.

Franciszek was nonplussed. Ren held her breath.

"What do you mean?"

"I can't forget about the monsters," said Lukasz, a bit indistinctly.

"*What*—what on earth are you talking about?"

Lukasz ran a hand over his mouth, down his neck. When he spoke again, his voice was hoarse, and the words hung in the cold air and Ren watched them cut, like a knife, into his brother's heart.

"I'm in love with one, Franciszek."

Franciszek's eyes flickered to Ren.

"Lukasz," he said, "we're the only ones left. We could survive. We could go back to Miasto. Or—or we could go to Hala Smoków. We could—"

"We will," said Lukasz firmly. "But first, we have to kill that Dragon."

Franciszek's face fell.

"Lukasz," he said, "no one else has done it."

Lukasz met Ren's eyes over the fire.

"No one else brought her."

⚘ 47 ⚘

THE QUEEN AND THE WOLF-LORD were long gone when, a few hours later, there was a knock on the Baba Jaga's door.

She crossed the cabin, her wraithlike dogs barking and the hands trying, unsuccessfully, to shush them. She hadn't always moved this slowly. Hadn't always felt this frail. Millennia of power, and all it took was some nameless demon underground to pull the rug out from under her.

The Baba Jaga opened the door to see twilight settling on her beloved hills. The mountain air was crisp and clean. The boughs of her apple tree bent in the soft breeze, and in her garden, bylica, *lipa*, and dziurawiec bloomed among her herbs, as they did year-round. It was all seasons at all times in the Baba Jaga's valley, and for now, her crocuses bloomed.

"My, my, I *love* what you've done with the place."

The Baba Jaga swung the door wide and cut an unpleasant curtsy. "Enter, Rodent," she said.

A furry foot crossed the threshold, into the light. The wraith-dogs fells silent. The hands became busy with their tasks. If they'd had eyes, they would have avoided his.

The Leszy stepped inside. His club scraped the floorboards behind him.

"Human bones in the fence," he said, adjusting his cap. "Nice touch. Couldn't help noticing one of your fence posts is missing a skull. Hurtful, you know. Seeing that I delivered you one, all gift-wrapped in your favorite flavor of flesh."

The Leszy smacked his lips, added: "*Favorite flavor of flesh.* My, my. That's difficult to say."

He cackled.

The Baba Jaga slammed the door shut with a bang. One of the hands dropped a glass in the kitchen, and it crashed to the floor. Unperturbed, the Leszy climbed, a little awkwardly, onto one of the Baba Jaga's chairs.

His gleeful little face became serious.

"Our mistress won't be happy, you know," he said.

The Baba Jaga sat opposite. Candlelight glittered off two monstrous faces. Gleamed off two frowns. Caught the glasses and vodka that the hands set between the two creatures, even though neither reached for them.

"I warned you," said the Leszy at last. "You weren't supposed to save him."

The Baba Jaga didn't answer. With a metallic click, the bodiless hands set down a cauldron of stew. The Leszy shook his head, as if in wonder. His eyes hadn't quite decided what color to be and hovered in a murky twilight between red and green.

The Baba Jaga spoke. "You gave them the sword."

The Leszy's eye twitched.

"It's mine, I made it," he said, banging a tiny fist on the table. "It's mine, I made it, I decide who gets it! And I had to, I had to do it! Bound me with a silly oath." He rubbed furry palms together. "Who knew they'd have a cross? Who knew he'd *know*? I heard he was the stupid one. I thought those strzygi would finish him off. But of course the lynx went bye-bye instead." He scowled. "I liked that pussycat, you know. I'm sorry he's dead. But then *you* . . . you saved the Wolf-Lord. You gave them *directions*. You granted them a *wish*, for the sake of the gods. Sometimes, I wonder," he finished, "whose side you're really on."

Fury spasmed over the Baba Jaga's face. It seized her watery old eyes, straightened out her puckered mouth. For a moment, it looked as if she might leap across the table.

But instead, she said, in a very calm voice: "I am on the side I chose a thousand years ago."

The Leszy ignored the jibe.

"And what side was that?" he challenged. "Can you even tell the difference anymore?"

"Do not question me," said the Baba Jaga. "Little god."

The Leszy's eyes swirled into red.

It was hard to look threatening with that potbelly and those skinny arms and legs. Hard to look threatening with a head that barely reached to the height of the table. Hard to have the upper hand in this room so dominated by another's magic.

But somehow he did.

"When they kill the Dragon," said the Leszy, in a very dangerous voice, "it will be your head on the chopping block. And cross my heart and hope to die, you old hag, but I will make *sure* the ax falls *exactly* where it should."

The Baba Jaga regarded him calmly.

"I am not afraid of you."

The Leszy cackled.

"In that case, you are even more foolish than I thought."

⚜ 48 ⚜

THAT NIGHT, THEY CROSSED THE valley.

Their way was lit by the stars overhead, by the bluish glow of the Mountain, and by the glimmer and sparkle of the armor of ten thousand dead knights. It smelled like metal and snow and death. They went at a steady pace, stepping carefully over the maces and the axes, their strides methodical. Focused. Ren avoided looking at her feet.

They were walking among ghosts.

Where have you gone? she wondered. *Has the Dragon devoured you?*

It wasn't a valley filled with death. It was worse: it was entirely devoid of life.

"Look at that," murmured Lukasz, more to himself than to either of them.

Franciszek made a noise of agreement.

Up close, the Mountain was even more daunting. It stood in the exact center of the valley. A circular moat, miles wide in every direction, surrounded it.

They approached, Ren's hand still on her sword. The water in the moat was clear, all the way to the bottom. Its floor was covered by armor, pennants, and more swords. Fabric and helmet plumes swirled far below them, ghostly and slow.

Unbidden, the Leszy's words sprang to mind.

Fire! Fire! The knights fall down.

Ren could have sworn she heard a cackle somewhere out here in this hopeless expanse.

"What?" said Franciszek.

"Something the Leszy said," she murmured. "The knights tried to climb the Mountain. But when the dragon breathes fire, the glass is too smooth, and they fall down. . . ."

Fire! Fire! The knights fall down.

Ren raised her eyes to the far shore, clouded with mist.

Lukasz had been pacing the edge of the lake. Now he returned, looking thoughtful. He had the easy, slightly sauntering prowl of an animal.

"There has to be a way across," he murmured.

Franciszek knelt at the lake edge and unsheathed his sword.

"You forget," he said, fishing around in the water with the tip of his sword. "I've been here for a while."

A silver chain lifted from the water, looped over the sword tip.

"Grab it, Luk."

Lukasz obeyed. As delicate as a water snake, the chain unfurled along the surface. He began to pull. Franciszek shielded his myopic eyes against the Mountain's glow as they fell into an easy rhythm. They were a good team. She'd had that once, with Ryś.

A boat appeared. The strangest boat Ren had ever seen.

It was a dragon skeleton, the spine forming the hull. The spaces between the ribs were filled with glass, and a long, articulated tail-bone formed the rudder. It was fronted with a silver skull, with an elongated snout and glass teeth set in its open jaws and glass in its eye sockets.

"What—" began Ren.

"Faustian," said Lukasz. "The Golden Dragon must have killed it."

Ren shuddered. The boat felt like a taunt.

Come and get me, the Dragon seemed to mock. *If you dare.*

"Stop," said Ren suddenly.

Thud.

Both brothers turned to her.

"Stop," she repeated. "Did you—"

Thud.

She looked up, craning back as far as she could. The mist swirled, unyielding overhead. The sky behind them was gray. It looked like it was going to rain. But . . .

"What is it?" asked Lukasz quietly.

"I thought I heard—"

Thud.

Thud.

"Damn," said Lukasz. "You did."

Thud.

⚹ 49 ⚹

A FOREST AWAY, THERE WAS another knock on another door.

Felka looked up. She listened intently for another moment. The house was silent, except for Jakub moving downstairs, unclipping his notes from the clotheslines. She picked up the sheaf of papers again. She went to the upstairs window, which, though small and round, looked down on the front door below.

There was no one there. A pit gaped near the front steps, occasionally spitting flames. Felka raised her gaze to the trees at the end of the road. The forest was closing in. In their absence, more streets had been swallowed. Instead of howling wolves, the night was broken only by thin, mewling wails.

Strzygi.

Ducha and the Leszy had been right. The monsters had converged on the village, getting into the streets and attacking the villagers. In answer, Czarn had rallied his wolves and driven them back into the forest. They all knew the victory was short-lived— it had only bought them enough time to get the humans to the

430

castle. At least there the walls were higher.

The last of Czarn's wolves patrolled the cobbles below with glowing eyes. She and Jakub had needed more time to pack, but it wasn't safe to be in the village alone.

One of the wolves stopped just outside the front door. It had a long, fluffy tail and a limp.

Czarn howled. Felka opened the window.

"We're almost ready!" she called down. "Just a few more hours."

As soon as they received the news that the Dragon was slain, Jakub would leave. Maybe he would go to Miasto. Felka knew he was hoping his manuscript would get him a professorship at the uniwersytet. Hoping his face wouldn't preclude him from the position.

She wondered if he would ask her to go with him.

"Don't rush," Czarn called back. "The strzygi are leaving."

"What do you mean?" she asked, puzzled.

He shrugged.

"Maybe Jakub knows," he said. "I have to get back to the castle."

Felka watched the black wolf lope back through the winding streets. Then she reached across Jakub's desk and found the special telescope he sometimes used to keep track of Ducha. She used a match to light the attached gas lamp. Then she trained it on the forest, and then on the Mountains in the far east.

The Mountains were too far away to see anything.

But, assisted by the gas lamp, she could see movement in the midst of the forest. The treetops rustled. A few stray creatures disappeared into the darkness at the edge of the village.

Strange...

The wind picked up. The window slammed inward, knocking over the telescope. The oil spilled, and a tongue of flame leapt to life on the hardwood. Felka rushed to stamp out the spreading fire, and outside, the wind howled in the eaves.

Someone knocked on the door.

"I'll get it," called Jakub.

She heard his boots tap the hardwood. The creak of the broken doorframe. The crackle of the fireplace.

A gasp.

"Kuba," called Felka, "are you all right?"

No answer.

She left the telescope and cautiously descended the stairs. For the first time in years, the house was clean. The broken table had gone into the fire, as had the half-filled tankards of beer.

Jakub was silhouetted against the darkness outside. Felka came up behind him and peered over his shoulder.

It took a moment for her eyes to adjust to the night. An old woman in a ragged cloak huddled on the threshold. Its hood was pulled low over her eyes. She supported herself on a cane that looked horribly like bone, and it must have been, because it was topped with a skull.

The woman did not look up when Felka joined Jakub at the door. She did not speak.

"Felka," Jakub was saying, "do we have any food? We should invite this poor traveler inside—"

The woman took off her hood. She revealed stringy black hair that hung like ropes around her hideous face. Her nose was long and covered with warts. There was malice in her eyes.

Felka's hand closed on his shoulder.

"Jakub Rybak," said the Baba Jaga.

Jakub shoved Felka back. Her heart skipped a beat. She crossed herself, said a quick prayer to the saints, and made herself ready to meet her god in the heat of a witch's oven.

"That's me," said Jakub.

The Baba Jaga gave them both a long, scrutinizing look. The moonlight cast her wrinkled, spotted face in ugly, yellow-green shadows. Felka wondered if she was assessing the meat on Jakub's bones or the measure of his strength.

"I am told you were once a father," said the Baba Jaga. There was a terrible cackling quality to her voice. A crow swooped down out of the blackness and alighted on the skull of her staff.

"Yes," said Jakub.

Felka did not move. She glanced up at him, noticing that the ghostly moonlight had made him look somehow younger. It seemed to scrape the scars from his face and smooth the ragged hair back from his brow. For a moment, it looked like he still had both his eyes.

"You have a merciful queen," said the Baba Jaga, her voice rasping from deep within her emaciated chest.

Felka wasn't sure what she expected. Monsters to crawl out of the forest? Black hounds to drag them away?

The Baba Jaga flung aside her cloak.

She revealed a little girl. She had long silver-blond hair falling over a red vest and a crisp white shirt. She was five years old. She was not ghostly. She was not mavka. She was not dead.

She was alive. She was smiling. She was holding open her hands.

"*Tata,*" said Jakub Rybak's daughter. "*Tata,* please don't cry."

☙ 50 ❧

ONE SECOND, THE MIST WAS swirling silver, and the next, it transformed. Lukasz watched the shadow take shape. A gleaming, glittering, whirling mass of gold and fury. The Dragon didn't hesitate. It was in its element. It was confident.

Lukasz grabbed Ren's arm. She was gaping up at the sky.

"Take the boat," he said. "We'll hold it off. Get to the Mountain."

"I'll help—"

With every wingbeat, a wave of heat hit them. Lukasz had fought enough dragons. He'd been burned, impaled, poisoned—

Every hunt up until now had led to this.

"No," he said. "Remember what the Leszy said? You need to kill it on top of the Mountain."

The dragon screamed overhead. It was so close that he could have counted the tines on its antlers. They were wasting time.

He looked back down at her.

"*Go.* We'll hold it off. Give you time to get up there."

"But—" Her eyes were flashing between lynx and human, and he knew she was panicking. "Your hand—"

"I'm fine." Lukasz shook her. "I can do this. It's going to be fine."

"Lukasz," she stammered. "Your brothers—this is your Dragon. You need to come with me. You were born to do this."

Beside him, Franciszek drew his sword. The Dragon was a hundred feet away and coming for them. But Lukasz wasn't afraid. He had survived mavka and he had lost eight brothers, and he had found one. He was the best dragon slayer in a thousand years.

But this was her Dragon.

"No." He took her by both arms. "You were."

Golden wings brought it ever closer. The blank black eyes stared down at them. And still, Ren wouldn't leave. She opened her mouth, ready to argue, and Lukasz cut her off.

"Ren," he said. "I love you, but I'm sorry."

Her face changed, from determination to bewilderment.

"Why—?"

And Lukasz shoved her backward toward the boat. He meant for her to fall into the boat, but he'd shoved her too hard. Ren hit the water with a splash, overturning the boat in the confusion. The clear water churned.

Lukasz winced and turned away. At least she could swim.

He weighed his sword in his right hand, tested his dexterity. It would have to do. Ren was splashing and shouting behind him.

The Golden Dragon hurtled down toward them.

He caught his brother's eye. He expected Franciszek to make a comment about him fighting right-handed, but instead, Franciszek asked, "You love this girl, right?"

Lukasz switched the sword back to his left hand. *No.* It would have to be his right.

"Yeah," he said, distracted.

"Word of advice," said Franciszek. "Most girls don't enjoy being pushed into moats."

Lukasz grinned at his brother.

"She's not a girl, Fraszko," he said. "She's a queen."

And the Dragon attacked.

✢ 51 ✢

REN HAULED HERSELF OUT OF the water, fuming. She had half a mind to turn right back into a lynx, swim across the moat, and kill Lukasz herself.

The Dragon was bellowing behind her, and the brothers were shouting. But the bank was obscured by black smoke, thick enough that her eyes watered. There was a sudden screech, and an enormous golden tail lashed out of the black and slapped the moat.

Water drenched her, and she nearly slipped on the slick glass. She flung out a hand, catching herself on the smooth side of the Mountain. The tail twitched once in the water, then flicked angrily and disappeared back into the smoke.

Ren held her breath. She couldn't stay. She had to move.

This wasn't that day in the river. It wasn't that day with the strzygi. It wasn't even that first day, when the Dragon had killed her mother and, perhaps without realizing what kind of enemy it was creating, had abandoned her to the care of the forest. Ren drew her sword.

She was going to kill that Dragon.

Ren turned back to the Mountain. *Too smooth to climb,* the Leszy had said. She didn't have much time. Five scratches scored the surface. Ren's heart soared. She put a hand flat on the glass.

Of course . . .

When she'd fallen back and caught herself, her hand had transformed.

Ren's fingers shortened and her palm widened. Five claws burst from lynx paws, each the length of a knife. They sank into the mountainside. Ren flexed them, and with a horrible screeching sound, they tore through the glass.

"Thank you," she whispered, to whoever had decided she would be this way. *"Thank you."*

She shoved the glass sword back into its sheath and stripped down to her bare skin. Then she rebuckled the belt around her chest, loosely enough that it would still fit when she transformed. Ren looked at her hands, felt the strength well up in her heart and spill into her limbs. The world slipped into focus.

She was a lynx.

And she climbed.

Ren climbed as she had never climbed before. She climbed until the sounds of the Dragon and the brothers faded below her. She climbed until black smoke turned to soft mist. She climbed until every bone ached, until the sword seemed to drag her down. She climbed for the dead king and queen. She climbed for the village. She climbed for her brother.

And she climbed because she had not been born a lynx, and because she would certainly not die as one, not here.

The Mountain leveled off sooner than she had expected, and she wondered if it was because she was climbing so fast. She was too exhausted to question it. She dragged herself over the edge, gasping, claws tearing through the glass.

She lay flat for a few moments, catching her breath. Then she got to her feet, muscles aching, and took stock of her surroundings.

Stunned, Ren took a step back.

The Glass Mountain was covered with golden trees. Oddly enough, they emitted the same eerie light as dragon bones. Ren glanced behind her, back over the edge, but snow-white clouds gathered and hid the fight below. The rest of the range surrounded the Glass Mountain like a purple sea, and beyond, the trees were green.

It was beautiful.

Almost hypnotized, she entered the copse of golden trees. She recognized them from her forest, all spruce and oak. Golden apples on their branches. Below the glass surface, golden roots intertwined, dancing and twisting under her feet. Fallen apples littered the ground.

Except for the *click* of her claws on the glass, the mountaintop was silent.

The trees yielded to a courtyard of sparkling, faceted glass. Two delicately wrought glass chairs faced each other, next to a floreted table with a glass chess set. Overhead, a weeping willow, with a thousand fronds of tinkling glass, swayed in a nonexistent breeze. And beyond the courtyard, glowing against the night sky, stood the most beautiful castle Ren had ever seen. And this, too, was glass.

It had tall ramparts and one turret that stood higher than the rest.

The mountain was unnervingly still. It struck her suddenly that the sky should have been lightening in preparation for dawn, but instead it was a strange dull gray. It looked like impending rain. There had not been a sunrise. She shuddered. It took a powerful enchantment to change the sky like that.

She crossed a glass drawbridge. Twin dragons, also wrought of glass, reared on either side of the castle's entrance. Its glass doors were open.

It began to rain.

Carefully, Ren wound around the door and entered the silent hall.

A banistered staircase coiled into the upper floors. Overhead, a chandelier swayed gently. It was all made of glass. Although, here at least, there was a tint of color. A flicker of life. Almost like a reflection—of what, Ren did not know, for she was completely alone—but it diminished the overall stillness of the place. The soullessness.

Curiosity stirred in Ren's bones. What use could the Dragon have for a *castle*? She glanced behind her. It couldn't possibly fit through that front door.

Ren climbed the staircase, feeling, oddly, that she was on familiar ground. Then she was on the second floor. She padded past another silent doorway, pausing to look inside.

The room was multiple levels, filled with shelves. Here, the glass was particularly lifelike. Especially filled with movement. Always in the corners of her eyes. Ren found her head swiveling in every way, trying to catch a clear glimpse of the blurred images. And when she was finally able to ignore the flashes of movement, she felt her eyes widen.

A glass chandelier, in the shapes of different animals, hung from the ceiling.

It was a library. And not just any library.

My library.

Ren turned slowly. Behind her stood a glass suit of armor, in the exact same place that Ryś had knocked it over, two years ago. Ren sprinted down the hallway. The alcove—where Czarn liked to sit—was flanked with shimmering glass banners and filled not with a black wolf but with a picture frame made of glass.

Ren ran past. It was all the same. The doors were in all the same places. The stairs led to the same empty hallways. The towers in the same precise locations. It was *her* castle. A perfect replica, on the top of the Glass Mountain.

And if I am right . . .

Ren was at the bottom of a set of spiral stairs, leading up a narrow tower. A strange feeling washed over her.

Familiarity? Relief?

She didn't know. She climbed the staircase, felt her legs growing more slender. Her spine easing out.

I am monster, she thought.

She felt like herself. She felt more like herself than she had since all this had started. She felt like the girl who had run wild through human streets and lain to sleep among lynxes. She felt like the girl who had feared nothing, had loved everyone, had defied all odds in an evil forest.

Ren kept climbing.

I am animal, she thought.

The fur rippled, disappeared. She entered a narrow hallway, rose to two legs. The glass sword must have looked ridiculous, hanging against her bare skin. Light, dull from the overcast sky, filtered through the windows.

This was the same passageway where she had kept a different room, in a different castle. Her hand closed on the doorknob.

I am human, she thought.

When she caught her reflection in the glass door at the end of the hallway, she saw herself as they must see her: magic eyes and wild hair and edges never quite substantial, never quite real. She was more than any of them expected. She was far more than any one thing. She existed beyond the witches or the monsters. She existed outside the realms of possibility.

I am queen.

Ren opened the door and walked inside.

❧ 52 ❧

"WELCOME, IRENA."

A woman sat on the other side of the room, behind an enormous desk of carved glass. It was supported by golden antlers instead of regular table legs. Snow-white furs covered the floor.

It was the first nonglass room in the whole castle.

Ren stared.

Whereas the castle was pale, the woman was pure intensity. Long, mahogany-colored hair cascaded over her shoulders, parting around a face of sun-kissed skin. At the point formed by the angles of her cheekbones, her lips were shellacked red. Her eyes, fringed with depthless black, were gold. She wore a silver-white gown with a high collar and sleeves that reached to her wrists. The gown sparkled, as if faceted, and Ren knew, instinctively, that somehow—some way—it, too, was made of glass. Its paleness only enhanced her color.

Into the silence, Ren asked:

"Who are you?"

The woman in the chair stood up. The gown chimed. She walked around the desk, the gown rippling like waves. Her hair caught unseen lights; like the Mountain, like the castle, it glowed.

"My name is Dagmara," she said. Like her gown, her voice chimed. Red lips over white teeth. "Irena, I am the queen."

Ren's stomach plummeted the entire length of the Glass Mountain. Probably hit the bottom of the valley floor.

"You're—"

"Yes," said Queen Dagmara. "Your mother."

She smiled. It was radiant. It bit Ren right to the core. Ren could hardly believe her ears. Her *eyes.* Shock had a hold on her, and everything else was pushed out.

Then Queen Dagmara said: "I'm sorry I wasn't there to tell you that, Irena."

Ren swallowed.

"Someone else told me," she said. Then amended: "Well, *something* else."

Queen Dagmara's lashes fluttered. She produced a soft, liquid smile.

"Ah, yes," she said. "The Leszy."

Ren was too surprised to speak. Queen Dagmara seemed to wait for her to gather her wits, reaching out, readjusting an inkwell on the desk. The gown was more like a cape, with tight, fitted sleeves and gossamer-thin glass between the sleeves and the bodice. It reminded Ren of the wings of a dragon.

The Dragon.

"So," said Ren, voice trembling with fury. "You've chosen the side of the monsters?"

The queen burst out laughing.

It was loud and beautiful, and with another ripple of glass, she raised her hand to her mouth. She smiled around the hand, eyes glittering. She looked . . .

Feline.

"Certainly not," said the queen. "You've got it all wrong, Irena."

Ren spoke through gritted teeth. "Enlighten me."

She didn't trust herself not to transform. Not to leap across the table and tear the queen to pieces, right then and there. She wouldn't have cared. Any sympathy she'd had for this queen was long gone. This wasn't her mother. Her *real* mother was home in the castle, mourning the death of her brother.

Ryś.

Unperturbed, Queen Dagmara smiled warmly.

She didn't seem to notice that her daughter's skin was rippling with suppressed fury. That fur was dancing in and out of sight. That her nails were slipping out, shifting back in. That her eyes were twitching between animal and human, wanting to be animal, not ready to change.

Yet.

First, Ren had to know.

"You've grown up to be a warrior," said Queen Dagmara. "So much more than we could have dreamed."

We.

Gold flashed outside the window. The Dragon was circling. Ren wasn't afraid of it, or if she was, then the fear rolled straight into fury. Became indistinguishable. Fed the roiling, burning storm inside her. The queen reached out, as if she was going to touch Ren's cheek. Ren twitched back, like a cat. The queen's hand fell away, and for the first time, her expression faltered.

Ren hung back. She'd seen enough monsters. Played enough games. Slipped through enough loopholes, made enough enemies. She prowled before the desk.

"I think," she said levelly, "I should hear everything."

The queen sighed. She gestured to one of the chairs near the desk, draped in more white fur.

"Very well," said the queen. "Sit down, Irena."

Ren did not sit. The queen did not seem to mind. Instead, she rested her chin on one supremely elegant hand and smiled. Her mouth was thin and feline. It took Ren a moment to realize it was *her* mouth, too.

"A little over seventeen years ago," began Queen Dagmara, "the evil crept in. It came from below ground. It was as if hell had opened beneath our feet. It started with small monsters—with nocnica and psotniki. I was concerned, but my husband reassured me. He said it would get better." She paused. "He said I was too beautiful to worry."

Queen Dagmara's lip curled. It was somehow elegant. It was an expression learned in schools and in ballrooms and in worlds lit by more than moonlight and shaped by more than fear.

In a different life, Ren might have learned the same expression.

"Then came the strzygi," murmured the queen, still staring out the window. "They came in such numbers, out of those pits. Evil spirits, wandering *my* world and hurting *my* people. They grew so numerous, and so quickly. They gathered like fog below the foundations of our kingdom. And they destroyed us."

Ren waited, silent.

"And no one did anything," continued Queen Dagmara. "My husband tried at first, but not very hard. He said there was nothing we could do."

What have the humans done? the Baba Jaga had asked. *They have given up.*

"But I loved our kingdom, Irena," said the queen. "I loved our village, with its Sunday markets and its houses, with their yellow and blue paint. I loved celebrating Christmas Eve with you and your father, and our villagers. I loved that castle."

Her face had become clouded, her lashes low on her cheeks. It was almost as if she was looking back seventeen years, into a world that Ren could not imagine existing. Beauty and color, she had learned, were for other cities. That warmth, that feeling of being home: that was for the magic halls of Hala Smoków.

That was for the Baba Jaga's cabin.

Those feelings were not for an angry village. A besieged castle.

"I tried to save us," said Queen Dagmara, and turned abruptly to face Ren. Her eyes were the most piercing gold. "But no one listened to me, because I was just a *queen*. And then came the Dragon. She warned me that ours would be the first kingdom to fall. The first battleground in a great war, a war that might sweep across this country, if we did not stop it here. I decided to go with her. Together, we would raise an army. We alone would fight. We would save this kingdom."

Ren stopped pacing.

"You listened to a *dragon*?" she demanded. The words came out harsh, spitting. "It's the worst evil—"

"When you met the Wolf-Lord in the river," said Queen Dagmara smoothly, "didn't you notice that the Dragon burned the psotniki in the trees? Or later, that she only burned strzygi? Filled those pits with flames? Did she not follow you every step of this journey?"

Ren stopped dead.

"And through all these fires," continued Queen Dagmara, "did you ever burn?"

Ren was reeling. She gathered her wits only enough to sputter:

"It's a *dragon!*"

Queen Dagmara smiled.

"You've been talking to Wolf-Lords."

She got to her feet. The gown chimed, and Ren took a step back. The Dragon had never touched her castle. Never hurt her animals. Never even the village.

"The Golden Dragon is not evil," said Queen Dagmara, closing the space between them. She was much taller than Ren, almost as tall as Lukasz. "She was made by something else. We don't know what exactly. Perhaps something trapped down there, in hell? Or maybe she was born from darkness and just couldn't bear to live in it."

This couldn't be happening. It couldn't be real. Lukasz's brothers couldn't have died for this, for *nothing.* . . .

"You destroyed my forest. You destroyed this kingdom—*and* Hala Smoków. They all went to save you, and your Dragon killed them." Ren could barely speak, she was so angry. "My brother is dead because of you."

"I wouldn't expect you to understand," replied the queen evenly. "The Dragon gave me a chance to do good."

She waved a hand. A small, clipped gesture that she seemed to think could negate thousands of ruined lives. Could negate eight brothers. *Her* dead brother. It was the gesture of a woman who had spent most of her life waving away servants. Giving orders and having them obeyed. A woman who had been born into power, and who had never truly had to fight for her life.

"I was the queen of this kingdom," said Queen Dagmara, when Ren did not speak. "And *still* no one listened to me. You don't know what that's like, Irena."

Ren threw up her hands.

"You're right," she said. "I don't know what it's like, to be born into royalty. I don't know what it's like to come into the world with power and wealth. Do you know why? Because it was taken away. I was just a baby. I was the weakest, most defenseless creature in that forest, and I *still* became its queen."

Queen Dagmara was suddenly quiet.

"You left me," said Ren, and her voice cracked. "You left me all alone."

The dim shapes on the wall began to resolve. The blurred reflections focused. They stayed pale, ghostly. But Ren saw them: A white eagle swooping across the glass ceiling. Her younger siblings skidding along the glass floor. Faint painted flowers trailing over the walls. A broken blue crib. An old spotted mirror.

A black wolf, head on his paws, lying on the ghost of a blue bed.

"You were never alone," said the queen.

Ren gasped. They weren't just memories. They were reflections of her castle.

"I was always there," said the queen. "We protected you."

Ren swallowed hard.

"We—?"

Ren broke off. Her eyes widened. How could she be so stupid?

It was all glass. The Mountain, the castle, the sword—everything was made of glass. Lukasz had mentioned the Leszy's forge, with its stained glass windows . . .

Ren's heart skipped a beat.

. . . he would have done anything to save his forest. He was its *god*. He had told them where to find that sword, and only after Lukasz had bound him with the cross.

"The Leszy?" breathed Ren.

The queen had a strange look of pride on her face.

"Yes," she said. She motioned to the sword at Ren's side. "Like you, he doesn't trust my Dragon. He made that sword and this castle—a weapon in case the Dragon ever turned, and a refuge in case I was in danger. We . . . we were surprised your Wolf-Lord asked how to kill the Dragon. We thought he would ask about his brother."

Ren knew her mouth was open. She closed it and asked: "Why bring me to the top of the Mountain? Is it true that the Dragon can only be killed here?"

Queen Dagmara spread her hands.

"The Wolf-Lord compelled him to tell you how to kill our Dragon," she said. "The least the Leszy could do was to ensure that we meet first, so I could explain."

The queen waited. Ren was dirty and bruised, but at least her skin had stopped rippling to fur.

"Wait," she said suddenly. "But I'm not human—"

The queen laughed again that. Her shiny lips were stark against the pale walls, the gray sky outside.

"Once again," she said, "the Leszy's idea. We thought you'd be safe with the lynxes, until you attacked a grown huntsman. After that, the Leszy thought it best to give you some claws. I think he rather likes you better that way."

The rain had thickened outside, and beyond the tower window, the sky was a wall of gray cloud. When Ren spoke again, her voice was quiet. It rasped, as always, because she had been born a human and because she had not been raised as one.

"What was the point?"

Queen Dagmara had moved back around the desk, trailing long white fingers along its surface. Ren wondered if they looked alike. She hoped they didn't. Then the queen said:

"To save the kingdom."

"You didn't."

Ren's words were harsh, made worse by her ugly voice, but she didn't care. Fury and pain had combined inside her, twisted around. Made her say the truth.

"People are dying. The Wolf-Lords are dead. No one has been saved. You sacrificed everything. Your throne, your husband, your child. And for what? The monsters are still taking over. Nothing is better. Nothing is saved."

The queen's eyes dropped to the desk. Rain rushed in to fill the void. The sky swirled, dull gray and stormy, outside the queen's tower.

"They are not dead," she said. When she hesitated, Ren saw the lazy, feline elegance falter. It was subtle: just in the tremble of her eyelashes, in the slight waver of her voice.

Outside, thunder rolled.

"I was waiting," she said. She kept her eyes on the desk. "I was gathering my army. They did not listen to me, seventeen years ago. I became terrified they would not listen to me again. But while I waited, the evil kept growing. And now I worry—I fear—my forces will not be enough."

She looked up, and gold stared into green.

And at the pain, suddenly stark on her face, Ren saw the queen with new eyes. As a queen, she had been helpless. She'd taken one leap of faith, sacrificed everything in one act of courage, and then found herself trapped once again.

Ren had only ever known loyalty from her animals. She'd never been afraid any of them would refuse her. She might have been raised in a war, but she'd never been scared of battle.

"It's too late now," said Queen Dagmara. "Strzygi are advancing on this Mountain, even now. We are under attack. No army is enough."

And just like that, like the images in the glass walls, everything slid into focus. No human could understand how to battle these monsters. No human queen, Ren realized, could rally the forces to defeat this. But Ren wasn't just a human. She was raised by beasts, made into a monster.

This was her world. This was her battle.

"It's not too late," she said. "Call up your army. They didn't listen to you seventeen years ago, but you're not the same queen you were back then. And—and anyway, they *loved* you. They sacrificed

themselves for you. And I have my own army—animals and monsters. Even a few humans. We can still win."

Queen Dagmara shook her head. She was almost painfully beautiful.

"You are just a girl," she said.

Ren held up her hand, long and white and so ready to turn back
to monstrosity. The silence filled with rain.

"I am so many things," said Ren. "I am mostly terrible things,
honestly. But of one thing I am sure: I am not *just* a girl."

Queen Dagmara shook her head. The glass gown chimed with the
movement.

"It would have been better if you had not come," she said. "Left
us to our own war. Better if you had stayed safe and sound in the
castle. But you didn't. You had to come looking for us."

Ren drew the glass sword.

"Well." She grinned. "I've been told I go looking for trouble."

❧ 53 ❧

REN AND HER MOTHER WALKED out onto the glass bridge.

Out in the open, Queen Dagmara's glass dress looked almost like armor. She had decorated her shoulders with a cloak of white Faustian fur, and her long dark hair was pulled back in a plait and woven with gold. The rain made everything slick and gray. The rain came down like dull thunder, bouncing off the glass sides.

She was beautiful.

Ren wore a similar gown, but her hair was once again too matted to braid properly, and it haloed her head in a giant tangle. Personally, she also found the glass itchy, but she wasn't about to take on a pack of strzygi with nothing but a sword.

Maybe she was more human than she'd thought.

Behind them, the castle glowed against the dull gray clouds. Ahead, the golden trees emitted the same golden shine as dragon bones. And there, silhouetted among the trees—

"Lukasz!" Ren shouted. "Lukasz!"

He broke into a run at the same time she did. They hurtled

toward each other, met beneath the golden branches, and Ren threw her arms around his neck. He staggered and almost slipped on the wet glass. Ren pulled away from him for a moment, trying to catch her breath.

"You—"

Lukasz interrupted her, smoothing the wet hair back from her face and kissing her forehead.

"You—" she repeated, gasping.

"Thank God you're all right," he said, pulling her close. "What happened? Did you kill it?"

Ren finally caught her breath. Then she shoved him off.

"You pushed me into the moat!"

Water was running in rivulets down his cheeks and dripping off his jaw. He laughed, held up his bare hands. No gloves anymore.

"Necessary evil," he said unapologetically. "And I'm fine, thanks for asking. Now, did you kill the Dragon or not? Franciszek's waiting for us. Had a devil of a time climbing up here, mind you—"

Lukasz seemed to suddenly realize something had changed. He stepped back and stared at Ren. White Faustian fur, glass gown. Then at Queen Dagmara, striding swiftly through the golden trees.

"Wait," said Ren. "Let me explain—there's so much to tell you. The Dragon—it's on our side."

His expression snapped from incredulous to unreadable.

"What?"

"This is the queen," said Ren, half turning away and pointing back at her mother.

Lukasz and Queen Dagmara gave each other a calculated

once-over. Lukasz took another step back, eyes narrowed. Then he repeated, his voice perfectly flat and without the inflection of a question:

"What."

"Lukasz," said Ren with a meaningful look, "this is my mother, Queen Dagmara. Queen Dagmara, this is Lukasz. He's . . . the Wolf-Lord."

Queen Dagmara didn't say anything.

Lukasz wasn't wearing his coat, and he was soaked to the bone. Queen Dagmara's eye lingered on the tattoo, slightly visible through his shirtsleeve. Her expression hovered somewhere between horror and disbelief.

If Lukasz noticed, then he didn't care. He turned to Ren.

"Just listen," she said. "I can explain."

She spared the details. When she finished, he put his hands in his pockets. Then he looked at her, rubbed his chin. She realized he looked just like he had the day they'd met.

He repeated, for the third time:

"*What?*"

"My God," said Queen Dagmara. "What a remarkable vocabulary."

"Are you serious?" he demanded. He looked over Ren's shoulder at the queen, and his accent was thick with rage. "What kind of queen are you? Do you realize what you've put this kingdom through?" He took a step forward. Ren put a warning hand on his chest, but he pushed it away. "What about your *daughter*? You left her behind in a world full of monsters—"

"She was protected," said the queen. Her expression was stone.

"She was alone!" roared Lukasz.

"Don't talk to me like that, boy," said the queen coldly. "Your family falls under my kingdom's purview. You are my subject."

"Bullshit," spat Lukasz.

"Oh my *God*, Lukasz," growled Ren. "That's the queen."

Lukasz rounded on her.

"No. You're the queen." Ren had never seen him so angry, and it scared her. "This woman abandoned her family. She left you with the likes of the Leszy and the Baba Jaga. And if those lynxes hadn't found you . . . And you know what?" He turned once more to the queen. "While you were busy with your pet Dragon, we were looking for you. Your husband *died* for you. And my father and mother. And *my* brothers. How did you feel, watching us all die at the foot of your precious Mountain?" There was a snarl in his voice that Ren had never heard, and it was climbing his face. Getting into his eyes. He looked demonic. "All I had in this world were my brothers. And they died, one by one, coming for you. To help you. Eight of my brothers are dead because of you."

They would never know what the queen had to say to all this. Because at that moment, a musical voice cut across the rain and the glass and the golden trees.

A voice that Ren knew all too well.

"Actually," said Koszmar. "Nine."

❧ 54 ❧

REN WATCHED, SUSPENDED IN DISBELIEF, as Koszmar crossed the glass mountaintop. He had changed. It was like she was looking at him through warped glass. Strangely distorted. Still familiar, not quite right.

For one thing, he was taller. His limbs were oddly graceful, and he took long easy strides, almost unnaturally surefooted on the treacherous glass. A glittering, slightly reddish beard wreathed his thin jaws, ran smoothly down his throat. His clothes were torn, braid hanging off his coat like sinews. His greatcoat was shiny with water, and the vila-hair plume of his dented helmet was stained red. His eyes were silver-blue, with the black pupils of an animal.

"Kosz." Lukasz looked momentarily relieved. "Kosz, thank God, you're alive—"

He froze, and Ren knew he was processing what Koszmar had said. *Actually. Nine.*

Ren pushed the queen behind her and Lukasz. Ensured her mother was protected. Even though Ren knew, instinctively and sickeningly, that Koszmar was after a different queen.

"Kosz," she pleaded. "Please. You have to understand—"

Koszmar smiled. There was a broken-off pipe in his mouth, and now he reached up and flung it away. More glittering red fur covered the backs of his hands; the long fingers were twisted into claws. He smiled, white teeth behind pale golden lips. He uncurled his claws.

Koszmar didn't have to shout. His voice carried over the torrent.

"I understand perfectly," he said. "You little monster."

The silver eyes found her, gleaming with hunger. This was not the Koszmar she had once known. This was not the same man who had lain by a fire and told her about his home. This was not the man who had chosen death over monstrosity. This was not the man who had shot himself to save her and Lukasz.

This was a strzygoń.

"Koszmar," she whispered. "Please. I know you're in there. Somewhere. You're a good person, Koszmar. You're my friend."

Ren felt her heart break.

"Friend?" repeated the thing wearing Koszmar's skin. "*Friend?* You left me there. You decided your precious Dragon was worth more than me. You—" He rounded on Lukasz. "You could have saved me. But you chose *her*, when I was dying."

In that moment, ragged and unshaven with his black hair glued to the back of his neck in the driving rain, Lukasz had never looked more like a wolf. He spoke in a low voice that carried over the rain.

"I will always choose her," he said.

The thing that used to be Koszmar sneered.

"Your brother is dead," he said.

Lukasz's face hardened. Leather scraped, and he drew his chipped sword. "Would you like to join him?"

"Charming." The evil in Koszmar smiled. His teeth were long and pointed looking. "But I already died once, Lukasz. I'm not interested in doing it again."

Then Koszmar stretched out his arms, palms to the sky. Before any of them could react, his claws twitched into fists.

And they came.

Beyond the golden trees, the edge of the Mountain shifted. The air was filled with a low mewling cry. It was angry, whining. Ren drew the glass sword. Dozens of feathery beasts gathered. Bald heads and hanks of red fur. They lined the Mountain's edge in every direction. They parted through the trees like a scaly river. They squalled and growled and paced.

Strzygi.

They were hungry.

They were always so hungry.

Lukasz spoke over his shoulder, addressing the queen.

"Where's your goddamned Dragon?"

"I don't know," stammered the queen. Her collected facade had cracked. "I don't know—"

Koszmar flicked his new fingers a second time. The strzygi lurched. Then, as Ren's heart slammed into her throat, they clambered, unsteadily, to their feet.

Some were burned beyond recognition, others had whole limbs hacked off. Some had parts of their skulls cleaved away, bits of gray brain and viscous blood spattering their shoulders. Their faces, frozen, still stretched into the tooth-baring, agonized grimaces of death.

With every twitch of Koszmar's fingers, the strzygi jerked and unbent. Elbows flung out. Heads swiveled and cracked. Jaws dislocated, relocated. Teeth gnashed. Knees jerked in the wrong directions. Spines bent at unnatural angles.

All these strzygi had already been killed once.

One lurched toward Lukasz, and his sword flashed out. The strzygon fell, but Koszmar flicked his wrist, and then the same creature, now lacking a top half, lurched back to its feet. Gray-brown entrails spilled over the glass.

Lukasz swore.

"We don't have a demon's chance in a church," he growled. "*Damn.* We are gonna die up here after all."

Both of Koszmar's new hands danced as he manipulated the strzygi. So what if he was a monster?

"No," said Ren. "He's mine."

She was one, too.

"Ren—" started Lukasz.

She smiled. Licked her lips.

I am human. I am animal. I am monster.

There it was. The rain was pounding, the strzygi were closing in, and fury burned her veins and tore through her blood. Power welled up in her legs, and strength seized in her jaws, and sound rained like music down on her ears. Her blood burned.

She leapt.

The glass gown exploded as she transformed midair. The sword crashed to the ground. Broken glass and Faustian fur cascaded over them. Ren collided with Koszmar, and he buckled. They hit the ground. A bone snapped, and Koszmar howled.

Their eyes met.

Her teeth grazed his shoulder, and she felt fabric tear. Then his clawed hands were around her throat. They thrashed, rolled over. Koszmar was on top of her, pinning her with his knees. He still had one of the old revolvers and struggled to load it while Ren twisted. He gave up, smacked her once with the unloaded gun. Ren hissed as pain splintered through her skull. Her vision blurred, stars dancing. She lunged up, blindly flinging out a paw. Koszmar yelped and she heard the gun skitter across glass. He jerked back, and at the same time, his knee slipped out from under him. Ren saw her chance.

She swiped, claws extended. Koszmar howled.

Five cuts blazed over his face.

He fell into the ground, writhing. Blood poured through his fingers. It was everywhere: spilled over the glass, smearing across his face. He crawled back onto his knees, then to his feet. When he turned back to her, one of his eyes was gone. The other hung from its socket, its animal pupil swiveling, constricting and dilating.

Ren circled, growling.

He hissed. Half his tongue was gone. He was madness. He was terror. He was nightmare. Whatever he was, he was not Koszmar. Not anymore.

Ren fell back, dug her claws into the glass. Then, with a strength she'd never had before, she leapt.

That was when she remembered: Koszmar had two guns.

Koszmar pulled the second revolver from his belt. For a moment, iron glittered. Fire flashed. Thunder cracked and her chest splintered. Ren heard, rather than felt, herself hit the glass. Pain. Unimaginable, blistering pain. People were shouting. And then—

Silence.

⚜ 55 ⚜

LUKASZ WAS FROZEN.

Ren didn't change back. She stayed what she was: a wet, battered lynx. Blood spread under her body and diverged in red rivers along the smooth surface.

There was a soft click as Koszmar returned the gun to its holster. He was staring down at her, half turned away, face partially hidden. His blood dripped steadily onto Ren's body.

Lukasz leaned down, never taking his eyes from Koszmar, and picked up the glass sword. When she'd transformed, the belt had slipped off her body. There was a soft hiss as he slid the glass blade free, and it glowed gently on the rain-swept Mountain.

For a moment, they were still.

The queen grabbed his arm.

"This is my fight—" he growled.

"Don't be stupid," she snarled, sounding a lot like her daughter. "This is my fight, too."

Koszmar moved. They both froze. His head twitched up, golden hair a little redder at the edges.

It's not him, thought Lukasz.

He turned fully toward them.

Ren had destroyed his face. Five gashes scored his pale skin, from hairline to jaw. They were worse than Jakub's. One cheek gaped fully open now, long yellow fangs showing through the shredded flesh. One eye hung from a a single fiber, dangling near his mouth and twisting in every direction. The other was completely gone, the socket ringed with dark red blood, dribbling off his chin.

This is not my friend.

Koszmar's second soul stared out of an eyeless face. Then he tugged at the golden emblem where it hung against the rags of his uniform. It was the exact gesture Koszmar had made the day they'd met.

Koszmar's claws flickered.

The strzygi danced back to their feet. One stumbled in to attack, and the glass sword arced out. This time, when the strzygoń fell, it did not rise again.

Thank you, Leszy, thought Lukasz. Finally something that could kill these horrible things.

Koszmar's fingers sprang up. The strzygi lurched toward them. Lukasz swung again, and four more fell and did not get back up.

There was a loud snap behind him; Lukasz spared a glance after chopping through another strzygoń. The queen had reached up and broken a branch off one of the golden trees, and now she wielded it like a club. When she met his eye, for the first time, he saw Ren in her.

Ren...

"What did I say?" he snapped. "This is my fight—"

"Bullshit," interrupted the queen, coming back to stand with him. "Crush that little cockroach, Wolf-Lord."

There was definitely a family resemblance.

Strzygi corpses flew aside as he carved a path to Koszmar. The glass was slick with rain and guts, but Lukasz had fought worse monsters in darker caves, and besides, he had already almost died once and come back from it.

Koszmar smiled as Lukasz approached.

Koszmar snapped his fingers. Suddenly independent, the strzygi turned on the queen as Koszmar drew his saber. The aristocratic blade sparkled in the gray.

Lukasz grinned.

Koszmar grinned back.

They lunged at the same time. Steel clanged off glass, the glass sword looking heavy and old-fashioned next to the saber. Koszmar was strong. Stronger than Lukasz had remembered. But he shouldn't have been surprised. He wasn't Koszmar, really. Not anymore.

Over the crossed blades, Koszmar snapped at him like an animal. Half his tongue was gone. Blood sprayed over Lukasz and he realized that Koszmar was now taller than him.

"What have you done to yourself?" he breathed.

"I let the magic in," whispered Koszmar. "I was undone and remade."

What remained of his lids fluttered over his sockets. The half-out eye swiveled against his cheek.

"How? You shot yourself," growled Lukasz. "I watched you blow off your face."

"But I didn't die," murmured the Wrony. "I didn't die, Lukasz.

And now . . . now I am so good at this."

Sweat and rain poured down Lukasz's face. He was fighting right-handed, and he knew he wasn't as strong as he used to be. But he was angrier. With all his strength, he twisted the glass blade. Koszmar's saber spun in his grip as he stumbled backward, slipping. He regained his balance, and Lukasz advanced.

Koszmar lunged again. The saber hacked down onto Lukasz's once-wounded side. The glass blade came up, knocked steel away. Wind slashed across the mountaintop like a whip. Lukasz pushed back his hair, snarling. Water and wind stung his eyes.

"So am I."

He pushed forward and Koszmar stumbled back. They were battling closer and closer to the cliff's edge. Koszmar's ruined face was shimmering gold in the gray. He went down on one knee, scrambled back to his feet.

Lukasz kept advancing. He tugged down his collar, showed the scarred expanse of brown skin over his shoulder.

"All better," he said, and grinned.

Koszmar smiled back. It was like he could not feel pain at all.

"So am I."

Koszmar lunged.

The swords smashed with superhuman force. Lukasz used both hands, but still the glass shuddered under the effort. For a moment, it looked like the glass blade might shatter. But then it shivered, glowed a little brighter, and held. They broke apart. Circled like wolves.

Koszmar was too strong. He was too fast. He had evil on his side, in his blood. The next time the saber hacked down, Lukasz could barely raise the glass sword in time to stop it. Lukasz fell back. Koszmar grinned, long teeth gleaming.

Lukasz fell back again. Koszmar swung hard and seized the advantage. He brought the hilt down, hard, on Lukasz's wrist. Pain shuddered up his arm, as the sword clattered out of his hand and spun across the glass.

Lukasz skidded after it. His bad leg twisted and gave way. He half fell, half lunged after the sword, but it skittered out of his fingers. Off the edge of the Mountaintop. Lukasz crashed to his knees. Watching, helpless, as the glass blade glittered and spun away, disappearing into the gray clouds below.

The voice was soft, musical. From lips that had once blown smoke rings at dark skies and shaped words of admiration.

"I'm curious, Lukasz."

Lukasz could hear every one of Koszmar's footfalls.

Looking over the edge of the Mountain, trying to wish the sword back, Lukasz watched the gray shifting and sparkling. The swirling fog gathered weight, gathered darkness. A dark shadow loomed, growing bigger by the second.

"How does it feel, Lukasz?" crooned Koszmar. "To have failed so completely?"

. . . *sparkling?*

Lukasz flipped onto his back. Koszmar loomed over him. The wild animal look was back. He snarled, the muscles of his face arranging, rearranging, drawing back from his teeth.

"Your queen is dead."

Koszmar had been utterly destroyed, from the toes of his scuffed boots to the last, unnaturally silver hair. Lukasz felt the saber's point slide up his chest to settle at the hollow of his throat. He could hear his breathing coming hard and fast.

Koszmar grinned down at him. The ice-cold, animal grin. Made worse by the rips in his cheeks, by the long fangs. By the blood slipping, unheeded, over his chin.

"Your brother is dead."

Thud. It was faint. *Thud.* Almost imperceptible. *Thud.*

But Lukasz had spent a lifetime in pursuit of one thing. And as Koszmar laughed, he couldn't help grinning, not even when Koszmar whispered, in that sweet, slightly nasal voice:

"You couldn't even kill the Dragon."

Thud. Thud. Thud.

"You're right," said Lukasz.

Koszmar hesitated, as if he could see the grin on Lukasz's face. That open-jawed, crooked-toothed, half-laughing grin. The grin a hundred other monsters had seen before they died.

Koszmar's head twitched to the side, almost quizzically. Water and blood dripped from his hair, down his wrists, ran down the length of the saber. The blade at Lukasz's throat wavered, for the barest instant.

"You're right," Lukasz repeated. "I never killed the Dragon."

⚒ 56 ⚒

THE GOLDEN DRAGON ROARED.

The Mountain shook. Lukasz watched as, reflected in its glow, Koszmar's face turned from triumph to shock, before transforming to terror. He stumbled backward.

Lukasz felt the rush of wingbeats behind him, sensed the shadow falling over him. The Dragon shot straight past the Mountain's edge. Lukasz glimpsed dead black eyes and six-foot black teeth. Then they were gone. He caught the underside of the Dragon's jaw, covered in serrated, armor-like scales. Then the expanse of pale gold belly, racing past, as if forever, punctuated twice by sets of legs and claws, before giving way to a long, tapered tail.

For a moment, the Golden Dragon blocked out the sky.

Lukasz raised himself on his elbows, looking past Koszmar. Queen Dagmara was walking toward them. The glass sleeves of her gown shimmered like dragon wings as she raised her arms. Koszmar was gaping at the sky. Then, as if in a dream, Lukasz watched him turn back to Queen Dagmara.

"This is for your soul," she said, in a voice that carried over the expanse. "And this is for my daughter."

She dropped her arms.

And, like an eagle, the Dragon dived.

Koszmar was fast. He dodged out of the way. The Dragon's teeth closed over air, its claws scraping the glass. Koszmar shot back to his feet, eyeless face twisting into a smile. He still had his saber.

Koszmar laughed.

Lukasz started to get to his feet, then stopped.

The Dragon's tail swung across the mountaintop. It cleared a path through the golden trees, splintering the trunks as it came. Lukasz watched the explosion of gold and glass. Still laughing, Koszmar turned around too late.

The tail caught him across the chest. His ruined face registered surprise.

The force sent him skidding across the mountaintop. He careened straight over the side.

But for a moment, he hung on. The clawed fingers scrabbled, carving bloody lines in water and glass. His shredded face leered over the edge. A crack was spreading, splintering up from under his hand.

"Help, Lukasz, help me—"

His old voice. His human voice. The voice that had made plans, had paid compliments. The voice of a strange, reluctant friend.

The crack gaped wider. Lukasz almost went for him. He almost hauled him back. Almost tried to save this second soul, when he had already abandoned the first.

But Lukasz didn't move. He couldn't. However many souls Koszmar had—whatever horror had brought him here—whatever bit of his friend was still inside, still trapped, still trying to get out . . .

Koszmar had killed Franciszek.

A rumble, and the ledge loosened. Koszmar was slipping.

Koszmar had killed Ren.

"Please, Lukasz, please—"

Glass screeched. The ledge came away. Koszmar screamed, disappeared, and then all that was left was his screaming, getting fainter and fainter, disappearing into the fog and rain. The Mountain was silent.

Lukasz walked slowly to the cliffside. Glass stretched downward as far as the eye could see. It disappeared into gray clouds and oblivion.

Koszmar was gone.

Lukasz turned away. He was suddenly aware of his pounding heart. No longer in time with the dragon's wingbeats, now hard and painful and constricting his throat.

Ren.

Queen Dagmara was hunched over her body amid the wreckage of the forest. The trees had been destroyed by the Dragon's tail. Golden trunks lay on their sides, the last bits of strzygi still twitching on the glass. A single severed foot hopped in a circle.

Ren was still a lynx. She had not changed back. Lukasz fell to his knees beside them. He couldn't think. He couldn't feel.

"It isn't working," the queen repeated to herself, over and over. She hugged her daughter's soaked body. *"It isn't working."*

Lukasz saw the golden apples on the glass, most of them wet with blood. One with a bite out of it.

Queen Dagmara was sobbing. Lukacz touched Ren's head. Then, carefully, took her from Dagmara's arms. She was heavy. Her fur was waterlogged. Her lynx eyes were closed and her shoulder was matted with blood. Her whiskers were bent. Blood and water swirled on the glass around them.

"No," he said hoarsely, smoothing back her wet ears. "Not like this."

It wasn't right. She was the queen. She'd conquered rusalki and banished mavka. She'd befriended the Leszy and charmed the Baba Jaga. Even the Dragon was on her side, for God's sake! To him, she had been untouchable. He had never worried, not for a single moment, that she would have—that she would be the one—who—

While he held her, she began to change. The fur disappeared and her ears changed to dark hair. She grew lighter in his arms, more fragile. The glass slithered up over her body, re-forming the gown. It trapped the blood from the bullet wound underneath, turning the gown crimson instead of silver. She had always been pale, but now she looked paper-thin. Nearly colorless. The blue veins of her throat stood out starkly. Blue circles hung under her eyes. Blue veins even spread out from her lips. Her hair was wet, flat, draped over his arm. It was lifeless.

This was his fault. Their fault. The villagers had thrown rocks, the soldiers had kidnapped her, and in the end—

When he took her face in his hands, her skin was cold.

Koszmar had killed her.

He couldn't tell if she was breathing. Intending to listen, he lowered his head. But he was worn thin. He wasn't thinking straight. His mind was full of blood and strzygi and everything they'd lost, everything *he'd* lost, and for some reason, hands shaking, he bent still farther and found her cold mouth.

For the last time, he kissed her.

A hand pressed into his shoulder. Then it transformed, fingers to claws and back again, and it took him a moment to realize what was happening. Ren's eyelids fluttered.

"Oh my God," he muttered. His trembling hands ran over her cheeks, through her soaked hair. Hope soared in his voice. "Oh my God, Ren—"

Her eyelids fluttered again. And then those cold lips twisted and smiled, and green eyes looked into his. A bit hysterically, she began to laugh.

And then, beneath branches of gold and upon glass washed clean by rain, Lukasz kissed her.

57

ALIVE.

Ren couldn't help it. She laughed, and Lukasz's mouth was on hers again. Her hands found his face, and she kissed him. Again.

Then they were both laughing. She wasn't sure why. Maybe she was relieved. Maybe she was just rattled. Maybe she was brave. She pushed herself up on her hands, still half supported by Lukasz. The queen leaned over and, unexpectedly, hugged her.

Mixed with blood, torrents of water washed over the ground, carrying golden branches, golden apples, and broken glass. A dozen feet away, the water parted around the Dragon's huge gleaming claws. Black smoke poured from its nostrils, down its body, caught in Ren's heart. She realized, with a start, that the rain was thinning.

The Dragon had saved them, she realized. So many times. It had saved them. It had escaped from an underworld of monsters and spent seventeen years at war. For her kingdom.

Gold scraped on glass, and the Dragon advanced.

The big equine head wove down from its great height. Ren got to her feet. She closed the distance between her and the Dragon until they were so close that she could smell the smoke on its breath.

When it looked at her, Ren recognized its expression. Its eyes were dull black, reflecting absolutely no light at all. They looked cautious. A little afraid. Curious. Hopeful.

She'd seen that look before, in a hundred other animals.

She reached out, and her hand met gold.

"Hello," she whispered.

It wasn't cold, like she had expected. Or slimy, or hard, or like the ice-cold armor of a stone-cold killer. It was warm, soft. Almost like fur. The Dragon closed its eyes. Then it purred. The whole Glass Mountain vibrated.

"I'm so sorry," she whispered. "I misjudged you."

The Dragon purred louder. Then, to Ren's surprise, it spoke. Inside her head.

You have done well, my queen.

A rumble shook the mountaintop. The ground lurched beneath her, and Lukasz's hand closed protectively over her shoulder.

The Mountain trembled. The last of the golden trees toppled, crashing into the glass. Golden leaves exploded, and apples rolled across the ground. Behind them, the castle was shaking, and blocks of glass were crumbling from the edges and tumbling down into oblivion. Ren turned to the Dragon.

"What's going on?"

The Dragon spoke again. *It is time for us to return.*

The Golden Dragon knelt down on its front knees. It took Ren a moment to realize what it wanted, and as soon as she did, Lukasz shot her a disbelieving look.

"Oh, no—" he started.

"Trust me," said Ren over the crashing of glass. "It'll be all right."

Looking very pale, Lukasz helped Queen Dagmara onto the golden scales before swinging up behind her. Ren came last.

As the dragon pushed off, the glass mountainside crumbled beneath its talons. They soared down to earth, weaving between hurtling chunks of glass. Cracks shuddered down the smooth sides and splintered up from its base. Ren resisted the urge to cover her ears, while the Mountain crumbled.

A gale surrounded them, strong enough to lift whole tons of glass as if they weighed no more than dead leaves. Like a spinning, twisting hurricane, the glass spiraled around the crumbling Mountain.

They landed in the field of armor, sliding off the Dragon's back. Ren stumbled on a fallen shield. She had almost forgotten about those poor knights.

"You said they weren't dead," she said, turning to Queen Dagmara. "Can you bring them back?"

"Wait." Behind them, Lukasz slipped off the Dragon's back. "They're not—?"

They have been sleeping, said the Dragon. *I will wake them.*

Ren watched in wonder as another gale lifted the armor. As if borne up by ghosts, the armor and swords and uniforms rose into the air. Shoals of shattered glass blasted through the valley, like torrents of rain. They shot through the floating armor, pinging off helmets and blades.

The gale rose to a roar, and Ren was suddenly aware of shapes forming within the armor. No, not shapes. *People*, formed of glass. Then the glass gathered color, and substance, and all of a sudden—

Everywhere, knights pushed back their visors and examined newly re-formed hands. Long-dead horses unfolded cautious legs. In the moat, a hand broke the water's surface. More knights surfaced, brandishing swords and pennants, and dragged themselves onto dry land.

Ren could hardly believe it. They'd brought back the queen. They'd raised an army—an army big enough to take back her forest. They'd resurrected the Wolf-Lords, brought them back from extinction. Raised enough of the dead to fill the empty streets and warm halls of the great lodge.

And there, a few feet away, at the water's edge—

"Oh my God," breathed Lukasz.

Before Ren could stop him, Lukasz had dashed away. She followed. He slipped in the mud and shoved aside the kneeling knights. Ren skidded to a stop beside him.

Slim in his black uniform. Facedown, black hair everywhere. The mud was dark. Lukasz fell, shaking, to his knees. Ren heard him sob, fell next to him. He ignored her.

Lukasz turned the body over. It was Franciszek.

He was dead.

"*No,*" he moaned. "No, God, no . . ."

The cold, wet body. The stained coat. The bullet, buried in this heart. Franciszek. Poor, frightened Franciszek.

"I'm so sorry," whispered Lukasz. "I'm so, so sorry—"

Then real tears came to Ren. People shifted, and Ren realized they were surrounded. Nine black-haired men and one black-haired woman looked down at them. The woman and one of the men wore silver crowns wrought from dragon bones. Most of the others wore black uniforms, but some wore leather and fur.

One of them was the spitting image of their father, with a beaky nose. A second looked almost exactly like Lukasz, but with sadder eyes. One with a bright, pretty face, now stricken with grief. Two men who could only be the twins, one with silver teeth and the other with a big purple scar. One as asymmetrical as he was mesmerizing. Another who was quite possibly the most perfectly handsome human Ren had ever seen. One brother who looked younger, a little different, from the others.

"What have I done?" Lukasz asked. He was crying.

Eight brothers, back from the dead. One lost forever. They fell to their knees, and Ren felt like an intruder.

"This is my fault," he choked. "This is all my fault—"

The twins flanked Lukasz, each with a hand on his shoulder. He had his hands over his face, and Ren didn't know what to do. The brothers crowded in, barely even noticing her. They went to Lukasz. Comforting him, consoling him. Telling him it wasn't his fault and Franciszek had known what he was doing.

Ren rubbed the tears out of her eyes, getting to her feet. Even after everything they'd done, they still hadn't been able to save their brothers.

Queen Dagmara stood a few feet away, beside a tall man with a dark beard. He wore a golden crown and a deep violet military uniform edged in gold. It took Ren a moment to recognize the insignia on his cap, so similar to the one Lukasz used to wear with his Wrony uniform.

It was the profile of a lynx.

Her father.

Ren approached them. The circled knights and soldiers parted as she passed. She felt their gaze on her. She imagined they were wondering who she was, dressed in glass armor.

Her parents—the parents she had never known—stood at the end of the gauntlet.

"Irena—" said the queen.

"Darling—" said her father.

They made as if to pull her in, but Ren took a stiff step backward. Her eyes shifted from human to lynx and back again.

The king drew back.

"My name is Ren," she said. "I am the queen of the forest."

The king and queen stared, and Ren realized, with a strange sort of detachment, that she did not even know her own father's name.

"Queen of the forest?" he repeated. He glanced at his wife. "My forest? Surely, she doesn't mean—"

The Dragon moved toward them. The knights shrank back. Even the king fell silent. The Dragon stopped just behind Queen Dagmara and her husband, and while the king turned a very pale green, it spoke:

She has been raised in the dens of lynxes, said the Dragon. *She has run wild with wolves. She is human, animal, and monster.*

Ren wondered if they, too, could hear the Dragon, because at that moment, the valley went quiet. The Glass Mountain had disappeared, and the lake was green with lichens and fish. Every resurrected knight, soldier, and peasant waited.

She is your queen.

There was a chorus of squeaking, of old leather and unoiled metal, and ten thousand knights took a knee. Ren glanced back at her human parents. Queen Dagmara was beaming. The king looked like he might be sick on his closer subjects.

Then the Dragon cautiously approached Ren. As it stepped over the king and queen, the king's face turned an unusual greenish color. *I will help you save this queendom.*

"Kingdom," Ren corrected automatically.

No, said the Dragon. *Not anymore.*

Ren held out her hand and stroked the golden nose, and the Dragon added: *I am sorry I could not save your brother.*

Ren's throat burned. She had hated the humans for thinking the worst of her, and she'd been no better. She'd been so blind to every one of those fires. She'd been so ignorant. She leaned forward and kissed the golden snout.

"I'm sorry," she whispered. "I'm sorry for everything."

I am not, said the Dragon. *I am glad you came for me.*

Then the dragon stretched its wings, pushed off, and disappeared over the Mountains.

The enormity of everything that was happening had begun to sink in. There were seventeen years of knights and soldiers gathered at the foot of the Mountain; they were kings and aristocrats, mercenaries and tradespeople. They were from every corner of the country, from every city and province. The best and bravest. The reckless, the expert, the ambitious.

And now, thanks to the Dragon, they were *hers*.

Ren looked at Queen Dagmara, who was shielding her eyes to watch the ascent of the Dragon. So she had been afraid, thought Ren. Overly cautious. Maybe she had spent too long thinking and planning, not enough time fighting. But in a way, Ren understood. Queen Dagmara did not come from the same world as Ren; she hadn't grown up fighting for her life, constantly proving herself to her subjects.

And all the same, she had made this possible. Queen Dagmara had built this army.

The queen glanced back and met Ren's eyes. Feline and beautiful, the queen gave her the smallest of smiles. Ren smiled back. The king looked between his daughter and his wife, brow furrowed.

At that moment, there was a tremendous commotion in the middle of the valley. The knights began hopping, as if they were jumping out of the way. There was a general chorus of *ouch*es and *oomph*s, and then the crowd parted.

"Oh God," said one of the Wolf-Lords. Ren couldn't tell them apart. "Not him again—?"

A very knobbly and very familiar creature appeared. He strode between the parted knights, jovially swinging his club, arm in arm with the lovely Leszachka. Eighty-six tiny Leshonki filed after them, leaving many of the knights rubbing their shins.

The Leszy and Leszachka strode straight to the feet of Queen Dagmara. Ren watched, hypnotized, as the queen leaned down and pressed her shining red lips first to the Leszy's cheek, and then to that of his wife.

The Leszy giggled. Then he turned to Ren.

"You . . . ," she said.

The Leszy heaved a huge sigh. He rolled his eyes. He crossed his arms. He sighed again. And then, looking supremely put out, he got down on one knee.

"Irena, queen of the forest. To you I pledge my undying loyalty. Your forest shall always be safe for animals. Your roads shall always carry honorable humans. Your children shall always be blessed, as you have been blessed, and above all other mortals, your family shall always be treated with respect and reverence." He rolled his eyes again. "As guardian of the forest, I promise that I shall also guard its queen"—here, his speech was somewhat ruined by the dirty look he shot in the direction of the Wolf-Lords—"and your *friends*."

Ren couldn't help it. He looked so pitiful, so grudging.

"Leszy." She spread her arms. "I was going to thank you."

He looked at her like she'd grown an extra head.

"You saved my life," she added, sinking to her knees, and hugged the furry little creature. His knobbly hands danced over their heads and his cap fell off.

"Hey, stop that!"

"You were trying to save our forest," whispered Ren. "I understand."

She kissed his cheek. The Leszy blushed a stunning shade of scarlet.

Ren released him, and he scampered back to his family, where his children were flexing tiny muscles and swinging tiny clubs. With expressions of complete terror, the knights backed out of the way of the fierce little Leshonki, and Ren wondered how many of them had dined at his table.

"Didn't think we'd see him again."

Ren turned. Lukasz was walking toward her. He was smiling, even if it was a little weak. His hair was drying, sticking up all over the place, but as he drew closer, he tugged his battered army cap back down over it. His eyes were dry.

Ren wanted to throw her arms around him. Tell him it would be all right. They were going to win. They were going to avenge their brothers. The war wasn't over.

Lukasz held out the glass sword. It must have fallen among the knights, at the bottom of the Mountain.

"You should keep this," he said. "You found it."

"Thank you," said Ren, awkwardly aware that they were being watched by most of the kingdom. Then she added: "I suppose we'll need it. I'm sure there are strzygi left in the forest."

"Oh good," he said. "I was so worried we were done with them."

Ren snorted. The return of his sarcasm was a good sign. He helped her buckle the sword around her shoulders.

"And then after that?" She glanced around at the clearing. "What then?"

Lukasz grinned, his teeth not quite coming together.

"I suppose I go back to the Mountains." He shrugged, then added casually, "And you marry one of these rich nobles."

"I'm not marrying a rich noble," said Ren, crossing her arms. "I'm marrying you."

He laughed and rubbed his eyes.

"You know I'm the one who's supposed to propose, right?" he asked.

She considered the idea and then dismissed it. After all, it was her queendom.

"No." She shook her head. "I think I will."

Lukasz took the last step toward her and put an arm around her waist.

"I love you," he said, and grinned.

He pushed the cap back on his head and pulled her close. She wrapped her arms around his neck. High in the sky above them, she was faintly aware of the Dragon circling among the white clouds.

"I love you, too," she whispered.

"Who the hell are you?" interrupted the king.

Lukasz leaned away. He turned toward the king. In the background, the Wolf-Lords watched with interest.

"Lukasz Smoków," he said. "Brygada Smoka. And I'm going to marry your daughter."

❧ EPILOGUE ❧

THEY BURIED FRANCISZEK AT DAWN, under the watchful gaze of the Moving Mountains, just beyond the great wooden gate, a stone's throw from the lodge where he had been born, the lodge he had not seen again before his death.

Out from under the wooden beams of the church they came, hefting the casket on uniformed shoulders. Down through the winding streets, snow scattering like faint dust under their feet, while from the windows the mountain folk watched. And then they came, too. In black flats and white jackets and skirts with green embroidery, they came; from under eaves, from taking down washing, from feeding horses and stringing herbs from kitchen rafters. And beyond the houses, with footfalls pattering like rain, came the wolves.

Before long they were all standing in the cool air, with the gate behind them and the Mountains ahead. Lukasz stood with his brothers, all of them now clad in Wrony uniforms. Nine brothers in the black of the Brygada Smoka. Nine black figures against the white jackets and blouses, against the embroidery and flowers, nine shadows in an otherwise perfect morning. Nine black horses stood in the hills beyond. No photographers attended this gathering of Wolf-Lords. No interviews were given.

Prayers were said. As one, the mountain folk and the soldiers made the sign of the cross.

"We shall be buried in the shadow of the Mountains," finished Lord Tadeusz the Elder, with his gray-and-black beard and his Faustian fur and chain mail. "Beneath the blessings of wolves."

A cry swelled around them all, encircled them, sank through their skin and echoed in their veins.

"When a wolf cries in the day," whispered Felka, in Ren's ear, "it is for a Wolf-Lord."

Ren didn't respond. She and Felka stood near the back of the crowd, with Jakub and his daughter. They had been the only outsiders invited, and a very small, very selfish part of her wished the Wolf-Lords hadn't been so generous. The streets reminded her of the fact that Lukasz had almost died, and the brothers reminded her of Franciszek's bloodied body, and the fresh cool air reminded her of glass and starlight and the songs of domowiki.

Someone squeezed her hand, and Ren realized it was Felka. Then she realized she was crying.

She watched, from their distance, as Franciszek was laid down in the Mountains that had called him back. They watched, from their distance, as each of the brothers stepped to the graveside to bid their brother farewell.

Lukasz leaned down from his great height and placed something in the grave. Gold glittered in his hand, and she squeezed her eyes shut, hoping to push back the tears. Lukasz stood back up, gaunt but dry-eyed.

Lukasz had thought of the gift. The Leszy had cast the glass. A melted dragon scale had served as the frame. A pair of spectacles, for the scholar who had died at war.

Afterward, Felka and Jakub took Anja to explore the Mountains with Czarn. The brothers followed their parents up to the great lodge, and although Lukasz had invited Ren, she had refused.

"They wouldn't mind," he'd said, almost pleadingly. He'd looked so different in this bright sunlight: freshly shaven, hair trimmed and pushed back neatly under his army cap. "You're family, Ren."

Ren had shaken her head. She tugged his collar straight, even though he didn't need it. She wondered if his uniform had ever been as spotless as it was now.

"You need to be together," she whispered.

Around them, the mourners parted like the sea. They kept a slight distance, but their blue-eyed glances were furtive, interested. The youngest Wolf-Lord had been a child the last time they'd seen him. And Ren . . . Ren had not even existed to them.

"My brothers—I—" He couldn't finish, and then started again. "It's my . . . it's my parents. I was four years old, Ren. I don't know them. They don't know me."

Lukasz glanced back up to the lodge. The collar of his jacket was buttoned tightly over the mavka's scars, and the fur-lined dress jacket was slung over the wounded shoulder. The Faustian fur caught slivers of sun, glittering and glowing against the black.

"I know," she said, thinking of her own parents. "I know. But the longer you stay away, the harder it will get. You have a second chance, Lukasz. If we had that chance with Ryś or Franciszek, I know we'd both take it. Don't waste this one."

"I don't know if I can do this."

Ren smiled. She couldn't know it, but it was the small twisty smile that he loved. The one that had been under all the dirt, framed with matted hair. The one that always seemed to appear right before her fangs.

"You killed a Faustian when you were fourteen," she whispered, taking his face in long, elegant hands. "You survived rusalki and mavka and you made deals with Leszys and Baba Jagas. You've cheated death itself. And you made me love you," she added, more softly. "You made me love you, when I was determined to hate everything about you. You can do this."

And he took her hands from his face and kissed them, and Ren couldn't know it, but a part of him missed the dirt under her nails.

Later, Ren walked the streets of Hala Smoków, feeling, for the first time, lost.

It would take time, she knew, to mend things with her mother. To know her father—Emil, as she had learned his name was. It would take time to stop flinching at the sight of the Dragon, winging up over the trees, speaking into her mind.

She was not sure what it would take to get over Ryś. More than time, she knew. Maybe she would never get over it. Animals were better at grieving than humans; animals were tougher, more accepting, more used to the cruelty of the world. Less obsessed with covering it up. But Ren wasn't sure which part of her would win out in this private little war. Worse yet, she didn't know which side she wanted to win.

Those damn strzygi. Easy to forget them, up here among these pretty houses and this clear air. Easy to forget them when you weren't constantly looking over your shoulder, peering at the shadows between the trees. Easy to forget them when there was nowhere for the darkness to hide and your world was defended by swords and wolves.

Ren turned off the main road, around the side of a barn. Against the wall huddled an old man, an empty tin saucer on the ground by his feet. He shivered in the chill, his hood pulled up and narrow shoulders quaking. Ren's heart gave a familiar little squeeze—the one she used to get for broken-winged sparrows and orphaned squirrels.

She knelt, fine skirt swishing over the dust, and unclasped the gold necklace from her neck and the bracelets from her wrists. They clattered into the saucer.

"Tell me," she said to the old man, "how did this happen to you?"

The old man turned toward her and took off his hood.

"I see the humans have yet to corrupt you, Ren," said the Baba Jaga.

Ren's hand flew to her heart. She watched, shocked, while the Baba Jaga gleefully gathered up the jewels.

"What are you doing?" asked Ren. Her heart hammered under her palm. "Why are you hiding like this?"

The Baba Jaga smiled her broken-toothed smile. Her black-and-red-striped dress was just visible beneath the beggar's cloak.

"You were so enamored with these humans," said the old woman. "You love their habits so. I wanted to make sure you hadn't picked up the bad ones, too."

The Baba Jaga cast an appraising eye over Ren's clothes, and Ren was suddenly self-conscious. She wore a somber skirt and jacket in deep blue velvet, with tight sleeves and a tighter waist. Ren had insisted on the subdued blue; her mother had insisted on the jewelry and the fashionably styled hair.

"I'm smarter than that," said Ren, although she touched her hair, a little anxiously.

"I know," replied the Baba Jaga. "I wouldn't bother with a moron." Then she continued: "Do you regret your wish?"

For a moment, Ren thought of Ryś, with a squeezing kind of nausea that seemed to accompany thoughts of him lately. But then she thought of Jakub and Anja, and of how oddly enough, the two of them and Felka were almost a family.

"I would never regret making someone happy," she said. "My brother knew what he was doing. Jakub's daughter didn't have any choice in the matter. I can go on without Ryś. Jakub couldn't."

The Baba Jaga nodded. Her ugly face softened.

"I am sorry about your friend."

The squeezing feeling tightened. Ren had been doing her best to separate the man from the monster, but every time she tried, she could only see Franciszek, dead on the edge of the moat.

"My friend died with my brother," she said, in a hard voice. "The thing on the Mountain wasn't him."

"But it *was* him, Ren," said the Baba Jaga. "Second soul or not, it takes a wicked creature to let that evil in. It takes a choice. Whoever he was, whoever he could have been—Koszmar chose his fate."

"No one chooses a thing like that."

Ren looked down. In her hands, she saw a black body, facedown in the mud. She saw her brother, falling straight down to hell. She saw the thing that had once been Koszmar.

"Couldn't you bring them back?" she whispered. "If not Ryś and Koszmar, what about Franciszek? Lukasz needs him—"

"Death is not sleep," cautioned the Baba Jaga. "One does not wake without consequences."

"But Anja—" began Ren. "And the apple tree—the cider—"

"No, Ren," said the Baba Jaga in a firm voice. "Let the dead rest. Their souls deserve peace."

"Gross," said Lukasz, wiping strzygi guts off his chipped broadsword. "Very gross."

It had been two months since the battle for the Glass Mountain. He was on the outermost border of Kamieńa, so close to the edge of the forest that he could see the trees thinning up ahead.

Czarn pattered toward him over the corpses.

"That's the last of them," said the wolf, and howled.

Waiting for the signal to regroup, Czarn's wolves filtered through the trees. His new Brygada Smoka troops—comprising Wolf-Lords, villagers, and a few nobles—followed suit. The Golden Dragon had taken care of every other dragon in the queendom, so apart from him and his brothers, no one else had antlers on their bridles.

Yet.

Beneath Król's hooves, the ground was carpeted with strzygi corpses, all of them beheaded, and they reminded Lukasz—a little nauseatingly—of the mavka. He was glad they were finished. The sooner he could get back to Ren, the happier he'd be. Overhead, psotniki still chattered from the trees, and there were still a few rivers that none dared enter. But the strzygi, at last, were dead.

"We should be heading back," said Lukasz, swinging astride Król.

Beside him, Raf reined up his own horse.

"Eager to get back to your pretty little vila, are you?" He grinned. He still had a poet's eyes and a devil's soul, but at least he wasn't as bent on leading them all to their destruction.

"Careful," said Lukasz as they turned the horses out to the path. "That's my fiancée you're talking about."

"Never thought my little brother would be the first to get married," observed Tadeusz, catching up with them. "I'll tell you what this is, Raf. It's damn embarrassing."

"Yes, well," said Raf, lighting a cigarette. "You and I have been dead for a few years."

"Hey—no smoking, queen's orders." Lukasz knocked the cigarette out of Raf's hands. "Besides, from what I hear, you've been making up for lost time."

Rafał grinned.

"Trying my best, little brother."

The forest gave way to a newly paved road. It wasn't just Rafał; the whole queendom was making up for lost time. Queen Dagmara was eager to prove that she could be a good ruler, and her husband was terrified that his wife might disappear again if he wasn't careful.

It had been difficult at first—a little overly political, in Lukasz's opinion. But backed by the Dragon and the Leszy, the king and queen had reached a compromise with Ren. Her domain would remain the forest itself, and they would continue to rule the castle and village.

Ren seemed happy enough with the result. Anyway, now that she was a general in the king's army, she had more than enough work to occupy her.

The trees fell away around the road, and the horses broke into an empty plain. The land beyond the forest. Lukasz had missed it. In the distance, a train billowed steam as it pulled into Queen Irena Station, the newest installment of the Royal Welona Rail. In the distance, the white tents of the Wrony army loomed on the horizon.

Lukasz kicked Król to a canter and pulled far ahead.

The tents flew past, their soldiers saluting. Lukasz barely noticed them. He headed straight for the far end of camp. Here rose the general's tent, larger than the others, bearing a gold crest on the awning: a lynx head back-to-back with a dragon. Ren's Dragon curled around the tent, long golden tail twitching while she slept.

And there, leaning over a table with Felka and Jakub, stood Ren.

Running wild in the woods, Lukasz had thought she was beautiful. But out here, in this perpetual sunlight, in the glow of her Dragon, in her black Wrony uniform, she was breathtaking.

The splendor of kings had transformed her. Her hair was piled under her cap, so dark and shiny that it sometimes looked nearly black. There was an intensity to her that hadn't existed before.

She wore a fitted black Wrony jacket with a long black skirt, both decorated with golden embroidery. She had a gold epaulet on either shoulder. An army cap with the lynx and dragon was crooked on her head. The fine clothes made her look wilder. More dangerous. More out of place.

After all, she wasn't just Ren, queen of the forest. She was also General Irena Khiva, of King Nikodem's army.

The Dragon woke as Lukasz swung off Król. His knee hurt less and less these days.

Ren moved away from the table and whispered to the Dragon, before kissing her equine forehead. With a rush of powerful wings, she lifted off into the sky.

Ren watched her take off. And then, as if they were both dreaming, she lowered her gaze to Lukasz.

And she smiled.

"Don't kiss the Dragon," said Lukasz, taking off his cap and throwing it on the table. "You don't know where it's been."

"I don't know where you've been, either," Ren pointed out, but she let him kiss her lightly before he glanced down at the table.

One of Jakub's maps was pinned flat to it. Over the last two months, she'd watched Jakub redraw it, again and again, with every offensive. Ren's armies were efficient: animal, monster, and human working in tandem. Lukasz and his brothers had even expanded the Brygada Smoka and offered their assistance.

And as their armies swept across the forest, fewer pits seemed to open in the forest floor. Evil bred evil, it would seem. Each time Ren's armies attacked, wiping out another pocket of monsters, fewer pits would open. She'd also found that when they settled the areas quickly with humans and animals, fewer monsters returned.

It was as if the presence of humanity—along with a few soldiers or wolves—kept the evil subdued.

Lukasz leaned down and tapped a black, shaded circle near the edge of the forest. It was the last dark mark on the map.

"You can cross this out," he said to Felka. "We finished them off this morning."

Ren grabbed his shoulder.

"Wait," she said. "We've finally finished? The monsters are gone?"

"For now," said Lukasz, smiling. "Tad and the wolves are heading back to the Mountains next week."

Felka gave a small cheer, and with a fountain pen, she drew an exaggerated red X on the spot. In contrast to Ren's black uniform, she was dressed in a pale green suit that brought out the amber in her eyes.

"Kuba," said Felka, turning to Jakub. "That will give us enough time to get back to Miasto."

Felka had just enrolled as a student at the uniwersytet, where Jakub was taking on a rather daunting workload as the other half of the department of Unnatural history.

"I have a short manuscript to finish first," said Jakub. "Perhaps next week? Anja is excited to see the city."

The Baba Jaga hadn't just given back Jakub's daughter. She'd also given him his face back. It was smooth and unscarred, and he looked ten years younger even with his spectacles and his dark suit.

"Oh good," said Felka, replacing her pen. "Ren can come with us. To prepare."

Ren was confused.

"Prepare for what?"

Felka snorted. Lukasz rolled his eyes.

"I think Felka is referring to your wedding," said Jakub helpfully.

"As you can see," deadpanned Lukasz, "Ren is incredibly excited to marry me."

Felka laughed.

"I didn't *forget*," Ren protested. "I just can't believe it's such an ordeal. I'd almost rather go after the Dragon all over again."

"I wouldn't," said Lukasz. "I barely survived the first time."

Ren smiled, but what she had said was true. She was much better at fighting monsters than choosing cutlery—and that was exactly what King Nikodem was expecting of her.

In fact, in awe of their recent victories, the Miasto king had personally offered the use of the Miasto Basilica for their wedding ceremony. Ren had been reminded by everyone—repeatedly—that refusing the invitation was impossible. She'd also been informed that the chosen venue came with entirely new sets of rules, reporters, and photographers. Ren would rather have been married in Hala Smoków, weeks ago.

But this, she had been informed, was out of the question.

Ren remained lost in thoughts of domowiki playing wedding marches and Leshonki strewing flower petals while the other three exchanged plans for the upcoming weeks. Before long, Felka and Jakub returned to their tents to begin packing for Miasto. Ren watched Lukasz's lips move, almost imperceptibly, as he tried to read a few of the words on the edge of the map. She watched his burned fingertips trace the letters, and in that moment of effort, she had never loved him more.

She slipped her hands over his shoulders and whispered in his ear.

"Let's get married," she said.

He half turned to her, like he had so many times in the forest, when they had been starting over and over. When they had loved each other without even knowing each other.

"As soon as possible," he agreed. He leaned against the table and put his hands in his pockets, grinning. "In case you forget again."

"I *mean*," she said, putting her hands around his neck. His hair was a little longer now, not as rough as it had once been. "Let's get married in Hala Smoków. Not in Miasto."

"King Nikodem wants us to get married in Miasto." Lukasz grinned.

"Hang King Nikodem."

He kissed her.

"You treasonous thing," he murmured. Ren kissed him again, and then he added: "Anyway, disobeying a royal decree would be asking for trouble. Calling the wolf, you know?"

Ren thought about it for a moment and then smiled.

"Oh, but Lukasz," she murmured. "I like wolves."

Pronunciation Guide

One of my most vivid memories of my Babi (grandmother) is of the two of us sitting on the living room couch, reading Polish children's books. I also clearly remember struggling with the pronunciation of many Polish words! After all, this gorgeous language can make for an intimidating reading experience, with its unfamiliar sounds, unusual letter combinations, and library of different accents. Therefore, I have opted to include a brief pronunciation guide for some of the words and names in *Don't Call the Wolf*.

Those familiar with Polish pronunciation will have already noticed that I have taken one enormous creative liberty: Lukasz's name. In Polish, Łukasz is the equivalent of the English Lucas, and is spelled with the "Ł," which transliterates to a "w." The correct pronunciation of Łukasz would therefore be "<u>W</u>OO-kash" instead of "<u>L</u>OO-kash." However, for the sake of accessibility, I've opted for a version that hybridizes both English and Polish pronunciation.

CHARACTERS

Word	International Phonetic Alphabet (IPA)	Phonetic Pronunciation
Agatka	[aˈgat.ka]	*ah-GAT-ka*
Anja	[ˈan.ja]	*AHN-ya*
Anzelm	[anˈzɛlm]	*ahn-ZELM*
Baba Jaga	[ˈba.ba ˈja.ga]	*BAH-bah YAH-gah*
Bieleć	[ˈbjɛl.ɛt͡ʃ]	*BYELL-etch*
Czarn	[ˈt͡ʂarn]	*TCHARN*
Dagmara	[dagˈma.ra]	*dag-MAH-rah*
Damian	[daˈmi.ən]	*dah-MEE-un*
Ducha	[duˈxa]	*doo-HAH (the ch transliterates to a guttural h, as in huge)*
Eliasz	[ɛˈli.aʃ]	*eh-LEE-ash*
Emil	[ɛˈmil]	*eh-MEEL*
Eryk	[ɛˈrik]	*eh-RIK (similar to English, but with a soft r)*
Felka	[ˈfɛl.ka]	*FEL-kah*
Frańciszek	[franˈt͡ɕi.ʃɛk]	*fran-CHEE-shek*
Henryk	[ˈxɛn.rik]	*HEN-rik (guttural h sound as in huge; soft r)*
Irena	[iˈrɛn.a]	*ee-REN-ah*
Jakub	[ˈja.kub]	*YAH-koob*
Jarek	[ˈja.rɛk]	*YAH-rek*

CHARACTERS

Word	International Phonetic Alphabet (IPA)	Phonetic Pronunciation
Koszmar	[kɔʃˈmar]	kawsh-MAR
Król	[krul]	KROOL
Leshonki	[lɛˈʃɔn.ki]	le-SHAWN-kee
Leszachka	[lɛˈʃax.ka]	le-SHAH-kah (guttural h sound as in huge)
Leszy	[lɛˈʃi]	le-SHEE
Lukasz	[ˈlu.kaʃ]	LOO-kash
Michał	[ˈmʲi.xaw]	MYEE-how (guttural h sound as in huge)
Nikodem	[niˈko.dɛm]	nee-KOH-dem
Ola	[oːˈla]	oh-LAH
Rafał	[ˈra.faw]	RA-fow
Ren	[rɛn]	REN
Rybak	[rɨˈbak]	rih-BAHK
Ryś	[rɨʃ]	RISH
Seweryn	[sɛˈvɛ.rɨn]	se-VEH-rin
Skuba	[ˈsku.ba]	SKOO-ba
Smoków	[smɔˈkuf]	smaw-KOOF (the f sound on the last syllable is a very soft v sound)
Styczeń	[ˈstɨ.t͡ʂɛɲ]	STI-tcheny
Tadeusz	[taˈdɛ.uʃ]	tah-DEH-oosh
Wodnik	[ˈvɔ.dɲik]	VAW-dnyeek

PLACES

Word	International Phonetic Alphabet (IPA)	Phonetic Pronunciation
Atena	[aˈtɛn.a]	*ah-TEN-ah*
Biblioteka Kwiatówa	[bi.bljoˈtɛ.ka kfjaˈtu.va]	*bee-blyoh-TEH-kah kfyah-TOO-va*
Granica	[graˈni.t͡sa]	*grah-NEE-tsah*
Hala Smoków	[xaˈla smɔˈkuf]	*ha-LA smaw-KOOF (the f sound on the last syllable is a very soft v sound)*
Kamieńa	[kaˈmjɛ.ɲa]	*kah-MYEH-nyah*
Kwiat	[kfjat]	*KFYAT*
Miasto	[ˈmja.sto]	*MYAH-stow*
Rusz	[ˈruʃ]	*ROOSH*
Szarawoda	[ˈʃa.raˈvo.da]	*SHA-rah-WOH-dah*
Ukrana	[uˈkra.na]	*oo-KRAH-nah*
Uniwersytet	[u.ɲiˈvɛr.sɨ.tɛt]	*oo-nyee-VER-si-tet*
Welona	[ve.lon.a]	*veh-LONE-ah*
Wieczna	[ˈvjɛt͡ʂ.na]	*VYETCH-na*

MISCELLANEOUS

Word	International Phonetic Alphabet (IPA)	Phonetic Pronunciation
Anglan Ływern†	[ˈan.glan ˈwɨ.və(ɹ)n]	*AN-glan WIH-vern*
Apofys†	[aˈpɔ.fɨs]	*ah-PAW-fis*

MISCELLANEOUS

Word	International Phonetic Alphabet (IPA)	Phonetic Pronunciation
bannik	['ba.nik]	*BAH-nik*
barszcz	[barʃʧ]	*BARSHCH*
bigos	['bi.gɔs]	*BEE-gaws*
Brygada Smoka	[bri'ga.da 'smo.ka]	*brih-GAH-dah SMOH-ka*
bylica	[bɨ'lit͡s.a]	*bi-LEE-tsa*
dola	['do.la]	*DOH-la*
domowik, -i (pl.)	[do'mo.vik, do.mo'vi.ki]	*doh-MOH-vik, doh-moh-VEE-kee*
dziurawiec	[d͡ʑur'a.vjet͡s]	*joor-AH-vyets*
gargulec, -i (pl.)	[gar'gu.lɛt͡s, gar'gu.lɛ.t͡si]	*gar-GOO-lets, gar-GOO-le-tsee*
gromnica	[grɔm'ni.t͡sa]	*grawm-NEE-tsa*
kikimora	[ki.ki'mo.ra]	*kee-kee-MOH-ra*
Lernęk, -i (pl.)†	[ler'nɛk, ler'nɛ̃ki]	*ler-NENK, ler-NENK-i*
lipa	['li.pa]	*LEE-pa*
Ływern, Ływerni	['wɨ.və(ɹ)n, 'wɨ.və(ɹ).ni]	*WIH-vern, WIH-ver-nee*
Malutka	[ma'lut.ka]	*ma-LOOT-ka*
mavka	['mav.ka]	*MAV-ka*
nav, nawia (pl.)	['nav, 'nav.i.a]	*NAV, NAV-ee-ah*
nimfa, -y (pl.)	['nim.fa, 'nim.fi]	*NIM-fa, NIM-fih*
nocnica	[nɔt͡s'ni.t͡sa]	*nots-NEE-tsah*
pierogi	[pjɛ'ro.gi]	*pyer-ROH-gee*
psotnik, -i (pl.)	['sot.nik, 'sot.ni.ki]	*SOT-neek, SOT-nee-kee*

rusalka, rusalki (pl.)	[ruˈsal.ka, ruˈsal.ki]	*roo-SAL-kah, roo-SAL-kee*
strzygoń (m.), strzyga (f.), -i (pl.)	[ˈʃʧ.gun, ˈʃʧ.ga, ˈstʐ.gi]	*SHTITCH-gon, SHTITCH-ga, SHTITCH-gi* *very difficult words for non-Polish speakers to pronounce. The first four letters (sh-tch) are pronounced as one syllable.*
Tannim, -i (pl.)†	[ˈtan.im, ˈtan.im.i]	*TAH-neem, TAH-neem-ee*
upiór	[upˈjur]	*oop-YOOR*
vila	[ˈvi.la]	*VEE-lah*
Wawel	[vaˈvɛl]	*va-VEL*
Wrony	[ˈvro.ni]	*VROH-nee*
Ząb lub pazur	[ˈzɔmp ˈlub ˈpa.zur]	*ZAWMP LOOB PAH-zoor*
zmora	[ˈzmo.ra]	*ZMOH-ra*
żywokost	[ˈʐɨ.vɔ.kɔst]	*ZHI-vaw.kost* *(zh sounds like the s in treasure)*

NOTES

†The words Ływern, Apofys, Lernęki, and Tannim are names of dragon breeds mentioned in the text, and are not of Polish origin.

The Anglan Ływern is a specific dragon slain by the Smokówi twins, while Ływern is actually a dragon breed. Ływern is a stylized spelling of "Wyvern," which is a two-legged dragon-like creature of western European tradition. The Ływerni of Welona are distinguished from Faustian dragons by their size, their amphibious nature, and the absence of antlers or a mane.

Similarly stylized, the Apofys dragon is inspired by the ancient

Egyptian deity Apophis (also: Apep), who was god of chaos and locked in eternal battle with the Sun God Ra. Although Apophis was traditionally represented as a serpent or crocodile, the exceptionally clever Apofys that Lukasz faces is known for its birdlike appearance and beautiful plumage.

Lernęki are the third stylized adaptation of a traditional mythical beast—the many-headed Lerneaen Hydra, defeated by Heracles using both fire and sword. Like their inspiration, the Lernęki of Atena prefer to nest in bodies of water, and they spontaneously regenerate when attacked with sword alone. Luckily for Kwiat, Lukasz has the inspiration to torch the Lernęki instead.

Finally, the Tannimi dragons slain by the four youngest brothers in Granica are also not of Polish origin. Adapted from the Hebrew *tanninim*, these mythical sea monsters symbolized chaos in Hebrew and Jewish tradition. In modern Hebrew, the word *tannin* means "crocodile." The Tannimi of Welona are also very much like crocodiles, but with a spiral "tooth whorl" on their upper and lower jaws. They also rely on the consumption of wood to maintain their ability to breathe fire. Understandably, the Tannim's arboreal diet wreaked havoc in the crowded harbors of Granica until the arrival of the Brothers Smokówi.

Acknowledgments

First and foremost, this book is for my family. This book is for my sister: you're the reason why I started writing stories in the first place. This book is for my brother: I don't think you realize it, but you're the greatest coach and cheerleader in the world. This book is for my fav BIL: you are so funny and so ready to help with anything and everything—I don't know how we got along without you. This book is for lil E: I can't wait until you're old enough to read this, and we can obsess over all the amazing books in the world together. Most of all, though, this book is for you, Mom. I could write a whole new book saying thank you. Actually, a lifetime of words wouldn't be enough for you. Everything in these pages, and everything in every page yet unwritten, is because of you. I love you.

This book is also for my grandparents. I like to think you have access to a copy, wherever you are now. I have been blessed to come from a long line of intelligent, loving, and fiercely independent women, and each and every one of them inspired this novel. But you, Babi, have inspired it most of all. I miss you, and I hope you don't mind that I named Ren after you. She is definitely the kind of person who would take good care of her plants and carry bugs outside instead of squishing them, so I think you would like her.

Over the last five years, this book has progressed in leaps of faith. Brent, thank you for your unflagging enthusiasm for this wild little book—sometimes I still can't believe that this gets to be the first story I tell. Stephanie, thank you for seeing the heart of this novel even before I did, and especially for encouraging me to go wild with all the blood and romance. To the team at HarperTeen, especially Louisa and Renée: thank you for your eagle eyes when it came to copy edits, and especially for tackling that beast of a pronunciation guide. To the team at Charles & Thorn, especially Kelly Thorn, and to Chris Kwon: thank you for creating a cover beyond my wildest dreams. To everyone else who helped in any way with this novel, thank you so much. You have made my dreams come true.

The folklore and monsters described in this story were inspired by my personal recollections, along with a huge number of books and websites. However, I owe a massive debt to the phenomenal *Polish Customs, Traditions, and Folklore*, by Sophie Hodorowicz Knab (New York: Hippocrene Books, 1996). Her knowledge of Polish herbs and folk tradition is truly encyclopedic, and it informed much of Koszmar's medical expertise.

Finally, I also want to thank you—the person holding this book. I am overjoyed to have met you—in some small way—through these pages. Thank you so much for picking up this unusual story from a foreign land. Thank you for holding on to the end. Now, sleep tight and don't let the strzygi bite.

It's a dark world out there, and we need the lights like you.